Back to the Wall

Steve Forbes

ISBN: 1-4392-2935-X
ISBN-13: 9781439229354

Visit www.booksurge.com to order additional copies.

Amazon books by Steve Forbes:

Kingdom Come
Hell and Gone
F2 (Effay Dos)
Back to the Wall
Back of Beyond
Southern Cross
Northern Cross
Neptune's Lance

Who is the Yega?

"Who do you think we're talking about? A wife-beater? An alcoholic who stabs a friend in a bar fight or plows his car into a crowded playground. A doper who blows away a family while robbing their house? No. No. The *Yega* kills. That's his life and that's all he lives for. He has no friends. He doesn't date. He doesn't go to the movies or out to dinner. He has no hobbies. He doesn't take drugs. He doesn't smoke or drink. Sometimes I think he doesn't even eat but of course he does. He eats. He sleeps. And when the Red Chinese give him a target, he kills. That's all he does and he does it better than anyone else in the world."

"But why," I asked, "is he after me?"

"Because you're the investigator, not him. You know how to find who you're looking for. He doesn't. But it's the same man he's trying to find. So he's following you, eliminating all of your leads as soon as you find them, murdering all of your witnesses after you've talked to them. And once you've found this friend of yours, the *Yega* will kill him as well. Naturally at that point you'll cease to have any value. And when that happens, my friend, the *Yega* will kill you in the most horrible way that he can imagine. I should add that there is no limit to the *Yega*'s imagination."

To my friends Lynn Stringfellow,
Dennis Rada, Charles Cantrell
Kelly Hogan (in memory),
and to D. W. Kang

Chapter Index

Back to the Wall

1. Flight to Nowhere

Had I known our aircraft was about to explode or what was going to happen to Huang Mu, I might have paid more attention. I was the only guy on board with any interest in him at all—or so I believed at the time—and when he left I missed it completely. I have three excuses, one of which is that it's tough to keep an eye on a passenger in coach while you're sitting in first class. Huang Mu was in coach. But the trip he was about to take I wouldn't even wish on a tourist.

There was also her. She was quite a distraction.

She had a seat in the forward section and across the aisle and every time she turned around I had to wipe a wistful smile off my face. She was that nice. She had a trim Asian figure, dark Asian features, butterscotch skin, huge almond eyes, and luscious black hair framing a pretty little oval face. Chinese for a certainty. I've been in the East long enough to know a Chinese girl when I see one. Nevertheless, I'd been standing behind this girl at the ticket counter when she grabbed the last non-smoking seat in first class and I'd seen her Thai passport.

Finally, there was the smoke. When I had presented my meager financial holdings to the ticket agent seconds after the Thai girl headed for the gate and minutes before the DC-10's final boarding call to Taipei and learned coach was booked solid, the agent had taken pity on me, accepted my Hong Kong dollars and upgraded me to first class. As luck would have it the last seat there was in the smoking section where I found myself surrounded by people who'd never read a surgeon general's report or were card-carrying fatalists.

Breathing wasn't even the worst of it.

Outside the plane visibility couldn't have been better. Our pilots were doubtlessly soaring along on visual flight rules but in there, navigation was conducted on instruments alone. Failing that, arms fully extended, hands patting the air to detect obstructions was the next best procedure.

From my seat I was having trouble making out the large galley area right behind first class as well as the two rest rooms on either side of the galley. And if I was having a hard time seeing that far, trying to see between the galley and the men's room back into coach to keep an eye on Huang was an exercise in futility.

He was smack in the middle of the center section with two passengers on each side of him. I liked that. It meant he wasn't going to do a lot of moving around.

Which was not the case with me at all.

Those of us who believed in going first class had our own, superior lavatory facilities forward and I would have enjoyed the occasional trips up there if only because the air was better. No sir. I dutifully made my way to the john in coach class to check on my man. He was in the smoking section, too. And as bad as the air was in first class it was ten times as bad back in coach. He looked miserable. I'll bet he was a nonsmoker. I almost felt sorry for him. He sat there squeezed into that cramped little seat with his lips pinched tight, his eyes narrowed to slits, and his tattered attaché case tucked under his arms.

The first time I went back there I stood and stared. The ticket agent had been right—the plane was packed. Nine seats wide, twenty-four deep. Two hundred talking, snoring, jostling, sweating, smoking human beings representing every age, every nationality, and every brand of tobacco.

"So this," I said to myself, "is how the other half lives."

I made four trips to the john in the first twenty minutes of the flight. The neighbors were starting to stare. I had earned their sympathy for a while but there's a limit. As I stood up a fifth time the American across the aisle from me looked over and I could tell by the smirk on his face he was within an ace of suggesting I go on dialysis.

That's when I spotted my wistful-worthy girlfriend leaving the women's rest room near the galley. She saw me at the same time and cut over to the starboard aisle. We'd already exchanged quite a few of what you might call fleeting glances. She would look back from her seat, see me smiling at her wistfully and then she'd turn quickly away. That kind of fleeting glances.

Now she was walking right up to me.

Of the several dozen men in first class I was the only one wearing tennis shoes and jeans and while I did have on a tie (that alone must have gotten me the upgrading) it had been years since I'd cinched one up tight or bothered to button the collar. Other than that the only thing she knew about me was that I had a goofy grin and a bladder the size of a teacup. But here she came. Is it any wonder I like myself?

"Ni shuo ying-wen ma?"

I regarded her little oval face, smiled into her large almond eyes, and gave myself a pat on the back. *"Wo hui shuo yidian,"* I replied. *"Ni shi naguo ren? Zhongguoren?"*

"Actually," she said, switching easily to English. "I am half Korean."

So I was right all along. She may have had a Thai passport and she may have been half Korean but she was speaking fluent Chinese.

Ten minutes had passed since my last check. I peered over her head into coach. I didn't expect to see very much of Huang from my seat and I didn't; in fact I didn't see anything. He wasn't in his seat.

I stood up.

Yes, he was gone.

The girl was following my glance and so I looked down at her to make some parting remark. Just my luck that I did. And hers too. Lucky neither of us was looking toward the back when the explosion came.

From the corner of my eye I saw a bright gout of flame lance from the men's lavatory. A wave of heat and pressure struck the side of my head like a wrecking ball.

In that enclosed space, the blast was horrific; it blew me and the girl off our feet and forward into nonsmoking. Lucky again. A fusillade of splinters, hunks of plastic and metal and sundry aircraft debris sprayed the entire central section. But as shocking as that was, and as terrifying, it was no worse than the immediate shrieking roar which followed. If I had rammed my head into a locomotive engine it couldn't have been any more deafening for that was exactly what it sounded like.

I had raised my head to survey the cabin with what I'm sure was an expression of proper horror. First class was a mess. I could see women screaming and some men, too—you couldn't hear them—grabbing at their chairs and each other or flailing their arms in the air. The process which had instantly scattered bits and pieces of airplane, personal belongings, and lighter material of every kind not nailed down or held onto—that process was now reversing itself. Now everything was being sucked out. The roar I was hearing then was the entire body of highly pressurized cabin air, as from a burst balloon, making an immediate rush from the aircraft. And all of the debris as well as every other light and likely item was going out with it. This was already well underway when I looked up for it had followed the blast by only a fraction of a second and continued for several seconds at least.

It was a spellbinding sight. Papers, cups, magazines, the lavatory wreckage, and unsecured clothes were all flying madly about and independently racing through the air to the place where the men's john used to be. It wasn't there any longer. What remained was a gaping, ragged wound in the side of the plane. Some clothes bags and hand luggage took to the wind and snapped out the two-foot diameter gash. A man who had been blown forward over the seat ahead of him was now hanging onto the seat back for dear life as the tempest caught him with what must have been several times the power of a cyclone.

The spell ended for me when I saw the Korean girl start to come up. At first I thought she was making a foolish attempt to get to her feet but she wasn't. She couldn't have weighed much more than a hundred pounds and when you're lying on your back it's no simple thing to rise horizontally. I held her down by throwing myself onto her stomach.

We were still in that position when the plane dipped at a rakish angel. The next thing I knew we started slipping forward down the aisle and I had to grab onto a nearby seat leg to stop us.

The rush ended as suddenly as it started.

But the freight train roar did not. I could understand that. A turbo-fan jet engine hung on the wing just a matter of feet from the hole and those engines require flight line crews to wear protective ear equipment to keep from going deaf while the pilots hold them to low idle. Add to that the wail of the wind itself as the DC-10 cut through the atmosphere at eight times hurricane velocity and you get a sense of the roar which assaulted our hearing. All that is a guess. I actually have no idea what speed we reached as the aircraft dropped its nose and dove toward the South China Sea.

The temperature plunged, too. It was ungodly cold. Every breath I took made my lungs seize though there was really nothing to breathe and I only kept trying so as not to get out of the habit.

With one shaking hand I clung to the girl. I gripped the seat frame with the other hand. My teeth clattered as I risked a second look around. Panic was dying down. People were beginning to react. The yellow oxygen masks, dangling like little puppets from their plastic hoses at every seat, were being used by those who had the presence of mind to do so. The mind I had but I lacked the presence of my seat. It was back up the aisle and so was my oxygen mask. The girl was already unconscious, whether from the shock or the cold or the lack of oxygen or my hundred fifty pounds landing on her chest, I didn't know. I was getting dizzy myself.

The aircraft seemed to level off a bit and I decided it was time to move.

I worked a hand under the small of her back and held her against my chest as I crawled up the aisle. Once at my seat I wormed myself between the arm rests and put her on my lap. Then I slipped the oxygen mask over her nose and mouth after first taking several deep drafts for myself.

Believe it or not that's the first time it occurred to me that we'd crawled right past her seat getting to mine. I could take her back to her seat, or go sit there myself. Or, I could get up and do something heroic. Except I couldn't think of anything heroic to do.

I slipped out from under the girl and belted her in. From underneath the seat I pulled out my camera case. It's the company camera, a 35-mm SLR motor-drive Canon that I always kept loaded and ready to go. I had my own duties. And while my job seldom calls for heroics it nevertheless pays the bills.

Now I looked around through the viewfinder firing off several frames as I panned coach and first class. Things had quieted down. Only occasionally did a scream rise above the roar. This surprised me for I would have thought the time for screaming had passed and anyway, where did they find the wind? The American couple across the aisle from me was doing okay. They were holding each other with both hands so at least they weren't smoking. That was something else. The clouds of smoke wafting about the smoking section had been sucked out along with everything else and now it was clear at last, and cleaner than the purest mountain breeze. Of course the problem was that by the time there wasn't any smoke in the air, there wasn't any air in the air either.

Judging by the look of the ground, we were maybe half the altitude of before and I wasn't likely to die from lack of oxygen. But the fact that I was seeing ground said even more. Instead of the South China Sea we were now looking down at the south China coast. That meant we'd changed course with altitude and were heading back to the west. Our pilots must have figured that Kai Tak airport was closer that Taipei and would be better equipped with emergency medical and fire-fighting equipment to handle our approach. Then too Kai Tak runway is built over a long bank extending out into Kowloon Bay and so if we didn't quite reach the field we wouldn't wipe out a slew of high-rise hotels when we crashed.

The screams were dying down.

A couple of men had left their seats and were working at the remains of the lavatory. I slid out from under the girl, stood, took some more frames and then moved over to inspect the site of the explosion and see if the men needed any help. A sink and a stool still hung against the outer wall just below the hole. Nothing else remained. All the tissue and towels and other paraphernalia had been sucked out into the near void by a very efficient vacuum cleaner. The pathos of a single torn scrap of paper floating in the toilet bowl amid such barren chaos, its inked writing slowly spreading out into the water like blood, seemed to warrant preservation on film. Pictures like that win prizes and get raises for people who take them. Having done so, I pitched in to help. We wrenched what was left of one partition from its mountings and engineered it against the ragged hole in the fuselage. I helped them because standing next to that damn opening was the most unnerving thing I'd done in some time. Across a few feet of stratosphere hung the intake of that mammoth jet engine. Its roar was several times as loud here. I thought the wind would have blown our small piece of partition away from the hole but it didn't. The aircraft's slipstream somehow sucked it against the outer wall and held it there.

None of us expected that to help matters materially but psychologically it did wonders. Just having the hole covered up, even if the roar continued only somewhat abated, made everybody feel better.

The men moved through the plane, comforting those who needed it and trading hopeful remarks with those who didn't. They may have been more heroic than I was. They certainly became more popular. A stewardess started working again too and finally got them in their seats. She insisted I sit down too until I flashed an ID.

I took pictures from one end of the plane to the other. That was where my popularity took the real beating. People don't like to have their photographs taken after their hair has gone through a wind tunnel and the skin on their faces has been stretched so badly it sags. However, in the course of my picture taking I was able to determine two things to my satisfaction, though there was nothing very satisfying about either one. First, Huang Mu hadn't come back to his seat. Second, he wasn't anywhere else on the plane either. I even checked the four other lavatories in the rear of coach seating and in both galleys. He'd disappeared.

I was still taking pictures when I noticed some people on the right side of the plane gesturing at their windows. I moved up to my seat.

My lap mate was gone too. I spotted her across the aisle and forward back in her own chair being belted in by a stewardess. After putting my camera away I cinched up and looked across my neighbor in the window seat. There it was—a mile below us and several miles off to the north; a smudge of brown in a gray-green sea. But even at our distance I could make out the clutter of skyscrapers that dominated Victoria Harbor and made it unlike any other city in the Orient.

I was glad the aircraft had come back to Hong Kong.

I was home.

2. Mysterious Passenger

That was a day for surprises.

I mentioned that I had no idea our aircraft was going to explode. Let me add that it came as no less of a surprise when the authorities at Hong Kong tried to tag me as the mad bomber.

The way my luck had been running I should have figured it but toward the end things seemed to be going my way. The unexpected flight to Taiwan had depleted my expense allowance for the week. The foul air in the cabin had likely taken a few days off my young life. The shock of the explosion had cost a few weeks. And, to top it off, I had lost Huang Mu. That could cost me my job. Still, the blast hadn't seemed to injure anybody too badly, including me, and I was among some two hundred and fifty passengers who cheered our safe, almost textbook touchdown at Kai Tak Airport. The roar didn't really peter out until the wide-body jet had coasted off the runway and rolled to a halt on a disused strip of taxiway.

It was then we heard wails of a different sort.

Fully a dozen emergency vehicles their lights flashing and their sirens bawling raced at us from every direction. Emergency doors opened; inflatable exit ramps ballooned outward and down; a self-contained stairway was extended from the forward undercarriage. Passengers began barreling out.

I hung around until everyone else had left. Then I pulled out my camera again, took a few frames of the empty aircraft, and finished off the roll from the top of the stairway of the emergency crews taking the steps toward me two at a time. I descended to the tarmac just as four police buses started across the runway.

Security people hustled us aboard under watchful eyes and away we went. I sat with the film roll in my clenched fist. I was trying to make up my mind whether the security people would confiscate my film and fighting a temptation to stuff it into the seat crack. There was little chance I'd be able to find my way back to this bus after we were turned loose and good odds that the officials would search the buses after we left them. So I swallowed the temptation by slipping the roll in my pocket even though I thought the odds were even higher that they would search the passengers, too.

A different urge, even stronger, struck me after the buses pulled up to a back entrance of the terminal guarded by armed sentries, and we began heading for it in a mass of four or five abreast.

A phalanx of men and women had positioned themselves on the second level, directly above the security guards. They were members of the news media. The Fourth Estate. Which sounds much more professional than "newshounds" and we journalists dearly love to sound professional. Reporters from all the local papers were there as well as the wire services and television news crews. I recognized several of them as they leaned against the rail shouting questions down to us and taking pictures with every kind of camera from 35-millimeter like mine to live radio-link video camcorders.

I spotted a particular one among them and grinned.

Tuan K'o stood out easily among a crowd of his fellow Chinese. Not all Orientals are short or slightly built and K'o—pronounced Koe, he'd told us again and again—was proof of the fact. He was well over six feet and had the widest set of shoulders I'd ever seen on a human being. I could not encircle his chest with my arms. While he lacked the quickness of mind I'd come to respect in the Chinese, he had a fundamental intelligence, a certain intuitiveness, and (just as important) he knew what to expect from his mental capacities. A lot of smarter people know less. Anyway, he'd worked with me enough that he also knew what to expect in that direction. He was the closest thing to a friend I'd ever known, East or West, but not until that moment had I ever felt the urge to embrace him, figuratively speaking of course. However, that wasn't the urge, the even stronger urge, which struck me the moment I saw him. You see, my giant friend had one other talent.

Kayo (as I called him and for obvious reasons) could run like a deer.

We were about halfway from the buses to the door when Kayo's lens found me. I gave him a wave. He lowered his camera. I waved again but this time the film roll was sticking out of my hand. His mouth worked into a smile; he seemed on the point of crying "hello"—or in his case "Wai"—when a certain intuitiveness on his part and a slight shake of the head from my direction shut him up.

Just as we moved under the canopy I sent the film high into the air with an unobtrusive—I hoped—flick of the wrist.

My aim was only so-so but my timing was perfect.

Kayo reached three feet out over the balustrade with a hand the size of a catcher's mitt and snatched the little capsule out of the air. A casual sweep of my head told me that none of the security people had seen me and only one of my fellow passengers was even looking my way. As we moved under the overhang I risked another glance upward; the other reporters were too busy taking pictures or asking questions to have noticed. And Kayo? My deer friend Kayo was gone.

We entered into a back area of customs.

I could drag it out as long as they did, but why? An official came and talked to us briefly in a clipped British way. Glad you're all safe. So sorry for the inconvenience. Your luggage will be coming shortly. Look forward to seeing you to other flights to Taipei or to quarters for the night. In the meantime we have to solve this nasty little mystery and won't you be so good as to make yourselves available for a short personal debriefing . . . there's a good fellow.

Exit official.

Thirty minutes. Enter another, a thin Chinese with a clipboard who began calling off names from a list. I made the assumption that his list was the plane manifest because that was the only record they had of our names. Also an assumption, they were using five different investigators. Only five names were called out and those passengers went to five different rooms. But here's a fact: it took them two hours to get to me.

The first half of the first hour was spent matching people with their luggage and personal belongings from the aircraft.

Things would have gotten pretty boring after that if I hadn't followed up on an item I neglected to mention on the list of things turning my way. My reaction to having someone like the Korean girl, conscious or otherwise, sitting on my lap and sharing my oxygen is positive and healthy. She was sitting across the room from me now. When I walked over to her she smiled and made room for me on the couch beside her.

Her name was Sung Kwon.

I asked if she was traveling on business or pleasure. Just visiting relatives, she told me. She was here for a family reunion. It seems her Aunt Ling and Uncle Sun, whom Sung hadn't seen in years, kept a flat in Kowloon. Ling, and Sung's cousin Sha Han whom she'd never seen but who had recently arrived in Hong Kong, were the only family Sung had.

She told me that her father had been a North Korean and her mother, Chinese. They'd moved to Hong Kong before Sung was born and then moved again, to Bangkok, where her father had a job. She spoke only a little Korean, what her father had taught her, and some Thai. Mostly she spoke Mandarin Chinese for she had lived in the Chinese community there after her father, and eventually her mother had died.

"But how did you learn such good English?" I asked her.

"From my Uncle Sun . . . when I was a little girl." Sung lowered her eyes and smiled. "Of course he's not really my uncle. I just call him that."

"Oh, yeah? What is he really?"

"He's my . . . aunt's brother-in-law."

Nothing Sung had told me explained what she was doing on a flight to Taiwan but before I could put the question, she decided it was time she learned something about me.

Fair enough. I truly would have given her the condensed version, leaving out the parts about my behind-the-lines work as a marine reporter in Vietnam and returning home with my collected writings a hero—the first man to win the Congressional Medal of Honor and the Pulitzer Prize in the same year, about becoming the youngest managing editor of *The New York Times,* about getting a blank check from Random House to write my life story and another for the movie rights from Sylvester Stallone who wanted to play the lead, and then giving it all up for a life of further adventure in the Far East. But I figured, what the hell, we've got nothing but time. So I gave her the whole story.

She didn't believe a word.

"Sylvester Stallone would play you!" she asked.

"Well . . . he'd have to hit the weights."

"And learn to speak Chinese, too!" she said smiling, and then added as an after thought. So how *did* you learn to speak Chinese?"

"I learned it from my Uncle Sam." I smiled back. "Of course, he's not really my uncle. I just call him that."

"What is he really?"

I had an answer for that but before I got it out somebody called my name.

Behind a shabby metal desk that shrieks bureaucracy the world over, a stout Chinese gentleman in a two-piece cotton suit introduced himself as Lieutenant Ming and extended a hand though only for the purpose of indicating a chair in front of his desk as a place for me to park my prat.

"Your name is Mulligan?" he asked.

I admitted it.

"Well, now," he said, "this shouldn't take too long."

"It's already taken too long," I observed. "The best you can try for at this point is that it doesn't take forever."

"My apologies. Before all the flight's passengers are scattered about the globe we thought it only prudent to take statements and determine what, if anything, of this tragedy could be learned." I nodded and he went on. "We are going to clear you through customs at the same time to expedite matters a bit," he said. "You were told to bring in your baggage. Where is yours?"

"I don't have any. But I've always wanted to say something to customs. Ask me if I've got anything to declare."

"To declare?"

"Yeah, you know, do I have anything to declare?"

"The plane didn't reach Taipei; you had no opportunity to buy anything."

"I know but just ask me."

"Do you?"

"Do I what?"

"Do you have anything to declare?"

I nodded brightly. "I sure do. I do declare it's good to be home."

No reaction. None. Not a hint of a smile showed on his face. I looked at the black-uniformed policeman with the black beret and the black shoulder-strap standing next to his desk. Nothing.

"I still need to know about your baggage," the lieutenant repeated in a humorless monotone.

I erased the smile. "I told you, I don't have any."

"No baggage at all?"

"Only this." I set my small camera case on his desk. He fingered open the top, glanced inside and then let it close.

"Where are your personal belongings, Mr. Mulligan?"

"I don't have any."

"None?"

"Not here. I do in my apartment, of course, but I didn't have time to pack."

The uniformed cop who stood at attention beside the desk maintained a mask of absolute inscrutability. That much I understood, the absence of a red flash on his shoulder lapel indicated he simply spoke no English. On the other hand, Ming's face had turned glaringly suspicious.

"Let me see your passport."

"No passport. I ha—"

"What do you mean, 'no passport'?" A black scowl descended upon me and his graveled voice was like distant thunder. But not too distant. "According to your ticket coupon you were ending your trip in Taiwan. There, or wherever you were going, you would require a passport."

"Oh, I have one. But not on me. I don't carry it with me wherever I go. I told you I boarded in something of a rush."

"Then where is your visa to enter Taiwan?"

I shook my head. "I don't have one of those either. You see I was—"

He placed both hands on the desk before him and rose.

"No passport or visa? How did you get an exit permit to leave Hong Kong?"

"I didn't."

Without dropping his mask, the uniform had come on the alert. No words were needed, in Chinese or English, to see that his superior was deeply disturbed. The time had come for an explanation. I reached into my jacket pocket for my press pass which I do carry with me wherever I go because it often proves useful. Being allowed to take pictures, for example, when everyone else on the plane is ordered back to his seat. Or skirting a line of travelers queuing up to get exit permits. But I never got to haul anything out. On a couple of occasions I'd seen mongooses in staged fights with the poisonous snakes of this region and as quickly as that little weasel could leap onto a snake's back and dig in his teeth close behind the head . . . that's how fast the policeman's hand came down on my wrist.

I never saw him move in.

Looking back, I probably should have just smiled, and then slowly bought out the press pass. But try and tell that to the snake with the mongoose screeching right in his face. I jerked my body back off the chair and the cop and I rolled onto the floor.

Do you know the trouble with Hong Kong? In Hong Kong every third guy thinks he knows how to fight. That's a fact. The trouble comes with the other two guys who really do know how and can beat the crap out of those of us who are better at thinking than fighting.

The little cop was back on his feet by the time I stood up. His open hands were making motions like he knew what he was doing. Mine were out too, trying to stop him from doing it to me.

"Now look—" I began. But it was too late.

He landed a fist across my face before I saw it coming and the second one struck before I realized the first was gone. I can take that for a while, don't think I can't, but it's no picnic. I swung and caught him on the side of the neck. Apparently that made him mad because he hit me three times again and I still hadn't quite figured out a strategy. Of course by then I was a little peeved myself, decided to use the extra twenty pounds I had on him to put him away, and sent my right fist for his jaw special delivery. It arrived in good time but before it did he'd changed addresses. He must have moved south because that's where I began taking a pounding, right below the rib cage.

It sounds messy and a little absurd too, I guess. All the time we were swinging away I could hear Ming behind his desk shouting in Chinese. I could have translated it had I not been preoccupied but I figured, why bother? If he were shouting tips to me, he'd probably be shouting in English.

I don't like to brag but I'd clipped the guy twice more on the shoulders before something struck me solidly in the solar plexus. Since his hands were engaged in bludgeoning my face at the time it must have been one of his feet. Whatever it was, it sort of froze me up. Then, when I wasn't looking, his best punch caught me just behind my left ear. For a short while I was airborne again and this time my landing was less than text-book. I crashed into a wall and slumped to the floor. Now I've lost enough fights that I rarely feel bad about it anymore. Like most fighters who are self-taught, I'm consoled by the fact that my failures don't really reflect upon my fighting abilities since they're merely the result of incompetent instruction.

But balled up in a corner with your brain doing back flips inside your skull is no time to ponder profound matters like these. It's no time to sleep either so I can hardly explain what happened next. I didn't black out, that much I know. And yet the next thing I knew somebody was shaking my head and when I opened my eyes, I found myself back in the chair in front of the desk. I looked at my watch and noticed it had been set forward about thirty minutes.

"Are you all right?"

There was a man, a hatchet-faced man who was not an Oriental, sitting on the desk, dangling a leg off the side. His hands rested casually in his lap, flicking a white card between his fingers. After a bit my eyes began to focus and I recognized the card as my press pass. Lieutenant Ming was still behind the desk and the same little cop was back at attention beside it; his black uniform was inspection ready and the beret again sat neatly on top of his head. Had he even lost the beret? If I'd winded him any he'd caught his breath nicely during the last half hour.

I rubbed the side of my head. It was already starting to swell. "I s'pose so," I said.

There was silence except for the clacking of the press card. "Since we now know," the newcomer continued, "that you were not reaching for a weapon, we're willing to allow that officer Chiang's reactions were a bit overdone and in that way we can also overlook your subsequent assault upon his person."

I expelled a dry liter of air.

"What a relief!" I said with feeling. "Do you think he's going to recover?"

"However, as concerns this other matter," he went on as though he hadn't even heard my remark, "you're in a bad spot of trouble. I think you'd better make a full statement to me. I'm Inspector Hawthorne, Mister . . .?"

He held the pass up in front of his face.

"Doyle Mulligan?"

"That's right."

"Eastern News Association?"

"Right. We're a news wire service for American and European newspapers." I continued rubbing the side of my head. "We also dispatch Chinese and Japanese-language copy through-out the Orient."

He nodded his head.

"And I suppose you're on a story now . . . ?"

Now and then you hear people described as hatchet-faced. I've used the term myself a few times. Never before had I known a man whom the description so perfectly suited. His nose was long and narrow, his forehead creased sharply just over his brows and his prominent chin like his starched shirt collar and cuffs, had an edge keen enough to slice cheese. When he bobbed his bean up and down as he did then he could pass for an axe in the process of splitting cordwood.

I admitted I was on a story. Then I said, "You know, Inspector, I thought I knew most of the Brits with Government House and the police but I never saw or heard of you before."

"I'm with Scotland Yard," he replied readily enough. "I've come over from England on a special assignment. Just happened to be around when this bombing business came up."

"You're here for the conference, huh?"

I'd said it casually because it was only a guess but I knew as soon as the words were out, mostly by the way he hesitated, that I was right.

"Er . . . yes," he said. "In a way."

"To look into the exodus of Chinese from Hong Kong?"

"More or less. To assist the Hong Kong police in their investigation, that is. But see here, Mulligan. Let's have your story. What can you tell me about this Mu fellow?"

"Huang," said the lieutenant deferentially.

"Nothing," I said.

Meanwhile Hawthorne had walked around my chair still flicking the press card in his hand. I sat and directed my gaze at Lieutenant Ming, who was back to being inscrutable, and at Officer Chiang, who'd never stopped.

"You never heard of him?" came from behind me.

"I didn't say I'd never heard of him; I just said I couldn't tell you anything about him."

The problem with having Hawthorne behind me was that I didn't know what he was doing. Was he watching the back of my neck where I usually flush when I've had too much to drink or when I tell my mother that I'm being good, eating right, and staying away from the Oriental girls? Would he find beads of sweat? Would he notice my hands fidgeting?

"Let me tell you something about him," said Hawthorne. "He was frightened of something. Noticably nervous. We know he was followed aboard the Taiwan flight by someone who, for want of a name, we will call . . . the bomber."

"Hang on, inspector."

"I'm not pointing fingers at this stage, Mr. Mulligan. This bomber sat in first class though his neighbors told us he continually twisted in his seat to spy into coach where Mr. Mu was seated."

"Mr. Huang," said the lieutenant patiently.

I didn't say anything.

Hawthorne went on, "The bomber used the lavatory in coach class, even though first class had separate facilities, in order to plant his explosive device which would detonate when Mr. Mu entered. Mu's neighbors said he went into the lavatory just seconds before the explosion and just minutes after the bomber had left it."

"Mr. Huang," said the lieutenant insistently.

Hawthorne was back in front of me now. I didn't know which was worse, staring at the hatchet face or having him whacking around behind my back.

"The lavatory blew up. Immediately after the blast the bomber hurried to the scene where others had begun sifting rubble. He searched the area and later scoured the length and breadth of the aircraft, apparently to be sure that no evidence existed which could tie him to the explosion. He must have found something incriminating and not daring to leave it there nor take the chance of having it found on his person he tossed it to a confederate who was waiting beyond the security area right outside of customs."

"Ouch!" I said, and I winced.

"Yes, I thought that might smart. Now I am pointing fingers. While you were unconscious—"

"I wasn't unconscious."

"You weren't—!"

"No. I was just . . . dozing."

"I see. Well while you were dozing we carried you back to your chair and paraded through here a number of passengers. They've identified you—"

"Wait a minute, wait a minute," I said. "You've left something out. You said Huang Mu went into the lavatory just before it blew up."

"That's right."

"Then where is he? I searched the plane. I found no trace of his body; if he was hurt, how did he get away?"

Hawthorne walked around behind Lieutenant Ming and stood looking out a window with his back to us as he spoke.

"Probably died instantly," he said. "I hope so, for his sake. But perhaps he didn't. It doesn't matter. The moment that hole opened in the fuselage he was no better than dead. He would have been sucked into the subfreezing, airless void of space nearly six miles above the Earth. In the seconds it took the passengers to recover their sensibilities enough to have seen anything at all he would have been no more than a black speck flopping his arms and screaming for all he was worth. It must have taken him several minutes to fall the distance to the ocean and I doubt if anyone could survive the psychological horror of such an experience. However, if the blast didn't kill him, if the cold or the lack of oxygen or the shock didn't kill him, the water would kill him. When you hit water at two hundred miles an hour it's no softer than concrete." At this point Hawthorne spun around, aimed his hatchet face at me, and chopped out the words. "But of course you asked where he is, not how he is, so the answer to your question is that he is now most certainly at the bottom of the South China Sea."

That was when I decided to talk.

"Okay, Inspector," I said. "I'll tell you this much. I'm investigating the same thing as you: how the Chinese are getting out of Hong Kong."

"Don't put words in my mouth. The police investigation is intended to establish whether or not a significant number of Hong Kong Chinese actually are leaving."

"Forget it," I said. "Your job is done. The Chinese are leaving. In droves. But that isn't really what you're here for. You and I both know what your real job is. To make a report that will placate the communists until they take over."

"Now see here, Mulligan, I want to hear about this Mu business."

"Huang," said the lieutenant doggedly.

By then it was all I could do to keep quiet. I had so much to say I didn't know where to start. I wanted to tell him what I thought: that he, and others like him, had already sold us out once. But that much he surely knew. Hong Kong Island and Kowloon had been granted to Great Britain in perpetuity. Only the New Territories to the north, on a 99-year lease due to expire in 1997, needed to be turned back to China. But the Reds wanted all of Hong Kong, all of its people and all of its commerce and cash. And the English wanted out of the colony business. So what had they done? They'd cashed in the island and Kowloon peninsula, too in exchange for some vague promises from Beijing. For fifty years the commies would do their best to give us a few little freedoms. Had London believed 'em? Hell no. But they could always claim they believed 'em. We didn't believe them and said so. Not from the first. And then came Tiananmen Square. The Reds drove their tanks over several hundred students who wanted only what we wanted, enough freedom to live their own lives. And after that, everyone knew Beijing's promises were nothing but lies. That had been three years ago. The story of Huang Mu really began there. But I didn't need to go back that far with Hawthorne, much as I would've liked to—that much he already knew.

"Well, Mulligan?"

I glared back. Part of the Huang Mu story had taken place far from the Orient, in North America, Europe, Asia. Even

England. Hawthorne sure didn't need to hear that part from me either. After opening the doors to the Red Chinese to take over the colony, the British closed the doors on their own subjects. English parliament passed laws prohibiting any of Hong Kong's Chinese citizens from immigrating to the United Kingdom. Other countries began closing their borders, too. NO VACANCY signs began springing up all over Asia and across the Pacific. The U.S. and Canada agreed to take in a few "Honkers," but only a few. Only those Chinese with personal fortunes could buy their way out. The rest, the overwhelming percentage, were stuck. But none of this would be news to Inspector Hawthorne.

"Are you going to talk or not?" he demanded.

"Oh, I'll talk," I said. "Just try and stop me. You know about the stories we've been running, don't you?"

"Naturally."

Then he knew the rest. In spite of everything, Hong Kong's population had been plummeting. Three months ago, Eastern News had launched a series on the exodus that had shocked the world. We'd documented the decline by random neighborhood polls. At a minimum, we figured, the colony was losing two hundred thousand Chinese every year and the figure was probably much higher. But nobody knew where they were going. Nobody knew how they were getting away. When Beijing complained that the British were letting the cream of the colony slip out before they moved in, Government House reacted by requiring exit permits. But that hadn't slowed down the exodus one bit.

"Well, one thing wasn't in any of the reports," I said. "We couldn't print it. But I don't mind telling you. This is your fault. Yours and the first British diplomatic team that negotiated the 'Handover.' As far as we're concerned you guys stabbed us in the back. And now we figure you're back to do it again."

Hawthorne's hatchet head arched up and down so that for a minute it looked as though he might cleave me in half. But he spoke instead.

"Listen, Mulligan. I'm not interested in hearing the local crabbing. If you want to point fingers, you know, I could remind you that these stories you're so proud of, the ones informing the whole world about the hordes of Chinese leaving Hong Kong, they're what started this whole mess in the first place. If you'd kept your months shut the Reds wouldn't be trying to muscle in early, the plane might not have been blown up, Huang Mu might not have been killed, and I wouldn't be standing here now trying to get you to give me facts instead of editorials."

So I gave him the facts.

We'd gotten an anonymous tip—it's always an anonymous tip—that a small acupuncture clinic in the Mong Kok area was involved in spiriting Chinese out of Hong Kong. All we had was the name of the clinic and the proprietor so I went to the place to scout around. It was one of the Celestial Acupuncture Clinics. A chain. You see them all over Hong Kong. This one, according to our informant, was run by a man named Huang Mu.

"Anyway," I said, "I checked out the clinic; Huang Mu was out. Nobody else in the place seemed to know what was going on so I got a description of the guy and then left."

Hawthorne interrupted at that point to exclaim; "Good lord! How amateurish."

I let it pass. "With Huang's description I set up shop outside the Shanghai Mansions where his clinic was located and kept watch. Huang showed up in the late afternoon, went inside, came running out with a briefcase half an hour later like the father of all collection agencies was on his tail. He grabbed a taxi, sped to the airport, and bought a ticket on Malaysian Airways's three P.M. flight to Taiwan. I was standing a few places behind him and got the last seat on the same plane."

"Clumsier and clumsier."

I let that pass too. "I figured he was going to meet some of his people at the other end of the line," I said. "Maybe he was making a payoff to some government official. I wanted to be there when he did. Naturally I kept an eye on him in the plane; there was always the chance he'd pass the money to someone then and there. I don't believe his neighbors told you they saw me watching him unless you suggested it but if they were half as observant as you say then they must have told you about his attaché case. He held onto it like it contained the crown jewels. He never let it go. Never set it down. After the explosion, naturally I went to look and take pictures but in the back of my mind I figured there was a chance that it could be just a diversion for him to disappear—"

Hawthorne interrupted. "Utterly absurd!"

"I guess so but at the time it seemed possible. He's in the disappearing business and you have to admit that he has disappeared." Hawthorne snorted loudly. "Okay, okay," I agreed, "maybe not, but now I've got another idea."

"I can hardly wait."

I turned over a hand. "Maybe the bomb was in his case. That could still account for the way he was holding it and for the fact that he didn't have any other luggage. Maybe he intended to commit suicide. Which would also explain how it happened there in the lavatory just as he went in. He didn't want to kill anybody else."

The inspector was shaking his head. "Then he picked a damn silly place to blow himself up. Why not at home? No. I'm not going to accept suicide. When a man boards a plane behaving as he did, nervous and clutching a case like that, he gets checked. We've talked to the security officer. He saw Mu and remembers. The officer didn't just run the case through the x-ray machine; he opened it up and examined the contents personally. No money. And no bomb. I considered it just barely possible that the bomb was in the case as you say only that it had been put there by somebody else and Mu didn't know it. That his going to the lavatory when he did was pure chance. But no. The security officer's testimony leaves no room for doubt."

I asked him if it wasn't possible the bomb was planted in the john by someone who had no connection with Huang and Huang's entering just before it went off was merely bad luck.

Hawthorne had thought about that and dismissed the idea. "I can swallow coincidence when I have to," he said, "but I don't think I can choke that down. Not after hearing your story. His sudden rush to the airport. Last-minute flight. No time for packing. His nervousness. His entire behavior. The man was running—toward something or from something, I can't say which, but he was running. And he didn't make it. So far as we know, only you, Mulligan, of all the people on the plane knew anything about him or had any interest in him. He bought the last seat in coach and you bought the last seat in first class. So it's black for you. And every minute you're not in my custody is just another 60 seconds of grace during which time I expect your complete cooperation. I want the address of the firm he worked for. I want a signed statement from you which includes everything you've told me here and more. And I want those photographs you took, the ones you say you threw to your friend, and I want them before they hit the wires."

"You want a lot."

He shook his head slowly. "What are you? Are you the bumbling reporter you seem to be? Or are you much more? Somebody is. If I accept your story then I'm left with no suspects. In fact, no one who could possibly have done what was done. And yet somebody did. Somebody got a bomb through the security net at the concourse—a damn good security net, I can guarantee you. And if it wasn't you, if it was someone else following Mu, here's what we're left with: the bomber boarded an aircraft even though he didn't have a ticket. He flew several hundred miles unseen by any passengers or flight personnel even though he didn't have a seat. He placed his explosive device in the lavatory without anybody seeing him and set it to go off when Mu went inside. Then that same somebody, somehow, got Mu into the lavatory without any of his neighbor's seeing a thing. And, when it was all over he slipped casually off the plane and through an army of emergency personnel. So do I start believing in bugaboos, boogey men and midnight beasties?"

The lieutenant had sat silently, stoically throughout our discussion. But when Hawthorne finished speaking Ming looked up suddenly and said with a kind of quiet alarm:

"Qu*yega*!"

Officer Chiang's mask of imperturbability shattered in an instant. He gawked at his superior.

One of us had finally spoken a word he understood.

3. A Hero's Welcome

Those words wouldn't stop banging around in my brain. Waiting to be turned loose, trying to find some wheels back to the office, and then all the way across town I couldn't stop thinking about them.

Not "Qu*yega*." I'd heard that one before, translating Red Chinese broadcasts as part of my indentured service to the United States Air Force. When I got my discharge and took a job with Eastern News Association rather than leave the Orient, I still ran into the expression now and then. The Chinese used it as a kind of crisis *gesundheit*. It was an explanation for the unexplainable and at the same time, a quick prayer that misfortune has ended. Mysterious deaths, particularly violent ones, and unnatural disasters such as explosions or destructive fires are quickly wished away and out of mind by that simple phrase.

I only wished I could get that damned hatchet-faced cop out of my mind half as easily.

No, it was Hawthorne's writing me off as a "bumbling reporter" that started me down. That hurt, I won't deny it.

Ordinarily I'd have shrugged off something like that in a minute. After all I was the regional desk's top journalist. Alex Stringer never held me up as his favorite character but he'd sure come straight to me when he'd gotten the tip about Huang Mu. As a matter of fact, in another eleven or twelve months when Stringer—who didn't speak a word of Chinese—was due for rotation, I felt I stood a good chance of being handed the directorship of the Hong Kong station.

On top of that I couldn't stop thinking how Hawthorne had blamed this whole mess on the ENA. That hurt even more. Not because I knew Hawthorne was wrong. It hurt because deep down, I knew he was right.

Hong Kong is a 24-hour Chinese fire drill. The energy of this town used to thrill me. I couldn't walk the streets without feeling the excitement. It was a fun town too before the British traded away our future.

It was busy before and it still is but these days folks don't go about their business with the same kind of vitality they once had. Vitality is a by-product of hope. It's hard to have hope when you haven't a future. And it's impossible to have fun without hope.

I stood on the curb at the airport pickup area looking around. It takes three dollars Hong Kong to ride the double-deck bus back to Causeway Bay and I didn't have it. A cream-colored minibus taking on passengers to the Ocean Terminal Complex could get me halfway but I didn't even have the two dollars Hong Kong for that or the six bits it would take to get me across the harbor to the Central District on the Star Ferry. That aborted flight to Taipei had cleaned me out.

I could either start hoofing or call the office and ask someone to come and get me. Neither option appealed to me.

The only guy at the airport I knew well enough to bum a few bucks from was an old newsie who ran the magazine stand. I did a feature on him once long ago and he'd liked it. How he'd slipped over the Chinese border to the New Territories twenty years before with no money and no possessions except for the rags he was wearing. How he's worked in the textile plants ten and twelve hours a day for three years until he'd put enough back to start his own business. How he and his wife bought their own home and had sent their son, who had never known communism, through law school. But the newsie wasn't anyone special, that wasn't the story. A million, maybe two million Chinese had come to Hong Kong the same way and done the same thing. That was the story.

I'd never been to the airport when he wasn't there at his newsstand. Wouldn't you know it—today he was gone; a middle-aged woman I'd never seen before had taken his place behind the counter.

"Where's Wu Wing?" I asked her. She was sitting there surrounded by black headlines from the *South China Morning Post,* the *Hong Kong Standard,* and *The Star*: "Conference to Pave Way for Early ChiCom Takeover", "Reds to Demand Closed Borders", "HK Stock Exchange Plummets on Eve of Conference—Massive Capital Flight Feared." There was even one story on the front page of *The Mail* that featured ENA's series on the Chinese exodus.

She glared at me and shook her head.

"He not here."

"When will—"

"I tell people all day. Wu Wing gone and he not come back. He not tell me where he go. He sell stand to me and he go. That all I know, sonny. You want to buy paper or not?"

My one inviolable rule is that I never bum money from women, not from women I've only just met, and especially not from middle-aged women who call me sonny.

So I was still in the dumps when my feet hit the road and my thumb began poking holes in the air.

Even the luck of having a cabby stop and give me a lift was no lift. Cabbies know everything. They know where to find the Wanchai girls now that they're no longer in Wanchai. They know where to turn off heading to the Dickens Bar once your concierge has stopped looking and immediately make for the more risqué Bottom's Up. They know where to find a "steal" on some really "hot" gems. They probably even know where the Chinese are running to but, being Chinese themselves, they don't talk about that to people who aren't.

We drove Hong Chang road to the tip of Kowloon. There we picked up the Cross Harbor Tunnel, shot under Victoria Harbor, and emerged Hong Kong side at Causeway Bay. Yes, I decided, sitting back watching the city go by, Hong Kong had changed. The towering office buildings amid the madness of neon advertising and Chinese banners were the same; so were the glass storefronts that lined every sidewalk, the barkers who shouted from each open doorway, the hustlers who worked in the crowds. Jamming every intersection were con artists, street artists, street vendors, street walkers, and hawkers. There were street stalls for fast food and streets stalled by eager windshield washers, eighty-year-old men who will shine your shoes and ten-year-old boys who can sell you a Rolls-Royce. The city was a free marketplace right down to the curbs, just like it always had been. And yet something was different. Something behind the signs, the storefronts, and the shouts. Perhaps it was no more than the lackluster smile of a jewelry merchant. A tailor who closed his shop half an hour early. The businessman slowly converting his assets to cash. For Hong Kong, 1997 wasn't just four years in the future, it was the end of the future. Every man in Hong Kong knew someone who'd already left; most would have left themselves if given the chance; many were making their own plans to leave. After Tiananmen Square our fifty years of freedom had dropped to four; after the conferences were over and the Red Chinese took charge of the docks and the airports as they wanted to do, and then later more and more functions in Government House as they'd try to do, our four years could be reduced to a matter of weeks or even days.

Yes sir, the fun had gone out of this town.

I hadn't perked up much when we reached our offices in the Causeway Building. I had the doorman phone up and have somebody come down and take care of the meter. Then I took the elevator to the seventh floor, walked to our door at the end of the hall, crossed the small reception area, and was almost blown over by the riotous welcome.

That was a badly needed lift.

No one had gone to too much expense. There was no confetti, no cake or party hats. But there was plenty of enthusiasm. Paper airplanes started flying about. A banner of fanfold computer paper saying: "Way to go, Doyle Mulligan!" was stretched across the wall directly over my desk. Everyone was on his feet, cheering, drinking, or clapping. A big mitt that turned out to be Kayo's slapped me on the back and ushered me into the center of the room. A drink was pressed into my hand. I sipped it, smiling modestly.

A really healthy ego doesn't mind taking a back seat to modesty.

When you're thrust into an accident of that magnitude and by pure chance you come sailing through with a strange beautiful girl on your lap but not the slightest ding on your bumper, you simply smile and credit your good luck. Modesty is behind the wheel. But Ego knows, even from the back seat, who's really doing the driving.

Apparently the pictures had been developed and were a big hit.

I was moved along by high spirits to the bulletin board where all 36 of the photographs were pinned. Stringer stood beside me while other reporters formed a circle around us. Stringer, a guy named Manuel, and I, were the only Westerners in the office. The others were what I call western Chinese. (There are two kinds of Chinese: the kind who talk to westerners and the kind who don't. The kind who don't also don't talk to the kind who do. So the Chinese who do, don't know anything worth talking about; only those who don't, do. We only hire western Chinese.

They also don't know anything worth writing about but at least they talk to us about what they don't know.)

"You're beautiful, Doyle," Stringer was saying. "And so is that."

He was looking at a single 8" X 10" print in the center, surrounded by all the others. It was the very first shot I'd taken, just as soon as I'd lined up the camera on the open hole through the pandemonium in first class. Even across the width of the cabin you could see the jet engine in the background. In the foreground, with papers and other light objects still swirling about in the air, the faces of fear-filled passengers were shockingly displayed. It was the kind of shot that a photographer would pray to have an opportunity to grab if only once in a lifetime. And there it was for me.

"That's the one you sent out?" I asked him.

"Hell, we sent out a dozen," Stringer was gleeful. "But that was the best of the lot." He'd been staring at the photo montage but now he turned to me. "There won't be ten major papers in the world that won't use it. They'll know we're here after today."

"That's good," I said and I meant it, even though all of our photos went out over the wire uncredited. It was enough just to know that I'd done it.

Someone from the back, Manuel I think, yelled, "How long after the explosion did you take that picture, Doyle?"

"This was after the initial panic was really over," I replied. "The explosion had occurred three or four minutes before."

Kayo grinned. "Why did you wait so long, Doily?"

The big Cantonese had accepted my well-intended moniker for him but for two years now he'd been pronouncing my name like some kind of lace napkin.

I smiled back at him. "It's like I told you, this was after the panic. I took the shot as soon as I recovered."

Everybody had a good laugh at that and we toasted a couple of rounds to the press and then they started moving off to their desks. It could have been Stringer's influence; he wasn't the type to let much time be lost to revelry, but that wasn't the case. It was after six-thirty and most had stayed overtime just waiting for me.

Manuel socked my arm as he swept by.

"You get that face in the explosion, Mulligan, or were you rolled by a midget?"

I never respond to that kind of crap.

Anyway, I'd spotted Kayo at the coffee bar grabbing the last of the donuts before they got stale so I headed over to thank him for getting out my pictures.

He waved my thanks away. "Any time, Doily." He pushed a big finger at my face. "Does it hurt too much?"

"No. Just enough."

"It wasn't because of me, was it? They didn't see me?"

"No," I lied. "They didn't see you, Kayo."

"Do you want me to get my needles?"

I winced.

Kayo was an acupuncture freak. He'd memorized the book by Lee Chung, *Ancient Ways/Modern Man,* and tried to get me into it too. I'd backed off gently but quickly. As far as I'm concerned, acupuncture is some kind of voodoo. In fact, the only difference between acupuncture and voodoo is that with voodoo you don't have to show up to get the treatment.

I'd worded it more kindly with him then and now.

"I almost met him today," he said.

"Met who?"

"You know. Lee Chung."

"Turn it around, Kayo. He almost got to meet you."

"Maybe next time he'll get lucky."

Ten minutes later I was in Stringer's office giving him my thanks for sending Kayo to the airport. He told me that he wouldn't have if he'd known I was on the plane. "We had to pull him off another assignment," he said. "Just a house fire up on the peak. It was nothing for us really, and yet..."

"Just another billionaire's mansion?" I answered almost absent mindedly. I wasn't really paying attention to Stringer. The high of my reception had passed and now I was swinging back down.

"Yeah. But not just another billionaire. It was some guy Tuan had rather admired. He caught it on the radio and I gave him the okay to cover the story. I guess he hoped he might get a peek at the guy. We would never have sent out a report on it. I just had a feeling..." He shook off the feeling. "Anyway, if I'd known you were aboard the plane I would have thought you could handle it alone but since Tuan got the film, out for you, I'm glad I didn't know." Stringer was shorter than I am, going both gray and bald prematurely. Alcohol had done awful things to his nose. He was getting fat, too. But he still came off as a better representative of the ENA than I did because he wore leather shoes and three-piece suits, he cinched up his ties and could never quite get used to the fact that I didn't. He also had a sixth sense about news, could juggle a hundred miniscule story facts in his head at one time and batted out copy faster than any man I ever knew.

"You'd better fire up a keyboard and put something out on this aircraft story," he said. "Feature it. A view from within. You know the kind of stuff I want. When we heard you were going to be several hours in customs, I had Manuel put out a general from the reports and we sent the photos along. We had to do something what with the other services breathing down our necks and even if what we had to say was no better than theirs, we had your pictures. Is there anything new?"

"You bet your wingtips, there is," I told him. Then I filled him in briefly on everything I had. It never paid to hold back on Stringer. He sat back in his chair and let it soak in. "So you see," I said, "it looks like the explosion was really murder and the one guy who buys it is our needle doctor. It's too good to ignore and no one but us and the police have got it."

Stringer agreed it was good but didn't think we could use it until we'd done some more checking. "If we're wrong," he said, "it could be very bad. So let's check it out fast because this aircraft bombing story is going to die. Her Majesty's aeronautics people will see to that. They always do. One, maybe two more headlines and it's gone for weeks. I can put one of our no-speakies at their outer offices and have him wait with the other wire-service flunkies. I don't have to waste you for that and I don't intend to. On the other hand, we've only cracked the lid on this emigration thing and see what it's gotten us. It's going to be good for a lot of headlines and as you pointed out, nobody else has anything on it. We've even got the inside track on the authorities. All they have is what you gave them."

Of course I expected that.

"I had my reasons," I told him.

"You always do. Let's hear them."

"For starters, my obligation as a citizen of Hong Kong. I had information the police needed in the investigation of a crime and it wasn't likely they'd get it unless I gave it to them."

"Okay. You obviously rehearsed that. Now what was the real reason?"

I didn't bother to take offense. "The other reason had to do with a quick review of what we had left after Huang Mu was gone. It didn't add up to much. Some woman calls and informs us a Mong Kok acupuncturist may be playing conductor in the underground railway selling fake documents or passage out of Hong Kong. He might be the first link in a chain that reaches beyond the East, to Australia, to Europe, or maybe even to North America. We'd hoped that his operation might account for a good fraction of the quarter of a million that are disappearing every year. But Huang was the only hook we had to hang our hat on and when you take him away, all we're left with is a lot of may be's, might be's, a possibly, and a hope or two. Well, somebody took him away."

"You think the police will give you something else?"

“I hope so. I brought that inspector up even with us as of today and promised him copies of the pictures I took on the plane. In exchange, he may be friendly to us when he finds out more about Huang.”

Stringer shook his head.

“It’s still not like you, Doyle. Turn your information over to the cops and let them do the investigating, then sit back and hope they let you in on what they find out. What’s the matter? Do you like this Inspector Hawthorne so much?”

“I don’t like him at all.”

“Then what’s your problem? You’ve been acting odd ever since you got back. Are you feeling all right?”

“I’m okay.”

“ “Well, what’s wrong?”

“I’m not sure I like this assignment too much either.”

“What the hell!” Stringer was aghast. “This is your big chance. The biggest story of your career.”

“It’s big all right. But look what we’ve done. If we hadn’t broken the story about the Chinese exodus two months ago Beijing wouldn’t be up in arms now. They wouldn’t have demanded this conference tomorrow and they wouldn’t be in any position to insist, as they’re certainly going to, that Hong Kong’s emigration policies be stiffened and that their own people be brought in to enforce them.”

“Now look, Doyle—”

“Government House will be arguing that no substantial numbers of Hong Kong Chinese citizens or Hong Kong dollars are leaving the colony and what are we doing? We’re trying to dig up the very proof the Reds need to make their point. It’s gonna be just like Macao. Their turnover date is two years later than ours: 1999. But the Reds found out about gambling money being funneled out and forced the Portuguese to accept some of their own military people at the ports of entry. Now they occupy major positions in the Macao police and government, banking and financial institutions as well as air and marine security. Hell, I think they've even got some of their foot soldiers down at the post office."

"The Portuguese didn't resist. They wanted out of Macao."

"And the British don't want out of Hong Kong? If we'd just kept our mouths shut maybe we'd have lost a good story but how many Chinese would have gotten out who won't now? You, me, everyone who works in this office is responsible for what's going to happen to Hong Kong."

Stringer leaned back, folding his arms over his chest. I could see a speech coming and I tried to forestall it by rising to my feet. But he waved me back down with the warning: "Now you're going to hear this."

According to Alex Stringer our only responsibility was to report the truth as accurately as we could. We may not always like it—he didn't always like it himself—but that was our job. He agreed I was right about the conference. What we learned would play an important part in how things turned out. But regardless of what we uncovered, we'd report the facts. If we kept quiet because we didn't like what we had to report then we needed to find a new job. If we told a lie because a lie suited us better than the truth then we might as well tell the communists to come in tomorrow and take over the new desk. That was their style, not ours.

I had to admit he was right about that but that was as far as I was willing to go at the time. His speech didn't mean very much to me until later when I had good reasons to be happy we'd stayed on the story. For that matter, everybody in Hong Kong had good reason to be happy we'd stayed on the story.

"The conference will continue for a week," he told me. "No more, I'm sure. That's how long you've got to find out what the hell's going on. Who's leaving and if they're leaving, where they're all going and what they're taking with them. If the answer is small potatoes and no big story well then, that's what we'll report. But it's no good just hoping, get out there and find out."

He didn't mean now. He meant after I finished my story on the aircraft explosion. Stringer got ready to go while I started tapping a tune on the alphabet synthesizer. Before going home, he peered over my shoulder. Ordinarily he read everything that went out but he was going to do me the honor of scrolling down only the first three or four graphs. Then, with a pat on my back, he was gone.

God it went slow. I could have composed a concerto more easily, but maybe not. Maybe the circumstances were wrong for inspiration of any kind. It was bad enough my story couldn't include any of the real meat about Huang and I was forced to settle for a corny feature. What was worse, I had to sit there by the window that overlooked Victoria Harbor and beyond it, Kowloon, where Hawthorne was still on the job. That was all I could think about. Daylight had slipped away from the city and electricity began to take its place. All of Hong Kong dazzled with neon and incandescence. I wished myself out there and suddenly there I was hovering over Causeway Bay with my computer terminal. The spirit of writer's block reflected in a pane of glass.

Sometime around ten-thirty I finished, proofed the file quickly, and then sent it to the wire operator's terminal for release. I made ready to go. As things turned out, it was lucky I had taken so long. If I'd been any faster the call would have come while I was en route to my flat instead of on my way out the door.

"It's for you," said the duty officer dryly.

I took the receiver and told it hello.

"Doll Mulligan?"

I screwed up my face. "Who's calling?"

"Never mind that. You're the reporter who was on the flight to Taipei? The flight with the bomb?"

"Yeah, that's me."

The voice was a man's. It was not a pleasant voice at all. The accent was Oriental but sounded like he was talking with a mouth full of rice and a fishbone lodged in his throat.

"I have information for you on the *de ha tit*. What you call the underground railway. Go the the Shin Lo Arena on Tak Ching Road. Give your name to the ticket seller."

"Tak Ching? But that's Kowloon City!"

"I will wait thirty minutes. No more."

"Could we meet out—"

"And no cops!"

The connection went.

I handed the receiver back to the duty officer. "Any idea where that call came from?" I asked him.

"Uh huh." He smiled at his own cleverness. "From the anonymous informant who called up this morning."

"Not the same one. Stringer said the first caller was a woman. Was this a local call?"

"I guess so. Why?"

I didn't take time to explain. The night shift people aren't trained for investigative journalism. Me, I already had several clues to the caller's identity. He was a man. Probably Chinese. He ate rice and fish, disliked cops and knew more about my story than I did. There couldn't be more than two or three million guys in Hong Kong who matched that description.

But if I wanted to meet him I'd have to go into Kowloon City. The Walled City. And given the choice I'd rather climb over the Great Wall of China and give Premier Dang a message from the unhappy citizens of Hong Kong.

It was the one place in Hong Kong that I'd never been.

The one place I had no business going.

I pulled my last coin, my lucky coin, from my pocket and threw it into the air.

Heads, I use my head and forget the call altogether.

Tails, I risk my tail by going into the Walled City.

It was tails.

You know, I told myself, this is too important a matter to be decided by the flip of a coin. I'll make it the best two out of three.

Up went the coin again.

Tails.

Damn!

The duty officer was looking at me as though he had nothing better to do. Which he probably didn't. He'd have the same stupid grin on his face when somebody called in to tell him that Doyle Mulligan had turned up dead in the Walled City and would somebody please come and pick up the body.

Three out of five.

I tossed it again and held my breath.

Tails.

You can't argue with fate.

I reached across the duty officer's desk into petty cash, scooped up a fistful of bills, cried, "For the taxi!" and told him to call Kayo Tuan at his apartment and have him meet me at the Kowloon City Market in twenty minutes.

I was in the hall with my finger on the elevator button before he could argue.

The advantage in wearing running shoes rather than dress shoes is that you're prepared to run and I believe in taking advantage of advantages. I raced out the building, flagged a red taxi and a driver who looked game and told him he'd get his best tip of the day if he made haste to Kowloon City. He didn't move. "You don't want to go there, Mistuh." He said after a searching look. "Not for *saiyahn*." I lied and told him I wanted to go there. "Well," he said, pausing again, "maybe I don't want to go there. Too dirty. Too bad. Too crime."

"You don't have to go into the city," I yelled at him. "Just take me to the market on Lion Rock Road. I'll walk in from there." I waved bills. "And you'll still get that tip if you hurry."

He fed gas.

The cabbie's hesitations did not extend to his driving. Once he decided to go he really went. Of course the Chinese are fearless motorists to begin with—very few Americans can hold a candle to them—but their tiny vehicles seem to fill them with a spirit of adventure as though the streets were just a big game of dodge'em cars. But actually it's more complicated than that. There's dodge'em cars and there's bump'em cars. The cars are the same and so are the bumpers. The difference is attitude. Here, half the guys play bump'em and the other half play dodge'em and you just pray that two bump'ems don't meet. They zip around like maniacs, take incredible chances, and are possessed of a total disdain for safety. Speed laws are routinely ignored. Lane dividers, when they're marked, mean nothing to them. No matter where you are in the city you're constantly subjected to the nerve-shattering squeals of slammed brakes, skidding tires and the screams of engines alternately revving and idling. Maniacal is the kindest way to describe it.

Either his doctor had already informed my cabby that he had but six days to life and he figured what the hell or the idea of a large tip had cast what small sense of caution he had into the night breeze. But I had to set my teeth when I thought about it. Here's a man who drives like he has six days to live and still won't go into the Walled City while mother Mulligan's boy Doyle with something like fifty years to look forward to, pays him to fly there as fast as he can.

The city is right across the road from the airport so really we were covering the same ground I'd just traveled under the pond and north up the peninsula. It doesn't show on the tourist maps because tourists are advised to stay away but it's there, an eyesore and a political embarrassment to the British. The walls are gone now but they might just as well still be standing.

When England leased the New Territories north of Hong Kong Island and Kowloon nearly a hundred years ago, Beijing retained jurisdiction over a small patch of ground across Boundary Street known as Kowloon City, a ghetto surrounded by a high rock wall. Eventually the British booted out the Chinese garrison stationed there on some silly pretext but in deference to the Chinese government, which was and still is, landlord of the lease, they never moved in and developed the town. The Hong Kong police have never patrolled there. The town became a haven for criminals and lowlifes. During World War II the Japanese knocked down the walls the stones of which were eventually used to extend Kai Taki Airport's runway into the bay. Yet the town remains as it was, a cesspool of dirt and crime, largely without electricity, running water, or modern services of any kind. Everyone in Hong Kong knows where the walls once stood for the lines are as clear as walking from day into darkness. And no one, no one that is, except the unfortunate few who must live there, or the untouchable many who hide there, ever cross over the lines.

The cab squealed to a stop in front of the Kowloon City Market, my door was already open. I stuffed a wad of Hong Kong dollars into the driver's hand and he roared off before he could count it, before I could change my mind, or before a Walled City denizen could step across the road to engage him. Anyway, he didn't need to count it. A good cabby can add up his tip while it's still in your pocket. My cabby, no slouch, had already vanished from sight before a squeal of brakes and a scream of revved engines informed he'd successfully dodged the first oncoming car.

It turned out to be Kayo. When he squealed to the curb beside me and pushed open the passenger door I could see the sleep on his face. He wanted a good explanation. I climbed in to explain and conspire.

4. The Walled City

If one can think of Hong Kong as an enclave of enterprise surrounded by a billion Chinese communists, then it's safe to think of Kowloon City as an enclave of anarchy amid a thriving, modern, well-governed metropolis. The contrast is as stark as a Stonehenge in St. James's Park.

From Kayo's Suburu we could see the mean little streets which lead to the city's interior. Most are too small for cars; some, even too small for the pushcarts. Drug dealers and thieves walk the maze of byways with impunity. There are no streetlights, no shoppers, no glass-fronted stores. There are places to eat and drink within the walls but not the sort of places that draw dinner crowds. The nightlife here is the kind that has people locking their doors. It was barely eleven o'clock in the evening and while Hong Kong and Kowloon blazed with electricity, Kowloon City was dark in the extreme.

"Let's go," I said.

We pried ourselves out of his miniature car and rose to our full heights.

I looked up at Kayo, whose full height was fully eight inches higher than my full height and I thought about that as we crossed the road side by side. I thought about how he was wider than me, too and heavier by at least eighty pounds. The shadow of night fell over us as we approached the first nameless cobblestone street. Kayo had probably never lost a fight in his life. I avoided them whenever I could. Frankly, I didn't recall having won any I couldn't. On this sort of job someone was going to have to assume the role of leader and I weighed all that as we paused on that invisible line where the stone wall no longer stood. I included my own age and experience, too. The original assignment had been mine and I wanted to keep it that way. This was my story. The anonymous call had come to me, not to Kayo. "Okay," I said with authority, "I'm taking charge."

He nodded back.

"You go first," I ordered.

Kayo marched off down the street like a resident. The darkness enveloped us before we'd passed the first building. Candlelight shone from a few open windows, barely enough to highlight the faces that followed our progress; never enough to illuminate the streets. Occasionally doors would stand open, too; numberless doors leading up narrow black stairways or down into rank basements occupied by God knew what kind of Oriental horror.

The place was a rabbit warren of walkways. The grimy stone walls of the dilapidated structures seemed to close in behind us and over our heads.

We turned up a sidestreet so narrow it was little wider than a sidewalk. A man could stretch out his arms and touch the buildings on each side of him. I heard Kayo say in Chinese: "Step aside!" and a small knot of excited men had to stop what they were doing and hug the walls of the buildings. In any other part of Hong Kong it would have been the ubiquitous mahjong game we'd intrerrupted with its inevitable gallery of kibitzers. Whatever these men were up to it wasn't mahjong. Slipping by them

I saw one man being held against the wall by three others, his face drained of all emotion except fear. I saw the flicker of knife blades and I knew if it hadn't been for Kayo, for his intimidating width and height as well as his undefiable manner, I'd have made it no farther than that.

Kayo hadn't slowed once.

I stopped him around a corner and asked him if he knew where he was going.

"No," he said, "do you?"

"No, but I'm not in the lead. If I were leading and I still didn't know where I was going, I wouldn't go so fast."

He shook his head. "In the Walled City it doesn't pay to look like you don't know where you're going."

As we spoke, a small boy raced by us carrying a pail in such a way I knew it contained neither water nor food. I had a pretty good idea what the pail did contain.

"Follow that kid," I told Kayo.

Two minutes later we were standing in front of the Shin Lo Arena watching other men and boys carrying wicker baskets or pails inside while others yet, barkers, moved up and down the streets shouting "*Tau shi shoo*." The words *Tau shi shoo* echoed down the labyrinthine streets.

"A cricket match?" asked Kayo.

"Right. But not the kind they play at the Hong Kong Cricket Club, old bean." Cricket fights—the large males found on the damp hillsides in the New Territories make the best fighters—are strictly illegal in Hong Kong. Naturally in Kowloon City, anything goes.

We joined the crowd soon working our way up to an old cashier behind a steel grill. I never had to say a word. He took one look at me, pushed his thumb over his shoulder and signaled a fat Chinese standing beside him to let us pass through.

In a filthy room barely thirty feet square and bare of furniture no less than two hundred people, all of them men, had gathered around a washtub on the floor, the nearer ones kneeling down, those farther back stooping over and those against the walls standing on their toes or climbing onto the backs of the men in front of them. The stench of sweat struck my nostrils with such impact it took me a second to realize that another of my senses was under an even greater assault. Everyone in that room, and I mean everyone except me and Kayo was shouting at once and the consequent noise level had soared past the threshold of pain. I had to stick my fingers in my ears. This worked well enough until I took another breath and realized to my horror I had no hand left to put over my nose. The problem became moot at best when more spectators pressed in behind me, crushing me so tightly I had to stop breathing altogether. Only my eyes could take matters in without feeling violated. I saw two hundred mad Chinese and four hundred fists pounding the air. Some were just shaking and some were filled with bills. As fast as the money went up another fist snatched it away and a bet was made. I saw a ruled chart in Chinese script posted on the far wall and decided this was a record of the competition. A single elimination event. When a man's cricket dies, he's out. Even as Kayo and I pressed through the crowd I could see two men bent over the tub. They had tiny brushes in their hands and seemed to be stroking their insects in the same way a boxing trainer will rub the back of his fighter. Both trainers came out of the tub together and as they did, the noise level doubled. I don't know what I'd have done if a hulking Chinese hadn't tapped me on the shoulder, turned and plowed a path through the human mass to another room farther along.

Two more Chinese hulks built to the same dimensions as the first and so much alike they might have been triplets were waiting for us there.

One of them glared at Kayo, turned to me and grunted:

"You were told to come alone."

"No, I wasn't," I said. "I was told not to bring any cops. Kayo's not a cop."

"What is he?"

“He’s an insurance man.”

He smiled. The way King Kong smiled before he put the grab on Fay Wray. “Like Lloyds of London?”

I smiled back. “No, like Rock of Gibraltar.”

The guy thought about that for a minute, decided it was possibly clever and therefore too much for him. “Okay,” he said. “You come with me.” He turned to the other two and said something which was neither Cantonese nor Mandarin. I got the point of it though when he led me away and the pair blocked Kayo’s path. From here, I would go on alone.

We went down a corridor, through a door, up a narrow staircase, down another corridor, through another door, and into a room.

By gosh, they weren’t triplets, they were quadruplets. Hulking brother number four stood against a wall with his arms folded.

“Doll Mulligan?” It came from behind me.

I turned around. Or rather, I was turned around. The first hulk grabbed my arm and spun me in a half circle and the second moved in behind me and took a hold on the other arm. The weight came off my feet until they were two inches above the floor.

I looked where they faced me.

At last, a Chinese of normal height and build. Here was my anonymous tipster. I took in what I could while he did the same to me. Forty to fifty years old, starting to go gray, turning to fat around the middle. Cigarette smoke had yellowed his fingernails and his teeth. With his pushed in nose, his flat face and his bulging eyes he looked like a Pekingese dog. He even made funny noises when he breathed. Any one of the hulk brothers could have trussed him up and toted him around under one arm like a pet. They might have too, if it hadn’t been for those big bulging eyes of his. Everything this character was that meant anything, I could see in those eyes. He was as mean as any one of the four; he was smarter than all four put together.

"Not Doll," I said. "Doyle. Doyle Mulligan."

"Do you know who I am, Mistuh, Mulligan?"

It was the right voice too. Half bark and half growl. Whatever had flattened his face had messed up his mouth in the process.

I shrugged my shoulders, which is no easy thing when you've got two hundred pounds hanging onto each arm and your feet are dangling two inches off the floor.

"Should I?' I asked.

"It's okay if you suspect; it's better if you don't know for certain."

I thought but didn't say: "Then it's perfect, because I haven't the foggiest idea." Still, I caught the implication. He wanted me to think he was a member of the "Big Circle," the legendary association of mainland Chinese criminals that pulled bank robberies and kidnappings from the safety of the Walled City. They also ran a refugee railway out of China and into Hong Kong. Maybe he was a member. Anyway, what I said was: "Okay then, you know me. I don't know you. Where do we go from there?" He said nothing. I went on: "Should I ask questions? You'll have to keep your answers simple because I can't take notes in this position. I don't want rush you, whoever you are, but I can't hang around all night. Get it? Hang around…?"

He said nothing so I went on.

"I told my insurance man I'd only be gone a couple of minutes. If this takes too long he's liable to get worried and come up here to cancel some policies."

I was talking just to keep up my nerve.

The Pekingese shook his head. His lips twisted into a sneer. After a pause so pregnant it had nearly given birth to a postponement, he murmured. "Walk with your mind, Mistuh Mulligan. Talk with your eyes. Save your mouth for eating. One gains no knowledge while speaking."

"That's good," I said. "Have you heard the one about the triple amputee whose doctor tried to charge him an arm and a leg—?"

"Enough! You were on that plane?"

"I told you I was."

"You saw the explosion?"

"Sure."

"Tell me what happened to Huang Mu?"

My mouth hung open but no words came out. That hadn't been in any of the newspaper reports. No one except me and Stringer and a few policemen knew a man named Huang Mu was missing.

"Who?"

"Huang Mu," he repeated. "You were following him, weren't you?"

"Oh, him. Yeah, I guess I was."

"Where is he?"

I made it sound casual:

"Huang took a gulp from the big drink."

He cocked his head the way a little dog does, stared at me as though he could look through my skull into my brain, stepped within a foot of my face and then hauled off and cracked me as hard as he could with his open hand. He did it once with the left, then again with the right. My head rocked hard to each side but not far to each side because it was playing bumper pool with my shoulders, which were nearly up as high as my ears. He backed off.

"You must be an American, Mistuh Mulligan."

My face was throbbing. But I didn't want him to know it. I was too rattled to come up with an argument for what was obviously a rhetorical statement and I didn't want him to know that either so I kept my mouth shut.

"There are many things about the British that I find objectionable, even intolerable," he went on, "but at least they have a grasp of the fundamentals of courtesy. They are polite. We

Chinese treasure good manners. It is a trait wholly lacking in the American people. Where is Huang Mu?"

"He's dead."

"The explosion?"

"Yeah. Of course there's no body. He was sucked out the side of the plane at thirty thousand feet."

The Pekingese closed his eyes. But the eyelids still bulged from his flat face. After a few seconds they came open.

"First Lee and now Huang. Do the police know who did this?"

I shrugged my shoulders and four hundred pounds again. "I don't know what the police know," I said. "When I left him, the inspector in charge of the investigation was talking about bubagoos, boogey men and midnight beasties."

The Pekingese's eyes bulged evcn wider. If they were talking now they were screaming.

As for me, my mind was all set to walk but the rest of me couldn't shake loose. "I thought I came up here to get information," I said. "Not so you and the Great Wall could slap me around. Do you have something to tell me about the Iron Underground or not?"

"Yes."

"What is it?"

"Your service is dropping the story."

"It is?"

"Yes. You want to live, don't you Mistuh Mulligan?"

I didn't even have to think about it.

"Only forever."

"Then talk to your editors. Convince them to drop the story at once."

"I talked to my editor earlier this evening about dropping the story. He likes the story."

"Talk to him again. Convince him."

"Just like that?"

"You will forget about Huang Mu and his silly clinic. You have no interest in whether or not Chinese are leaving Hong Kong. You have no interest in where they may be going. Forget the *de ha tit*. You will find yourself a new story."

"If I don't have any interest in this story, why did I come here? Was it just to see a couple of bugs battle to the death in a washtub? Maybe I came for the atmosphere."

"You didn't come here."

"I didn't?"

"No. You've never been to this room. You've never been to the Shin Lo Arena. You've never even been to Kowloon City. And you've certainly never spoken to me."

"...whoever you are," I added for him.

"Correct. In that way you can go on living. If not forever, at least a little while longer."

"I get you. It's kind of a health thing. This story is bad for mine."

"Exactly."

"What about the conferences?"

"You're not concerned about them. If you're assigned to cover them, you'll refuse.

"In a minute," I agreed. "It may tie in with this *de ha tit* business and I don't have any interest in that. I get a little queasy just thinking about it."

"Very good, Mistuh Mulligan."

"Maybe I could cover some Kowloon restaurants for the food editor."

"Yes. That would be a good idea."

"I had lunch at a place on Waterloo Road that makes the best Mongolian hotpot you ever tasted. I could write about that."

The Pekingese man stood up and gestured to the door with a paw. "My men will show you downstairs. Stick to your Waterloo restaurant, Mistuh Mulligan. Otherwise you will find yourself in a pot much hotter than anything the Mongolians ever concocted."

"It was nice not meeting you."

"Good by, Mistuh Mulligan."

Arm in arm they started me toward the hall. Halfway there I dug in my heels and turned my head around until I spotted the Pekingese about to leave through another door on the opposite wall.

"Tell me one thing," I shouted to him.

He stopped and came slowly around.

"What is it?"

"Just between you and me and the Great Wall here, where do you think all those people are running to, huh?"

His bulging eyes narrowed to mere slits. He turned to one of the hulks and said in Cantonese: "Take this foreign devil out into the alley and kill him."

I understood every word of that and though it sounds silly, the "kill him" part of it didn't hit me until later. And my minds glossed right over the foreign devil thing too. The term "gweilo" has been used against westerners so much in the last several years it's almost earned itself a kind of respectability. All I could think of was that we'd come in on a back street the size of a sidewalk and if it had an alley out back, how in the world could it be big enough for two hulks and me at one time?

That was my first concern.

Then the "kill him" part hit me and I began to scream like a madman.

One of the hulk brothers wrapped a hand over my mouth and together they wrestled me into an adjoining room where I was pushed down a back stairway. I practically tumbled all the way down. Somehow I reached the bottom in one piece and scrambled to my feet. And here came the brothers moving in to take hold of my arms.

There was nowhere to run except back up the stairs or out into the alley. They wanted me out in the alley and I'd have to fight my way through them to get back to the stairs.

So that's what I did.

It was a battle I dared not lose for like the cricket match this fight was single elimination. I became a flurry of motion, blocking their blows, showering them with every nature of strike, swinging, kicking, dodging, parrying, and moving. Always moving. I was on them like bad weather—a storm of fighting fury. My feet struck like lightning; my fists pounded them like hailstones. The outcome was never in doubt. But I bet that before they'd dragged my bruised and battered body into the alley and dumped me in a broken heap on the cobblestones, they knew they'd been in a fight.

"Just do it and let's go," one of them growled.

"Not for this one," snarled the other. "Look what he did! I'm going to slash his damned throat."

"He bit you, too?"

"No, he got blood all over my jacket. Lift him up."

I felt one of them kneel down beside me, turn me over, and raise my back off the stones. He grabbed a handful of my hair and yanked my head back. This is it, I said to myself. My heart leapt into my mouth and I swallowed it back down as fast as I could because I didn't want to be stabbed in the heart while having my throat cut.

It was too dark to see what happened next. At least, it was too dark to be sure of what I was seeing—that alley was a montage of shadows formed by the oblong of half-light from the arena's back door. One shadow separated itself from the others and glided behind the hulk brother holding the knife. I sensed as much as saw the thing hovering over his kneeling body. I heard a grunt and then a plop when the knife fell into a puddle. When my head was let go, it dropped back onto the cobblestones. I didn't go out but I felt like I weighed half a ton and none of it muscle. Not until later did I realize the hulk had landed on top of my chest.

I tried to roll over.

The shadows of two men stood over me. The larger one windmilled his arms wildly at the other. This smaller man swung once. A body blow. It sounded like a sledge hammer smashing a ripe melon. I didn't really see it. What I saw was the big one stop swinging, bundle his trunk in his arms, teeter a bit back and forth, and then slump to the stones like a two hundred pound bag of rice.

The remaining shadow vanished as suddenly and quietly as the moon scudding behind thick clouds.

All I got after that was the sound of heavy footsteps slapping the wet stones like gunfire from the back door of the arena. In only a second or two, Kayo was pulling the weight off my chest and helping me to my feet.

I stood there while my head slowly stopped spinning. I rubbed my neck just to satisfy myself it was still attached.

"You took your damn time," I mumbled at my friend.

"There were those two others," he explained by way of apology. "They tried to stop me and I had to hurt them bad."

As though that made it okay. Jesus! I could have been killed!

"I think you hurt this one a little too bad," I said turning the first hulk brother over on his back.

"What?" Kayo was suddenly beside me.

"He's dead," I told him.

"But Doily! I didn't hit him. The other one either."

"Somebody hit him. Somebody was here. I thought it was you."

"Didn't you hit him?"

"Well…I fought with him, but—"

"There's not a mark on him," said Kayo.

And Kayo was right. Not a bruise. Not a knife or a gun wound. Nothing. He had a few smears of blood but according to him it had been my blood. There was no reason at all for him to be dead. Nevertheless, he was dead.

I crawled over to the other body. Here was a different story entirely. The blood on this one was his own. It boiled out of a hole in his chest the size of my fist. I wouldn't have believed a wound like that could have been made by anything quieter or less destructive than a bazooka and yet I'd heard nothing except for that melon being smashed.

I stood up.

"Let's get out of here, Kayo."

"We can't just leave a dead body. It's against the law."

"This is Kowloon City."

"Still..."

"We can call the Hong Kong police but they won't come. Not here, they won't."

Kayo and I hashed it out and decided that there was only one cop in Hong Kong who was dumb enough to walk into the Walled City and that was Inspector Hawthorne. Kayo would have to go because it was his car. I would go too because I wasn't staying one minute here by myself.

We started walking.

As we neared the city's boundary Kayo asked if I knew where Hawthorne was. I told him I had a pretty good idea.

"That guy up there said something about how somebody named Lee had got it first and now Huang."

"Jesus, Doily, that's like Smith. There must be half a million Chinese in this town named Lee."

"But half a million Chinese didn't just get it. Didn't you go to a fire this afternoon...before Stringer pulled you off and sent you to the airport?"

"That's right. Lee Chung's mansion up on the peak."

Lee Chung.

I'd already guessed it. Lee Chung wasn't a billionaire in the British sense. He didn't have a million million dollars. He had only a hundred thousand million or so Hong Kong dollars. Which meant he was worth a paltry fifteen or twenty billion bucks U.S. Kayo idolized the guy. To an acupuncture groupie like Kayo, Lee Chung was the head guru. Before writing his book, Lee had piled it up poking holes into sick people which, even at a hundred dollars a hole must have made Lee about the holiest man in the east. Figured that way I could well understand my friend's idolatry.

But Lee was much more than a billionaire acupuncturist with franchised clinics all over the world, upwards of a hundred in Hong Kong alone, and at least half a dozen in every major city on every continent. With royalties from these clinics he'd bought into hotels and casinos. He owned an airline in Australia, a containerized steamship company in Japan and a Pacific cruise line that sailed out of Hong Kong. Lee was also the colony's finest example of refugee to riches; so it surprised no one when he became the colony's most outspoken critic of the Handover. Like most wealthy Chinese he had made his "arrangements." His money and interests were safely overseas, in London, New York and Tokyo banks. Unlike the others, he had announced his imminent departure. And he advised other Chinese in Hong Kong to do the same thing. Even the not so wealthy. In fact, to anyone who could afford to get out of Hong Kong, Lee Chung's advice was always the same—Get out!

And if that wasn't enough, it was at least a reasonable surmise that Huang Mu's acupuncture clinic was owned by Lee Chung.

Thirty minutes later Kayo was downshifting through the Subaru's gears up the winding Magazine Gap to Peak Road and on from there to the peak.

At 1800 feet, the highest point in Hong Kong, Victoria Peak overlooks the Central Business District on the island. Much of its summit is taken up by the Victoria Peak Gardens. The swank mansions are across a gap to the east where the summer temperatures are still ten to twenty degrees cooler than the city. Lee Chung's digs were just up from the tram station terminus so he would enjoy a good view of the gardens, the business district as well as Victoria Harbor and beyond it, Kowloon. Hell, he could probably see halfway to Beijing. This land is the most expensive ground on the planet and Lee had more than anyone else living up here. He hadn't put up a mansion; he'd built a palace. A twelve foot high wall broken only by an electrified gate informed us we'd reached our destination. The gate was standing open. We caught the red flash of emergency strobes at the end of a long drive and the glow of several fires just coming under control.

"Just a house fire up on the peak," Stringer had said. "Nothing for us really and yet…I had a feeling."

My sixth sense about Stringer's sixth sense was tingling. Kayo's too. I heard hs intake of breath as we entered the front gate.

There were cars all over but only official vehicles were getting through. A fireman waved us onto the grass. We advanced on foot through smoke laden darkness so dense even a battery of flares, flashlights, spotlights and occasional headlights couldn't suppress it to a police barricade which restrained a group of civilians from the actual site of the fire. I recognized reporters from the Standard, the Morning Post, the Sun, as well as some Cantonese language dailies. I saw no one from the other wire services because, as Stringer said, a fire is strictly local news. Naturally there were reporters from the "mosquito press," the Chinese dailies which normally concentrated on gambling and sex but tonight saw a story in a fire at the home of the world's wealthiest celestial. Kayo moseyed across to some mosquito reporters he knew to dig up some dope.

Beyond the barricades, a once magnificent estate lay in ruins. Fire trucks had positioned themselves to put out what fires still burned in the structures and grounds. The manor itself was nothing but a gutted monolith with piles of still glowing embers throughout. Behind the house, where we were standing, we could make out the remains of a multiple car garage where the black carcasses of several expensive automobiles smoldered. Flames had consumed a potting shed and reduced to ashes a once formal garden neatly terraced on the hillside. Only the twelve-foot stone wall surrounding the several acres had contained the blaze.

But thirty yards from the press, in the middle of this garden was the core of official activity. Flagtone steps led to a circular concrete foundation. Charred perimeter posts and the twisted black skeletons of shrubbery outside the circle convinced me that the structure had been a kind of Oriental pavilion or gazebo called a *fangzi*. Of the roof and the sides nothing remained. We could see the heads of several men working inside. But what they were up to was anyone's guess.

Official or press, I was the only foreign devil on the premises with the exception of two men just this side of the *fangzi* who were deep in conversation. One a tall man with a hatchet-face and a quick angular way of moving, was apparently getting a report from the second, shorter stockier man who was wearing spectacles and a tan Burberry weatherproof like I'd seen in the window at Lane Crawford CBD. A cop and a coroner if ever I saw them. There aren't so many Westerners in public service that I hadn't met Mortimer Braithwait the medical examiner before. And of course I had only that same afternoon made the acquaintance of the charming and well-mannered Inspector Hawthorne of Scotland Yard, London.

"Inspector!" I shouted.

The taller of the two men turned, saw me, frowned, and returned to his conversation with the doctor. After another minute they parted company so the M.E. could trudge back into the ashes and Hawthorne could make his way over to the ropes.

"What are you doing here?" he growled.

I grinned. "Do you want to see my press card again?"

"No, I don't. I don't want to see you again either." He narrowed his eyes as he got close to me. "My lord, I didn't realize that officer had fisticuffed you quite so professionally. You look wretched."

"I'll feel better if you'll tell me what's going on."

"I wouldn't." Hawthorne turned his back on me—showing no graps of the fundamentals of courtesy—walked away and as he did muttered under his breath, "Bloody Irish stew!"

I swear that's what he said.

For a moment I was too astonished to reply and when I did my mind hadn't recovered sufficiently to do better than shout, "Tell it to the queen, copper belly!"

He stopped and whirled around.

"You notice I don't ask what you're doing here," I added in a slightly less belligerent tone. "Flash! Visiting Scotland Yard Official Supervises Dousing of Local House Fire. I don't have to ask why you're here because it's the same reason that brought me and we both know it. It's all one big mess, isn't it? We both know that, too and I'm going to get to the bottom of it with or without you. Only don't come asking for any more of my help."

If that sounds arrogant, then that's the way I was feeling. Hawthorne glared. I thought he was going to have me arrested and so did he, but when Hawthorne turned to the police officer just across the ropes that was not the order he issued. His face had softened a bit from rage to resignation.

"You say you speak Chinese, eh, Mulligan." It wasn't a question.

"Some," I said angrily.

"How much?"

"Not how much. How many. There is no Chinese language. There are several dozen Chinese dialects. I speak Cantonese and Mandarin. Cantonese is the official language of Hong Kong. Mandarin is the official language in Beijing. I'm hazy on the others."

"All right. Come on."

I grinned, saluted my brother reporters and stepped over the rope. When the officer moved in to stop me, Hawthorne signalled it was okay for me to cross. Then the inspector waited until he and I had moved well out of hearing of the others before he halted and glared down at me."

"How long have you been here?" he demanded not exactly politely but almost civilly.

"About ten minutes."

"Not here, dammit. Here! China."

"I've been in Hong Kong three years; including all of the East, about five."

We'd moved along the flagstone steps toward the *fangzi*. If I hadn't been concerned with catching a glimpse of the official activity I might have marveled at the view of midnight Hong Kong which the *fangzi* had obviously been situated to provide. Hawthorne, in a brooding silence, was regarding neither. He had paused, waiting for a group of officials to pass.

When they had he muttered:

"All right, tell me about the 'dee hah teet.'"

"*De ha tit*?"

"Yes."

"There's no secret to that. It's a Cantonese variation of the Japanese. It translates as Underground Iron. That's what they were going to name the MTR here, the Mass Transit Railway, in particular the section under the harbor between Kowloon and Hong Kong Island. However, the Chinese—always a superstitious lot—objected because the term *de ha tit* also has a rather morbid connotation."

"Like what?"

"Iron crypts or tombs."

"Go on."

"That was a few years ago. Earlier this year, as word spread that an underground railway was spiriting thousands of Chinese out of Hong Kong, the name cropped up again. This time *de ha tit* seemed to fit."

"How's that?"

"Whoever takes a ride on that underground...they never surface again." I raised my brows. "Chinese 101 recessing for today?"

"Not quite yet. What do you know about this 'yaygah' business?"

"Yaygah? Never heard of it." I thought for a second. "Oh, you mean the expression. '*Queyega*!' It's ***yega***. Like Vega, except with a 'Y.'" I laughed. "What of it? Don't tell me you're becoming superstitious, too?"

"What does it mean?"

"Nothing much. It's sort of a blessing. Qu is just 'scat' or 'go away' ***Yega***, I don't know exactly. It's an evil spirit of some kind. You know the thing. When disaster strikes they say that quickly and it scares away the demon."

"What kind of demon?"

I shrugged. "Who knows? The word isn't Cantonese or Mandarin. In fact, I doubt if there is a literal translation. I heard it more often back in Red China quite a few years ago where I think it got its start." I raised my brows and grinned at him. "If you really want in on all the spook stuff you know they put gargoyles on their rooftops to scare away evil spirits and pointed corners on the eaves to stop them from getting inside. Do you want the lowdown on that, too?"

Hawthorne merely snorted. I was to find that he would do that often in conversation me.

"Well," I began brightly because, after all, an affirmative snort sounds much like a negative one, "the evil spirits drop out of the sky." I was gesticulating wildly, swinging my arms in big circles. "They hit the gables of the houses and slippery slide down." My hands swept in a great arc and then hung, shaking in the air just inches from his face. "But see how the upturned corners catch on their shirttails as they go over the eaves?"

"You know, Mulligan, you act rather slippy for a man who blocks with his face. You have been of no help. Now go back behind the barricade. And no more disparaging remarks about the queen, do you hear?"

"I could be more help," I offered.

"All right." He squared off with me. His piercing blue eyes stared right into my swollen black and blue ones. "Tell me what you're doing here."

I thought about it. Hawthorne knew good and well there was a connection between these two incidents, the bombing of an airplane and the burning of a Victoria Peak palace. I did too. He just didn't know what I knew and I didn't know what he knew and it didn't look as though either of us ever would unless one of us opened up first. It was right aabout then I remembered Kayo, the two bodies in Kowloon City and why I'd come in the first place.

"I got a tip that Lee Chung was tied in to Huang Mu," I offered tentatively. "I talked to a guy who's involved with the *de ha tit* and he knows both of them."

"Who is he, this guy who knows Chung and Mu?"

"Lee and Huang," I corrected him. "The Chinese put the surname first and the Christian name last."

"Who is he?"

"I don't know." I held up my hands. "Honest inspector that's the truth. I almost got killed finding out that much and a couple of other guys did get killed. Some goons who tried to cut my throat. That's what I've come for. To take you to them."

"Where are they?"

"Kowloon City. It's near the airport."

"There must be several police stations between here and the airport."

"Not any that will send cops into Kowloon City. Ask Doctor Braithwait. We're talking sleaze bucket big time."

"All right, all right, give me a minute."

He turned to the side when he heard footsteps and then gave me his back to confer with the medical examiner.

"Extraordinary," said Braithwait. "If I'm right and I think I am. You should see this, inspector."

The two of them turned and began wading back through the thick bed of ashes toward the *fangzi* and since I assumed my invitation to tag along was a continuing one, I hurried to catch up. On the steps Hawthorne stopped, glared at me and snapped:

"You can come, Mulligan, on one condition. You don't tell anyone about what you see or hear. Not your boss, not your big friend, not any of the people you work with. And you don't print anything until I give you the all clear."

"No deal," I declared. "What if you fall in the harbor and drown?" He snorted. "Or just lose your voice. Suppose another wire service or newspaper picks up the story? I can agree to hold on as long as possible. Beyond that, you'll just have to trust to Doyle's discretion."

When they joined the others in the *fangzi* I followed at a discreet distance, showing discretion. Once I mounted the steps I could see what I hadn't been able to before. Seven Chinese knelt in a circle on the flagstone floor, a network of interconnected white lines had been carefully swept clean of ashes. It looked for all the world like another game of mahjong in progress but it wasn't mahjong this time any more than it had been in that Kowloon City back street. Honkers love playing or watching mahjong but these boys were having no fun at all. They viewed the object of their work with gruesome distaste. The players/kibitzers were actually fire and medical officials and the network of lines were not the domino-like rows of white mahjong tiles but the bones of a full human skeleton.

We got closer and stood over them looking down into the center of their little circle.

No clothes remained, little skin or internal organs and what was there merely adhered to the blackened bones like so much burnt leather. The flesh had been consumed not by worms across the span of months or years but by a fiery furnace in a matter of minutes.

Yet the bones themselves told a horrifying tale.

The figure lay on its back. The legs were together. Curiously though, the forearms lay over the rib cage and the fingers were neatly intertwined. The finger bones and the ribs below them were terribly distorted, almost as though they were made of gray putty.

"The ribs fractured down here," said Dr. Braithwait, bending and pointing to the two lower ribs on the left side, "are the result of a beam falling on the body after death. We removed it along with the other debris. There just isn't enough flesh left to determine cause of death here or in the laboratory. Nothing's left but bone. We'll never know for certain what killed him just as we will never establish with certainty who he is."

"Dental records?" snapped Hawthorne.

Braithwait looked up and gave a superior little smile. "Ordinarily, yes, but look at his teeth. The fillings have melted right out of them. What's left is too misshapen to be of any clinical value." He added, "But since you know it to be—"

"We know, Doctor Braithwait, that a few minutes before the fire, the cook admits seeing Mr. Chung rise from a half-completed breakfast and walk out to this pavilion."

"*Fangzi*," the doctor corrected him. "And the name is Lee. These Chinese chaps put the first name—"

"Yes, yes, never mind all that. You said you had something extraordinary."

"Indeed, I do. For there is something. When you search for the source of the fire, I believe you will find it is right here."

"We've already assumed the *fangzi* was—"

"Not the *fangzi*, inspector. Him. I have talked to the fire marshal," Braithwait indicated one of the Chinese standing to the side, "and we are in agreement that everything points to it. The direction of the burning, the obvious intensity of the blaze in this specific area."

"What are you saying?"

"I believe that this man was himself set afire."

"How?" Petrol?"

"I doubt it. The heat was too intense for that. God, look what it's done to him. I've seen bodies hauled out of blazing buildings before but nothing ever to equal this. He burned like a fireball at an incredible temperature and only a very high incendiary could accomplish that. If we had not tended to the fire when we did, I shouldn't be surprised if even the bones would have been consumed. Those ribs and the metacarpals and phalanges…er, the finger bones, they're not just burned, they're actually melted. Fortunately, for us the rest of the skeleton was saved because that is not the worst of it. See here." Braithwait knelt again and pointed through the crater of dissolved rib bones to a point on the spine. "The fourth thoracic vertebra here—vertebral body shattered neatly just laterally to the superior costal pit; and here, the fifth cervical vertebra—poterior tubercle fractured cleanly."

"You're telling me his back was broken?"

"Yes. Twice."

"Then that killed him?"

I was edging to one side of the inspector, trying for a closer look. I got more than I'd bargained for. I thought I had a strong stomach and I guess I do but I was swallowing hard and tasting Mongolian hotpot. I hadn't been lying to the Pekingese. I'd had it for lunch and I'd loved it. But. Like so many other things it's only a treat the first time around.

"No," I overheard Braithwait say. "No, I would say not. The breaks are clean. Unbelievely clean. I could almost believe these vertebrae were severed as part of a surgical operation. Except they were caused by a blow or blows while this man was erect. Before the body was burned. And it was done so skillfully that while there would almost assuredly have been extensive—probably even total—paralysis, I don't think it would have killed him. He could not have moved at all. In fact, the first person to come along and help him to his feet would most likely have finished him off by shifting the spine."

"I don't buy that," said Hawthorne. He indicated the intgerlaced fingers. "You can see for yourself he's praying. Begging for his life. How could he do that if he couldn't move?"

"He could not have done that," said Braithwait with renewed force.

"Then…"

"Someone did it for him."

"You said if somebody came along and moved him—"

"Unless it was the same person who broke his back. Lee was alive. Probably even conscious. It's my guess that he lay there watching helpless and in extreme pain as someone, whoever the monster was that did this to him, methodically prepared some type of thermite explosive, placed it on Lee's chest, and locked his fingers on top of it to keep it from falling. Then he walked away. Whether it went off in ten seconds or ten hours, Lee couldn't have done anything but watch the clock count down until the damnable thing ignited and set him ablaze."

The hotpot won. I managed to slip behind a couple of burn piles before it hove but I doubt anybody was fooled.

A little while later I found Kayo behind the barricade, took him aside, and broke my promise to Inspector Hawthorne. I owed Kayo that much. I didn't want him to read about Lee in the morning papers. I didn't tell him how Lee had died. Kayo was upset enough without that.

Anyway, as it turned out, I didn't need to.

Before we were finished Kayo would learn it for himself firsthand.

5. The Boy from Tiananmen

I marched through the front doors of the Arsenal Street Police Headquarters Building in Wanchai, stopped just inside, and stared.

A juvenile delicious wearing bluejeans and tennis shoes sprang off a seat in the waiting area and bounded toward me. I almost didn't recognize her. Sung Kwon looked so much like a kid I had to remind myself she was the same girl to whom I'd been giving whistful smiles on the Taiwan flight only twelve hours before. In spite of that, this outfit seemed to fit Sung's character better. I don't believe she was wearing makeup (with those dark features she hardly needed to) and her long black hair was entwined in two billowing pigtails which bounced off her shoulders with every step she took.

I guess I looked different to her, too. "Doyle!" she cried as she got close enough to make out the rainbow of bruises on my face. "What happened to you?"

"I'm okay. What are you doing here?"

In one way I was happy to see her here and in another I wasn't. Seeing her made me happy. Seeing her here confirmed my suspicions.

She came against me. "I came looking for you; they told me you'd be here." On an impulse Sung started a hand for my face but drew back without making contact. "I waited for you at the airport but you must have left another way. Did you get into another fight? You weren't so messed up when I saw you in that room. The policeman did that to you, you know. They said so." She looked cautiously around and lowered her voice to a whisper. "Did the police beat you up again?"

"Not this time. There were four of—"

"Don't you ever win any fights?"

Only a woman can shoot a guy down as fast as that.

"Just once," I said. "The toughest fight of my life. We went at it all day and into the night: punching, kicking, biting, and clawing. Blood was everywhere. Broken teeth were flying like Chicklets. It could have gone either way. Only my extra height and reach gave me the edge. Yes, I won that one, all right." I smiled down at her. "And no little kid has ever lipped off to me since."

Sung made big eyes, the way women do when they pretend to believe and be shocked by what men say.

"You beat up a child!"

"Well . . . she was big for her age."

We broke it up when Inspector Hawthorne came marching out of a back room with two other Royal Hong Kong policemen in plain clothes. I braced myself for a remark and would have got one if he'd been the one Sung had talked to about finding me because I'd asked him about her on the way back to Kowloon City. No remark. Not even a Cheerio. He just reached out a hand for the Manila envelope I was carrying and snatched it away. Oh, they have manners all right!

He pulled out the reprints and started leafing through them, handing each one in turn to a lieutenant beside him as he finished. I'd put each picture in proper sequence so the first ones showed Huang Mu emerging from his Celestial Acupuncture Clinic, hailing a cab to the airport, entering the terminal and then no more until after the explosion. Those were in order too, ending with the fire and security people racing toward the DC-10 once it was down and the passengers were out on the tarmac. I expected a crack about the one print, that first one I'd shot after the explosion because it had been in at least two of the local papers, but no, they passed it by. In fact, none of them spoke a word until Hawthorne was shoving the pictures back into the envelope and then he muttered at me:

"Negatives?"

That's every cop in the world rolled up into one. You lay before them such a feast of information they can't even get it down at a single setting and instead of "Thank you" they growl for a doggy bag.

"What about the acupuncture clinic?" I asked to change the subject. "I thought you were going to let me tag along when you went through the place?"

"We're not going through the place."

"Why not?"

"Because last night while you and I were out searching for bodies in Kowloon City, a fire went through the place—the clinic is gone. There's nothing left."

I felt the same way I had when the Pekingese slapped my face good and hard. My mouth had plenty to say but my brain had gone slack-jaw.

"What about the others?" I said shortly. "There must be a hundred Celestial Clinics scattered all over Hong Kong and Kowloon as well as the New Territories."

"Eighty-seven, to be precise. But which of them do you have evidence against tying it into the *de ha tit?* We'd need evidence to obtain a warrant."

"Lee Chung owned 'em all?"

"Apparently."

"So what are you going to do?" I said.

He half-smiled. "I'll remind you, Mulligan, I've come to Hong Kong in order to look into this matter of IE's, and report what I find at the conference which, I needn't remind you, starts this afternoon."

"How about me?"

"I haven't time to nanny the press."

I asked him what that was supposed to mean.

"You've been advised to forget your story and stay out of this affair altogether," he replied. "It was good advice, regardless of who gave it to you. This is a matter for the police. Let us handle it."

"But you said—"

He dipped his hatchet face and chopped off my words: "We needn't detain you any longer, Mulligan. Now, if you'll excuse us . . .?"

With that, he and his two Royal flatfeet passed by us and swept through the front doors.

I swear to God if Sung hadn't been there, I'd have made a few disparaging remarks about the queen that would have had the most ardent anti-colonialist blushing.

As it was I kept my mouth shut.

I heard her saying: "So what are you going to do now?" However I ignored the question because I was thinking about how to word what I needed to ask her.

"I'm still on assignment. This is my case whether the Hong Kong police like it or not. Somebody's been burning my bridges before I can cross 'em." I grumbled. "I've only got one lead left. Hawthorne doesn't know anything about it and I'm darned if I'll hand it over. I'll check it out by myself." I was feeling pretty darn cold until I gave Sung a good look. Then I melted. The pigtails were wonderful. I couldn't imagine anything looking better on anybody than those blue jeans and blouse looked on her. But it was the tennis shoes that did it. On impulse I said, "You don't want to come along, do you?"

"No," she replied with sheer delight in her eyes.

"That surprised me. "You don't?"

"No," she repeated.

There went all my suspicions. I didn't know whether to feel relieved or let down. I asked her where she did want to go.

"With you," she said.

I took a mental step back. "Didn't you just say you weren't coming with me?"

"Yes."

"Well, make up your mind."

She took me by the arm and led me through the front door explaining: "You asked me if I don't want to come and I answered, No, because that was wrong, I do want to come. You asked if I didn't say I was not coming and I answered Yes because that was correct, I did not say that. Now do you understand?"

I answered, Yes, because I didn't. Still, I was starting to get the idea. Sung replied to statements rather than questions. This was a gift from her father, the Korean way of replying to what my fifth grade teacher back in Kansas used to call the "Negative Interrogative."

I would be a long time getting used to it.

Once we were outside, I suggested we get something to eat first because it was almost noon and I'd nothing in my stomach but the remains of yesterday's Mongolian hotpot and what of it I'd managed to keep down acted like leftovers. Sung suggested taking a rickshaw. That's when I gave her a smile and put it down in my book that she hadn't been long in Hong Kong.

We walked to a *dai pai dong* near the "Suzie Wong" area where the red lights are dimmed but not nearly extinguished. The *dai pai dong* is the Hong version of a fast-food restaurant. Fast in this case applies not only to the food but to the restaurant itself which sports two big wheels and a vendor who pushes it around. We carried our goodies to a park near the docks and watched cruise ships dodge steamers and walla-wallas out on the pond.

"The government hasn't renewed a rickshaw license since 1975," I explained to her over Peking Duck, the official food of the colony, or it would be if the colony had an official food. "There's only about half a dozen of 'em left," I said, "run by seventy-year old men who sit down at the Star Ferry Pier charging the tourists ten dollars Hong Kong to have their photographs taken." She thought that was sad. There were still lots of rickshaws in Singapore and Bangkok, she told me. I knew for myself that Macao still had pedicabs galore.

"Yes," I agreed, though I'd never even thought about it till then. "It will be kind of sad when the last rickshaw is gone."

I really did feel sad. I was sitting on a park bench in Wanchai eating Peking Duck with a beautiful girl—not one of those porcelain perfect Oriental beauties but a real girl with butterscotch skin and large almond eyes—and I was sad. Or, looked at another way, The Chinese communists were poised to take over Hong Kong, the colony's very existence had an expiration date stamped "Long overdue," every year a quarter million desperate Chinese were packing their lives into bags and running away…and here we were worrying ourselves about six rickshaw "boys" who were way past the age of retirement.

I could understand about me. I didn't much like this story of mine. I wanted to quit. I'd been told if I didn't I'd be killed. The cops wouldn't cooperate. Every lead I'd found had been blown up or beat up or burned up but one: the beautiful girl with butterscotch skin and large…no, enormous almond eyes.

So I was sad.

But Sung's curiosity was bursting. After we'd settled the rickshaw matter she started asking questions. The more she wanted to know, the less suspicious I was, and the more certain.

She wanted to know about this IE business. I explained that it meant Illegal Emigrants. That at one time the only thing Government House worried about were II's—the Illegal Immigrants. Chinese had been slipping over the border from China to the

New Territories for decades. A few thousand or so each year, mostly old, homeless, or unskilled people that Beijing didn't mind losing. But Hong Kong's population had already swelled to the point there was no room for more when the Reds got the idea of throwing open the gates every once in a while and letting ten, twenty, even as many as thirty thousand come south in a week. The Hong Kong police had no choice but to truck as many as they could catch back to the People's Republic. "At one time, the city was a base." I explained. "If a guy could get past the Chinese guards and the British guards all the way thorugh the New Territories to Kowloon or Victoria, he was home free. He'd be granted citizenship. But no more. Now they go back. Since they started that policy, the flood of refugees had dwindled to a trickle. The big thing now is the IE's" I told her. "A lot more are trying to get out than are trying to get in."

Sung wanted to know about the big conference she'd been reading about. I explained it to her. How the Red Chinese had tried assuring the people of Hong Kong it would be business as usual after 1997 because they needed the city to remain an entrepot for Chinese goods. Half of everything that goes into or out of the People's Republic goes through Hong Kong. This colony wouldn't be worth taking over if all the professional people and most of the qualified workers walked out. The Chinese would only inherit another Canton or Shanghai, nice tourist stops but cities without vision or enterprise. Don't think for a second Beijing doesn't know that, I said. And then came Tiananmen Square. Naturally Sung knew about that. She'd been in Thailand at the time but there weren't many Chinese anywhere in the world who hadn't heard what the People's Liberation Army had done in Tiananmen Square. I explained how, after that, we Honkers knew we were living on borrowed time. That it would be business as usual for the communists, not for us. China's only hope now to take over a port of any value to them was to do to Hong Kong what they already do in China: lock all the doors so no one can go in or out. That's why Beijing had called for the conference. If the British diplomats couldn't prove the emigration situation was blown out of proportion—which they couldn't, because it wasn't—and if they couldn't hang tough against Chinese intercession—which they wouldn't, because they wasn't—the doors might be locked any day.

She wanted to know about Huang and everything that had happened to me since I'd last seen her. I filled her in on all the essentials. The second anonymous tip, my sally into Kowloon City, Lee Chung and the fire on Victoria Peak which had been started even before our flight had taken off for Taiwan, and finally, Hawthorne's and my trip back to Kowloon City to recover the body of hulk brothers number one and two. The Pekingese along with hulk brothers three and four had long since disappeared.

"According to Braithwait," I closed my report, "the big Chinese was so healthy he should have climbed off the table and walked away. There wasn't a thing wrong with the guy with the possible exception that he was dead."

"You don't know who killed him?"

"Who? We don't even know how. With the second one we do. Sort of. He died of a heart seizure. Something rammed under his rib cage inside is chest, seized his heart, and yanked it right out of his body."

"That's so terrible. And you were right there when it happened?"

"Yeah."

"You didn't see?"

"It was a very dark alley, Sung. You can't believe the Walled City until you go there."

"And you went there alone! Oh, Doyle, you should have taken someone with you to help you fight those men. Promise me you'll never go there alone. Not ever again."

Well...like I said, I'd only covered the essentials.

"Oh, Kayo was with me," I assured her. "For all the good he did."

"But you said you had one more lead that the inspector doesn't know about?"

I knew she'd ask about that. "That's right, "I said.

"Huang Mu is dead; Lee Chung is dead; the man who tried to kill you in Kowloon City has disappeared. Who is left?"

I cleaned off the last of a chicken wing, swallowed it, threw the bone into a trash can, licked my fingertips, faced her politely, and as nicely as I could I told her that she was.

"Me?"

Uh huh, I thought to myself. Enormous eyes.

"You," I said.

"What is there about me?"

"It's not much, I admit, but you're all I've got left. Hawthorne told me that Huang Mu had bought the last seat in coach and I'd bought the last seat in first class. He said no one but me could have followed Huang onto the plane."

"I see."

"But think back. You were in the ticket line behind me, Sung. I gave you ups because I was trying to hang back a little from Huang and I didn't know seats were so scarce. Your first class seat in nonsmoking should have been mine."

"You were very nice."

"Hawthorne said I was the only one on the plane who had any interest in Huang. He made a big deal about how I kept going back to use the coach rest room. And yet just before the explosion you were coming out of the women's rest room in coach. You could've used the first-class rest room, too."

She was nodding her head. Saying nothing.

"I went back to keep an eye on Huang Mu," I told her. "Why did you go back there?"

"For the same reason."

"You were watching him, too?"

"Yes."

"Did you follow Huang to the airport?"

"I followed you. You were following Mr. Huang."

"Go on. Tell me the rest of it, Sung."

She had lowered her head. When she did her bangs had fallen over her face and I couldn't tell if she was crying or what. She wasn't making any noise but some of them don't. Suddenly she straightened, shook her bangs aside, and faced me clear-eyed and determined.

"Don't be mad at me, Doyle. I did what I had to do. I was … I am looking for my cousin. He's trying to get out of Hong Kong. Maybe he's already out. I don't know. I knew I couldn't find him myself but I thought someone else might be able to if I told them what I knew."

I was more hurt than mad.

"Why not just go to the police?"

"I couldn't. I promised my aunt that I wouldn't."

"This is the cousin and aunt you were telling me about? I thought you came here for a family reunion."

"I did."

"All right, tell me what you know."

"Han went—that's my cousin's name, Ping Sha Han but we call him Han—he went to a Celestial Acupuncture Clinic run by a man named Huang Mu. He didn't have travel papers. No passport or exit permit, nothing at all. So he couldn't have been planning to leave legally."

"Something clicked in the back of my brain.

"Did you call our office?"

"Yes."

"You talked to a man named Stringer and told him about Huang Mu."

"Yes."

I was getting a little hyped up in spite of myself.

"Go on, go on," I urged her, "what else do you know?"

"Nothing. Just nothing, Doyle, I swear."

"There's got to be more, Sung. Your cousin didn't say anything to you about where he was going or how he would get there?"

"I didn't see him. I never have. We've only written to each other. We used to write often but I haven't heard from him in several years."

"Then…?"

"My Aunt Ling—Han's mother, my mother's sister—told me about Han. She sent for me. To come to Hong Kong to help him. I think she wanted me to take him back to Bangkok with me. But when I got here, Han had already disappeared. She told me he'd gone to that acupuncture clinic and he never came back."

"How much does your aunt know?"

"I don't think she knows anything more than she's told me."

I didn't believe that for a minute but I let it pass. There was plenty of time to talk to the aunt.

"Let me get this straight. You say he didn't have any papers. Everybody here carries some kind of ID. It's the law."

"He'd only just got here, Doyle. A few hours before he disappeared. He was what you were calling an II, an illegal immigrant."

This was too crazy to believe. The guy sneaks into town one minute and sneaks out again before he can say hello and good-by to his cousin who's come a thousand miles to see him. It was screwy!

"Did Han know you were coming?"

"Of course. My aunt told him she'd sent for me. I was excited about getting to meet him."

"Why did he leave before you got here?"

"He was frightened."

"Of what?"

"I think it was the Red Chinese."

"He had to leave before the conference ended, is that it?"

She shook her head positively. Positively negatively.

"No, he was supposed to arrive before the conferences started," she said. "But something happened. My aunt said

Han told her he couldn't stay. He believed that Beijing had sent someone to get him."

"Someone? You mean like the People's Liberation Army?" I was only half kidding.

"She didn't say PLA. She said someone."

My heart was thumping. I didn't know why. Or maybe I did know. I have a kind of a sixth sense, too.

"It doesn't work that way, Sung. Sometimes the PLA let refugees through the border. More often the poor slobs have to sneak through. If the PLA catch them they throw them in jail. Once they're over the border the British or Gurkha battalions may get them and hand them back over to the Reds. Some refugees make it as far as the city only to get caught by the Royal Hong Kong Police without identity cards. They still go back. All of that can happen. What you're talking about can't. Not yet anyway. The Red Chinese simply don't track down refugees who make it into Hong Kong."

"They did Han. They had tracked him all the way here from Beijing and they didn't stop when they got to the Hong Kong border."

"Why?"

"Don't you see? He was there. At Tiananmen Square. Sha Han was one of the twenty-two student organizers of the demonstration. He was there when the PLA moved in and massacred all those children. The PLA killed them all. The other twenty-one organizers were executed. Hundreds of students too but they searched for those student leaders and one by one found them and killed them."

My mind was racing. The surprise of what I was hearing sent it scurrying on ahead.

"I'd heard two made it to France," I interrupted her. "And one was hiding in the U.S. Embassy in Beijing."

"Not any more. The two in France are missing and presumed dead. The Americans announced a few weeks ago that the student who'd sought sanctuary in their Beijing embassy had died. They didn't say how. No, they're all dead. All of them except Han. He ran. He's been on the run in China for almost three years."

"Was he there? Inside the square those last hours?"

All Western newsmen and photographers had been moved out before the massacre. I knew that. The Chinese government claims to this day that no students died and though everyone knows they're lying no one's turned up any hard proof.

Sung tossed her hair. "I guess he must have been," she told me. "He's got pictures."

"Photographs? Of the massacre…?"

It was too good to believe.

"Video pictures. I don't know what's in them. He's trying to trade the video tapes for asylum."

She'd opened the bag and let me have it all. I asked questions for another five minutes but by that time I knew she was dry.

It didn't matter. What she'd given me was enough.

More than enough.

"Will you still help me to find him, Doyle? After what I did, I mean. I can't bear to think anything's happened to him."

"Just try and stop me!" I grabbed her shoulders and shook her. "Don't you realize what your cousin is?"

"Yes." And then after a pause. "What is he?"

"He's the answer to a prayer, that's what he is."

"I don't—"

"Where does your aunt live? Ling, did you say? We've got to talk to her right away."

"She's got an apartment in the Mong Kok." Sung held out a hand to stop me." "But Doyle, she's not there. She went to stay with her brother in-law after she talked to me. My Uncle Sun. I told you about him. She's there now. In Aberdeen somewhere."

"Junk town? Do you know how to find the place?"

"I've never even been there. As a child I spent every weekend on Uncle Sun's junk but back then he lived in the typhoon shelter."

"That's okay. We'll find it. But first things first. Let's run over to the office and get more copies of those pictures I took on the plane. There's always the chance your cousin was aboard the same flight as Huang. Your aunt may spot him for us. If so, we'll know he's back in Hong Kong now looking for another way out. Don't worry, honey, we'll find your cousin, too."

We could have walked to Causeway Bay. It's only a few blocks and I loved watching Sung's pigtails bounce. But I had no time for walking now. We took a taxi and hang the expense.

I hadn't been this pumped in weeks.

The near-impossibility of the search hadn't even begun to hit me yet. Not until later when I was talking it over with Stringer did I realize the difficulties that lay ahead. All I saw at first were the opportunities. Hong Kong glowed with sunshine. Scintillas of blinding light lanced off the waves in the harbor, off the glass walls of the skyscrapers on both sides of the harbor. The road ahead of us looked so bright we forgot for the moment it was a light that blinded as well as brightened.

Sung sat beside me, wanting perhaps, but not daring to smile. Maybe she thought she'd done something wrong in not telling me more from the start. I didn't think so. She may have thought I was sore but I wasn't. I wasn't even sore at Inspector Hawthorne. Not any more. I just pitied the guy. After all, for the rest of his life he'd have to be him, whereas for the rest of mine, I'd get to be me.

On the way up in the elevator I kind of bragged just a bit about the level of activity in our office and about my own role of leadership there. So when the elevator opened and we crossed through the reception area I guess my chest was out a little. I expected to hear the frenetic patter of printers, the clatter of a dozen computer keyboards banging out the day's crop of news and the chatter of reporters hashing over their scoops. What a disappointment! No patter. No clatter. And no chatter. There were typists at their terminals all right and hands in some cases even poised over the keys. There were small groups of reporters in apparent mid-conference and other signs of bustle in abeyance but no one was moving and no one was talking and no one was working.

We were halfway down the aisle that separated the rows of desks from the partitioned wall with its cubicle offices for Stringer; Ben Kao, our China observer; and then two more for the telex machines and darkroom, when someone cried out" "Hey, Mulligan!"

I glanced sideways at Manuel.

"Where'd you pick up the China doll?"

So they had all been staring at us and with such an intensity that it precluded any other activity. I say "us" though to be accurate they—and they were all men—had all been staring at Sung; still, she was with me, wasn't she? By the time we'd reached the rear of the room where the red light over the darkroom just flickered out the door opened suddenly and Bobby Ching, our photographer, emerged. I placed an order for a complete set of 8 × 10's of my roll of film and with a nod of his head he jumped back inside.

Before we got back to my desk at the front—they're arranged by seniority—Manuel had risen and was blocking the aisle with his two hundred pounds of which, to be fair to him, at least half was not fat.

"I asked you, Doyle, where'd you find her?"

"I heard you," I replied. "But where we met is none of your business. Don't you have a Man bites Dog story to type up?"

He ignored me, stepping around to face Sung. "What are you doing with a chump like Doyle when you could go right to the top, little girl?" I grimaced, but really, what kind of an approach can you expect from a guy called Manuel? Any mother who names her kid that has got to expect him to play with his hands. The two of us had never been close. Still, we had worked together for a few months and I was reluctant to try anything physical. However, if we had not been close before we were growing distant by the second. He owed Sung a little respect. And me too. After all, his desk was fully half a room back from mine.

I inserted myself between them.

Maybe Manuel thought I was going to shove him, as he later told Stringer, but I didn't. He shoved me, and hard. I wound up on the floor with an "out" basket over my head and papers all over the place. Furiously I whipped them aside and leaped to my feet, fists at the ready. What I saw then I almost couldn't believe. Manuel was sitting meekly in his chair with his arms pinned by a computer terminal which had seconds before been on his desk. Somehow it had ended up on his lap. There was Sung standing over him, shaking a finger and giving him what for.

I would have laughed if I hadn't felt so ridiculous but decided not to let that stop me and gave out a guffaw as I gently took Sung by the waist and led her forward to my desk.

When we were out of earshot I asked her how she'd done it and she replied that she'd lived too long in the Chinese section of Bankok not to have handled men of that type. I acknowledged that sad state of affairs but reminded her that she had now moved up. "You meet an entirely different kind of people in first class," I said.

Stringer was waiting for me.

"What's going on?" he asked.

"Ask Manuel." If I knew Stringer he would anyway.

He was still frowning at me. "How many times have I told you to wear a tie in this office and on the job?"

"What do you call this?"

I flicked the pointed ends at him.

"It's a tie, all right...but I don't call looping it around your open collar, wearing it."

I jerked my thumb over my shoulder. Why don't you move Manuel up to the front and have me take his desk. He wears a tie and slacks and leather shoes. Of course he doesn't bring you goods like this." I urged Sung into our conversation and Stringer, who's got a lecher's sense of propriety, smiled so wide his tongue nearly fell out. "Not her," I said quickly. "I'm bringing her. She's bringing the goods. And you can take Doyle's word for it this is gonna make everything else we've sent out this year look like filler."

He led us into his office.

"Hot damn!" said Stringer after I'd unloaded.

"No less," I agreed.

"The last survivor of Tiananmen Square. And pictures to boot. If you could get an interview with him that would be something indeed."

"I'll get it. But that's not all I'm after. If I can get Sha Han into that conference to tell his story there's no way the British will let the communists push them around. They'd have to stand firm on the 1997 takeover deadline and the fifty years of freedom guaranteed after Handover."

Stringer was nodding.

"Yes, you're probably right. And that'd be a whopping good story in itself. But, Doyle, you've got only one week. Maybe less. Have you thought it through? There are thousands of Chinese who've taken the Iron Underground and never surfaced again. You're going to try to find one, just one man, and bring him back to Hong Kong."

"I'll find him," I vowed. "I'll find him if it kills me."

Sung's eyes grew so big I thought they would pop.

"Jeez," I said laughing. "Don't you know a figure of speech when you hear it?"

She said no.

6. The Nowhere Man

We took the bus to Aberdeen.

It's not much farther from downtown than the airport. In fact, it's just over the peak from the Central Business District. But the bus takes the shoreline around Hond Kong Island, a thirty minute trip that seems shorter to me only because of the scenery. Not today. Blue skies had turned gray, the pale yellow water of the Sulphur Channel was gray, Green Island off Mount Davis point was gray, and Lamma Island was lost in low gray clouds. I guggested to Sung we use the time to fill in the background on her story and because of this the journey dragged on for at least thirty seconds.

She was twenty-four.

She weighed a hundred and ten pounds.

She had a room in the Nathan Hotel in Kowloon.

The room was a single.

"How about you?" I asked her. "Are you a single, too?"

"I'm not married if that's what you mean."

I fixed my eyes on my notes. My pencil was poised over the pad.

"Boy friends?"

"Really, Doyle. There are some things nice girls are not supposed to discuss with gentlemen."

It was a new one on me. And I'd been out with quite a few Asian girls. That may say something about my choice of girl or it may even say something about me. So I put down "Old Fashioned Values," which sounds better than "Old Maid" and means the same thing. I knew enough about girls to know if they've got someone hooked, or even nibbling, they don't mind telling.

She worked as a social savior for the government of Thailand helping to bring modern services and lifestyles to the rats' nests of Bangkok, the refugee slums inhabited by dirt poor Vietnamese and Chinese. It was the same slum Sung had been raised in. The slum her mother and father had died in. She worked there because she hated the slums as much as she loved the people who lived in them. And it seemed reasonable to her that if, by staying, she helped as few as two others get out, staying was better than going. So she had stayed. She had stayed until the day before yesterday when she'd gotten a telephone call from her aunt in Hong Kong begging her to drop everything and come at once. Sung had dropped everything and come at once.

By the time the bus had deposited us and a gaggle of tourists in front of Aberdeen's Tin Hau Temple and grumbled off leaving a contrail of smoke in the direction of Repulse Bay, I'd decided she was one gutsy woman with all the right instincts, all the right intentions, and for all the right reasons. The only thing she lacked being perfect was the right guy. And now that she'd found me, she was.

We walked down to the bay past small shanty structures that didn't stop when we got to the water. They just became floating shanties. The Chinese call Aberdeen *Heung Keung Tsai,* Little Hong Kong. I call it junk town.

Hundreds, maybe thousands of junks and sampans filled the bay between the inland village and the off-shore island of *Ap lei chau.* The vessels are anchored there in a pattern of apparent chaos. Maybe there is a system to it but I never found out what it was. A few short docks extended into the bay but none of the floating domiciles were berthed to them. Those were for the myriad little sampans which for a price would ferry tourists out.

Clustered out there is the most impressive collection of wooden sailing boats imaginable. Most of them were junks, two or three masted but bare of the raked four-corner coarse cotton sails braced flat by bamboo battens. They are high pooped with broad flat bows cluttered by the trappings of living quarters instead of fishing vessels. Many sport tarpaulin or even galvanized tin roofs that make them almost unbearably hot through the dry season and almost dry through the rainy season. In spite of this, they're the mansions of the community. Their little sampan cousins are the floating cottages. Flat bottomed with high rake transom sterns and bows close to the water, these square unmasted fishing boats have been converted into residences by matted roofs on their box-like cabins amidships.

I guess there are Venetian streets and avenues among and between the vessels but it loked like one giant logjam to me.

We split up at the wharf, working both sides of each pier asking the *xiangdaos* sitting in their sampans or on the pier of they'd ever heard of a fisherman by the name of Ping Sun Lien, who, according to Sung, was her aunt Ling's brother-in-law. I got no bites till I was nearly to the end of the pier on my side and one enterprising young man whose shabby little craft hardly the size of a rowboat boasted an outboard engine, nodded his head emphatically.

I didn't believe him.

If I'd gone down the row of taxis at Chicago's O'Hare International and asked each driver in turn if he knew where Cuthbert Applewart lived and one of them said, "Yeah, sure; hop in,"

I wouldn't have believed him either. But the guy had a motor and we had to take somebody. My own private horror had been that we'd be consigned to skulling our way around that zoo all through the evening and into the night. It took long enough as it was.

After some mandatory haggling we headed out across cool but calm waters. Our *xiangdao* took us to a good-sized junk on this side of the loating city on a course so direct that I thought for a while I might have misjudged his integrity. He maneuvered our vessel alongside the larger one and hailed an old woman working on the decks above us.

Sung looked at me and shook her head to let me know the woman was not her aunt.

I smiled to myself when our guide asked the woman in Cantonese if she had any idea at all as to where a Ping Sun Lien was anchored.

She didn't. Had she ever heard of the gentleman? She hadn't.

We took off again, undaunted.

"You do know where Ping's boat is?" I asked the guide.

"Yes, most certainly," he answered immediately.

Neither did the next seven people we rousted.

We putt-putted our way into the logjam at times heading through nests of junks moored so closely together we could hardly squeeze between them. Often we had to turn back. Occasionally we tried to proceed and got stuck. If we needed help turning or pushing through, the help was always eagerly forthcoming. Whenever we asked for directions the residents were pleased to tell us what they knew. The Chinese are a friendly people though they tend to be closed-mouthed around *saiyahn* and to view us with humorous contempt and suspicion. These tendencies, stronger here than in the city, were more than overcome by the fact that our guide was local, that I, the only *saiyahn,* spoke Cantonese, and Sung, whose excellent Mandarin was practically useless, had the power to charm.

Finally we came to a man fishing on a sort of floating fruit stand who identified a single smallish junk several up from his position toward the big floating restaurant as the one we sought.

We motored there directly.

A man was standing in the bows, holding a string of fish when we pulled alongside and I asked him if he was Ping Sun Lien. Of all the Aberdeen residents we'd talked to he acted the most suspicious. Suspicious and scared, too. He was a weathered little guy. His hands were gnarled, his back was bent, his skin was parched and wrinkled, whispish white hair that fell out from his coolie hat was as fine as spider's web, and if he had more than four teeth to call his own they must have been in his pocket because when he opened up to demand what we wanted they clearly weren't in his mouth.

But when Sung introduced herself his face brightened. He hung his catch on a wooden bulkhead and shuffled over to welcome us aboard.

I helped Sung up first, told our *xiangdao* to wait, then climbed up behind her. The old fisherman met her hesitantly. They exchanged respectful, almost ritual greetings. Sung's uncle seemed to have trouble adjusting his memories of the little girl he had known with the young woman he was seeing. Yet, after a short while, when he turned to me, there were tears filling his eyes. I liked what I saw. From a distance I'd have guessed him to be in his seventies. Closer, I could tell he was much older. You don't get eyes like his in just seventy years. Like the Pekingese in Kowloon City his eyes were all that mattered. But where the fat man's were mean, Ping's were kind, where the other's were smart, these eyes were wise. They hadn't seen everything, these eyes of Ping's but they'd seen almost everything and they had a pretty good idea what the rest looked like.

He led us into a small cabin and down a wooden ladder to the lower quarters. It was as cluttered belowdecks as it was topside and with naval and fisherman's wares in addition to the habits and handicaps of household life. Still it was not a random clutter for if a race can share a common trait then the Orientals are by nature a tidy people. Everything seemed to have its place, there simply weren't as many places as there were things. We passed through a curtained doorway and here where we found Ling, it was very orderly. The room was brightly lit by dozens of candles and hanging lanterns. Sung's aunt, wearing red pajamas, squatted in front of a short legged table surrounded by red pillows. There was a red cloth spread over the table and, on top of it, were red artifacts that looked like *ta chiu* icons for placating evil spirits. I recognized the dish-like device right in front of her. It was a *fung shui* compass, a kind of Chinese Ouija board whose eight ancient trigrams represent nature and its elements. Proper alignment of the natural forces makes for a positive prediction of future events. A brass statue of *Tin Hau*, goddess of the sea and the protector of fisherman, stood off to one side while a Chinese gong and mallet hung close by to the other. All in all, it was as complete a collection of horseshoes and rabbit's feet Chinese style as I'd ever seen.

Ling stood up when she saw Sung. Something like fear had etched itself into her face but these lines softened a bit now into a poor excuse for a smile.

They embraced. Then they both started yakking at once.

Half an hour later they were still yakking and none of it was much to the point if you ask me. Sung was telling her all that had happened since she'd started following me at Huang's acupuncture clinic. I knew about that. I wanted to know what had happened before then. It was a bad time. For old Ping too. He sat on his heels the way Chinese can, walked around the room with his mind, and talked to the wall with his eyes.

Finally he turned to me and in English so good it surprised me until I remembered he had once taught it to Sung he said, "You are seeming most patient for a young American. Are you content to listen?"

"I'm here to learn," I said. "One gains no knowledge while speaking."

His face brightened again. "Confucius!" He inclined his head at me by way of applause. "Do you read Confucius?"

I wanted to say that I read Confucius with my ears, but I didn't. I told old Ping instead that I didn't read him as much as I should, which was true, because I'd never read him at all.

I handed the photographs to Sung. She moved beside her aunt so they could study the prints together and one by one they went through them. Those of Huang Mu meant nothing to Ling. She flipped past those. They spent a lot of time with the interiors of the aircraft, especially those that showed the most passengers, dozens of blurred faces in each print. After the last print was back in the envelope Ling had to admit that she'd recognized no one.

I was a little disappointed but not surprised; it had been a long shot.

"*Deui miyuh*," said Ling.

"That's all right," I told her. "You can't see what's not there. We'll find your son. But we'll need everything you can remember. Everything you did and saw and everything he said to you."

"I cannot."

I thought she mean she would not. She had tied the fingers of both hands into a single knot and lines of anxiety were cutting back into her face.

"Because I'm *saiyahn*?" I asked.

"No. Not that. Because my memory is not so good."

But she was better than she thought and after some of Sung's encouragement, she started in.

Sha Han had appeared without warning one day at Ling's Mong Kok apartment. He had not written to tell her he was coming. In fact, she'd had no word from Han since before the massacre. He'd never written much. Relations between them were strained because Ling and her husband had fled to Hong

Kong and Han had elected to remain behind to complete his degree at Beijing University. She had only been able to keep in touch with him through Sung. The cousins had continued to correspond frequently right up to the time of the student uprising. I asked her why Han had stayed in Beijing instead of coming south with his parents. Because he was due to graduate in 1990. I pressed the point, saying that Hong Kong University is better than B.U. B.U. she told me is free, while the colleges here were beyond their means. Pressed still further Ling admitted her son was a communist. I backed off. When 1991 came and Ling still didn't hear from Han she worried he might have become involved in the student uprising. She thought he might even be dead. I stepped in again at that point to ask why he would have gotten involved with the student democracy movement if he was a communist. And Ling begged the question. Han, she said, always kept a finger to the wind. I thought of the Chinese expression, "He changes his mind like he changes his shorts." But kept quiet when I remembered the way my mother had sent me off to the Air Force with instructions for daily shorts-changing. I figured that mothers being the way they are about their sons and their sons' underwear, the remark was probably inappropriate.

But there was Han. Five years older and looking more like forty than twenty-five. He was nervous, fidgety and very high-strung. He asked about his father and Ling explained that her husband had left Hong Kong. That he was preparing a home for them in the West. Ling had bombarded him with questions. What had he been doing all these years? Where had he been living? And (mother Mulligan's favorite) why had he not written? Han told her that he had, in his last year at the university, come to share the view of many of his fellow students that communism had seen its day. They looked to Eastern Europe and the U.S.S.R. and perceived a new wave of freedom. He had participated in organizing the student movement which began in Tiananmen Square in May 1989 and spilled over to the whole city of Beijing and eventually to all of China. In the early hours of June 4, 1989 when the PLA had rushed in with their tanks and their troops and machine-gunned hundreds of students, he'd gotten most of the action on videotape. He also had tapes of the massacres in other parts of the city and in other parts of China. Beijing wanted him back. They wanted the tapes, too. But for three years he had managed to elude the PLA and the god of plagues by running from one tiny village to the next, finding refuge with people who had lost sons or daughters in the massacre. Sha Han had little left. His friends had all been murdered. His money had been spent in making his escapes. His degree was lost for good. All he had was the tapes and as long as he had them he knew Beijing would never stop searching. Then a wealthy businessman here in Hong Kong arranged to slip him out of China. The man was going to pay him a lot of money for his story and for the tapes.

"Who was the man?" I asked her.

"I don't know."

"Did Han ever mention the name Lee Chung?"

"He mentioned no names except…"

"Yes?"

"…no names."

Han told his mother he would have to leave Hong Kong as soon as the conferences ended. Ling telephoned Sung because she worked for the government of Thailand and Ling felt sure Han's cousin could arrange something. Sung promised to take the first morning plane. She would arrive in Hong Kong by ten. But Han was up before the sun. He was gone for almost two hours. When he returned, his entire manner had changed. His nervousness of the previous day had multiplied ten-fold. He was panicked. He would not eat or even sit down. He kept saying he had to get out of Hong Kong at once. If he waited even the few hours for Sung to arrive he would be dead.

"What about the conferences? And his money?"

"Ling shook her head.

"He had no mind for the money. All he could think of then was to get away." Ling didn't know what to say or do. She knew very little about the arrangements her husband had made to leave Hong Kong but eventually, she told Han what little she knew.

I interrupted to clarify something.

"You mean your husband left Hong Kong illegally?"

She and Ping exchanged glances. Ping smiled a smile without humor and nodded to her.

"Yes," she admitted.

"Why didn't you want to tell Han?"

"Because I was frightened. My husband had heard that the *de ha tit* was very expensive and very efficient. No Chinese had ever been caught leaving Hong Kong on the *de ha tit*. But he was worried. He'd had friends who'd taken the Iron Underground weeks before. They'd promised to write to Chen once they'd reached their destination. They never did. My husband talked to someone. The man told him all of the people who left were discouraged from writing or phoning because the British might find out where they had gone and what their new locations were. They would be deported back to Hong Kong. This did not entirely satisfy my husband. He paid the fare and told them he had no wife or children. You see the *de ha tit* only takes entire families. Parents and children, even wives and husbands, cannot leave separately. Chen assured me that once he reached the West, or wherever he was going—for he did not know—he would find some way to communicate with me that it was safe.

"Has he?"

"No. I have heard nothing."

"How long ago did he leave?"

"Four weeks. Almost a month now."

"And that's why you hesitated to tell Han the route your husband had taken?"

"Yes, but in the end I had to tell him because his fear was greater than mine."

When she said that I thought, "Man, that must have been some fear!" I crossed my fingers and plunged ahead:

"What did you tell him?"

"To go to the man my husband had talked to. Huang Mu. He ran the Celestial Acupuncture Clinic near our Mong Kok apartment."

"You gave him Huang's name?"

"Yes. But of course he could have gone to any of the clinics. Huang's was closest."

"Any of the Celestial Acupuncture Clinics in town?"

"Yes. That is what my husband told me. A man can get out of Hong Kong by walking into a Celestial Clinic and paying the price."

That, at least, was something new for me.

"What was the price?"

"My husband took five thousand dollars from our bank account. It was very nearly everything we had saved since we'd come to Hong Kong. Huang Mu told him the price varied according to one's ability to pay."

In other words, I thought, whatever the market will bear.

"Han had no money?"

"I think he did," Ling said nodding. "I think the rich man had given him something to live on when he first came to Hong Kong."

"But he didn't come back? Not after he went to talk to Huang Mu?"

"No. He rushed out immediately. And I never saw him again."

"What was he frightened of?"

"I don't know."

"Please tell me, Ling."

"I have told you—I don't know."

Sung wrapped an arm around her aunt and glared at me. I traded looks with old Ping. I think he knew. I was sure he knew

Ling was lying. Ling had said she didn't know but what she meant to say was she didn't dare tell me.

"It doesn't make sense," I told her. "Your son runs away because he's frightened of something. You hang around only until Sung comes to town and then you race out here to little Hong Kong to stay with your brother-in-law. Your flat is empty now, huh. Meanwhile Sung is paying eighty dollars a night for a hotel room that's just down the street. It's an insult to my intelligence to tell me you don't know what Han was scared of. Let me rephrase the question. What are you scared of?"

Ling shook her head and said nothing.

This was silly.

My mind walked over to old Ping and my eyes asked him for help. Nothing. His eyes knew what I wanted all right. I saw in them the same fear I saw in his sister's but the mood of his mouth was strictly knowledge-in, not knowledge-out.

I turned to Sung.

"Well?"

She found her aunt's face and made an appeal. "Please, auntie. I've asked Doyle to help me find Han. It's not fair to hold back."

Ling's gaze fell."

For a moment there was silence. Then Sung looked at me and took sides. "She wouldn't let me stay in the apartment," said Sung. "She tried to get me to go back to Bangkok; when I refused she told me what I said, about Han and Huang Mu's clinic. She made me promise that I wouldn't go looking for Han alone. That I would get help. But not the police. She said she was coming out here to stay with her brother until it was safe to return."

"That's it?"

"No. You're right when you say she is frightened. She was frightened yesterday, too. I knew it. But she wouldn't tell me why."

I looked from one to the other of the two elderly Chinese.

"What the hell!" I said at last, "Is it Nein?"

They both stared at me.

"You know about Nein?" exclaimed Ping.

I shrugged. "I know Ling keeps talking about some god of plagues. I knew Nein is an ancient monster who destroys crops and homes and kills people. That he's only repelled by loud noises, bright lights and the color red. I see all these candles, red objects, the gong, a protective goddess, and a lot of good joss hanging around and what else can I think?"

"You are well-versed in Chinese ways," said Ping. "But Nein," he added, "is a myth."

"Tell that to your sister."

"She's very superstitious."

"And you're not."

He tried to smile. It was pathetic. "The demon that threatens this family is no myth."

"What is it?"

"Are you a courageous man, Mr. Mulligan?"

I grunted at that. "I'm as brave as the next guy," I said, "as long as the next guy isn't Audie Murphy."

Ping swallowed.

In doing so he seemed to make up his mind about something. He said slowly.

"Have you ever heard of the ***Yega***?"

Ling stared at her brother in open-mouthed amazement.

"You mean like in Quyega?" I replied rather plonkingly. "Yeah, I've heard about that myth, too."

"And if I tell you the ***Yega*** exists?"

"He's real, huh?"

"Real. And not real at the same time. Do you know what the word means?"

"No. It's not Cantonese or Mandarin."

Ping nodded slowly. "That is correct. It is a Hakka variation of a Mongol expression."

"What does it mean?"

"It means he who is not here."

"Not here? Where is he?"

"Not any here. He is every here and no here all at the same time."

"You mean nowhere?"

"Yes. Nowhere."

"You're telling me this ***Yega***...this nowhere man, whatever you call him. He's after Sha Han?"

"Han thought so."

"What do you think?"

Ping blinked. I noted it because it was the first and only time I'd seen him do it. He glanced at his sister-in-law, looked back at me and spoke carefully.

"I think Han is already dead."

"But you don't know."

"On the contrary, I know exactly when and where and how my nephew died."

"Let's hear it."

"Han died as soon as the ***Yega*** began looking for him. He died at the place where the ***Yega*** finds him. He dided in the most horrible way the ***Yega*** can imagine. I should add that there is no limit to the ***Yega***'s imagination."

Ling began weeping. Sung tried to comfort her while the old man and I batted it back and forth a bit more.

Where did the ***Yega*** come from? Who controlled him and why was an evil spirit after Han? What proof did they have that such a thing as the ***Yega*** even existed?

Ping's answers became monosyllabic, later nothing but murmurs. He was more and more evasive. When he closed his eyes I knew we'd stopped talking altogether.

Ling was more than ready for us to go; she must have said or done something to impress this upon Sung.

We couldn't just leave. There were traditional good by's to be said.

We said them.

And then we just left.

Nobody suggested we come back again soon.

Sung and I saw ourselves out. We slipped over the side and settled into the sampan giving our *xiangdao* directions—or rather instructions, for my directions then would have been absolutely valueless—to return to shore. But we only got as far as the floating fruit stand before it occurred to me I'd forgotten the envelope with the prints. I asked him to go back, told Sung to wait in the sampan, and climbed back over the gunwales into the junk. Neither brother nor sister was on deck.

I hailed. No one answered. I presumed they were still too upset to come topside. However, I noticed Ping's string of fish wasn't hanging by the door where he'd left it. Four of the fish were on a bench. The fifth had spilled its guts on the deck. Ping must have come up to clean one and rushed back below. I knew I hadn't seen that mess when we'd left.

I stepped over the pile of innards and tiptoed into the cabin calling out at the opening.

Nothing.

They couldn't be as preoccupied as that.

I climbed down the ladder calling their names as I descended and then called out again before stepping through the curtained doorway. At first I didn't see them. The room seemed dimmer than before. Most of the candles had gone out. Then I saw them. Old man Ping was stretched out lengthwise. His sister was curled up behind the little table where she'd been sitting. An almost disgustingly sweet odor hung in the air. I've never smelled anything like it before and I don't suppose I ever will again. Which is fine with me. I took a couple of careful whiffs, felt nothing , and crossed to the woman. The brass gong was beside her; the mallet was in her right hand. I felt for a pulse. She had none. I plucked some fibers from the table cloth and stuffed them under her nose. They didn't move. She was dead. There wasn't a mark on her but she was dead. I turned to the old man and almost collapsed. My knees were turning to jelly.

It couldn't be a case of the stomach again because I've seen my share of bodies and these two were clean. Had they suddenly sprang to their feet and shouted "Surprise!" the only thing which would have surprised me is how well they could hold their breath.

But my legs were turning to jelly.

I'd like to say that right then and there I was feeling guilty about my role in this damned burlesque but frankly my head was getting a little wuzzy. I checked Ping but not long enough or well enough to have taken an oath he was dead. He looked dead to me. Not that my eyesight was worth a damn by that time. I couldn't make out anything clearly. And I was starting to see things that weren't even there.

A waft of candle smoke hung in the air near the brass statuette. Even as I watched a vaguely human form appeared through the haze. Of course everything in the room was hazy by then. Why that one apparition scared me so much, I don't know. Maybe, in my delirium, I believed it was the spirit of *Tin Hau* herself coming down to take charge of the bodies. But the fact is, it looked more like the shadow I'd seen in the Walled City alley.

Anyway, that's when I knew it was time to get myself, by means of the jelly legs, the hell out of there.

Halfway to the door my knees buckled.

I wound up on my stomach. Fine, I thought. That form of locomotion is at least basic. I remember crawling a ways and getting a hand on the curtain that led to the ladder way before the room went from dim to dark and my brain sort of fizzled out.

7. Like a Mackerel

I should have died; in fact, I thought I had.

I inhaled. A stench of rotting wood and dead fish and regurgitated Peking Duck filled my head. My eyes came open. The deck was a brown blur at the end of my nose. Damp and decaying. But I couldn't raise my head high enough to focus. I started groping with both hands. My fingers dipped into something warm and wet to my right and I was exploring the gooey stuff when a horrible thought struck me: suppose it's the duck! Was I playing in my own barf?

I turned to look. No, thank heaven, it was the gutted mackerel. Hooray! I had tracked down the dead fish.

For some reason I couldn't understand at the time this discovery filled me with relief. Wasn't one mess the same as another? I thought the thing through. The fish had been topside. And I'd collapsed below decks. What did it mean?

I exhaled. My lungs felt like two blocks of ice though the air itself was warm. A fresh breeze set the deck gently rocking. I breathed a bit more. When my insides started to thaw I got adventurous, decided to give crawling another try, and worked to my hands and knees. I wobbled, lost my balance and fell, rolling to one side so that I landed flat on my back. Gray clouds floated high above the mizzen.

I had made it out! Somehow I'd climbed the ladder and reached the upper deck.

When I looked around in order to relish this happy news I saw Inspector Hawthorne sitting in the bows of the junk. I wasn't aware I'd been smiling but I must have been smiling because the moment I saw him I became aware that a smile was leaving my face.

Maybe it was just Hawthorne himself or maybe seeing him reminded me of what had happened to the Pings. Whichever it was, I stopped smiling.

"Welcome back, Mulligan," he growled.

I said nothing.

He wasn't alone, there were other figures milling about the junk but it was his voice I heard again. "How do you plan to explain all of this?" he asked.

Good question. I was still working on a plan to stand up; brain busters like talking and explaining were not even on the calendar of events.

I mumbled something.

"What was that, Mulligan?"

"I said, 'They're both dead!' "I pointed back through the doorway. "They killed themselves."

More carefully this time I rolled over, got to my hands and knees, and pushed myself into a kneeling position. A man came out of nowhere, bent down beside me, shone a light into my eyes, and took my pulse with a practical hand. It was the coroner, Mortimer Braithwait.

He used a cloth to wipe something off the front of my shirt. The smell of regurgitated Peking Duck grew stronger.

"You'll make it," he said.

I glowered at him.

"You call that an autopsy?"

Hawthorne asked Braithwait if he'd decided what it was.

"Some type of gas I should imagine. No traces of it left now. I can't tell all that much until I get the bodies back to the morgue."

"Perhaps Mulligan here can give you an idea."

My mind was just starting to clear. "There was a sweet smell," I said. "So sweet it was nauseating. My lungs froze up. It only took about thirty seconds to drop me."

Braithwait murmured slowly, "Could be several things, Inspector."

I looked around for Sung. The coroner was moving off. Cops were everywhere. They were taking photographs, dusting for prints, making notes. They were going in and out of the cabin. I fully expected to find an outline of chalk on the deck where I'd lain. When I didn't see one, I knew for sure I was still alive. I threw both hands onto the gunwale and hoisted myself to my feet. Then I could see Sung. She was sitting in a small police launch to starboard being grilled by two cops. I caught her attention and nodded to let her know I was all right. She pulled a handkerchief away from her cheeks and showed me a tired, joyless little smile in which her eyes wanted no part. They were too red and too wet to smile.

My heart went out to her; but I was eternally grateful for the attempt. When a girl takes a guy to meet her only living relatives and they commit suicide as soon as he walks out the door, well, it's not like he's won their blessing.

So I was grateful for any little sign that she didn't feel about me the way I felt about myself.

"What the M.E. means," Hawthorne told my back, "is that it might be one of three or four things he's heard of or one of maybe a hundred that he hasn't."

I turned.

"How did I get out of there?"

"You tell me. Your lady friend found you right there, she says, and couldn't bring you to. She went ship to ship until she found a Chinese fellow with a transceiver. When your name came across the speaker I thought I'd better come along knowing there would be bodies to deal with. If your wits are returning you'd better answer some questions."

I spotted a seat within staggering distance, released my hold on the gunwale and hiked over. My head was reeling; once I was safely down, I tried to steady the damn thing in my hands.

"What makes you think it was suicide?" Hawthorne wanted to know.

"What else? I didn't kill them. I might have driven them to kill themselves but I sure didn't pull the trigger. There was no one else here except Sung and she left with me. I came back alone two minutes later and found their bodies."

Hawthorne rubbed his chin.

"Why would they want to kill themselves?"

"They were scared. Scared out of their minds, the two of them."

"About what?"

I looked up.

"They had a crazy idea that some kind of evil spirit was haunting them."

"Did they name it?"

"Yeah."

"Let me guess, was it the yahgah thing?"

A Chinese lieutenant standing nearby went stiff. His walkie-talkie fell to the deck with a bang.

Hawthorne and I eyeballed the guy; then I muttered to Hawthorne, "I suppose you've already got this from Sung."

"No. From you. Just before you woke up. You talked in your sleep. I know you're never unconscious but you do sleep, don't you, Mulligan?"

"I used to," I said.

"All right, you'd better tell me everything."

I told him everything.

Well, not quite everything. I held out one little item because it didn't have anything to do with the deaths of the Pings and I wanted a chance at it myself while it was still fresh. Looking back, I don't believe it would have made any difference if I'd told him. At the time I thought it might help me to find Sha Han. I've never been madder at myself than I was right then. That I'd pushed those nice old people to the edge and then over just so I could get a good story was an unforgiveable mistake. All I could do now was try to make it right.

They brought Sung aboard. She sat beside me mopping up tears with her hanky. Considering what she'd gone through however, she was holding up fine. I explained to her we were cooperating with the police, as always, and they wanted to know about the conversations we'd had with the Pings earlier. She'd probably just told it to the cops down in the launch but she told it again now. I crossed my fingers and held my breath when she came to the part I was saving; fortunately she didn't give it away. By that time Hawthorne could see that our stories matched and he was hurrying her along. He wanted to get to the kicker. She repeated the word properly and distinctly but made nothing of it and was going on when he stopped her.

"What the devil did the old man mean by this nowhere business?" he asked.

"I don't know any more than he told us," she replied. And here she stopped to dry her eyes again.

"You're Chinese?"

"I'm Thai. My mother was Chinese and my father was Korean but I have lived the last several years in Bangkok."

"Don't you speak Chinese?"

"No."

Hawthorne glared; then he aimed the glare at me. "You told me she—"

"She does," I said. I turned to Sung. "Don't lie to him, Sung, you speak excellent Mandarin."

"Of course, I do."

"Why did you tell him you don't?"

"I didn't. He asked me if I don't speak Chinese. I answered, No, I do speak Chinese."

It was the Korean answer thing again. I looked up to find Hawthorne still glaring at me as though I'd put her up to it.

"And yet," he asked her, "you don't know what your uncle was talking about?"

"Yes."

"What do you know?"

"I meant, Yes, I don't know what he was talking about. He was frightened. You say 'What the devil!' but do you look for creatures with horns and goat feet under your bed?"

Hawthorne sat back resignedly and heaved a large sigh. Turning to the lieutenant—who hadn't uttered a sound since dropping his radio and didn't look as though he had much to say even now—Hawthorne barked at him to begin a canvas of the neighborhood, such as it was, to determine if anyone had observed another party boarding or leaving the junk.

"It will be time wasted," muttered the officer.

"Do it anyway!"

The officer gave in grumbling, "All right. I'll assign a man to it."

"Didn't I just tell you to do it?"

The Oriental's eyes blazed for a moment before he drew away and climbed back over the gunwale to the police launch. As he scaled down the ladder and disappeared, he muttered a remark that was both guttural and gutter Cantonese.

We listened to the high-pitched roar of the engine as he and the driver motored to the nearest junk.

"What did he say?" snapped Hawthorne to me.

I shrugged. "I'd better not tell. You might consider it disparaging to a member of the queen's police force."

And so he would have.

"You've nothing to add to your statements?" he asked, "Either one of you?"

I debated telling him about my hallucination, the hazy human apparition I'd seen down there. I decided against it. He'd surely think I was only feeding his fancy.

But there was something else. That's what I told him about.

Hawthorne eyed me suspiciously.

"When I first came aboard," I said, "there were no dead mackerels on the deck. At least they weren't gutted. Ping had them hanging on a string." We looked at the disemboweled creature at the doorway and the pile of viscera nearby which my fingers had explored.

"It can't be a mackerel," said Hawthorne; "the mackerel is an Atlantic fish."

"Have it your way. It looks like a mackerel to me; it smells like a mackerel and it's as dead as a mackerel. But I know it wasn't gutted until just before I came back to get my photographs. Which reminds me, inspector, they're still in there . . . my pictures."

Sung and I got ready to go—informed by Hawthorne that we would, after all, be allowed to do so. Hawthorne refused to return the photographs that the police had recovered from the cabin even when I reminded him they were the same as the ones I'd already given him that morning. He muttered something about fingerprints and turned his back. After I told him that my prints and Sung's, as well as the Pings were all over them, he ordered our prints taken and gave me a receipt for: "thirty-five eight-by-ten black-and-white glossies in like-new condition."

And then, with black fingers and black faces, we went. The police launch took us as far as the shore.

As we were walking through town to catch a double-decker back to the Central District, an ancient pumper truck roared by. We followed it with our eyes to a little street frontage shop several blocks down. Smoke and flames spilled onto the sidewalk.

Locals gathered to mourn the loss of the business and to pay their respect even before the firemen performed last rites over the cremated carcass. I thought, how sad it is that structure can only die flagrantly—in a tempest of flames, a blast of high explosives, or a crash of collapsing stones—brazenly for everyone to witness. While two people slip away without a sight or a sound, or a soul to see them. It had been that way all along. The DC-10 had been blasted out of the sky but Huang Mu's death had gone unnoticed. Lee Chung had died as horribly as a man can die; yet it was the death throe screams of his burning mansion that had brought the help that came too late to help him.

"Not a good day for junk town," I said.

Sung merely nodded her head in understanding.

When we had our tickets I told her that I'd understand if she didn't want to ride back with me. I was even willing to wait for the next bus if she'd be more comfortable.

She said she'd be more comfortable if we were someplace alone where I could hold her very tight and keep holding her until all the dying stopped.

I was standing beside her—not too close—with my hands in my pockets but when she said that I wrapped an arm around her shoulders.

"I'm glad you don't blame me for your aunt's suicide," I said. "But I do blame myself. And I want you to know I'm going to do something about it."

"But, Doyle, you are doing something."

"Just wait. You haven't seen anything yet."

But I said no more until we got off the bus together in the CBD. It was late. The electricity was just starting to come on around town. Hong Kong never runs down day or night but somehow that night was different. I could feel it. The air seemed to crackle with a kind of static excitement like a charge of high voltage about to touch ground. People were running when they should have been walking. Anxiety and fire trucks and other emergency vehicles—screamed through the streets with their sirens howling. Everywhere I looked I expected to see newsboys on the sidewalks waving special editions of their papers and shouting "Extra . . . extra." It was the sort of a night when you felt you should accost some hurrying stranger and demand to know, "What the hell's going on?"

Neither one of us felt like eating but we didn't want to be alone either. I didn't like the idea of going to her hotel or taking her up to my flat so soon after what had happened so I suggested we ride the Peak Tram up to Victoria Peak and walk through the gardens.

We were near the Hilton Inn then; the Peak Tram station is just a hundred yards up the hill from the hotel.

Despite a short line it took us forever to get tickets. The cashier traded news with every Chinese who stepped up to the cage, whispered words and worried sidelong glances. Was my imagination working overtime or what? Could it be that I knew what was happening to this town and read my concern in their faces? Or was it the other way around? Maybe these people knew more than I did. When our turn came I took one look at the cashier's nervous little mug and asked him what the gab was all about. "Only the weather," he said. When I observed that the monsoon season would have to come awfully early to justify this kind of interest, he pretended not to hear me and I pretended not to care.

It's actually a funicular railroad, which means there's two cars tied to cables and when one goes up the other comes down. During morning and evening rush periods the trams are jam-packed with Peak commuters; this late however Sung and I shared the seats with a few tourists and lovers and that was about it. Still, I didn't tell her what I had in mind.

Not even when we'd left the tram at the upper terminus, walked along the road to the Victoria Peak Gardens, and lost ourselves on a meandering garden path called the Governor's Walk did I reveal my plans. I could have told her then—I'd planned to tell her then—but something was wrong. The time and the place were right. Yet for some silly reason I stood there surveying the grounds and sniffing the air. What was it? The air stank like a soaked campfire. Smoke and dust-sized particles of airborne ask hung in the mountain mist. Then I remembered that Lee Chung's palace, which had burned to the ground only a few hours before, was just across the saddle. I set my distraction aside. And that's when I told Sung I was glad she hadn't mentioned to Hawthorne about the Celestial Acupuncture Clinics.

"What about them?" she asked.

"You know, what your aunt said about how a person could walk into any one of the eighty-seven clinics and catch the Iron Underground out of Hong Kong. Eighty-six, I guess, now that Huang Mu's clinic is out of business."

"Inspector Hawthorne doesn't know?"

"I hope not. He thinks it was only the one clinic. At least, that's what he told me this morning."

"What difference does it make?"

"A big difference. If Hawthorne knew, he'd investigate them. And probably scare them into closing down. If he was smart, he'd try putting a Chinese cop into the pipeline and see where it comes out."

"You don't want him to?"

"Hell, no."

She asked me why not.

"Because I'm going to follow Sha Han into the pipeline myself."

We'd stopped beside a pagoda near the overlook to talk my plan over. Hong Kong was laid out below us, an electrical bonfire floating in the black South China Sea. By contrast, the People's Republic to the north was hardly any brighter than the water around our won shores. Just over the Chinese border, Canton, whose population was greater than ours, was hardly visible. It glowed like dying coals on a burned out land. To the northwest nearly the same distance away shone one other flame of human enterprise: Macao. The Portuguese colony was a fraction of Canton's size or population, but it blazed brightly against the midnight horizon like a beacon. These two enclaves, Hong Kong and Macao, were truly islands of fire in a frigid, black void. Which would be consumed first, I wondered, the firelight or the darkness? With the Soviet Union in shambles and communism on the run everywhere else in the world I couldn't help thinking that fires like these might someday burn in the People's Republic as well. Or would the hardliners in Beijing manage to extinguish the flames here before their own people began to see the light and feel the warmth? By comparison, the few hundred students at Tiananmen Square were lighting a candle.

As we talked a number of people were gathering at the edge of the overlook. They were pointing out the sights in the city below them. They were making noises too. Not the oohs and ahs of happy tourists overwhelmed by an incredible vista but more like the muted, shocked, and even strangled cries of witnesses to an unexpected disaster.

"It sounds very dangerous for a *saiyahn*," said Sung.

"Maybe. But after today, I've got to do something. Anyway there's only another five or six days of conference left and this is the first solid lead I've got."

"You want the story that much?"

"I want Sha Han that much. What good will it do us to find the Iron Underground if we can't come out of it with your cousin, alive, to tell his story at the conference?"

She said suddenly, "I could go."

"Go? What are you talking about?"

"Into the *de ha tit*."

"Forget it!"

"I am Chinese. There would be no danger—"

"No danger! Are you nuts?"

"It was my family that died. My family! Sha Han is my cousin. If anyone has a right to go, it is me!"

Just like a woman. Sung was so wrapped up in this thing she'd overlooked the obvious reason why she couldn't be the one to go, and I'd stopped to consider what the reason might be when I was again distracted by the people at the bluff.

Excusing myself, I stepped over closer to the edge.

Even from up here the sounds of sirens carried clearly. I could see the blaze of the city. But for the first time I realized there was smoke down there, too. Two fires burned right below us in the Central District. Over in the Wanchai, the flames from half a dozen more leaped into the sky. More in Causeway Bay and Sheung Wan. There were fires across the Victoria cityscape—not big fires but small determined ones. And across the harbor in Kowloon, even more of them. In the Tsim Sha Tsui, To Kwa Wan, Haung Hom, and Mong Kok districts. I lost count before my eyes advanced up the peninsula where Boundary Street marks the beginnings of the New Territories. And I saw fires off in the distant New Territory towns, too.

Sung had come up beside me. She'd seen them now.

I was too shaken to speak.

Not Sung. She spoke all right. But she was so shocked she leaped, very understandable, to three wrong conclusions as fast as the words reached her tongue.

"My God," she said, "The whole city's on fire!"

"No," I said, "not the whole city. Just certain parts of the city."

Then she said:

"There must be a hundred fires out there."

"No," I said, "only eighty-six. Or rather, eighty-five, there must have been a clinic in Aberdeen, too."

After that she turned to me and almost whispered: "Doyle, this can't mean what I'm thinking . . ."

She didn't even finish. She didn't have to, any more than I had to correct her unspoken words. I knew what she was thinking. And we both knew that's exactly what it meant.

Standing there on the peak watching all of Lee Chung's Acupuncture Clinics burn . . . it should have ended the chapter on our ill-fated journey to junk town. It didn't though. The next morning we got a postscript. Inspector Hawthorne brought it to the Eastern News office with him just as I'd finished bringing Stringer up to date.

"Somebody, or some *thing*," I said, "came to Hong Kong looking for Sha Han. He must have known that Lee Chung had sneaked Sha Han out of China. Lee planned to use the boy's evidence and testimony about the Tiananmen Square massacre to stall off Beijing's attempts to wall up the city."

"Just as we do." said Stringer.

"Yeah. But not for the same reason. Lee was running the Iron Underground. He knew if the Reds walled up Hong Kong it would put his railway out of business."

"And this somebody . . . or some *thing* . . . killed him?"

"Right. Not too nicely either. I'll bet the killer didn't even know the old man ran the Iron Underground. His orders were simply to get his hands on Sha Han. Lee must have given him the name and maybe the address of Sha Han's mother before he died. The killer went to the Mong Kok to get him. Maybe Sha Han witnessed the murder; maybe he saw the fire. He raced back to his mother's apartment and told her there was no time to wait for his cousin Sung. He had to leave right away. Reluctantly, Ling told her son about Huang Mu and the Celestial Acupuncture Clinic. So by the time the killer showed up, Sha Han had left. His mother had gone too. The only person still around was Sung. This guy followed her to the clinic. He followed both of us to the airport where he boarded the plane and killed Huang Mu. He's been following me ever since."

"He killed the Pings?"

"Yeah. But it's even spookier than that. He must have been right there in the junk when Ling told Sung and me that all of the Celestial Acupuncture Clinics are involved with the *de ha tit*."

"How do you know that?"

"I saw him. I thought it was a hallucination of some kind but it wasn't. A couple hours after she told us about the clinics, every one of them was on fire. I'm telling you this guy is trying to make sure Sha Han doesn't get out of town."

"Or that no Chinese get out of town."

"I'm sure you're right, Alex. He's got new orders now to close down the *de ha tit* when and wherever he finds it. But he's still after Sha Han, that's the big thing—he wants the boy bad. Which means we've got to get to him first."

Stringer sat there nodding his head in understanding. "Is that the only proof you've got . . . that the Pings were murdered, I mean? Hawthorne will be here in a few minutes and when he finds out you held out on him he won't like it unless you've got something else."

"I've got this. But I'm not going to give it to him." I leaned forward and placed the receipt Hawthorne had given me onto Stringer's desk.

He read it over.

"I see."

There's nothing slow about Alex Stringer.

"Then that's why Hawthorne's coming here. He must have found fingerprints on some of your photographs."

"Yeah," I said.

"And he wants to see Ching to get his fingerprints. So he can eliminate those."

"Yeah."

Stringer waved the receipt.

"And this is why you asked me to have him bring along your photographs. All thirty-five of them."

"Yeah."

He straightened himself in his chair and placed both palms on his desktop. It's what he does when he's about to pull rank.

"You know what this means, don't you, Doyle?"

"It means Hawthorne is more interested in getting his hands on this killer than in finding Sha Han. It means it's going to be up to us—"

"Us maybe, but not you. You're out of it."

I started to argue, but Stringer didn't even slow down.

"We'll have to shift you to some other phase of this story," he said. "I don't like it any better than you do—you're the best reporter I've got. But dammit, until they catch this lunatic who's following you around, we can't afford to let you get close to any more leads or witnesses. He's eating them up as fast as you find them."

"What about Sha Han?"

"It won't do you any good to—"

"Forget about me. Find Sha Han. Everything depends on it." I slammed my fist on his desktop. "The Iron Underground was news and we printed that, even though it hurt Hong Kong. Sha Han is news, too. Big news. And he can save this town. Somebody's got to find him."

"Somebody may. But not you, Doyle. I'm sorry, that's how it has to be. You know I'm right."

He was right, I did know. I also knew that if I didn't find Sha Han, nobody would.

That's when Hawthorne arrived, bringing with him the PS which put me out of the picture for good.

"We figured out what killed those two down at Aberdeen. Or rather," he said, "Braithwait found out. He rather liked Mulligan's notion about the bloody fish. You'd called it a mackerel?" he said looking at me. "Braithwait asked around. The local name is Spirit Fish. Can't pronounce the Chinese. It seems the flesh is something of a delicacy. And highly toxic. Have to take great pains in preparation. Even then one can only eat a little. The fingers and toes go numb. That's the signal to go easy. Anyway, Braithwait took the carcass and innards back to the lab along with another one of the same species off the junk.

He dissected the second fish and compared the organs with that pile you landed on. When he finished he had a little blob of blue he couldn't account for. Its function, I mean. And it didn't have a matching organ in the gutted one. He assumed it had been removed by someone."

"Or some *thing*," said Stringer.

Hawthorne shrugged. "Braithwait ran some tests, but it didn't appear toxic. Then he remembered about the candles in that cabin. He held the organ over a Bunsen burner for a few seconds to see what would happen."

"What happened?"

"We don't really know. Apparently he dropped like a stone. There were three lab technicians in the room with him and they died too. Two must have tried to go to him while the third ran for help. Took six steps and collapsed in the corridor. A policeman saw him fall and stepped to the laboratory. Just barely cracked the door so he could peek through. He may or may not live."

"Damn!" I said.

"Yes, all of that."

"Inspector," I started, "I don't know what to say—"

"I do," Hawthorne growled. He got to his feet and stood over me. He took so deep a breath his hatchet face rose like an executioner's ax over my head. "You're through with this story, Mulligan. Do you hear me? Finished! If I find out you're in any way involved with finding the Iron Underground or IE's I'll throw you in jail. And I'll make sure you don't get out until after the Red Chinese come marching across the New Territories."

Terrific, I muttered under my breath, the way things are going, that ought to be about one week from now.

8. The Myth and the Monster

I believe I mentioned earlier that Ben Kao's office was next to Stringer's while I occupied a desk on the main floor but that I had aspirations of getting the directorship when Stringer was rotated back to the states.

It's not as absurd as it sounds.

Ben Kao was stuck in that office before Stringer came and before the man Stringer replaced. He'd probably still be stuck there after I was long gone.

Kao was ENA's China observer. His territory included everthing north of Hong Kong (although in a few years his territory would unhappily include Hong Kong) while Stringer, who was in overall charge, directly supervised everything south. Ben Kao was also liaison for the employees Stringer called the "no speakies," the Chinese of the office whose struggling English was not yet fluent enough that Stringer would even attempt to wage communication with them.

The China observer is supposed to know what's going on in the People's Republic. To do this he has to talk to the refugees who come south across the border. He listens to Beijing radio programs and watches Beijing TV. He reads every newspaper that comes out of China. He reads every Red magazine, every communist bulletin. His contacts behind the bamboo curtain send him official speeches. He reads diplomatic guest lists when he can get them, menus and waybills when he can't. He reads the lines, then he reads between the lines, and after that he checks out the margins, the ink and the paper itself. If he's good, like Ben Kao, he might get an inkling of what's going on in the People's Republic.

Ben was one of the best.

The old man was a lot like his office, well-used but well carred for. His thick hair was combed back precisely. His inevitable three-piece suit was always sharp. He had a clear face that gave no hint of his sixty years and either he shaved three times a day or his skin just didn't have the genes for beard.

He and I got along fine although we were probably more opposites of habit than were Stringer and I. He appreciated the fact that I loved the Orient and tried to grasp its life as well as its languages, while Stringer truthfully hated it and spoke not a word of Chinese. Alex Stringer was here in the East only as a condition of remaining with Eastern News while I was with the ENA only as a condition of remaining in the East.

Ben and I had talked at length about the Chinese exodus of Hong Kong. I think he could have told me things if he'd been willing. But he wasn't. He had the money to flee Hong Kong but he wasn't doing that either. "The British," he used to say, "are like our adopted mother. We ran from our real mother because she was too strict and at times even cruel. Both say they want only the best for their children; neither seems to realize that the time comes when children must make their own decisions. We have tried for self-rule here in Hong Kong but the British won't allow it. They own all the land just as the government in Beijing owns the land of China. The British made all the decisions here just as the communists do in the People's Republic.

When Beijing takes over Hong Kong, we will be under communist rule again. But at least it will be Chinese rule. Sometimes a real mother, even a strict one, is better than an adopted mother who does not want her child to grow up."

Then I would remind him that it was Chinese rule he'd run away from thirty years earlier to come here.

"Now," he used to say, "I am too old for running. And Beijing, also, is thirty years older."

"But still cruel," I would add, making an unnecessary reference to Tiananmen Square.

"Yes. Still very cruel."

Our arguments usually ended there but today I was able to provide him with more Beijing cruelty.

He already knew about the murders of Huang Mu and Lee Chung. Every Chinese in town knew of the simultaneous burning of the Celestial Acupuncture Clinics. Now I briefed him on the Pings. I finished up by relating my conversation with Hawthorne about the deaths at the coroner's office that had tragically revealed how the old Aberdeen couple had been killed. He sat back and soaked it all in, although with Ben you could never really tell how much of what you were giving him he already knew.

"Doyle," he said in a fatherly tone, "you've been told twice now to abandon this story, by the police and by those killers in Kowloon City. You've been threatened with everything from death to incarceration if you don't."

"Yeah."

"I warned you against it from the beginning."

"I remember. Maybe I should've taken your advice, Ben, but I didn't. Now it's too late."

"But now that you've lost your last lead what possible choice—?"

"I got another lead. The police found only 35 prints in Ping's junk. I'd taken a full roll of film. That's 36 exposures. Somebody," I said, "whoever killed the Pings, took one. And I think I know why. The killer was on that flight to Taiwan when he blew up Huang Mu. I must have gotten his face on one of my shots. He didn't want me to find it. So he stole the picture.

Before I could go any further there was a knock at the door and it came open. Bobby Chin walked in with several still warm prints. At a nod from me and with no comment from Ben he began laying them out on Ben's desktop. "I wanted the missing picture," I said, "the one he'd taken, not realizing or maybe forgetting we had the negative and could just print up another. But, like Braithwait and his pile of fish organs, I needed the discards to know which one had been removed."

Bobby Ching caught my eye and continued. "I just compared them with the original proof sheet," he said. "This print was the only shot not included; I ran off some more copies." There were three 11 x 14 prints, all of the same negative and so fresh from the dryer they curled up on the desk.

We gave it a good look.

Ben made a sound like "humph."

Ching winked at me.

I don't know what I'd expected. A shadowy, sinister-looking fiend hiding his face behind a broad brimmed black hat, a slavering man-beast or maybe even a Darth Vader type. This wasn't it. We were looking at my art picture. The one with the scrap of paper floating in the men's commode.

"Are you sure you got the right one?"

Ching nodded sheepishly.

"Well, there goes that idea," I said. "right down the toilet."

"What was written on the paper, Doyle?" asked Ching.

I said I didn't know.

"Where did it come from?"

Again I didn't know. I told him presumably it came out of Huang Mu's briefcase. The three of us sat there awhile in silence. Finally I said, "Bobby, do you think you could blow this up enough to make out the words on the paper?"

"This high speed film is too much grainy," he answered. "But I can try some things." He scooped up all the prints except mine and left.

"Now what?" Ben asked me.

"I'm still going after him," I said.

"Him? You mean Sha Han?"

"No. Stringer's pulled me off that part of it."

"Then who are you going after?"

"You know. This Yega guy. Anyway, the guy who calls himself the ***Yega***."

"Don't be a fool!"

"The son of a bitch killed Sung's aunt and uncle; he killed Huang Mu and Lee Chung, and God only knows how many other people."

Ben was shaking his head. When he spoke, his words were graveled and his voice quaked with emotion.

"He's out of your league, Doyle."

"Well then, tell me what league he's in. What team does he play for and who owns it. I already know his batting average because I've been keeping score."

"Is this why you've come to me?"

"I need help."

"Indeed, it has often amused me that it takes only one man to dig a grave but six to transport the body. Since you are apparently prepared to do your own digging I assume you wish to enlist my aid as pallbearer."

I leveled my eyes at him.

"You know, Ben, I think you've got the wrong idea about this. I'm not dumb enough to try to tackle this ***Yega*** all by myself and drag him back to the inspector. Look at my face for chrissake! But I've got to do something. The conference will be over in five or six days. Meanwhile, the guy's been following me around, grabbing my clues as fast as I find 'em and killing my witnesses before I can get their stories in print. Maybe if I can get a line on him I can follow him for a change. He might even lead me to Sha Han. Don't tell Stringer, but that's really what I'm hoping for. If I can't look for Han, I'm going to look for the guy who's looking for Han."

"I urge you in the strongest possible terms, Doyle; don't do this."

"I thought you might be able to tell me something about the word ***Yega*** or at least give me a start."

"No. Don't even ask me. I cannot." Again Ben's head moved methodically back and forth. "More to the point, my friend, I will not."

"Why?"

"Doyle, I will tell you this much. As you know I lived most of my life in China and its ways are too firmly rooted in me to make adaptation facile. We exchange stories about those subjects which are to sacred to be dealt with directly. You would call them rumor but to us they are much more." I sarted to interrupt but he stopped me by holding up a hand. "I know what you think. That this is merely religious nonsense, and for the most part I agree with you. As you know, I am converted to Christianity. You and I have discussed at length much of the mythology to which I refer. *Shea Kung*, the earth god, *Sing Wong*, god of the city; *Tai Sui*, the sixty gods of the year, *Nein*, god of disasters; *Tam Kung; Tin Hau; Pao Kung; Wong Tai Sin* and dozens of others. Fine and good. I am able to do that because unlike many of my countrymen, I have come to realize the irrationality of those myths. The ***Yega*** is different. His legend is the outgrowth of stories that were too substantive to be forgotten and too dangerous to be retold. It represents forbidden knowledge."

"The big taboo? Come on, Ben. You sound just like Sung's Uncle Sun. Can you really believe that?"

"I do believe it. But the point I am making is this: No man dares call himself ***Yega***. Such a man invites certain death. There is only one ***Yega***. And he is no myth."

"How do you know?"

"I won't say."

"You won't give me any steer at all?"

"I will go this far. I will give you no information about that subject directly, but I will give you the names of some people who can. Outside of China, there are only a handful who would have some knowledge of this. I can name four or five who might be able to help a little. Do not think badly of me, Doyle. I simply will not help you dig. If the two of us shovelled together we would only succeed in opening a grave of sufficient size that our bodies might be buried side by side. I will bear your casket as a friend, but not until you are dead."

"But like you say, Ben, we're friends and you still won't help me, what makes you think these other people will give me anything?"

Ben shook his head again.

"I don't for a moment suspect that they will."

So I settled for names in my notebook and addresses too after Ben consulted a personal black book in his desk. And I didn't even get that until he'd exacted a promise from me that I wouldn't utter his name to any of those people or to anyone else in connection with my investigation. I'd never known him to be so cautious. I always thought Christianity was as far as his spiritual beliefs took him but something had put the fear of god in him and it wasn't God.

For the rest of that morning and into the afternoon I tracked down the five people in my book. Never have I had so many doors slammed in my face over one issue. The names were all Chinese so it didn't come as any surprise that the people were Chinese, too. Neither did their reluctance to talk. And yet before the day was out I found myself wishing that somewhere, somehow a *saiyahn* would surface with some of this information. About the only thing I managed to learn was the reason none did—the Chinese weren't giving it out.

Hong Kong is a funny kind of a town. In appearance it's a modern city. But in many ways this appearance is merely a façade. Houses are blessed by priests before residents dare to move in. Billion dollar skyscrapers are designed in cooperation with geomancers according to centuries old theories of yin and yang. If a site has bad *fung shui*, the Chinese workers will strike. Inadvertently bulldozing into the nest of a sleeping dragon can cost a construction firm hundreds in "exorcising fees." The alternative is "bad joss" for the whole neighborhood. This is Hong Kong. We have scores of newspapers and yet the silliest rumor can sweep through the town like a monsoon without once appearing in print. Every holiday here is tied to some kind of spirit; spiritual icons fill the walls of Chinese churches and homes. A respect for traditional beliefs remains with the Chinese for life. It may even follow them after they're dead. Thousands of graves are broken into each year by relatives in order that the bones of their forebears can be meticulously sorted and cleaned.

In a setting like this, just hours after a bizarre wave of "officially" unexplained fires had swept through the city it should not have surprised me, the reception I got.

But after a while, it did start to piss me off.

The first on my list was a skinny little guy who ran a thriving fishing service out of *Lai Chi Kok*. He was easy to find but hard to approach. After waiting almost an hour for the crowds to disperse enough for me to have a private chat with him I had to come right out with it. He was too busy to listen to me pussyfoot. I no sooner had the Y word out of my mouth than his face paled, his eyes bugged, he pivoted on a heel and raced into his private office, slamming the door. In my face.

The second name turned out to belong to a real estate developer working out of an office in the Central District. I had to send in word through his secretary that I wanted to talk to him and then take a seat. You can guess what word I didn't send in. I spent forty minutes in a waiting room that needed developing, reading analyses from the local papers on how the Sino British conferences were going. The Sun banner "Reds throw British on Defensive" pretty much summarized the first day. If the writer knew what he was talking about it didn't look good. I recognized Manuel's writing style on an ENA sidebar in the Standard that was headlined "PRA Presence Likely by Mid-Year," and started reading.

"Beijing's negotiators, like determined door-to-door salesmen, know what they want from Hong Kong and they're not prepared to take "Thanks but no thanks," for an answer. They've got their foot in the door and they've dumped a mess on our carpets which only they can sweep up. Once inside they'll produce a bewildering assortment of appliances from their trunks. First we'll see a small detachment of bureaucrats at the airport and harbor office. Soon they'll have men at the important financial centers, the banks, the Hong Kong Stock Exchange, and post office. Before you know it, PLA regulars will be drilling on the square in front of Government House.

"The British negotiators, on the other hand, don't want Beijing's help in cleaning house any more than they care to insult the communists for fear Beijing will take it out on Hong Kong after the British have gone. They just want the whole mess to go away. And yet they seem to have lost sight of the fact that it was Beijing which dumped the mess on us in the first place."

Even Manuel's hokey style couldn't mask the fact that my time was running out.

Finally the wheeler dealer admitted me. I really tried sneaking up on it this time, but how? All I had was the name. How do you sneak up on a name when merely pronouncing it has the same effect on people as telling them you've got leprosy. He went cold, called his secretary and told her to go to her desk and wait thirty seconds before telephoning the police. I barely made it out in time.

The third fellow was also on Hong Kong side. He was a jeweler in the thieves market who owned a shop called the Nine Dragons Jade Factory just around the corner from Ladder Street which is nothing but steps. They say if something is stolen from you one day you can find it the next morning in the thieves market. Most of the stuff comes from Red China so the tourists only come to look. Not me. I was ready to deal. The guy wasn't too busy. I had him get out several expensive rings and began chatting with him as we discussed in Cantonese the merits of each. I swung the discussion to thieves of such gems and then to other criminals and before he knew it we were talking about the murder of the couple in Aberdeen just the other day. I had haggled him down a bit on one little jade ring which I thought would make a nice gift for Sung but I didn't want to get him down too far. I wanted him hungry. While fingering it casually I mentioned that now the police were closing in on the murderer they'd put to rest any suspicion that the you-know-who had been involved. My hand was relieved of the ring; the ring, returned to the tray; the tray, replaced in the glass counter; and the counter door slammed shut and locked.

I tried reasoning with him. I tried begging.

Eventually my insistence paid off. He let me put the ring on layaway at the original exorbitant price. But as for the information, try the dealer next door.

Number four was a manager in a plastics manufacturing company. His waiting room was so crowded I had to take a number just to talk to the receptionist who wasn't letting anyone in anyway. I'd already read the papers and I could tell something odd was going on so I spent my time picking up hints from suits and ties. The rumor mill had it he was gone for the duration. I gathered that, while my man was in no position to tell me about the ***Yega*** (though he wouldn't) because he was gone, he was in an excellent position to tell me about the Iron Underground (though he couldn't because he was on it.)

That left but the one name.

So I was not jaunty when I crossed Reclamation Street to the little storefront address near the typhoon shelter and recognized the place as a martial arts school. There are hundreds of such establishments in Hong Kong, most of them Kung Fu and Tai Chi Chuan styles. The glass front of the kwoon was painted with Oriental figures performing kicks and throws and was lined at the bottom with samples of the trophies won, supposedly, by members of the school.

When a paunchy little character with long black belt cinching up his uniform and equally long, equally black hair tied up by a head band stepped up to me, naturally I asked if he was Wang Chen.

No, he said, Master Wang was busy. What did I want?

I'd been given too many brush-offs. I was playing fair and getting kicked in the teeth. Well, I decided, the gloves were coming off.

"Have you heard of the National Geographic Society?" I asked him.

He had.

I poked my chest with a thumb. "I'm a member," I said.

"Good pictahs!" he replied smiling.

"Thank you. We're doing a spread on Hong Kong this month and thought we'd spread a little of the publicity on you guys. How about it?" He disappeared after showing me to an observation window where I could watch a karate class in progress. I knew without asking that the instructor was also not Wang Chen. He was big and he had a black belt but he looked like an American to me. At any rate, a Westerner. Seeing him in the white uniform, calling out instructions in Chinese and demonstrating kicks and punches set me thinking about gooks and geeks. I don't like the words, either one of them, but there they are. Put an Asian on a horse with a bunch of American cowboys and he's a gook. Put a Westerner in a *gi* with a bunch of Asians and he's a geek. Even this guy. He knew his stuff, I guess, but karate is their stuff not his and even though he wore a black belt and the others wore every color except black, he was the geek. That's the reason I couldn't bring myself to take karate classes as much as I tired of guys beating me up. I can't even ride a horse. In a *gi*, I'd geek out completely.

"Master Wang will see you."

I followed the paunchy guy down a corridor, past some small rooms where private lessons were underway and finally he stopped and held open a door. I stepped in. I was prepared for more rows of swinging legs and fists launching in unison toward invisible targets. But no, what I saw was nothing like that at all. Master Wank, chopsticks in hand was flat on his stomach devouring a plate of rice and what appeared to be chicken testicles. It's one of the dishes like the shark's fins, bear paws, monkey brains and birds' nests that the Cantonese eat and I don't. I stick with the Mandarin here because it goes down as easily as it comes up.

He wore the pants to a black uniform. The top half was laid out beneath him like a beach blanket exposing a compact well-muscled body. I figured him for forty but there wasn't a hint of gray in his shaggy head of hair. As he ate a young woman practiced little chops along his back. Her yellow belt indicated she was probably a novice at punching and kicking but as a masseuse she seemed quite expert.

"You are National Geographic," barked Wang.

I waved my subscription renewal notice in front of his face and told him that Gilbert Grosvenor himself had sent me out here to interview the great Master Wang. With a growl he sent the girl packing. I watched her skamper out on her bare feet while Wang sat up slowly and slipped on his top. He wrapped and knotted the wide black band of cotton with a speed and dexterity that comes from many years of practice.

I worked into the conversation as gently as I could, determined not to lose him before I'd gotten something for my trouble. My notebook was out, my pencil was poised, my earnest phiz was in place and my photographer, I told him, could return tomorrow if that would be convenient in order to take pictures of Wang, his staff, Wang, his school, Wang, his students and, of course, Wang himself.

Once the interview got underway, I realized I'd heard of him before. He was one of the senior stylists in this small country with a reputation for flair and toughness that was unmatched. Having studied more than thirty years in China he claimed to be the most advanced technician in Southeast Asia and no one had stepped forward to dispute his claim. We went on a short tour around the place while he showed me records and pictures of himself at a variety of festivities, tournaments, and demonstrations and if he were capable of all the things I saw him pictured doing, then he was damn good. Certainly he had a big school with junior instructors all over the place. We ended up back at the observation window watching the big American put the class through its paces.

Wang explained that he maintained strong ties to the traditional methods of instruction and placed great emphasis on mental development along with physical training. I interrupted to ask him how he could be sure, what with the large number of students passing through, that he ws not teaching someone who might misuse the skills. He shrugged it off.

"How would you know, for example" I ventured "that one of your students would commit a murder such as the papers reported yesterday?" The Lee Chung killing had been released by the medical examiner's office as an accidental burning death but the mosquito press had cornered someone in the fire marshal's office and the truth was out. Few may have understood why Lee had died. But how Lee had died...? Every Chinese in Hong Kong knew about that.

As we talked an occasional shout would erupt from the big American instructor followed by a chorus of shouts when the class bellowed out their response. "The killer" I said "was obviously someone well versed in the martial arts." I pointed through the glass. "How can you even be sure that one of these students here didn't do it?"

"No student of mine did that, Mr. Mulligan."

"How do you know?"

"Because no student did that. That was not the work of any student of any organized style of martial art."

I persisted. "You mean to tell me you don't have any students who could punch hard enough to break a man's back."

"That's not the question," he snapped.

Wang had a way of glaring that was more than a little unnerving. I couldn't figure out why. His wide flat face was hard and unyielding. But then many Oriental faces are. He looked tough, even a little mean. But I've interviewed mean, tough types before. There was just something about him that bothered me. Something I'd heard and forgotten.

"It was my question," I said.

More glare.

"If you walk with your mouth, Mr. Mulligan, you will lead yourself into trouble. Listen and learn!"

I nodded.

"That's me," I said. "I'm a Confucious man all the way. 'One gains no knowledge while speaking.'"

That surprised him.

"Yes, of course. The I-Ching. You've read it?"

"Are you kidding. "I've got a first edition signed by the author."

He narrowed his eyes and marked me down as someone to watch. He continued:

"I was explaining that a large man with some training or a slighter man with much more can learn to break bones. Arms. Legs. Backs. That is not a problem. We begin with the heavy bag. When we have punched the bag ten thousand times we go to boards. We break ten thousand boards before we advance to bricks. Once we have broken ten thousand bricks we have the power and skill to break bones." He spread his hands. "But Lee Chung did not suffer a simple broken back. I am told he was hit in such a way as to crack the backbone and paralyze him. How is that done? I don't know. How does one learn that technique? How can he perfect it? That much I do know, for there is only one way. After breaking the ten thousand boards and bricks, the aspiring technician begins breaking backs. He breaks the backs of ten thousand men until his strike is so deft he can affect their spine as he pleases. He can kill instantly, injure badly, or merely paralyze completely and let the first person to come to the victim's aid complete the assassination by their assistance. Unfortunately, Mr. Mulligan his education has meant the loss of ten thousand people who are willing to sacrifice their lives or whose lives have been sacrificed in a most horrible fashion that one man's skill might be perfected. I have never attempted to learn this technique. I do not want to do so."

I was starting to figure this guy out little by little. Over a late lunch with Sung Kwon that afternoon I described Wang's attitude during the interview as one, not of disgust, but of jealousy. She didn't understand. Wang, I told her, was bothered by any suggestion that he was not on top of the heap. He was humble in the tradition of the Orient and the martial arts but only because everyone else that he met in his business was obliged, by virtue of his superior talents, to display even more humility to him. The idea that there was somebody out there who was able to best him at his own mastery gave him an itch in a place he couldn't scratch.

So it would have been bright to drop it there. Sung asked me why I didn't and I could only tell her that it's not in my nature to give up on an interviewee until he has given up on me and Wang wasn't giving up, just the opposite in fact. He was about to strike back.

"Do you mean to say," I persisted, "that there's no way to determine a man's size or weight or even strength by his ability to perform such a trick?"

Wang's eyes narrowed to black slashes.

His mouth closed. The lips pressed into a thin line.

His blunt instrument of a fist moved toward the glass. It knocked twice. Once Wang had the instructor's attention his fist made a little signal. Immediately the instructor arranged for a lot of bowing and scraping. The ranks of students broke. All the white uniforms headed for the back of the classroom where they sat down and folded their legs Yoga fashion with their fists on their knees and their eyes staring directly ahead. Wang was already moving to the entrance door some distance away. Just before disappearing inside he crooked a blunt finger at me. Reluctantly I followed. He was conferring with the big instructor when I entered. At the same time a large heavyweight punching bag was being hung on a chain in the center of the room.

Wang turned to me.

"Have you any training in the martial arts?"

"A little," I admitted.

"What kwoon do you belong to?"

"Well…" I lifted my shoulders modestly. "I usually just work out on my own." He regarded me curiously without seeming very impressed and only later did it dawn on me he had been studying the still fading mass of bruises and cuts that had covered the better part of my face.

"How can you train alone? How do you stay in shape?"

"I run a lot."

Wang smiled "But not fast enough, uh?" He planted himself right in front of me and pointed a finger at his own nose.

"Let me see you punch," he said.

I felt like a damn fool, but what choice did I have? He was standing there pushing his fat face at me and his students were all watching. I made a half-hearted jab at him. Wang jerked his head back in an instant. "No, Mr. Mulligan. Punch fast."

So I did. I threw a right and, thinking he'd probably block that one, I followed with a quick left. He got them both. I guess he'd most likely done this ten thousand times, too. His blocking hand, cocked in front of his face, whipped at my right fist and flicked it aside. Then it snapped back in time to do the same with my left fist. He was far too fast for me. I swear he never even looked at my punches. I think he could have whacked my fists out of the air blindfolded.

He straightened up and shook his head smiling.

"Did you beat yourself up, Mr. Mulligan?"

Very funny.

Wang walked to the heavy bag where the American stood. "Dennis," he explained, indicating the same man, "is one of our most experienced instructors and he is also probably the strongest man in our school." With no warning he shouted something to Dennis in what must have been Chinese but was so guttural I didn't catch it. The guy immediately jumped back in a fighting stance, stiff from head to foot. When Wang shouted again, Dennis, screaming, lashed out with his right fist, caught the bag right in the midsection and sent it rocking back about three feet. The big bag continued to swing back and forth until he stepped forward and clasped it with both palms.

Wang looked at me and gestured to the bag. "You're lighter than Dennis and without experience, Mr. Mulligan. Would you like to try? The answer was no. But I scanned the sea of faces around us and decided that that would be a bad answer for any man whose ego was driving even though it did so from the back seat.

My stance wasn't much but I stiffened up good and aimed for a point about where Dennis had hit it. I didn't shout as he had but I sure felt like it when my fist encountered concrete and my wrist bent hard at an angle that it was not designed to bend. The leather was thick and the stuffing must have been sand. The thing could not have weighed less than two hundred pounds. It moved back, all right, about a foot or so—nothing like it had with Dennis, but at least it moved. I gritted my teeth and folded my arms trying not to let it show that my wrist was sore as hell.

"Not too bad," offered Wang. "You're stronger in the head than in the body. Your mental is good but your physical is uncoordinated."

I would have had to interrupt him to take offense, and why bother? He was going on. "You are both stronger and heavier than me; now it is my turn." With no preparation Wang stepped back from the bag in a casual ready stance and then bounded into it, slamming his fist forward at the same time his shrill cry cut the air. That bag seemed to bend nearly double with the sudden force and rocketed away from his fist. It thundered against that stout chain. It swung the full length the chain allowed, just missing the ceiling nine feet overhead by mere inches. The room quaked as the bag pounded against its restraints. Swinging back down, it shuddered to a stop against Wang's stiff arm.

Wang turned to me with a smug smile.

"Size and strength mean little compared to technique, Mr. Mulligan. Not tricks...technique. This is the breaking punch, a punch that can shatter boards or bricks or...bones. But it is only one technique. There are many ways of force."

With no further explanation, Wang stepped back again and faced the bag as before with his right fist cocked. I had no idea what the man could possibly do for an encore except perhaps knock the blasted bag off the chain, but that wasn't on the program. His cry began and just as the fist started forward, I caught a quick glimpse of it opening up and the middle finger retracting slightly until the three central fingertips formed a blunt knife edge. Then it was away like an arrow and I didn't see it again. It exploded into the bag with an incredible eruption of what turned out to be sawdust instead of sand and drove inside the leather almost to this elbow. Brown dust sprayed the room and poured from the rupture but when the split second had ended and we all watched Wang start to withdraw his arm, we could see that the bag had not budged by any measurable distance. His arm slid out and out and at last his hand appeared gripping a fistful of sawdust which he turned on me and held in front of my face.

The stuff poured out from between his fingers.

I was too stunned to speak.

"You left then, didn't you?" Sung prompted me when I reached that point in the retelling. No, I told her, but I did swallow a remark. I had suddenly remembered where I'd heard of

Wang Chen, the thing that had been bothering me all along. A year or so before I'd caught him on a Hong Kong television special performing the same trick…er, that is to say, the same technique, on a bull. The show was taped; the bull was live. His fist had withdrawn on that occasion clutching what close up cameras revealed to be the bull's heart. The bull, needless to say, did not survive the telecast. There is something, something rather disturbing about standing next to a man who is capable of ramming his hand into your chest and ripping out organs at random that makes swallowing remarks seem the practical thing to do. So I did not ask him how he had gone about financing the loss of ten housand bulls or heavyweight bags.

Meanwhile, Wang's hand became drained of sawdust.

"Tricks, Mr. Mulligan?"

I raised my brows.

"No," he said, answering his own question. "Not tricks. This is the result of decades of patient practice, countless hours of work and pain. And even then, it is a technique that goes only a short distance along the full reach of the martial arts. It is merely the limit to which we can allow ourselves to go in a civilized world. There are scarcely a handful of men, perhaps no more than two or even one, who dare go farther…who have the facilities and the capabilities to go beyond. Men who can shatter spines without killing. Men who, it is said can literally remove limbs with so quick a strike—not merely dislocate bones for that is fairly easy, but actually dismember limbs from the body. Men who, it is also said, can kill without striking at all—by mere contact alone. This is *tien-hsueh*, delayed death touch. A warrior so skilled can cause his opponent's body to anguish and his spirit depart against the momentary touch of the death hand. This is technique, Mr. Mulligan, not tricks and not fantasy. Technique. But you will not find them taught or studied here."

I looked down at Wang. He was talking and talking only because I'd provoked him. His temper was the chink in his

I-ching. But even though he was talking, he was hiding behind the obscurity of a subject without a specific name.

"Let me get this straight," I said slowly. "This one man you're talking about—is he the **Yega**?"

I swear it was as though somebody had reached in and snatched the heart from *his* chest. The blood drained from that man's face as the sawdust had from between his fingers. If he'd been mad when he'd arranged for this little demonstration, then he was way past it now. He turned to Dennis, muttered something in hasty Chinese that I could translate and stormed from the classroom.

"And then finally you left?" asked Sung sipping tea.

"Yes. But I was not giving up on my interviewee. He had just given up on me."

Dennis squared off at me but he didn't need to say it—I was to be asked to leave and, if I hesitated for a moment, assisted bodily to the door. With the remnants of my pride, I left the classroom and the studio and didn't begin nursing my wrist until I was outside. It was only the silence of a door not slammed at my back which made me turn and so to see Dennis still standing behind me on the sidewalk.

He told me no hard feelings. My nod seemed to satisfy him. After a moment he started to withdraw and then paused. "Tell me something," he asked, "I've studied with the master for ten years. I thought I'd seen all his moods. I've seen him so happy he claps his hands, so sad he cries. Jealousy, pride and anger I have seen. And sometimes even humility. I thought the only emotion he lacked was fear. And now I've just seen him frightened to death. What did you say to him? ...that word?"

I shook my head. "It's the big taboo, Dennis. Master Wang was discussing a living legend. What I asked him about was a mythological monster. The hell of it was we were were both talking about the same guy."

Dennis nodded as though he understood. But how could he? I know I didn't.

9. A Short Run to Macao

"Back breaking and dismembering I can at least understand," said Stringer dryly. "But what the hell is this death hand stuff?"

"Wang didn't explain how it works," I told him. "He may not even know." I could've added that because I was talking from a public phone booth I didn't care to speculate. I could've said that I'd already made a report and now it was his turn. I could've reminded him that Sung was waiting for me in the restaurant where my food was getting cold. All of that was true. I could've just told him I'd never heard of it before. Unfortunately, I had.

More than a decade had passed since the martial arts craze had been responsible for the rash of charlatan talents purveyed in the back pages of cheap magazines, among them the "masters" who could teach ultimate fighting methods of poison finger strikes and death touch techniques to anyone with the price of a paperback book. Ten thousand willing sacrificial bodies not included. I'm embarrassed to admit those ads had stung me twice before I enrolled in a really good home correspondence combat course. They were frauds. Something told me however that what had inspired them was not.

"You think Wang knows our man?" Stringer asked me.

"Hell no!" I replied. "And what's more, he doesn't care to make his acquaintance."

"Are you any closer to finding this creature?"

"I don't know where he is now, but I've got a pretty good idea where he trained. If there is such a guy and if he can do what Wang says he can, he must have studied in China."

Stringer observed that if he was down here after Ping Sha Han and closing up the *de ha tit* at the same time it was a sure bet he'd come from China. We needed to know where he was now.

"Have you done any better?"

"A couple of things," he said. "First Bobby Ching has that blowup for you to look at. It's legible but incomprehensible. Some kind of code. It might mean something to you; it doesn't to me."

"And the second?"

"We've been going through Lee Chung's holdings here in Hong Kong. It seems he owned a couple hotels; half a dozen restaurants, an automobile agency and several warehouses. The police are checking them out too; they're ahead of us everywhere we go. Manuel just left a warehouse over at the Ocean Terminal Complex owned by Lee A. Chung Hua Moving and Storage Company."

"What about it?"

"The owner's an odd character by the name of Chang Li. Manuel said he was acting strange."

"Manuel has that effect on people," I said.

"The description sounded familiar, that's all. Forty to fifty, graying, overweight, flat face with bulging eyes. It sounded like a description you'd given me."

"How was he dressed?"

"Manuel didn't say."

"Well, was he wearing two bodyguards that look a lot like the Great Wall?"

"Apparently he did have some muscle."

I tried to sound calm but I felt my pulse picking up.

"All right," I said. "I'll swing by there on the way back to the office and ID the guy."

I rejoined Sung in the dining room and wolfed down the rest of my *dim sum* and hundred-year old eggs while she eyed the goodie cart. The eggs are really only about as old as Sung but they don't look as tasty. As for the *dim sum*, it's a variety of tiny dishes: won tons, steamed dumplings, rice rolls, like that. The waitresses wheel trolley carts around laden with one dish or another, calling out their offerings. Everything's the same price. Diners take what they want and when they're done, collect their little dishes so the cashier can add them up. Sung had perked up when a waitress started calling out *nor mai chi, chien chang go, yah jap go,* and *daan* tart—the coconut snowballs, thousand-layer cakes, pudding squares and hot custard tarts. There were no fortune cookies on the trolley. The fact is, you can't buy a fortune cookie anywhere in Hong Kong, thank God. Hong Kong may be a tourist town but it's a Chinese town too and the food here is real.

"No time for dessert," I told her.

"Are we in a hurry?"

"Uh huh. I have to make a stop on the way to the office."

"Where are we going?"

"Not we, me. This time you're absolutely positively not coming with me."

"But, Doyle—!"

"Don't bother saying a word. My mind's made up."

She frowned at me as I slid the dish away and wiped my mouth. I stood up and so did she. The way she was dressed who needed dessert? She looked good enough to eat. The pigtails were gone now, replaced by long flowing curls that swept down nearly to the middle of her back and poured over the shoulders of her crème-colored knit sweater like hot chocolate over vanilla ice cream. It was the first time I'd seen her face made up. Her cherry red lips, dazzling candy bright eyes and butterscotch skin were an irrestible delight for any sweet tooth like mine. She had traded in her tennis shoes for high heels and her jeans for a miniskirt revealing the kind of mouth-watering pastry that would never be found on any dessert tray. Funny thing, whatever she was wearing was the thing I liked her best in. But this really was my favorite.

When we picked up a taxi outside I gave the driver the name of the Chung Hua warehouse at the Ocean Terminal and held the door open for Sung.

"But you do understand now," I lecturered her, "you're to stay with the cab. If I get into trouble, you run for the cops."

Oh yeah. She understood.

The Chung Hua Storage warehouse was surrounded by fancy hotels on the north and south. In another few years it'd be torn down to make way for another hotel because the land was too valuable for storage. It stood near the wharf where the cruise ships dock and just across the street from the famous *Tsim Sha Tsui* shopping district.

We cruised past without stopping. I had the cabby pull over in front of a nearby hotel and slipped out of the car.

I'd just started along the sidewalk when the cab gunned passed me. I whirled. There was Sung, standing on the curb stuffing change into her purse.

I wanted to scream. I glared at her. She smiled back. I could either make a scene or move it. Moving sounded more sensible and a darn sight less conspicuous.

We cat footed to the back of the warehouse. Here, we were looking out and down at the docks. Two cruise ships were tied up there with room for two more. The back side of the warehouse was even less impressive than the front.

"Look, Sung," I explained when we were safely ensconced behind the neighboring hotel's garbage dumpster. "I'm going to slip in the back door. If these are the guys I ran into before, they're killers—they tried to kill me once and they may try again. They may even get me this time if you don't do as I say. Wait here. All I want is a quick look and I'm gone. But if anything happens to me in there you being out here and going for the cops may be the only bargaining chip I've got. Now will you do that?"

She nodded.

I ran in a kind of crouch across the space between the two buildings. The back door of the warehouse was standing open. Not wide open, but cracked.

I poked my head in and waited for my eyes to adjust to the acres of darkness. In the silence I could hear my heart thumping out a wild drumbeat.

A hand grabbed my shoulder.

I whirled around.

"Damn!" I couldn't believe it. I was trying to whisper but the curse came out in a hoarse scream.

Sung had a finger to her lips.

With her other hand she was pointing down toward the docks.

I looked.

"Are those the men you were telling me about?" she breathed in my ear once we'd both ducked down.

There must have been an underground passage leading from the warehouse to the docks. A door had opened in the wharf wall and three men were sneaking out. Two were big hulking things. They marched on each side of the third man, a bit of a guy with a pushed-in face and big Pekingese eyes. Well, well, I thought, the little dog is taking his boys for a walk.

It couldn't have been easier. I had my ID; it was him. Now I could go.

"Where are they going?" asked Sung.

"I don't know or care," I told her, but I watched them head north toward the King George Memorial Park and I wondered where the hell they were going.

If they were leaving the warehouse, I could step in and look around. Who knows, I might even find a few hundred IE's waiting to catch the next train.

But why were they leaving? And why was the door open?

The three of them followed the wharf wall down past the next building before scrambling over and heading toward the street. The hulk brothers looked right and left, front and back as they walked. A gnat couldn't have gotten through to the Pekingese without getting slapped. I decided these guys weren't just leaving. They were leaving for good. In fact, they were running. Like Huang Mu.

They disappeared behind the hotel.

Sung got up and tiptoed a few yards up the alley while I pulled my lucky coin from a pocket and sent it spinning.

Heads, I head into the premises and look around.

Tails, I tail the trio.

It landed tails.

I exercised my veto. If this was Huang all over again I didn't want any part of it. I was in no mood to get blown out of the sky twice in one week.

I flipped again.

Tails.

Just because the Pekingese was running didn't mean he'd end up at the same place as Sha Han. In fact, Sha Han could be inside the warehouse right now, waiting to catch the next train out. I didn't really believe it but the possibility was enough to warrant a second veto.

I tossed the coin one last time, caught it just as Sung came running back over, said to myself, "Please…be heads, "and slapped it onto the back of my hand.

"Doyle what is it?" sung cried.

"It's tails, dammit.!"

"I mean what are you doing?"

"What else? I'm going after them."

I grabbed Sung by the wrist and away we went. We took a peek around the side of the warehouse before showing ourselves. Sure enough, the trio was just then getting into a waiting Rolls Royce down on the corner.

We started flagging taxis. At last one whipped to the curb. I shouted at the driver those words that every cabby secretly longs to hear one day and we squealed away from the curb to follow that car. We could just barly make out the Rolls still going north on Ferry Street. I told myself if it turned east on Argyle and headed for the airport it really would be Huang Mu all over again. But it went straight. We soon sped near the Mong Kok District and I began to believe they were going to visit the Shanghai Mansions. Wrong again. The Rolls turned left into the *Kai Koki Tsui* district and all but lost itself in traffic.

We barely caught sight of them peeling south again for the waterfront. This time it was going to be by sea. But to where? There I was, asking the same questions I'd asked myself with Huang Mu. Was this the escape route that the others were taking? Were we on the *de ha tit* now?

The Rolls deposited the Pekingese and his two pals in a parking lot right across from the Macao Ferry Pier. During the day it's a parking lot. At night the minstrels and fruit sellers, fortune tellers and fortune takers take over and it becomes the Open Air Market. But that was still hours away. As our taxi pulled up we spotted them heading for the ticket office on the dock, the hulk brothers carving a path through the crowd for their boss. They were shoving old men and women aside. Yeah, I thought to myself, you treasure good manners, all right. You treasure good manners like you treasure your diamond tie tack and only drag both out for Chinese New Year. I shelled out for the cabby feeling my heart sink as I saw how my financial reserves had dwindled. "My God, not again," I muttered. My plan was to give the guy enough to take Sung to the police but

I didn't have it and now I was too late; she was piling out the other side. The taxi zipped off.

My eyes stayed on the ticket line at the counter and those three men. From here they could catch a ferry to any one of a dozen destinations around Hong Kong including the Central District, the New Territories or one of the islands. But they didn't. With their tickets in hand, the trio made a bee line for the hydrofoil docked off to one side. They were going to Macao.

"Sung, quick, have you got any money?"

"Yes. Some."

"Have you got enough to loan me ticket fare to Macao and still get yourself another cab?" I was moving through the small crowd, pulling her along.

"No."

"How much have you got?"

"Just enough to buy tickets for both of us."

I stared down at her. "Gosh, Sung, the ride in the cab won't be anything like as much as the Macao ticket."

"I know," she said flatly, "But if you don't let me come with you, I'm not going to loan you any."

I stopped to plead with her. "Look, Sung. Don't you see what's happening? Didn't you learn anything the last time? I don't want you anywhere around if this is a repeat of the Huang Mu fiasco. I don't even want me anywhere around but I've got to see where he's going and you've got to get to the police and tell them what's going on. Find Hawthorne if you can. Tell him who we're following and—"

"I don't know who we're following."

We had moved to the head of the line and the ticket seller put the question to me. An amplified voice announced the hydrofoil departure in five minutes. Like Huang Mu, the Pekingese was cutting it close.

"Chang Li," I said, suddenly remembering the name that Stringer had given me.

"We have no destination Chang Li," said the cashier.

"Two tickets to Macao."

It was Sung. She reached up and put the money on the counter, scooped up a pair of ticket stubs and pulled me off toward the dock.

Hand in hand we crossed the pier and jumped onto the accommodation ladder. The door promptly closed at my back. Wide and two stories high, this monster didn't look any more like a ferry from inside than it had from outside. And it wasn't. The hydrofoil could travel at close to fifty miles per hour on three giant wing-like skis extending below the hull. It could make the short run to the Portuguese colony of Macao in under an hour carrying a hundred and sixty passengers.

We'd no sooner stepped inside and joined the milling throngs all searching for their seats in typical Hong Kong confusion than a public address speaker announced departure.

Sung staked out our seats while I looked around for the Pekingese and his pals. They were nowhere to be seen. Could they have doubled back on the pier and gone to another ferry without my seeing them?

Too late.

The powerful engines ignited. The ship eased out into the typhoon shelter. It picked up speed once we cleared the other crafts. Soon we were thrown against the backs of our chairs as the hydrofoil kicked into overdrive and shot ahead like a rocket. Slowly, ever so slowly, we felt ourselves begin to rise off the surface of the sea until we were just skiing along smoothly six feet above the water.

Another time I might have actually enjoyed it.

Right about then I had a knot in my belly and a feeling I was making a wasted trip to Macao. The feeling wasn't so bad. I could stand losing a couple of hours and the two-way fare on the hydrofoil. But suppose they were aboard. Then the record seemed to favor the odds that someone else was aboard, too. Which meant—here was the part that knotted my belly–that these of us who survived would likely be swimming home.

This may be a good place to explain that my idea of swimming is to flop near the surface for ten or twenty seconds until my strength and my air give out and I go down. I have this negative buoyancy problem. In spite of that I was silently grateful the Pekingese had decided against flying. Once had been enough. If you're blown into the water you can always try to grab a seat cushion or another unfortunate passenger and take him down with you. But when your plane is rocketing into the sea and you're scrambling around for something to hang onto or, worse, you're flapping your arms in the sky, negative buoyancy takes on a whole new definition.

After a while our speed decreased and the craft began settling into the sea once again. I spent the short docking time at the island community of Ma Wan monitoring everyone who got off and later, new arrivals. There were few of the former and fewer of the latter and very soon we were back in our seats and heading west again on the long open stretch of sea that separated the two European colonies.

That short stop had also given me a chance to survey the occupants of our section and I was convinced that our quarry was not among them.

When the seatbelt lights went out and we were permitted to move around, I knew that's what I'd have to do. Telling Sung to stay put, I slipped across into the aisle, looked up and down, decided to try the upper deck first turned around and collided into her.

This was getting ridiculous.

"Don't you hear well?" I asked her.

"No."

My brows went up. It couldn't be that simple.

"You're not deaf?"

"Yes."

"You are?"

"No."

I shook my head to clear away the cobwebs.

"Sung, can you hear me now?"

"Oh, yes."

"Aren't you going to do what I tell you?"

"Yes."

"Then stay in your seat."

"No, Doyle, I won't."

Another thirty minutes of this and we'd be in Macao.

"What do you want me to do?" she asked.

"It beats me," I said. "I think I knew when we started this conversation."

"I'm going to help you, Doyle."

"If you want to help," I suggested, "you can check the forward seating. There are more seats yet up front. If you spot 'em, don't let on; just come and get me. I'll be on the upper deck."

By golly, it worked. She turned and headed forward. That was the trick then, I decided—tell Sung to do what she was already planning to do anyway and then convince myself it was my idea.

I rubbernecked my way aft.

A door at the back opened onto an emergency exit and stairway to the upper level. Before climbing up I stepped to the exit door and watched the boiling wake of those twin propellers and decided it would take quite an emergency for me to exit there. I had no way of knowing that in another five minutges I'd be frantic to get out this same door. At the top of the stairs I pushed through another door and found myself in first class. Here was now my proper station in life. The more luxurious accommodations didn't put me off a bit. Several dozen chairs had been scattered around an area that was fully as large as the cramped coach section below. A forward bulkhead just like the one in coach class gave it the same dimensions but rather than leading to additional seating, I suspected the door to this bulkhead opened onto the wheelhouse and captain's quarters. I moved forward. The windows up here were larger than below too and offered better views. But my concern was with the people occupying the chairs. A few were empty, just like economy, but not many. The hydrofoil business between Hong Kong and Macao was brisk. Most of the passengers were going to Macao for the gambling and I had to ask myself how many of these high rollers in first class would be coming back coach.

Nothing. No sign of the Pekingese.

At the door to the wheelhouse I had to resist an urge to knock and speak to the captain. To warn him of possible trouble or enlist his help. If my quarry wasn't even on the ship then what trouble could there be? I decided to wait until I either found him or verified he wasn't aboard.

My walk back took me down the opposite aisle.

Still nothing.

I climbed down and stopped at the lower level emergency door as I'd done before. Through the window I could see the rugged rocky coast of Lantau Island settling into the sea as though our high speed wake was the trail of a torpedo which had sunk it.

I entered economy class.

Sung wasn't back yet. I walked the length of the aisle and passed through the bulkhead to the forward section which was every bit as cramped but smaller and it took no time at all to see that neither the fearsome threesome nor Sung was around.

I was just coming back into our assigned section when I heard the thing that tightened the knot in my belly. It was loud down here. Chinese chatter is like that. It carries. It's tough to pick out one word or phrase from the confusion of sounds. But there was something special about the shrill scream of that little Chinese kid speaking to his parents.

"Look, Daddy. An arm."

Nobody else seemed to hear him. But I heard.

Neither his father nor his mother turned.

I turned.

The little guy was standing in his window seat looking back pointing out his small porthole. I lthought he meant that there was an arm outside the window perhaps somebody crawling along the side of the ship. I bent down and stared. I straightened up again without seeing a thing.

The boy had attacked his father, who was ignoring him for the sake of a book by Tao-yuan, a kind of Chinese Goren on Gambling. "I did see it, Daddy," he said. "I saw an arm fall into the water."

I went stiff.

The monkey's fist in my stomach balled itself tighter.

The kid's parents still hadn't looked up. Nobody else was paying him any attention either. Even the boy semed to think it was all a joke. I was the only one who knew better.

I brushed someone aside very rudely, put my face to the glass, and craned my neck overhead. Nothing there. "Sorry," I snapped, raced back to the rear, slammed through the door and launched myself up the stairs. I don't know what it was I expected to see in first class but I didn't see it. Here was the same sedate group of travelers I'd left only moments before, reading, chatting, sleeping, and enjoying the scenery for which they'd paid.

I leaped to one of the large windows on the left side. Port. Nothing. I looked ahead and astern as much as the glass permitted. Nothing. Not a damn thing.

And then, just as I'd decided the kid was as crazy as I was something flew by.

I was looking for it. I expected to see it. But when it streaked past my window I just couldn't believe it. My brain couldn't accept the possibility of such an outlandish event in the real world.

It was a human limb. Bloodied and with bone protruding at each end, it was unmistakably the thigh of a man from hip to knee. The thing sailed down from overhead, tumbled back in the hydrofoil's slipstream and pitched into the sea well astern.

I should have moved immediately. But for a moment, I wasn't even breathing. The seconds ticked by. Eventually I breathed. Then I stood up. Someone later reported to the police that I remarked very calmly. "The son of a bitch is dismembering them."

But I don't remember saying it.

I do remember thinking I had to get to the captain. He could stop the ship. He could arrange for a party of men to storm the weather deck over first class.

I remember diving through the wheelhouse door, throwing myself along a narrow passageway. The wheelhouse itself was fully forward. A door on my right was open revealing a room the size of two telephone booths pushed together, probably the captain's cabin. The ladderway leading up to the weather deck and down to coach class was off to my left but I didn't know that because this door was closed. If I'd known about it, I'd have climbed up fast and either saved someone's life or gotten myself killed. As it was I did neither.

I rushed forward. A helmsman sat in front of the controls staring out his windscreen at the onrush of sea and a bright ball of afternoon sun hanging high over Macao. Another man standing beside him—undoubtedly the captain—turned when he heard me coming. He was quick. When he whirled, he already had a pistol in his hand and before I could say a word he'd lined it up on my head.

I shouted: "There's somebody being murdered up on the roof." At least that's what I started to shout but I only got as far as "There's somebody—" when a slug smacked into the passage wall beside my left ear.

The explosion twisted my head around so hard I almost went down.

"Wait! Don't shoot!"

But he wasn't going to wait. And he was already lining up his pistol for a second shot.

I doubled back and crashed through the passenger door. As I fell through, barely staying on my feet, I clenched my teeth and tensed my back muscles waiting for the impact of the bullet or the deafening sound of the second explosion. They never came.

I floundered back down the aisle to the rear exit. The looks I got from those people didn't mean a thing to me. If the captain was still chasing me, let him. That didn't mean a thing either. I had to get up to the roof.

And then I was going down the stairs. There were more steps than before and they were steeper. I stumbled, caught a foot and plowed the rest of the way on my side. I smashed into the emergency exit.

I pulled myself up and pushed against the door bar.

It didn't budge.

I pushed harder.

It still didn't budge.

I threw myself against it like a maniac.

"Christ!" I screamed, "what good is an emergency door if you can't get it open in an emergency?" Of course it was probably rigged not to be opened while the ship was in motion—no emergency could present more danger than stepping out the back of this rocket over those mammoth twin screws and that mad froth of sea. But that logic didn't occur to me then. It didn't seem to apply.

I grabbed a fire ax beside the door and heaved it at the window. The glass shattered. I watched the thousand little tempered cubes as well as the ax go flying back into the hydrofoil's wake. The resulting hole was too small to crawl through so I'm not sure how I made it. But make it I did. The next thing I knew I was hanging by my waist with buckets of water being thrown at my head. Somehow I got a grip on the ladder off to the side. When I had both hands on it my legs came through and I swung for a while until my feet could find a rung.

The difference between this world and the one I'd just left was not to be believed. From the quiet and comfortable I was instantly assaulted with the most tremendous roar I'd experienced since standing beside that open hole in the side of the DC-10.

The engines for those twin screws must have been just below the lower seating area in the after compartment for it to bellow as it did. The howl was horrific. And the swell and hiss of the sea below me was every bit as frightening. I looked down—don't ask me why—and saw the ocean sweeping beneath my feet at an ungodly speed.

I didn't look down again.

My head was already spinning like a top. The noise and the sea rush were physically draining. What little strength I had left was going fast.

Rung by rung I climbed up to the roof. A continuous railing surrounded a wooden weather deck; it was only open at the stern where my ladder ended.

That's where it ended for me.

I didn't think I'd ever get that far and I damned near didn't. I got both hands on the deck but my arms wer too tired to hoist myself up. It was all I could do to hang on.

By inches my chin came over the top.

And there he was.

I was staring eyeball to eyeball with the Pekingese.

He lay less than three feet away, stretched out on his stomach with his arms thrown out to the side. His left leg was thrown to the side too. About ten feet to the side. As for the right leg, it was nowhere around. I could see the empty hollow of his right pants leg soaking up blood by the pint.

He should have been dead.

But he wasn't dead. Not yet, anyway.

His bulging eyes were looking directly at me. That was more than bad enough. Much worse though, he was seeing me.

He was talking to me with his eyes. I knew what he wanted even before I saw his lips moving.

I tried to look over and behind him.

Something ghastly was going on at the forward end of the deck but the ship was still flying into the sun and I couldn't see what it was. I guess I really knew what was going on but I couldn't see it. There were people moving around. Black silhouettes. Two of them were up and one of them was down. And then two of them were down. Every once in a while a scream was carried back to me on the wind and I could identify human parts sailing off the side of the ship.

Blood and other visceral fluids were flowing back over the deck. The wind was whipping them up and spattering them in my face.

I knew what was going on all right. Two hulking humans were being turned into chum.

When the screams died away I watched a dark figure come scuttling back toward the Pekingese and me.

It came right up to us, standing over me and eclipsing the sun with its blackness.

This time I was staring eye to eye with the killer...Uncle Sun's demon, Master Wang's ultimate technician, and the character who'd been following me around Hong Kong for three days.

I saw black arms and legs. I saw a face mouth, nose, ears and eyes. But once I'd seen those eyes I couldn't see any more. I couldn't look anywhere else.

I'd never seen eyes like those before. Like big balls of black glass. I could see right through them, right into the black mass of a mind behind them. The eyes didn't walk over to me, they pulled me inside. The mind didn't talk to me once I was there. It issued instructions.

Doyle Mulligan didn't know who or what he was seeing.

Doyle Mulligan would forget what he was seeing.

Doyle Mulligan had seen nothing.

I don't know what would have happened next if Doyle Mulligan hadn't fallen over the side. I lost a foothold. Then the other foot slipped too. All of a sudden my body ws flapping off the back of the hydrofoil like an ensign blowing in the wind.

Precious seconds passed while my feet fought for a hold on the ladder.

Somehow I grabbed hold of a rail stanchion. My head came over the deck edge again.

The Pekingese was being dragged forward. Even then he was nearly outside of my failing vision. I saw his eyes lock on mine. I saw his lips mouth the words "Help me...please help me," in Chinese over and over again. He was running away in his mind. Running as fast as he could run. But it wasn't fast or far enough.

And then the two of them were just a blur.

One blur stood over the other propping the helpless body beneath it. The Pekingese screamed once when he lost his right arm. He barely whimpered when his left arm went over the side.

Before the rest of him went I'm sure he was dead. I hope to God he was dead.

I couldn't help it. My mind started thinking about the triple amputee whose doctor tried to charge him an arm and a leg. I think I said aloud: "Keep the change, doc."

But by that time I was half gone myself. I saw dishes of dim sum go flying past me. How could I pay the bill if the **Yega** kept throwing away all the dishes?

Steamed dumplings.

Rice rolls

Won tons.

It was all coming back to me now.

The black, blurred figure disappeared down through a hatchway and it seemed like forever before another figure emerged, looked around and then moved back to me and helped me up.

The wooden deck was treacherous with the slime and fluids that covered it, all that was left of the Pekingese and the two men who were supposed to have kept him alive and in one piece. I'd wanted to too. I'd needed him in one piece to see where he was going. It's true the hulk brothers had paid a higher price for their failure than I had paid for mine.

But then, I wasn't through paying.

10. A Macanese Lesson

The Red Chinese were waiting when we got to Macao.

There were some Portuguese cops too and a Portuguese superintendent of police was in nominal command but the way the Reds pushed the customs people and the passengers around left little doubt in anyone's mind about who was calling the shots.

It was my first encounter with the People's Liberation Army. I had to swallow a dozen remarks. "Get used to it, Mulligan," I kept telling myself, "this is what's waiting for Hong Kong."

That came later.

The hydrofoil had anchored outside Macao harbor.

I was still at the rail, tossing the cookies I hadn't eaten for dessert when the hatch opened for the second time and Sung climbed out. Was that embarrassing! I was getting tired of hv-ing her catch me with egg on my face. This time it was one hundred year old egg and *dim sum*. Honestly, the way this story was going I'd about decided to start phoning in reports to the of-fice with a cryptic: Veni. Vidi. Vomiti. I came, I saw, I puked.

We went back below. The hatch accessed a narrow shaft with a circular stairway that wound all the way down to the engine room below coach. We exited on the first class deck across from the captain's phone-booth sized cabin.

The captain, whose name was Yun, met us there.

He still had the gun and he looked like he'd still like to use it but luckily for me, he was finished with gunplay. Without asking a single question, he urged me and Sung into his cabin, closed the door and left us alone.

We were there when the Red Chinese boarded.

Through a porthole I saw their launch come alongside. Several dozen armed and uniformed men climbed aboard and dispersed through the ship.

I heard them burst into first class and begin shouting orders as though they were commandeering the vessel in the name of the People's Republic.

The cabin door slammed back on its hinges and three of them crowded in. They pointed their weapons at our chests. Others were tramping into the wheelhouse and climbing up to the weather deck. I knew by their tan uniforms and insignias that they were People's Liberation Army. I would have known without the uniforms. It was written all over their faces—In Red Chinese characters, of course.

They took all the passengers by launch to the customs building on the dock in batches of two dozen or so. An hour after they boarded the hydrofoil, all hundred and sixty of us were ashore.

Two Red soldiers moved Sung and me into a separate room. A PLA officer came in. He ordered the soldiers to frisk us. My pockets were turned inside out and the contents piled on a table in the center of the room. Sung's purse was dumped upside down on the same table.

"Now, see here!" I started to say, "I'm a card-carrying member of the Press..." The officer ordered me to shut up. So

I shut up. He told us to sit down. We sat down. After that he and his two lackeys left.

Another commie captain popped his head in a little bit later to be sure we were still shutting up and still sitting down. He popped back out without having said a word.

We waited in there for three hours. Nobody wanted our story until a pear-shaped little guy with a funny little hat on a hairless head, a faceful of scars, and a voice to match came in to talk to us. He introduced himself as Superintendente de Policia Maldonado. “Call me Donado,” he said in a comical quack. “Everybody does,” he added.

It wasn’t a put on. He actually quacked.

Maldonado, it seems, was Inspector Hawthorne’s counterpart in Macao. With a few important differences. The major one being that Maldonado had to kowtow to the Red Chinese instead of having the Chinese kowtow to him.

But there were other differences. For instance, the superintendent had a sense of humor as well as a grasp of the fundamentals of courtesy, both of which Hawthorne lacked. He was Portuguese instead of British, short and fat instead of tall and thin and instead of a hatchet-face, he had scar tissue stretched tight across his head and neck. It looked to me like his hair had caught fire and someone had stubbed him out. And, of course, he quacked when he talked.

“I’m sorry this has taken so long,” he apologized. “I have only just now received permission to take statements from you. Unfortunately, I have been denied permission to have one of my detectives assist me and so you will have to endure my absurd appearance and voice.” Donado placed palms on his bulbous belly. “The result of Macanese food—” he moved one hand to the scars at his throat, “—and burned vocal chords.” His smile robbed his words of any self pity. “You will understand when I tell you that I am known here in Macao by the rather bizarre name of Donado O Pato. ..Donado the duck.”

I raised my brows.

Sung shook her head slowly.

"You know," he prompted us, "like Donald the Duck."

Sung's head still wagged back and forth.

"The cartoon...?" He swirled a hand in the air the way the Europeans do.

I spoke up. "I can explain it to her later, superintendent." He smiled at me and actually bowed by dipping his head two millimeters in my direction..

With that behind us I told him my name was Doyle the Mulligan and this was Sung the Kwon and I gave him my story from beginning to end, ending with my diving out the emergency door, scrambling up the ladder to the weather deck, and finding the Pekingese and his pals being disassembled and tossed into the sea like someone returning a jigsaw puzzle to its box.

"Did you see who did it?" demanded Maldonado, excited in spite of himself. "Can you describe him?"

"I don't know who or what I saw," I told him.

He glared at me. "How can you not know?" he said.

"Well, I guess…I forget what I saw—"

"You forget!"

"I guess I really didn't see anything," I said. The hell of it was, I really didn't remember.

And so it wasn't until I listened to Sung telling her story that I began to understand what must have taken place aboard the hydrofoil. It says much about what was going on in my brain that I hadn't asked her about it in those three hours.

She'd checked out forward tourist seating as I'd asked her to and then turned her attention to the two rest rooms, looked in the ladies room personally and impressed a stranger into checking out the men's She found the stairway between the two rooms. Like a brave but silly fool she had ventured down to the engine room, found it unmannded, and then climbed up to the wheelhouse. She was there with the captian when they heard screams coming from the upper deck. They'd sent a mechanic up to look around.

After hearing her story, Maldonado prevailed upon the Reds to send in Captain Yun.

When the captain was flinging lead past my skull it was easy to believe that the hydrofoil was the first leg in the Iron Underground. Captain Yun, I'd felt, had tried to kill me to protect this secret. But now, even before Yun came in and sat down, I decided it just didn't add up. The Chinese had built a higher wall around Macao than the British would ever build around Hong Kong and even if the hydrofoil could have smuggled a significant number of IE's over here they'd only be getting in deeper instead of getting away.

The captain didn't want to admit he had allowed three men to make the trip to Macao in the privacy of his cabin. Regulations forbade it. Even if they were scared senseless of traveling with the other passengers and insisted that a lunatic killer may have followed them onto the ship. Even if the captain bumps the price of a ticket. Particularly if the captain fails to report the bump to the ship's owners. He wouldn't ever admit that. Nevertheless, he did admit it. Maldonado, despite his appearance and voice, proved himself to be a skilled, dogged interrogator.

Yun looked over at me when he spilled that part about the lunatic killer. He didn't think I was. Not any more. But the glance was the nearest thing to an apology I ever got out of Yun.

Before he was finished the only movements that weren't known but which could be pieced together by the movements of everyone else were those of the killer. He must have boarded right after the Pekingese and his pals. Nobody came aboard after me. While I was wandering around, he had sneaked into the captain's quarters unobserved, enticed the three men up to the weather deck, and proceeded to deal with them in much the same way a garbage disposer deals with left-overs. When he was through, he locked the hatchway behind him, climbed down the stairway and returned to his seat, still unobserved.

Then when we reached Macao, he got off the ship.

Unobserved.

That didn't seem to impress Maldonado too much but it sure impressed me. The passengers had passed single file aboard the PLA launches. Our papers were checked as we boarded.

Was he still hiding on the ship?

Had he dived overboard?

It was too much for me.

"Oh, that's easily explained," said the superintendent once the hydrofoil captain had breen escorted outside and we were alone again.

"I'd like to hear it," I said.

"They let him go."

Sung and I exchanged startled glances.

"They?"

"The PLA."

I started to say something and stopped. It made sense, by gosh. After all, the guy was working for them. I said as much to Maldonado.

"That's right, he agreed. "The same as you."

"Me!"

"You."

"What kind of Mickey the Mouse is that?"

"Not at all. You're after a story. But you're looking for the same thing as this killer. He's not a professional investigator like you are. All he knows how to do is kill. So he's following you around letting you do all the looking and when you find who you're looking for he'll step in and do what he does best. He'll kill the man you're looking for. Then he'll kill you and your lady friend, too."

But the PLA—"

"—want to close down the *de ha tit*, Mr. Mulligan. And you're helping them do that."

"They why are they holding me here?"

Maldonado shrugged like a European. "They're not. As far as they're concerned you're free to leave. They wanted to release you three hours ago. It took me that long just to convince them to let me talk to you first."

I turned to Sung.

"You were segregated," Maldonado told my back, "so that the customs people wouldn't disturb you. You've been given royal treatment. You should see what the other passengers have gone through."

"We can both leave now?"

"I can't stop you, Mr. Mulligan. And they won't."

I moved towared the table which had all my belongings on it and started stuffing things in my pockets. Sung did the same with her purse. "Well did you get what you wanted from us, superintendent?" I asked him.

"Not all. I think you know more than you're telling."

"Try reading tomorrow's newspapers."

"I've been following the Hong Kong press, Mr. Mulligan. I could learn more from any Chinese off the street."

I forced a laugh.

"So could I. But they won't talk to me."

"Nor to me, Mr. Mulligan. What I know I have learned by dint of chasing it down the same way you're doing."

"You're interested? Professionally, I mean?"

"Very much."

I wasn't sure I wanted to hear this.

"Do you know this guy, superintendent? The killer, I mean?"

His absurd head and funny little hat dipped twice.

"I do."

What do you call him?"

"I don't know his real name. Only the name he goes by."

I grinned. "All right. If you won't say it, I will. Is it ***Yega***?"

He winced. "Yes."

"You've seen him?"

"Oh, no."

"But you know he exists, don't you? I'll bet you could tell me some things."

"I might too. If you were to tell me some things."

"I'll tell you this much," I said. "The guy can waltz from murder to murder without being seen. He can get a bomb through a sterile concourse and onto an airplane with no one the wiser. He carries dozens of incendiaries and fire bombs around in his pockets but nobody ever notices. He terrifies his victims so much they run like the devil. But as soon as he catches 'em they take his hand and stroll off with him to be torn to pieces, blown up, or cremated. He works the poor bastards over like a combination Bruce Le and Dr. Christian Barnard. He poisons old men and women. And he makes people like me—people who've watched what he's done—sick to their stomachs. You want a description? All right. He's got poison fingers and death hands. He has no face and no soul. He may be a man. Or he may be two men or a handful of men. He may even be an evil spirit. He's here; he there; he's everywhere and he nowhere all at the same time." I took a breath. "And if you can catch him, I'd be grateful. I'm getting awfully tired of looking over my shoulder."

"I don't blame you. So am I?"

"You?"

"Yes, me. I've been looking over my shoulder for the last two years. And I'm not a man who likes to look over his shoulder. I've made it my business to find out what I could about this murderer. He's no evil spirit. He's evil, all right, in every sense of the word, but he's also a man."

"Just one man?"

"Yes. There's only one ***Yega***. We can pray there will never be another."

"If praying would do it," I told him. "I'd pray the one right out of existence. I don't kinow about you but the guy scares the hell out of me."

Maldonado smiled a scarred smile.

"I have been a policeman for forty-two years. I don't frighten easily. I've chased every sort of criminal in the book. Killers, butchers, lunatics, sadists, mass murderers, and torturers. This ***Yega*** is something else. I'll tell you the truth, he scares the hell out of me, too."

"Then you must know as much about him as I do," I said. "because the more I find out, the more scared I get."

He nodded. "I know enough to frighten me," he replied.

"Like what."

"The ***Yega*** doesn't waltz. He walks like you and me. He doesn't carry incendiaries or explosives around with him for the simple reason he doesn't have to. He can find whatever he needs when he needs it. I doubt very much if he slipped a bomb onto that airplane. From what I know of the fiend he slipped himself aboard—taking the boarding pass from one of the other passengers perhaps—and assembled an explosive from materials he found at hand."

"At hand? On an airplane!"

"Certainly. Who do you think we're talking about? A wife-beater? An alcoholic who stabs a friend in a bar fight or plows his car into a crowded playground. A doper who blows away a family while robbing their house? No. No. The ***Yega*** kills. That's his life and that's all he lives for. He has no friends. He doesn't date. He doesn't go to the movies or out to dinner. He has no hobbies. He doesn't take drugs. He doesn't smoke or drink. Sometimes I think he doesn't even eat but of course he does. He eats. He sleeps. And he kills. That's all he does and he does it better than anyone else in the world."

"You mean he's an assassin."

"Not at all! An assassin sneaks up behind his victims with a sawed off shotgun or picks them off with a telescopic rifle from half a mile away. Take away his weapons and what it he? Nothing. The ***Yega*** is an enforcer. He's a master of unarmed combat, of course, but a master of pyrochemistry and explosive physics as well. He could walk into this room now with his pockets empty and fashion any kind of incendiary or explosive he needed."

I looked around. The four walls of that tiny room were utterly bare. Except for the table and two chairs the floor was bare too. Who was Maldonado kidding? And then I looked at Maldonado's scarred face and I couldn't help but believe he knew exactly what he was talking about.

The superintendent stepped to the table.

He pointed to Sung's purse and raised his eyebrows at her. "Do you mind, miss?"

With her permission he dumped the contents back onto the table and began stirring the pile with his fingers.

It couldn't have been a more innocuous collection: nail polish, hand lotion, hairbrush and hair spray, mascara a bag of cotton balls, keys, a wallet. The standard pharmacy found in a lady's handbag.

"There's nothing explosive there," I said.

Maldonado just chuckled.

"You think an explosive is some strange matter scraped off the wall of a cave or dropped from a passing meteorite? Most explosive materials are simple chemical compounds made up of elements like hydrogen, carbon, oxygen and nitrogen and others that appear in substances you regard as everyday products. For example, the military name for the explosive nitrocellulose is guncotton because cotton," he lifted the small plastic bag of cotton balls, "is 90 percent cellulose and the best source for it commercially. I've seen guncotton blow and I'll guarantee you it'll knock the wings off a plane let alone a little hole in the side."

I couldn't keep the skepticism out of my voice. "Are you saying he could make a bomb from those cotton balls?" I asked him.

"Of course it would have to be nitrated."

I snickered.

"How would he do that?"

Maldonado looked from me to Sung and then back at me. "I suppose he would urinate on it, Mr. Mulligan. Urine is an excellent source of nitrogen."

That shut me up fast.

He tossed the cotton balls aside and picked up a deck of playing cards. "He could sure as the world make a bomb of these. The red spots of all the diamonds and hearts contain both the nitrates and cellulose so no nitration is required. They're in the dye and the card already. All you have to do is soak the cards in water and compress the red residue into a container. It's been done before…in American prisons by convicts trying to break our or commit suicide. In fact the American playing card companies changed the formula for red dye for that very reason."

I stepped in closer.

"Look at this." He handed me a small can of hair spray which Sung wasn't wearing and to my mind never should.

"Look what it says here. 'Keep away from fire or flame.' That's good advice. Check the ingredients. Alcohol, isobutene and propane. All flammable. All explosive in the right conditions. What do you think would happen if he'd put a can of this inside a jet engine or into a microwave oven in the plane's galley.

The superintendent scooped up another container.

"This hand lotion contains glycerine. In the presence of nitric acid it becomes glyceryl-trinitrate."

"Is that flammable?" Sung wanted to know.

"It'll burn. But I don't recommend lighting it. You see its more popular name is nitroglycerine."

He'd got me and Sung going now. I picked up a jar of Vaseline and Sung ws running down the list of ingredients on a bottle of nail polish.

Toluene," she said. "What's toluene?"

Maldonado blew up his chest. "A distillate of coal tar. Highly poisonous once it's nitrated. After three nitrations it becomes tri-nitro-toluene, more commonly known as TNT. I won't kid you. I couldn't make a bomb from that stuff. But the ingredients are here for someone who does know how." He held aloft a bottle of nail polish remover. "This is different. It's pure acetone. You don't need to do any distilling or nitrating or separating to get this stuff to blow. Acetone is itself an explosive when properly contained and detonated. I believe a bottle this size would put a hole in the pressurized fuselage of an airplane but we'd have to try it to be sure."

He gestured at me.

"That Vaseline in your hand? Pure white petrolatum. A jelly-like hydrocarbon derived from petroleum. Mix in a bit of potassium chlorate and it'll give you very good results."

"Where do we get the potassium chlorate?"

"You can distill it from common laundry bleach right in your kitcfhen. If we were restricting ourselves to ther stuff here in front of us....the tips of these matches are about 50 percent potassium chlorate. You can soak the heads in water and skim off the surface or filter it through a dry cloth."

Maldonado dropped the bottle and signaled Sung that she could return the stuff to her purse.

"The kitchen is another source of explosive materials," he went on, rubbing his palms together. "Potasium chlorate from the bleach mixed with ordinary granulated or powdered sugar yields an extremely volatile brew. In the garage, a compound of fuel oil and fertilizer, like ammonium nitrate, becomes a high explosive with a power equivalent to that of dynamite. Fire bombs? Try throwing ordinary soap flakes into a can of gasoline, mix potassium ntrate with sawdust, kerosene with wax, or cellophane and iron filings. You can make a form of plastic explosive by cooking diesel oil and powdered laundry detergent. The possibilities are endless and he knows them all.

"The point I'm trying to make is that the ***Yega*** doesn't need to carry bombs around. He doesn't need to store his munitions and he has no use for supply lines, all of which can be used to trace him. He works alone, without any help from anybody, anywhere, just using what he finds along the way to accomplish his end."

"Then how can you ever catch him?" I asked.

"You mean the police?"

"Yeah."

Maldonado shook his head. "I don't think he'll ever be caught. Certainly not by the police. We only came close to him once. And that was pure luck."

"The ***Yega*** was here? In Macao?"

"Two years ago."

"What happened?"

Maldonado folded his arms and leaned back against the table.

"The syndicate which supervises the gambling operations here as well as some of the hotels began funneling out their profits in preparation for the eventual takeover by Beijing. When the communists complained we tried to stop it but there wasn't much we could do. Beijing wanted to move in their own people to watch the docks and the post office. Lisbon didn't like that idea. Talks stalled. Money continued to flow out of the colony. And then the ***Yega*** moved into Macao. Almost overnight fourteen of the syndicate's managers were brutally murdered. There were many fires. At the homes of syndicate people and at the casinos. Explosions, too. After a while the Chinese employees refused to work any more no matter how much the syndicate offered to pay and when the Chinese quit here or in Hong Kong, you're out of business. That was it. The syndicate gave up and so did Lisbon. The ***Yega*** moved out, the PLA moved in. And the money stayed."

"So that's how it happened. I never kinew," I said.

"The British and the Portuguese have different notions about free press. What I've just told you never appeared in any newspaper."

"You said something about getting close to the ***Yega***."

"Too close. I went to the home of a casino manager to offer him protection. I'd no way of knowing he was next on the list. Hs house went up before I could get him out. He and his family were consumed by the flames while I..." the inspector gestured to the scars covering his neck and head. "I was merely disfigured. But make no mistake. Had I been meant to die, I too would have been consumed. As it was, I merely learned a lesson."

I believed him. When it came to lessons, the ***Yega*** was an education in himself. He made the school of hard knocks look like a kindergarten class.

When Sung was moved to say something sympathetic to Maldonado he told her to save her concern for herself.

"Until now," he said, "no one has ever gotten so close to the ***Yega*** and lived. Your young American friend here has done so not once but three times, on the plane the junk and the hydrofoil. The ***Yega*** regarded my entire Macanese Police Force as no more than a minor annoyance. I hate to think of what will happen to Mulligan here—and you if you are still with him—when he's reached the end of his investigation and his usefulness."

Maldonato had more to say. But after a while I was listening with only half my brain.

The more he told me the more I realized that Ben Kao was right. I didn't have any business playing in the same ballpark as this nowhere man. And it didn't take any Billy Martin to know that if, compared to him, guys like Wang and Maldonado and Hawthorne were in the minors, then Doyle Mulligan was still playing little league.

I tried to explain this to Sung after we'd been turned loose. Superintendent Maldonado had offered to take us on a tour of Macao. When we declined he couldn't keep his relief to himself. He was convinced—as I as—that the killer was still following me. He wanted us both out of town.

Another hydrofoil took us back to Hong Kong.

"You knew all that stuff I'd fed you about me was just baloney," I told her on the way back. "All that hero stuff. You want the truth? My father died in childbirth. From the shock, I suppose. I'm an only child. Raised by my mother. No good friends until I came here. And before I started this story the most excitement I ever had was watching old movies starring guys like Alan Ladd or Gilbert Roland. A thrill for me was filling out my collection of videotape classics."

"But Doyle, why are you telling me this?"

"I'm studying martial arts by mail for chrissake!"

She touched a hand to my cheek.

"What are you trying to say?"

"I don't know. I just wanted you to know…about me. That you shouldn't expect too much of me. This *Yega*…his ancestors spawned in a different ocean than mine.

11. A Well-Earned vacation

I toss this out first because it was the first thing that met me when I came into the office the next morning. The print itself had been blown up to 11 x 14. The words were in Chinese script. Someone, one of the "OK speakies" most likely, had transcribed it into English and somebody else had typed it out on a plain piece of bond.

Fire Little Yang	Sun-Moon
Water Strong Yang	Dog
Earth Light of the Yang	Star-Passing
Fire Strong Yang	Light-Morning
Wood End of Yin	Circle
Fire End of Yin	Stop-Line
Metal Strong Yin	Open-Tiger
Earth Strong Yin	Burning-Point
Wood Little Yang	End-Stop
Water Little Yin	Good-Change
Metal Light of the Yang	Ox-Down
Fire Little Yin	Soft-Time

This paper was in my hand. I was sitting in a chair across from Stinger's desk. We were alone. The door was closed. Nevertheless, I was talking in undertones.

When we got back from Macao I'd taken Sung to her hotel and told her to lock her door. I ran, not walked, to my flat and looked under my bed before going to sleep, something I haven't done since I was four. On the bus ride to work I'd spent most of my time checking out the other commuters and the rest of it scrutinizing traffic through the rear windows. At the office I'd peeked at the kneehole of my desk and even—if you can believe it!—in each of the drawers. That's what I'd come to. Now I was sitting in Stringer's office behind a closed door and I was whispering.

Stringer wasn't.

"Does it mean anything to you, Doyle?"

"Not much. Of course I've heard of the yin and yang—female passive and male active…that sort of thing. These first words: fire, water, earth, wood, and metal. They're the five ancient Chinese elements. The rest of it is just so much mish-mash to me. Except the animals—the dog, tiger, and ox. They remind me of something. I wonder if it's tied in to *fung shui*?"

Stringer shook his head.

"No. We thought of that. Ben Klao knows *fung shui* and he couldn't make anything out of it either. He says *fung shui* recognizes eight natural elements, not five—hold on a second, I made some notes…okay, here they are—rain, fire thunder, heaven, wind, ocean, mountains, and earth. But no wood or metal. And the corresponding animals they represent are the pheasant, goat, pig, fowl, dragon, horse, dog and ox. *Fung Shui* doesn't list a tiger."

"Well, it must be some kind of code."

Sure it's a code. I told you it was a code. Do you thinik you can figure it out?"

"Not if Ben can't."

Stringer leaned back in his chair and expelled air.

"Well it's too bad. I thought you might."

"Why me?"

"You're the bright boy of the office, aren't you?"

"Oh, that."

"And our friend obviously thought you could figure it out."

"Our friend? I didn't know you and I had any mutural friends, Alex."

"You know who I mean. This ....***Yega***?"

"What the hell are you talking about?"

Stringer tossed hids head in a casual sort of way. But he was secretly enjoying the possibility that he'd guessed something I hadn't.

"He gave you the clue didn't he?"

"He didn't give it to me, I found it."

"But you wouldn't have if he hadn't stolen the print. Now see here, Doyle, you're too close to this thing. Either that or you're too personally involved. He's been following you around everywhere you go—you said that. He could have killed you any time. Yesterday on the roof of that hydrofoil would have been a good time. But he didn't."

"Why should he? I'm doing his job for him, aren't I?"

Stringer's hands flew up. "That's my point! He could have killed you on that airplane. But he didn't. He could have let Chang Li's bodyguards slash your throat in that Kowloon City alley but instead he saved your neck by killing them. He saved you again in Aberdeen by dragging you topside on that junk after you'd collapsed below deck."

While Stringer talked, I'd folded the paper, pocketed it, stood up, crossed to the window, and looked down at the street. I remained there after he'd finished. He was right of course. This was what Maldonado had tried to tell me the other day in Macao.

He went on:

"We pulled you from your assignment. Sent you off on a tangent, looking into the ***Yega*** himself. What you've learned makes it pretty obvious that the police aren't going to get this character any time soon. If at all. And they won't be able to stop him from wiping the Iron Underground, and the people who run it, out of existence. Agreed?"

I muttered agreement without truning.

"As long as he's in Hong Kong," Stringer added, "we'll get nothing out of this story. He'll see to that. And we've only got a few days. So the obvious thing to do is get him out of Hong Kong."

"How do you plan to do that?"

"By getting you out of Hong Kong until after the conferences are over. And hoping he follows."

It was a dreary morning outside Stringer's window. A fog had moved in off the sea. It would probably burn away later on, but at the moment I felt the dispiriting damp of the mist come right through the glass by a kind of osmosis. This had been my big story. I hadn't liked it too much but it was still mine. When Sha Han came into the picture and it looked like we could use the story to help the people of Hong Kong I'd wanted it even more. Now I felt it slipping away. Alex Stringer, editor and mastermind; Manuel Fuentes, investigative journalist; Bobby Ching, photographer; as well as a host of ENA reporters and contributors. Oh, yeah, and Doyle Mulligan, diversion.

"You've heard of Zodiac Cruises?" asked Stringer.

"Yeah," I said. "Isn't that Lee Chung's Hong Kong-based cruise line?"

"That's the one. The police walked through one of their ships yesterday evening. It's docked at the Ocean Terminal. They figure all of the acupuncture clinics were Lee's ticket offices. The Chung Hua warehouse was a holding place, like a boarding platform. The only question is, where did the IE's go from there? The cruise ship was an obvious possibility. It was docked right off the warehouse when Chiang left. But the police gave it a clean bill of health. They checked the passenger list—mostly American and English travelers—and the crew.

The crew's Oriental but their papers are in order and all of them have shipped out with the company before. That leaves a few other possibilities. Lee has an interest in a container terminal up in the New Territories. He owned a transport company that trucked between the warehouse and the airport as well as the container terminal. Lee also had that airline which flies out of Australia and which services Kai Tak. He owned a containerized steamship company out of Tokyo. It has contracts with his container firm in the New Territories. So there's plenty of investigative work to be done. But I'll be frank, Doyle, I don't even want to have my people get started until you, and your lunatic shadow, are out of Hong Kong."

I nodded assent.

Maldonado had wanted us out of Macao; Stringer wanted us out of Hong Kong.

"I can't just fly you to Rio or Acapulco—this ***Yega***'s not stupid. However, he may not know that the Zodic Ship's been checked out and cleared. If we book passage for you under an assumed name and with a cover story he'll think we suspect the cruise ships of running Chinese and that you're there to investigate. It's at least a good bet he'll sneak aboard too. And once he's on the high seas there's nothing he can do but lie low."

"After he's killed me, you mean?"

"Why should he kill you?"

"Because I suckered him onto the cruise ship. When he finds out he's apt to get mad. He went through the gambling syndicate in Macao and the *de ha tit* here in Hong Kong like a ginsu knife through tofu and as far as we know he wasn't even mildly annoyed."

"He's never killed without a good reason. Unless his killing advanced him somehow. I wouldn't send you if I felt there was any real danger."

I had to agree that Stringer's plan sounded good. As much as I hated to admit it the thought of getting away from bombings and burnings and butchering rather appealed to me. The rest of his argument was pure bunk. The ***Yega*** always had a good reason for killing. He liked killing. And Stringer wouldn't send me if he felt there were any real danger—to Stringer. There wasn't, so it looked like I was stuck. But the worst part would be explaining it to Sung. I'd promised her I'd find Sha Han. I could tell her that this might help someone else find him. On the other hand it might not. And I'd promised her I'd do it myself.

Stringer was still talking.

"Now, I couldn't just phone up the company's Hong Kong representative and ask for a discount pass for you on the basis of a story we're doing. We've got to play this like we mean it. They mustn't suspect you're a reporter. Which means we have to pay the fare. Fortunately, Zodiac Cruises are very reasonably priced considering their accommodations and their amenities which are first class." Stringer was leaning back in his chair puffing on a pipe. I knew that at times like these he thought of himself as something very much like Ian Fleming's M at England's MI6. He was probably wishing his eyes were battleship gray, that I was taller and a little better in a scuffle. This was Stringer's big disappointment, he didn't have a good James Bond on the payroll. "Zodiac's got twelve ships in the line," he briefed me. "All fairly small as cruise ships go—a hundred and fifty passengers or so—but new ships and very classy. Comfortable and fast. For passengers who like to travel in style. First class all the way."

Sounds like a ripping good show, I thought. But I said to him: "That's me," and I tried to get into the spirit.

"You don't look it."

"I'll grow a mustache."

"You won't have time." Stinger puffed on his pipe. "The ship sails this afternoon. Name's the Lao Shu. She's been in the harbor for two or three days. I booked a vacant cabin for you on the return leg to Hawaii. Little over half full circle fare, which is reasonable but still not cheap. Your fellow passengers will have money. They'll talk money; they'll act money, and they'll look money."

"I'll get a new pair of sneakers."

"No, you won't! You've got the morning to get some decent clothes. This is not a love boat where singles run around in cutoffs and bikinis and sleep in other people's cabins. These cruises are for respectable, sophisticated couples with the emphasis on 'couples.' "

"I'll take Kayo along."

"Like hell you will! When you two get together there's inevitably trouble. I mean married couples. You'll need to have a girl along or stand out like..." He eyed me with his plain brown eyes wishing I looked as distinguished in a cutaway as Sean Connery. "Like you do right now. Cinch up that damn tie, Doyle. What is this anyway?" I pushed it up a little. "No," he went on, "I was thinking about that young woman you brought in here the other day. She'd be just fine. She's pretty enough that no one would mind she's Oriental and she could be an in with the stewards and the other crew members who, as I said, are mostly Chinese."

I aimed a finger across his desktop.

"Look, Alex, you can shove your damn prejudices." Bond would never talk to M like that. It made Stringer screw up his lips in disgust. "I'm leaving Sung out of this," I said.

"You took her to Macao yesterday."

I wondered how he knew that. "I sure did," I admitted. "And darn near got us both killed. The next time we may not be so lucky. Kayo can take care of himself if anybody can. Me, too." I meant by that Kayo could take care of me, not me take care of me. "Besides Sung doesn't like boats; she gets seasick. I practically had to Shanghai her to get her on the hydrofoil."

"Well, I already called her up this morning at her hotel and she agreed to go."

I swore at him again. He'd had no right to do that. I told him it wasn't his decision to make.

"You're right," he said. "It was hers. When I let her know you were going and it would help with the investigation and the search for her cousin she jumped at the chance."

"Ask her again. She's never given me the same answer to a question twice in a row."

"She's an adult."

"She's an airhead! She's a…a chocolate Easter bunny. Cute as can be and sweet too but when you take a nible you can see there's nothing inside but air."

Stringer grinned lecherously. "That explains it then," he said with his eyes twinkling. "When I talked to her, she kept hinting around you'd been nibbling."

I ground my teeth and shut my mouth.

If nothing else that proved my point about women—there might be some things nice girls like Sung aren't supposed to discuss with gentlemen like Alex Stringer but whether or not they've got someone, someone like Doyle Mulligan, hooked, or even nibbling, isn't one of them.

In the end we decided that Sung would go because she'd been with me right along and that would be more apt to make the you-know-who think we weren't on to him yet; at the same time we'd have someone else go along too in case we ran into trouble.

At that point Stringer offered graciously. "I'll give you Manuel."

"Forget it. Manuel is more likely to cause trouble than to handle it. He'll spend all his time trying to get Sung in bed, which is probably his idea of working under cover, and I won't be able to leave the two of them alone. Anyway, he's big, but he's just fat. What's he going to be worth in a fight?"

Stringer took two puffs on the pipe. "He told me he decked you the other day with just one punch."

I blew up.

"Punch? He barely touched me. I fell back and tripped over the desk. Ask anybody in the office."

"I did. They seem to think he handled you pretty good, and that the girl handled him even better. That's the story I got. As a matter of fact, Doyle, that was primarily what I had in mind when I asked her if she'd go along. I figured she could protect you in case you did run up against this nowhere man of yours."

Ha. Ha. Ha. That was Alex Stringer to a T. He enjoyed his concept of comedy and he enjoyed trying it out on office subordinates which was exactly the reason he didn't have any of those double-oh types on the payroll. Stringer was smart enough to realize what kind of ideas his peculiar humor was likely to give any man with a license to kill.

So we went back into conference and came up with Kayo as a candidate.

The big guy was called into Stringer's office and he agreed, giving me a sidelong smile because he knew good and well he wouldn't have been picked if it weren't for his ol' buddy Doyle.

Stringer sent us both off with his well-wishes. "Ive got a feeling," he said, "that you'll have enough excitement you won't even give Hong Kong a thought." I wondered if that was his instinct at work or his sense of humor.

I didn't spend the morning getting accoutered but with an expense allowance burning a hole in my pocket I did get a couple of things. I thought about getting a tweed cap and suit of plus fours but then decided it was too much to pay for a laugh. No wingtips either because I had a pair of Nikes that hadn't even been broken in. What I did was go back to the Nine Dragon's Jade Factory in the thieves market and get Sung's ring out of layaway. Then I obtained a small caliber automatic pistol quietly and illegally from a Ladder Street pawn shop.

The hopes and fears of Doyle Mulligan. That's what those two items represented.

I met Kayo about noon and together we headed for Sung's hotel. The three of us wanted to have lunch and make plans for the upcoming voyage. Sung was dressed and packed by the time we entered her suite. I had on my new Nikes, blazer and brown denim pants. But she looked even better than me. She had rolled her hair into a bun on the back of her head and poured herself into a neat little pants suit which immediately took honors as my favorite of the outfits I'd seen her in. Whether or not she could talk like money or act like money I didn't know but as for look, she looked like a million bucks. Yes, if there was ever a perfectly matched couple we were it, which was, after all, the whole idea.

"Sung and I are newlyweds," I explained to Kayo after we'd given our orders to the waitress in the Hotel's dining room. "We're going to the United States to start a new life. You're her big brother—now, my brother-in-law—who's coming along with us to carry things and to tip over people who step on our toes. Think of yourself as part porter and part Doberman pinscher. Okay?"

He shook his big head. "You think the ***Yega*** will follow you onto the ship?"

"Why not? He's followed me everywhere else."

"Then he knows you and Sung aren't married. And he knows I'm not her brother."

I took a deep breath. I didn't know where I'd lost him so I'd have to start over from the beginning. "Okay, I'll go through it once more," I told him. "Try to pay attention this time. Remember, one gains no knowledge while speaking. Confucious pointed that out in the I Ching."

"Yes."

"You know about that?"

He nodded. "Oh sure. The Book of Changes; twelfth passage: A wise man listens, a fool speaks."

"Exactly. So listen up. We don't care what the ***Yega*** believes. We only have to fool the people running the Lao Shu into thinking that we're not working on a story—which of course we aren't—and to act as though we don't suspect the Lao Shu of being a part of the Iron Underground—which of course it isn't. If we can do that, then the ***Yega*** will believe that we are on a story and that the Lao Shu really is involved with the Iron Underground and he'll board the ship too. Now does that make sense?"

"No. You said we don't care what the ***Yega*** believes."

I glared at him. "I'm sorry. I shouldn't have."

"Then why did—?"

"I lied, okay?"

"Whatever you say, Doily, but…"

"What is it?"

"I've never lied to you."

I shook my head dragged both hands across my face, and pressed on. "All we have to do," I said, "is keep up the act for a few hours. A day at the most. Once we're on the high seas, he's stuck. We won't drop our cover—there's no sense in twisting the knife—but it won't matter so much after that. Any questions?"

"I have one."

"Go ahead, Kayo," I sighed.

"Lao Shu. It means rat. What kind of a name is that for a cruise ship?"

My mouth hung open. I have trouble with conversation shifts as abupt as that.

"It's the Zodiac Cruise Line," Sung answered for me. "All the ships are named after signs of the Chinese Zodiac. Rat, she said, "is the first sign."

She was right. I couldn't have listed all the animals in the Chinese zodiac off the top of my head but I knew them when I heard them and I was kicking myself for not putting the two names together. Kayo, at least, could say he hadn't been told the name of the line but I'd known both for eight hours.

Meanwhile Sung was proceeding to list them.

""Next comes ox, tiger, hare and dragon." She spread the fingers of her left hand, turned her eyes skyward and began counting them off. "Snake, horse, sheep, monkey, chicken."

She switched hands. "Dog and pig." She smiled. "There are twelve ships in the Zodiac Cruise line and each is named after a Chinese sign."

"I've always thought those were odd names," I said, "even for astrology."

"No, Doyle. Do you know what Zodiac means? It's Greek for Circle of Animals. The western system is the one that's odd. Look at all the signs that aren't animals." She went back to her left hand. "Gemini is twins. Virgo is a virgin. Libra is a scale. Sagitarius is an archer. And Aquarius is a waterbearer. The Egyptians have a similar system but the Aztecs of South America adopted the Chinese 12-year cycle."

"What sign are you, Sung?" Kayo asked her.

I didn't hear that part. I had already been impressed with her knowledge on the subject of astrology and I didn't need to know what zoological house she was born in to know whether or not she was bright. I polished off my plate of Mandarin fish and I never tasted a thing. I spent the rest of the meal listening to her talk and I didn't hear a word. But I perked up later when Kayo asked her about her Chinese year sign. "I'm 24," she said. "That means I was born in the year of the chicken. I'm a pioneer in spirit, devoted to work. I quest after knowledge. I'm selfish and a little eccentric. I avoid hares, and I'm supposed to marry a snake or an ox."

"What about you Doily?"

"What? Oh...I'm a snake," I said without thinking.

Sung furrowed her little forehead. "So you were born in either 1953 or 1965. If you were born in 1953 you'd be 40 years old."

"No, not that one," I said. "The other one."

"You mean 1965? But then you'd be 28. I thought you told me you were in your thirties."

"I meant, not the snake. I'm the...the ox. That's it. I'm an ox."

"Then you were born in 1961?"

"Yeah, " I said quickly. Then I smiled. "Hey! I was born in 1961."

Sung and Kayo burst out laughing. Me too. I laughed harder than either of them.

"Then you're insatiably curious," Sung told me at last. "You can be content with your own company though you should look to a snake or a chicken for true contentment. But the sheep will bring you trouble." Sung stopped talking and I noticed that she was looking through me. I asked what was wrong. "I just remembered," she said. "Sha Han is 26. He was born in the year of the sheep."

"Then it's just as well," I replied, "that someone else will find him before we return." When I said that her eyes found mine again, she smiled sadly and said that was true. It was true. Suddenly I knew it too. And that was the point I started looking forward to the trip. I made up my mind if I couldn't contribute so much as another column inch of copy to my big story I could at least enjoy a well-deserved vacation, have a chance to be close to Sung, and get to know her better.

Of course I'd failed to reckon with Stringer's sense of humor on that. Or his instincts.

I could leave out what happened next, our little detour on the way to the cruise ship and the thing that eliminated any possibility I would enjoy my well-deserved vacation. I never did tell Kayo or Sung about my personal little detour although Sung sensed something was wrong and Kayo may well have guessed.

He'd talked to Ben Kao and Ben had given him the name of a priest who specialized in blessing ocean voyages. We had an appointment for one o'clock. Kayo was serious about this sort of thing. And even Sung seemed to like the idea. Maybe she believed; maybe she just didn't care to take any chances. Me, I was going because Ben was convinced I needed all the blessing I could get and had made Kayo promise he'd drag me along.

So we drove north into the New Territories about five or six miles to the town of Sha Tin. There's a racecourse up there, a tidal cove and a reservoir as well as exploding high rise apartments that are part of the government's plan to shift Hong Kong's population away from the harbor. We parked at the railway station and climbed what the tourists are told are five hundred stone steps to the monastery.

I'd kidded Sung that I would count every step because I figured there were either more or less than five hundred. The Chinese, being a neat people, like to round things off, like those hundred year old eggs and thousand layer cakes Sung and I'd had for lunch. As it turned out, I lost count, so when we got to the top and went inside the immense white edifice I was determined to make up for it. Sha Tin Temple is known as the Ten Thousand Buddhas Monastary but I've heard it said there are as many as 13,000 Buddhas in the place.

There were Buddha statues around the outside, fronting the entrance and along both walls as we ventured in. There were Buddha painting, Buddha tapestries, Buddha figurines, Budda wood-carvings and even a few Buddha rugs. Buddha was in ivory, bronze, brass, stone, and crystal from floor to ceiling in every chamber we saw. That place was lousy with Buddhas.

Several Buddhist priests and their acolytes were going from alter to altar performing their duties. They ignored the crowds, devotees as well as tourists.

Kayo and Sung went off to find Li Chao, the priest who had a way with bon voyages. I hung back, telling them I was going to count every last Buddha in the joint. I'd made it to twenty-four and was examining a little statuette of a guy with eleven faces and eight arms wondering whether or not to include him when I found a tag that said: "Avalokitesvara the Bodhisattva," which, as I understand it, is kind of a valet, and which seems like a good job for somebody with eight arms and eleven faces.

Something distracted my attention.

I looked up suddenly. The wall to my right had begun to move. Except it wasn't a wall. There was an opening to another room barred by a rich velvet tapis emblazoned with golden buddhas. As I watched, the tapis parted a few inches and a scrawny hand snaked through. It came as far as the elbow before a single bony finger with two inches of dirty nail curling from the tip pointed in my direction and then crooked three times, beckoning.

I raised my brows.

I looked around but no one else was even close to where I was standing.

When I looked back the hand had disappeared through the tapis.

There was a"Public Not Admitted" sign in front of the opening. After a moment's consideration I decided the sign did not apply to me because I'd been invited. I took off my blazer, draped it over Avalokitesvata the valet, cracked the tapis and pushed my head through the crack. Then I stepped through.

It was a room about the size of Wrigley Field. Quite dark. Illumination came from a tiny pair of windows on the far end. Like a grand ballroom, the center of the room was bare though statues and busts lined the sides and thousands of pieces of Buddhist art filled the walls from floor level to twenty feet high. I made a slow circle. I figured if I started counting now and skipped dinner, I wouldn't finish with the room until sometime in the Year of the Slug.

I was so enthralled it took me a moment to realize that my mysterious beckoner had disappeared. In spite of this I felt as though I were being watched. I'd felt it ever since coming into the temple but the feeling was stronger in here. Maybe that's what several thousand Buddhas in the room will do to your head. Just then I spotted a small panel door in a side wall standing half open and I crossed the room to it. I could hardly believe what I saw. I was standing at the top of a narrow twisting wooden stairway even darker than the room. About fifty steps down was a tiny landing and at the landing was a candle which lighted the next flight of steps to a second landing and a second candle. I counted at least a dozen candles descending into the darkness.

Did I go down? Yeah. Why did I go down? Who knows? Maybe I'm stupid. Maybe I'm just insatiably curious like all of us born in the Year of the Ox. Anyway, after taking off my tie, knotting the ends and hanging the loop beside a pair of crossed Buddhist staves I started down. The room was so incredibly busy there was no chance an odd bit of clothing would ever be noticed. I'd reached the second landing when I heard the door close behind me. There was nothing to do but keep going.

I wouldn't have been surprised if the stairs had come out below the railway station at the bottom of the hill.

But it didn't. I came out in a dungeon, a damp stone corridor more poorly lit than the stairway. The feeling that I was being watched never left me as I tried all the doors along the corridor, finding all of them locked except the last door but one which was standing open.

I looked in.

This was the darkest chamber of all. The only light inside came from a single candle behind me on the corridor wall. It was scarcely enough to furnish the dark room with shadows.

"*Step in and close the door*."

I froze.

The order had come from one of the shadows. Somewhere inside. I'd been suckered down here. Suckered the same way Lee Chung had been suckered outside to his *fangzi*. The way the Pekingese and his pals had been suckered onto the upper deck of that hydrofoil.

I thawed enough to look behind me. The stairs were far away; the surface, an infinite distance. For all the help Kayo could give me he might just as well have been back in Kowloon. If I shouted at the top of my lungs I'd be dead before my cries reached the monastery.

"Don't be a fool," the voice said, "come in and close the door."

I stepped through and then closed the door at my back. What little light the room held vanished in an instant and with it the shadows. Now it was completely dark. I didn't understand that. I never had. Light travels for billions of years through space bouncing off planets and asteroid belts and when you close the door you'd think some would still be bouncing around off the walls. Where does it go? The only thing bouncing around in here was my heart. I felt like I'd swallowed a rubber ball the size of my fist.

I had to stall for time. Stall until help arrived or my wits returned. "Who are you?" I managed to get out. My lungs had quit altogether so my heart hammered the words out of my chest.

"Never mind that. You've booked passage on the Lao Shu leaving Hong Kong today."

It wasn't a question. Nevertheless the speaker expected an answer.

I felt like saying. "You're not getting anything out of me, you chink bastard," but I didn't. I don't like the word "chink," I didn't know anything about his parentage and the whole point of the cruise was for this guy to know we were going. So I said instead: "Yes sir."

"You're leaving at four o'clock this afternoon."

"Yes sir, but it's not too late to cancel if you think it's a bad idea."

"Just listen. You believe the Lao Shu is not involved with the *de ha tit*. You're only going because you want to draw the… the killer out of Hong Kong."

"You mean," I said, and there was relief in my voice, "…you're not the ***Yega***?"

His reply was a sharp intake of air.

As soon as I heard that I treated myself to a breath of my own, letting it out long and slow. Apparently he wasn't. But who was he? The only thing I could think of was someone else from the Big Circle or the *de ha tit.*

"I'm here to warn you," he said.

"Warn me?"

"That's right."

This sounded familiar. "Let me guess," I said. "My wire service is dropping the story."

"What?"

"You think I should forget about the silly cruise. I have no interest in whether or not Chinese are leaving Hong Kong. I have no interest in where they may be going. I'll forget the *de ha tit.* I'll find a new story. How's that?"

"It would be fine if you'd do it but somehow I don't think you will. You'll go on the cruise and you'll pretend to investigate the possibility that the Lao Shu is involved with the *de ha tit.* In doing so, the chances are you'll be killed. You and the others."

"What others?"

"You know who I mean. Tuan K'o and the Kwon girl."

"Why should we be killed?"

"Because the Lao Shu is involved with the *de ha tit.* It is the final leg in the underground. And the people who run the operation are understandably ruthless about keeping their secrets from being discovered."

Whenever he stopped talking I was struck by how quiet this dungeon could be. I could hear my heart bouncing off the walls of my chest.

"The police already inspected it from top to bottom," I said. "They couldn't find any illegal emigrants. Not one. There were no extra food supplies on board. There was no evidence that anyone had ever stowed away. The police even posted guards at the dock to see that there won't be any."

I waited for the voice to break the dark silence.

"Obviously," he said at last, "the *de ha tit* is closed. Nevertheless, this is the underground route out of Hong Kong. Where the Lao Shu goes there have the Chinese gone. You'll be leading the...killer right to them"

It had taken a few minutes for this to sink in. Now it had and I knew. If this wasn't the ***Yega*** I was talking to, neither was he a member of the *de ha tit*. He was Chinese, one who knew more about this story than anyone else I'd met and he seemed willing to talk to a *saiyahn* like me. Before thinking it through I blurted out:

"You know about him, don't you?"

"Who?"

"The ***Yega***. You know who he is and what he looks like, don't you?"

Silence. Profound silence. And the darkness was equally profound. It was a scary combination, like sitting around a campfire with friends telling ghost stories except you've no friends and no campfire and the ghost is doing the telling.

He said: "That was not what I came to discuss."

"But you know," I said.

"No one knows what he looks like. No one has ever seen him."

"Why do they call him the Nowhere Man."

"Because he is anywhere, everywhere and nowhere."

"What do you know about him?"

"There are stories. But one doesn't tell such stories and speak the word Ye—speak his name in the same breath."

Here we went again. I said, "Talk to me. Call him Fu Manchu if it makes you feel any better."

The voice dropped to a whisper.

"The stories are about the son of a shaman."

"Shaman? You mean like a medicine man.,..or a priest?"

"Both. And neither. It was once believed that shamans could communicate with the gods and sprits. They were able to conjure demons and rid the community of evil. By the late 1950's all of the shamans in China were gone. All except one shaman named Onan. They say he was the greatest of all the shamans who ever lived."

"Go on."

He went on. Reluctantly, but he went on.

"No one ever questioned where Onan's powers came from. A shaman could be trained by another shaman, or be guided by the favor of a particular spirit, or he could inherit. This last is how Onan gained his abilities, for it was known that his father was shaman, too.

"What kind of abilities are we talking about?"

"It was said that with a glance Onan could cause men to tremble. Were Onan to stare, men would shake violently until they fell to the ground in a spasm. Enemies and spies could be brought before him and after moments they would surrender all their secrets and swear allegiance to him. In the same way a snake charms a bird into its mouth, Onan could charm a man. Women were his, not for the asking, but merely for the wanting. If he looked at them and willed it, they willed it too."

"That's a neat trick," I said.

"You're *saiyahn*," he replied. "You want to understand but your heritage will not permit you to believe."

"I'm still listening."

"It was also said he could vanish. Disappear before a large crowd of people and not reappear for days. He could change his appearance without using costumes or cosmetics, even become someone else known to the people of the village to be absent or…dead."

I'd heard this stuff before. Maybe there was something to it. Some of the shamans worked a kind of stage act. They were lttle more than sleight of hand artists and magicians. Onan sounded more like a spellbinder. A mesmerist. A man who could hypnotize someone, two or three people at once or even a small crowd of people without their knowing it. They say Nostradamus could do it. Rasputin and even Houdini. If Onan was a born hypnotist and he passed on the gift to a son…

"But for all his ability," the ghostly voice went on, "Onan remained childless. None of his wives had ever borne him an heir. He went to a healer who was known to cure impotence. Her name was Chao M'ing and in her own way she was just as unique as Onan. She used no potions. She made no incantations. She erased wounds, relieved all manner of pain, even healed madness with a touch of her hands."

Uh, oh, I thought. When warlock meets witch. "And did she cure him?" I asked.

"More than that. She gave birth to his child."

"This child," I said. "Was he, you know, Fu Manchu?"

I sensed he was having to struggle for each utterance. The words he was speaking he had never spoken before. "It was the custom of the time," the voice said, "for disciples to send word among the people that a child was born to the shaman. The people would celebrate and be joyous, unfettered by the knowledge of the child's sex for only if it were a male child could the legacy be passed on. The next day the disciples would send word that a boy child was born to the shaman and again there would be celebration. On the third day they would declare to the people the light of the spirit was seen in the eyes of the boy child. That would be a time of greatest joy, for the people would know they would not want for a spiritual leader in their lifetimes. Unfortunately, in Onan's case none of this came to pass. Twenty-four hours after the announcement that the child was born, Red soldiers from Beijing swept into the village and stole the child away. Onan and M'ing were murdered. And the child was never seen again."

The voice stopped talking abruptly,

When was this?" I asked.

"Who can say? The revolution was also a child at the time. Mao was in power. And no one questioned."

"Is that the end of the story?"

"Yes. Of course, there are more stories."

"Let's have another. We may not have too much time."

I'll spare you my effort to drag the thing out of him. The next story took place in Beijing several years later. It was the story of a boy's education. He was consigned to instructors at an early age for what was, by any account, a very singular education. No math, literature or history. No religion or philosophy. There was no time. For six hours a day, seven days a week the kid studied chemistry and physics, the chemistry of poisons and drugs; the physics of combustibles and explosives. China's most renowned scientists were sent to his private school. In his physical lessons, another eight hours each day, he studied with the country's most accomplished martial arts masters. Every technique of every style of unarmed combat was presented to the youth and with a ruthlessness and a thoroughness not possible in any other place or time.

In the story, and in China of the time, there was great turmoil. China was still trying to pull itself from the devastation of revolution, massive over population and famine. A single man's life, or a thousand lives were virtually without value. Every day, buses transported large numbers of men and women into a private athletic facility in the very heart of Beijing and every day bodies were secretly removed by the truckload. Those lives at least had found value in a boy's extraordinary education.

He learned to use knives and swords as well as firearms of every type. In all they could teach him they molded the boy into a veritable weapon. He was destined to surpass the combined mastery of his instructors. Once his expertise and brutality exceeded theirs they too were without value. Like the others they had come by bus and left at graduation in the bed of a truck.

It was only a voice in the darkness, in a dungeon deep underground. And yet I knew the words it spoke must be the truth. This was the story Master Wang Chen had only hinted at, what Superintendent of Macao Police Maldonado had tried to explain. But the voice knew much more than they did.

It knew how the boy—now a man—had then become an arm of the government, an arm that could reach out anywhere, at any time and strike the enemies of Beijing.

"If a certain intellectual's criticism displeases the state but the critic is well known by the masses," said the voice, "then it is more beneficial for him to have a heart attack than to suffer prosecution. When a commune defies a directive in quotas, a mysterious fire that sweeps through the sleeping quarters will kindle more energy than chastisement. A foreign newspaper that constantly prints defamatory stories about the People's Republic may suffer an explosion of unknown origin. If a Chinese agent is captured and is on the point of passing his secrets then how convenient if he commits suicide in his cell. No one," said the voice, "can know when the lightning will strike and no one can stop it."

The puzzling and gruesome death of a liberal party boss several years back—ironically I'd run across the incident translating Red radio transmissions—this voice now credited to the ***Yega***. …I beg your pardon, to Fu Manch. A mass murder of factory workers believed to be organizing a union, a case never solved, was also the work of the Fu man.

Then came Tiananmen Square.

The voice told me about the student leader who had fled to the American Embassy in Beijing. It knew what Washington wasn't admitting, that the student had died after being poked in the eye. I asked him if he was kidding. But he wasn't. A finger, not the students, had rammed into his left eye so hard and so deep it had penetrated his optic foramen at the back of his eyeball and punctured his brain. It knew how the other students had died too. Those who had run to Europe as well as those who hadn't gotten out of china. In every case they had died violently. And alone. And no one had—

My ghostly informant stopped speaking. Before I could urge him on I heard a faint sound. No more than the crunch of a pebble on stone beyond the door of the room. I ceased to breath.

"*One is in the corridor.*"

That wasn't the voice. Not the same one. It was spoken in Mandarin Chinese and it came from the room next to ours.

I heard footsteps crossing our chamber. A door coming open.

"Quickly!" said the voice. "This way."

I turned, threw open the door behind me, and stepped into the corridor. A huge shadow moved toward me. As it reached the single candle and the light fell upon its face, I said: "Dammit, Kayo, you picked a find time to show up."

"I thought you might be in trouble." He was holding my brown blazer out to me.

I ignored it, snatched the candle off the wall, and dove back through the doorway. Kayo was at my heels.

But we were too late.

The only other door in the room—a wooden one but solid and three inches thick—was barred from the opposite side. Even Kayo's and my combined weight couldn't budge it.

After a while we retraced our steps to the corridor and climbed the long narrow stairway to the top where we found Sung waiting in the big ballroom. She smiled when she saw us. "That was really quite clever," she said, pointing to the loop of my tie before the crossed staves which formed a bold "OX" beside the little door.

"A little too clever," I said.

"What were you doing down there?" she asked. "What did you find?"

"Yeah," said Kayo. "What *did* you find?"

"Just a man who wanted to bless our cruise," I said.

We left the monastery and sped back to Kowloon. Having dropped off the Subaru in a parking garage we proceeded by cab to the Ocean Terminal. The three of us hadn't exchanged a dozen words when we strolled out along the wharf and found the Lao Shu, the smallest of three cruse ships at the wharf wall and one of two I'd seen the day I came looking for the Pekingese.

It was 450 feet and fifteen thousand tons of luxury accommodations gleaming white and brass.

Once on board, the three of us went straight to the purser and learned that we had cabins on the lower of the two passengers levels. An outside stateroom. All cabins on the Lao Shu, he told us proudly, were outside staterooms. We saw what he meant after we'd taken the elevator down and discovered there was a single passageway running the length of the Leo Deck. There were a couple dozen cabins on each side. Such an arrangement would have spoken clearly for the small size of the ship had the cabins not been so spacious.

Our cabin was amidships on the port side. I say ours but actually Kayo had an adjoining cabin which was, except for being slightly smaller, identical.

Like typical tourists the three of us stood on the rail and waved good-by to the docks and the junks, the high rises and the shacks, and watched Victoria Harbor disappear behind us as the ship swept south down the west side of Hong Kong Island. We passed junk town and later, the magnificent beaches of Repulse Bay. Soon Hong Kong was just a memory and a dusty smudge on the distant horizon.

12. The Good Ship Lao Shu

Stringer's instincts took a real beating in some ways. I did bring cutoffs and Sung did bring a bikini and neither she nor Kayo spent a single night of the cruise sleeping in their own cabin. My expectations were no closer. Still, if I were wrong in every other respect of what that voyage was going to offer I was at least correct in that it gave me an opportunity to spend some time with Sung and get to know her better.

There was that first evening shortly after we departed Hong Kong. That was a good example.

I had just folded back the setee to reveal a twin bunk across the cabin from Sung's and turned to find her watching me with growing alarm.

"It could be worse," I said quickly. "At least they're separate bunks."

"You're not going to sleep there, Doyle?"

I looked from one to the other. "I'll flip you for it."

"You said this was a single cabin."

The question was, how would a respectable couple who talk money, act money, and look money handle a situation like ours? "No, I didn't" I corrected her. "I said the ENA had booked a single and a double. This is the double. Kayo has the single. There's nowhere else I can go."

"You can't sleep in the same room with me!"

"We're supposed to be married, Sung. We have to sleep together." Her startled face gave me the whole story. Stringer's sense of humor. He had told her nothing of the arrangement. "I mean in the same room," I added quickly. "Look, we can put up a curtain. Pretend we're Claudette Colbert and Clark Gable. It worked for them. We ought to be able to make it work for us."

"Who are those people?"

I told her never mind. I admit that a person can be unacquainted with Claudette Colbert and still have a right to live, but it's not possible to have a rational discussion with someone (even someone with whom you'd like to sleep…in the same room, that is) who's never heard of Clark Gable. Sung suggested she move into Kayo's cabin and that he and I sleep in this one. I argued that the cabin stewards would get suspicious if her and Kayo's personal things were in the wrong rooms. "We've got our cover to protect," I begged her. At that point in the argument, she walked out into the corridor, rapped on the door of the adjoining cabin, and returned moments later with Kayo towering behind her.

She asked him point-blank if he'd be willing to switch beds with her on a nightly basis. They could sneak into each others cabin before going to sleep and sneak back again in the morning.

Kayo turned on me with his most threatening glare.

"Have you," he demanded menacingly, "been trying something funny with my kid sister?"

I could see it would be necessary to re-evaluate my opinion of his sense of humor. Being in continued close contact with me should have had a beneficial effect and yet his first feeble attempts at comedy sounded suspiciously like Stringer's.

Anyway, that's what we did.

Another example under the heading of Getting to Know Sung came the following morning when the persistent heat had driven the three of us to the Pisces Deck where a saltwater pool was surrounded by several dozen reclinable deck chairs. That's when I came out in the cutoffs—I never wear a swimsuit—and Sung made her appearance in the bikini. A yellow string bikini. At least that's what I thought it was until she turned to level her chair for sunbathing and I saw that the rear was all string and no bikini. I guess the best way to describe it would be to say that after she'd been sunning herself for a while her tan lines were—well, they were just lines!

All the healthy guys immediately headed for waist deep water. I'm healthy enough myself but I stayed where I was and enjoyed the scenery. That's why I always wear cutoffs.

When Sung looked over and caught me giving her the goofy grin again I asked her if all the girls in Bangkok wear bikinis like that and her face turned red. "It's not a bikini," she told me, "it's a tonga. And they're very popular." She was a little embarrassed but trying hard not to show it.

Oriental girls are generally short and rarely busty and Sung was and wasn't. But she wasn't skinny either. She was Just toned and tanned and curvy and everything that the tonga revealed, which was almost everything, added up to one slick figure. After her performance the first night working out the sleeping arrangements I'd expected something showing a little less cheek and a bit more prudence but no. Sung was proving that Old-Fashioned Values and Old Maids are not the same thing after all. She was good. She was bright enough to know she was good and proud enough not to care if everyone else knew it too. In fact she was too good, too bright, and too proud to share bunks with any bumbling reporter just because he'd arranged to take her on a cruise.

All that I'd gathered in the first two seconds watching her slip out of her warmup. And one other thing—watching her tan her behind—I also decided that my favorite of her outfits so far was the yellow string bikini. Er…tonga.

Still another example:

I knew she was cute and sweet as a chocolate bunny and regardless of what I'd told Stringer I never really thought she was an airhead but her way of answering questions had about convinced me she was uncomplicated until she taught me a leson about that, too.

First I have to explain something about me.

Despite my carefree exterior I was the same guy who'd checked out the kneehole and the drawers of his desk before starting to work, who'd looked under his bed before lying down. I assumed the ***Yega*** was aboard. I had to. That was the whole point of the trip. Of course, by then I expected to see the son of a bitch every time I looked over my shoulder though I never did. But that meant I had to appear to be investigating even though I knew good and well the ship had been a leg of the *de ha tit.* I knew the ship had been checked out by the police who'd found nothing, and that I was just wasting my time. Furthermore, I knew that if the ship's crew caught us we'd be in big trouble. The kind of people who run operations like this one would deal with us severely certainly and permanently probably.

So I had to be seen nosing around. . . without being seen to be nosing around. I felt this subtlety was too much for Kayo and that's why I didn't tell him what I'd found out in the monastery. I felt it would take away any pleasure Sung would get from the cruise and that's why I didn't tell her.

I'd go off by myself to explore, leaving Sung and Kayo on the upper decks to whack golf balls or play shuffleboard. I'd wander around rubber-necking like a landlubber who's on his first cruise, a "Golly-gee whiz!" kind of investigation, which if I do say so myself, I'm rather good at.

The trouble being every time I turned around, there she was. Take that same afternoon. I was strolling down the row of life-boats, lifting the tarpaulins one by one and peering inside at the well-stocked interiors, when I heard footsteps behind me.

"Golly!" I said. "Just lookit all that stuff. Gee whiz!"

"Find any stowaways?"

I turned. "Sung. What are you doing here?"

"Looking for you. Doyle, what's going on? You told me and Kayo that you'd changed your mind about sneaking around. That we were just going to act like regular passengers. And yet every time I turn my back you go out exploring."

"I'm an Ox," I said. "We're curious, that's all."

"There wouldn't be any people hiding in there, that's the first place someone would look. They'd have to be somewhere in the bottom of the ship, wouldn't they? And if you want to explore, Why don't you take me or Kayo with you?"

"I'm an Ox," I said. "We're content with our own company."

"What are you looking for?"

"I'm an Ox," I told her. "I should look to the chicken or the snake for true happiness. But the hen won't leave me alone so I'm out looking for snakes."

She might not have heard a word. "You've been acting funny ever since we left the monastery," she said. "I think you saw something or heard something down there that you're afraid to let us know?"

"What a silly idea."

"What was it, Doyle? Did you learn something about the *Lau Shu* and you're trying to protect me and Kayo by keeping us in the dark?"

So in addition to everything else she was psychic.

I pooh-poohed her worry, took her back to her room, and made up my mind that the little wanderings should stop. If any-one on the ship's crew, or worse the ***Yega*** himself, had as much intuition as Sung I wouldn't be fooling him no mater what I did.

Sung and I and about a dozen others had been invited to dine at the captain's table. I was there, despite my tennis shoes, denims and brown blazer because the purser had seen Sung around the ship and he was in charge of the selection. Personally I didn't care much for the purser. He thought he was good looking and so he spent a lot of time in front of a mirror. He thought he was awfully clever and so he liked to hear himself talk. He thought he had an eye of the ladies and so he'd been eyeing my wife.

Sung didn't disappoint us. She was wearing an evening frock that captured my vote for current favorite. It had a high front and back long sleeves and a floor-length hemline. It had a slit on the right side that explosed her leg all the way up to her hip. It shone like silk. It fit like Saran Wrap after an hour under a hot-air blow dryer. How she ever squeezed into it I hadn't the courage to ask her.

Captain Hsiao would have appreciated it I'm sure but he couldn't make dinner and so the purser, who took his place, expressed the captain's regrets without once taking his eyes off Sung.

We moved out after the first seating to make way for the second group of diners. While Sung and I were in the lobby waiting for Kayo she pointed out the wall lined with large framed poster pictures.

"These are the ships I was telling to you about," she informed me.

Each of the twelve vessels had been photographed from overhead while under full steam. The Lao Shu was the first one. Next to it was the Gon Nu, the Ox. I followed the photographs until I came to the end. The Goul, Dog; and the Zhu, Pig neither of which sounded much like ship names to me in Chinese or English. Below each of the photographs was a complete little history of the ship's design, manufacture and specifications.

All were generally of the same size and configuration, 15,000 tons displacement, 450 feet in length, about 50 feet beam width, 25 feet of draft, all were cable of 27 to 30 knots and made the run across the Pacific from Honolulu to Hong Kong in seven days with a full complement of 150 to 225 upper crust passengers and crew. They'd been built from the keel up to Lee Chung's precise order.

By the time I'd gotten that far, Kayo had joined us. Together we headed into the Lao Shu's nightclub, the Galaxy Club, in which it was possible to dance until early morning.

You might suppose that for those people who talk, act and look money, a waltz or a tango would be the step. At least a sensible five piece orchestra. But you'd be wrong. Disco.

Instead of a band they had a compact disk player wired in to speakers all over the room. Instead of soft, romantic lighting we suffered the staccato flashes of several strobe lights. And instead of an intimate dance floor we had to tap-toe and trip across a mesmerizing, computerized, illuminated platform. The huge speakers were woofing and tweeting a wild clatter, strobes were flashing a terrible barrage, and the dance area was going crazy.

I could only take it for brief snatches. Then I'd have to retreat into a corner where the decibels were down nearer the threshold of pain.

Sung loved it.

Even alternating dances with me and Kayo, she couldn't get enough. Finally Kayo got interested in a nice-looking unattached blonde and I used the opportunity to suggest to Sung that the two of us go out for a stroll around the deck. I felt my pocket to make sure the jade ring was there. And then, just as she was about to say yes, the damn purser came by and asked her to dance. I could have socked him. Sung was just too nice to refuse. He took her out to the dance floor and started gyrating. It killed me to see him looking so good, looking so clever, looking at Sung. In addition to his other gifts he thought he knew how to disco and to prove it he spent the next half an hour showing her steps.

When I couldn't stand it any more I waltzed out to rescue her. "Don't forget," I warned her once we'd made it to the quiet and calm of outside, "we're supposed to be married."

She said she hadn't forgotten.

"We should act like it," I said.

"What are we doing," she asked, "that married people don't do?"

The moon was high. The breeze was cool. We had the deck to ourselves. Sung shivered a little leaning against the rail so I put my arms around her.

"It's not that," I said, "it's what married people do that we don't."

She lay back her head, closed her eyes, pushed her lips up within a centimeter of mine, and whispered: "What don't we do?"

We did it.

It went so well we did it some more and when we finally stopped I started thinking about other things married people do.

"Look, Sung," I said, "you don't think it'd be better if you slept in our cabin tonight?"

She thought hard.

Her head moved up and down."Yes," she said.

I was ecstatic.

"You do?"

"Then I watched in dismay as her head began shaking back and forth.

"No," she said.

"If you're not sure," I offered in exasperation, "we'll just forget it for now."

"I'm sure," she replied. "For now."

"How come I'm not sure what it is you're sure about? Don't you know I'm crazy about you?"

"No."

"Well, I am."

"I know. I'm crazy about you too, Doyle."

"But you won't let yourself love me?"

"No. It's too late for that."

"Why is t too late?"

"Because I couldn't stop myself from loving you now no matter how hard I tried."

When I shook my head then I could almost hear my brains rattling around. No matter how many times I promised myself I'd stop wth the negative interrogatives, they'd still slip out every once in a while. And no matter how many times Sung explained the Korean answering system, she always managed to sucker me in.

"A woman," she went on, "likes to know that her man is good. That he is also brave and humble and kind and patient. Only then can she give her whole heart. To learn this takes time."

I said, "Sung, you take as much time as you want. When you've made up your mind, I'll be waiting. Patiently. Also kindly and bravely and with goodness and humility. Because that's the kind of a guy I am."

She reached up and did that married thing again.

"But you know," I said, "we almost blew it last night. Another one of those and our cover will be shot for good." She gave me the huge eyes. We'd been told to expect a fire drill early in the cruise and at four o'clock that morning it had come. Sung and Kayo and I along with the other 150 passengers had spent a shaky hour against the outer rails with the ship dark as a tomb and crew members racing around waving portable floodlights. Whoever had planned the drill had gone so far as to have smoke gushing out from belowdecks and mock emergency orders in Chinese blaring over the public address. Most of the other passengers, seasoned by many cruises, had taken all this in stride. To me it had seemed very real. And very scary.

Then suddenly, the announcement had come. Everything was fine. Power was restored. Lifeboat davits were turned in.

Life jackets were replaced in the lockers. It was only a test. The fire crews had responded well. The passengers had passed. We could go back to our cabins.

"Has someone said something to you?" Sung asked.

"Not yet, but I sure got some strange looks last night. You have to admit it looks kind of funny when Kayo and I come running out into a crowded passageway and us with our night clothes on and then you race out of the next cabin. Everybody knows that we're supposed to be married. Kayo's too big for anyone to suggest he's perverted but what about me? I'm barely five, ten."

She said. "I'm only five, one."

That's the kind of an argument you can expect from someone who's never heard of Clark Gable. "Oh, yeah?" I said. "What did you say your sign was?" I don't remember what house she was born in but I do remember what cabin she slept in and it wasn't mine.

I told her I was going to bed and that if she wanted me to I'd escort her back to the Galaxy Club.

She wanted to know why.

"Don't you want to dance the night away with the ship's purser?" I asked. I could affort to be big about it. He was a better dancer than I was, he was better looking and maybe more clever too. But I had it all over him in patence and kindness and goodness and bravery. And humility, too. Humility I got if I do say so myself.

"Yes!" she said with feeling.

I couldn't believe it.

"You do?"

"Of course not, Doyle."

She'd done it again. I called it quits, escorted her back to her cabin and filed the whole night away under the heading of Getting to Know Sung.

It was the next day. The three of us had just eaten lunch so it was too early for a dip in the pool and too hot for sunning. We decided some exercise was in order and had ordered a steward to run after some mai tai's when a loudspeaker broke in with the day's headlines. This was our one concession to reality, a glimpse of the world as seen from the clouds. The Middle East was boiling, Eastern Europe was dragging itself from the depths of communist depression, Donald Trump was staging a financial comeback, and the Sino-British conference in Hong Kong had temporarily broken off.

Kayo and Sung and I exchanged glances.

After six days of talks Beijing's allegations that many thousands of Chinese were being allowed to slip out of Hong Kong each month had gone unanswered. The British had been sympathetic, even acquiescent of demands by the People's Republic that they themselves oversee the colony's ports of entry and exit. The talks had reached the stage of how many PLA would be assigned and how soon they would take over the ports when a British negotiator had the gall to suggest that the Reds supply proof of the mass exodus.

The gallant Britisher wasn't named, but I could see Inspector Hawthorne's hatchet face in this as clearly as if he were standing beside me.

Beijing's people walked out. They would be back, their spokesman assured the media on the following Monday at ten o'clock sharp at which time the proof would be supplied and their demands would be met. "The world," the Red spokesman had declared, "will witness the shocking truth."

As I traded glances with Sung and Kayo I wondered if they were thinking what I was thinking.

"That could be good," said Sung optimistically. "Won't it give your people more time to locate Sha Han?"

"Yeah," I said. "It'll also give our nameless friend, if he's aboard, time to get back to Hong Kong and kill him. Maybe that's what Beijing is counting on."

"When do we dock in Honolulu?" Kayo asked me.

"According to the brochure, about four o'clock, Sunday afternoon," I told him. As soon as I'd said it I knew something was wrong. So did Sung.

"But that's Hawaiian time," she said. "Hong Kong time is six hours behind, isn't it?"

I shook my head. "It's eighteen hours ahead. We cross the International Date Line some time tomorrow." I did the math in my head and didn't much care for the answer I came up with. "Four o'clock Sunday in Honolulu is ten o'clock Monday Hong Kong time," I said slowly. "We'll be docking at the exact hour Beijing says the whole world will witness the shocking truth."

Our little trio grew quiet.

"Who would have thought that a sheep could be so much trouble," said Sung, finally breaking the silence. "If only Sha Han had been born a dog or a tiger."

Something clicked in my brain. A connection that should have been made three days before and wouldn't have been made yet if it hadn't been for the radio announcement and Sung's little speech. I told them I'd be right back, went to our cabin and found the coded paper that Bobby Ching had enlarged from my art photograph. There it was. Dog, tiger, ox. I raced back to the upper decks.

"Sung," I said, sitting down beside her. "Look at this, will you? See if you can make any more sense of it than I can."

She took the paper and read down both columns.

"You mean this dog, tiger and ox?"

"Yeah."

"They're animals of the Chinese Zodiac."

"But does it mean anything more to you?"

"No, I'm afraid not."

"What about the rest of it?"

"Yin and yang. You know about that, Doyle?"

"Yeah."

"And these others: fire, water, earth, wood, and metal. They're the five elements."

"Yes, I know about that, too."

"I'm sorry, Doyle. I guess I can't help you."

I started to reach for the paper. Kayo was looking over her shoulder now trying to see it for himself.

"It was worth a try," I said, stuffing it back into my pocket. "I thought it might be *fung shui* but it wasn't the right list of animals. Then you explained about the Zodiac the other day and it occurred to me it might be some kind of zodiacal code."

"Is it important?" she aside.

"I don't know. It must be if it's coded. Either that or it's just a collection of Chinese odds and ends and means nothing. But the guy who gave it to me must have thought it meant something that tied in with this *de ha tit*."

"Can I see it, Doily?"

I pulled the paper back out and handed it over to Kayo. "I'm sorry," I told him, "I thought you did see it."

He took one quick look and said very matter-of-factly, "This doesn't have anything to do with the *de ha tit*. It's not a code either."

"It's not?"

"No."

"Well, what is it?"

"Sun-Moon…Dog…Star-Passing. They're acupuncture points."

"What?"

"Sure. You know about those, Doily. From Lee Chung's book. The 365 traditional acupuncture points. He lists the traditional names along with their number and position."

"What about this other column?" I leaned across Sung and read several at random. "Wood, end of the yin; water, strong yang; fire, little yin; earth, light of the yang. What are they?"

"Meridians."

"Huh?"

"You know. Meridians."

"Like longitude lines?"

"No, no. Didn't you read the book when I lent it to you?"

"Well...I guess I skipped over that part."

"They're pathways. Twelve different routes that the *ch'i* takes in traveling through the body. Each of the five elements has a corresponding yin and yang organ. This last one. Fire. Little Yin. The heart meridian is linked with the fire element. And it's yin in character. Little yin, because it gets its energy from the spleen meridian which is also yin in character but belongs to the earth element. You get it?"

"No."

"Think of the meridians as highways. The acupuncture points are stops along each high—"

Sung, who'd remained quiet until now, burst in with an idea. "Or as sea lanes."

"Okay," Kayo allowed. "And then the acupuncture points would be ports of call."

"Not ports," she said excitedly, "departure dates."

"I guess..."

"Three hundred sixty-five points," Sung continued. "And 365 days in the year. Twelve merdians—"

"For twelve months," said Kayo.

"No, no; for the twelve ships in the Zodiac line."

"Say, you're right, Sung."

"Is there a definite order to the meridians, Kayo?"

"Oh, yes."

My head was swinging from one of them to the other in a vain effort to keep up. I'd had them both labeled and filed. Kayo: good friend, certain intuitiveness but not especially sharp. Sung: a chocolate Easter bunny, sweet and cute and no airhead, but Doyle Mulligan...he was the office's bright boy. And here they were putting the finishing touches on a problem that had stumped Alex Stringer, Ben Kao and me. Or had it? Ben Kao knew acupuncture, too. He was the one who had turned Kayo on to needlework. What if Ben had translated the code: Suppose he wanted to warn me what he'd found out but didn't dare to get involved directly as long as the ***Yega*** was still following me around. Might he not have arranged the meeting with me in the bowels of the monastery? I was now convinced that ghostly voice I'd talked with for nearly half an hour was none other than Ben Kao himself. Ben was not a "Western Chinese." He was a friend. And he'd decided to violate the code of silence in order to help a *saiyahn*.

"Let's see," said Sung. "Lao Shu the rat is comparable to Aries which is the first sign of the Zodiac. What's the first meridian?"

"That would be the lung meridian. Metal, strong yin." The three of us scanned down the list. "Open-Tiger." That's an acupuncture point all right but I don't think it's on the lung meridian. I'd have to check the book to be sure." Kayo turned to me. "What do you think, Doily?"

I was startled. "What? Me? Am I still here?"

Sung asked my big friend if he had his book with him.

"Of course. It's up in my cabin."

He left to get it and Sung ran off right behind him. I didn't know why until she'd returned with a complete cruise schedule from the lobby.

We watched Kayo flip through the pages of Ancient Ways/ Modern Man by Lee Chung. None of the days or points seemed to match until Sung suggested that it wasn't the published departure dates from Honolulu which were important but the dates of departure from Hong Kong and even then we almost missed it. The Lao Shu "point" number missed the Hong Kong departure date by two days. I told him to try another one and that one was also two days shy of the printed schedule. In fact, they all were. It couldn't possibly be coincidence. The thing was coded in a way that no policeman investigating a Celestial Acupuncture Clinic would ever suspect what it was. I'd have been willing to bet that their other files and accounts were coded much the same way. But clearly the sheet was a list of the twelve ships of the Zodiac line and their current month departure dates from Hong

Kong minus two days. Ben had decoded it all except for the difference in days. I knew now he hadn't figured that part because I'd figured it out for myself. And any minute now Kayo or Sung would figure it too.

The two of them were still talking over the implications of this when I stood up, stepped to the rail and sent a coin spinning high.

Heads, I put my head in a hole and forget everything.

Tails, I grab the tiger's tail and get back to work.

I snatched it out of the air.

I slapped it onto my wrist.

Tails.

"You know what, Doily?" Kayo was shouting. "I'll bet these point numbers are boarding days instead of departure dates. It makes sense they'd board the IE's a couple of days before sailing."

I muttered back something.

Darn that guy. He'd interrupted my train of thought. I couldn't remember now which I was flipping for. I'd have to toss again.

I sent up the coin.

Looking for heads, I said to myself. Come on heads.

It was tails.

Kayo spoke up again. "If that's true, Doily, it means the IE's were already on the Lao Shu before the acupuncture clinics burned. Before Li Chiang's warehouse was shut down. They were already here when the police walked through the ship and posted guards at the dock."

"Yeah, yeah, Kayo, I know." Dammit, he'd messed me up again.

This was it. One last toss.

I sent the coin up especially high just as the two of them crossed over to the rail.

"Doily, said Kayo, grabbing my arm. "this is the only Zodiac ship to leave Hong Kong since Sha Zhan bought his way into the *de ha tit*. If he got out, he must be somewhere on board."

I looked at him.

I looked at her.

They looked back.

And then together all three of us looked down.

The coin hit the deck with a ping, spun in a circle one or two times and then rolled under the railing, sailed over the side and plunked into the Pacific Ocean twenty-five feet below.

"What was that?" asked Kayo.

I said:

"It was tails."

"No, I mean, what was it?"

"Just my lucky coin, that's all."

"How do you know it was tails, Doily?"

I was firm.

"Take my word for it, Kayo." I said. "It was tails."

From that moment on, the vacation was over and we were back on the story.

Somehow we got Sung into her cabin and then Kayo and I started searching the Lao Shu from top to bottom. We didn't meet many passengers. Some were still at the first seating for lunch; others were at the pool or the bar or in their staterooms. We practically had the corridors to ourselves. No stairway we could find went further below than the deck of our own cabin. Our search took us forward but, oddly enough, the outside doors giving access to the bridge, navigation and radio rooms as well as the quarters for the captain and his senior officers, were locked. We went back to the lobby and tried the passageway. Here we had no more luck. Underneath the sign "Bridge" had recently been posted another notice which announced that passage was allowed for "Authorized Personnel Only" and a Chinese ape was standing by in case we had any question about who was authorized and who wasn't. We wasn't.

Eventually we located a freight elevator that probably went all the way down to the engine room but we couldn't try it because the summons button had a combination keypad.

We returned to the passenger elevator and pressed the button for the Leo deck. I sure wasn't looking forward to reporting no success to Sung. Kayo, meanwhile, was giving the elevator controls a good going over. Despite the fact that there were only three decks, there were four buttons. The upper three were marked with the deck names; the lowermost button had no markings.

Kayo raised his brows—Shall we?

I raised mine back—Why not?

The doors whisked shut.

They opened again on a deck much like ours but shorter and less ostentatious. It was a single corridor with doors along both sides. As we moved forward we could see through the few open doors that they were quarters for the crewmen. They were nearly as spacious as the passenger cabins though there were half a dozen or more bunks in each cabin.

As we walked by one open door I saw the purser inside gyrating in front of a full-length mirror. So complete was his fascination he never even saw us go by.

At the end of the corridor we found watertight hatches to the holds. Four altogether. One was a refrigerated hold with a label that said Reefer #1. The others contained nonperishable stores. I had Kayo act as a lookout while I went inside. The reefer had a ladderway that went up (probably into the galley) but I didn't climb it. I didn't open up crates of stores either but I checked all four holds well enough to have sworn there weren't any stowaways.

I returned to the corridor and to a disappointed Kayo Tuan. My face must have told him everything. But what did we expect to find? A sign posted on one of the crew cabins saying "Illegal Emigrants Only?" Maybe a family of Chinese huddled together in the reefer wearing parkas and living off frozen vegetables.

We walked side by side back to the elevator.

"What's back here?"

Kayo peeked behind a corner where the elevator bulkhead failed to block the entire corridor. I followed him around.

We found a small alcove for another elevator but it was occupied. Not the elevator, the alcove.

A uniformed seaman who'd been sitting at a tiny desk leapt to his feet and came over to us. He was wearing a side arm. One hand was on the butt, the other pushed outward at us, urging us back. He had a quarrelsome nature and a fat face to match.

"What are you doing down here?" he growled. "Passengers aren't allowed on this deck."

Kayo went stiff.

That's not to imply he didn't know what to do. I hadn't written him a script so it was simply a case of not knowing what to say. As far as doing, he'd already balled up a fist and picked out a spot on the seaman's fat face.

"We're just looking for someone," I said quickly.

"Who?"

"My wife. She's missing. I thought she might have come down here."

"Passengers aren't allowed down here."

We told him we'd look somewhere else, turned around, and walked around the corner to the main elevator.

Then we raced back to Sung's and my cabin to scheme.

I was thinking diversion. This whole cruise was nothing but a diversion. Now we needed another one. Of course that meant using Sung because she was the most diverting thing on the ship. We came up with a plan, everything was agreed on except what she would wear.

Kayo suggested the yellow tonga but I was unalterably opposed.

"She could wear that warmup over—"

"Not the tonga," I declared. "No way!"

We finally settled on the miniskirt and white blouse.

From the elevator Kayo and I watched her move down the crew corridor and I decided that dumping that outfit off the number one spot of my personal hit parade had been nothing but impetuous folly. She checked the numbers as she walked and stopped in front of the door I'd given her. Apparently it was still open. She stood in the doorway. She smiled. Then she stepped inside.

I counted off sixty seconds nice and slow.

"Okay, Kayo," I hissed.

He was checking his watch. "It hasn't even been half a minute yet, Doily," he whispered back.

"Close enough. Get Going!"

The big guy marched purposefully down the same path Sung had taken. I wasn't expecting any Oscar winning performance and I sure didn't get it. Kayo was all ham. He stopped at the open door, drew up his chest, pointed an accusatory finger into the purser's cabin and shouted, "What are you doing to my sister, you Chinese Cassanova!" The truth is I did write that script but it sounded better when I said it.

I heard other shouts coming from inside.

Desperate denials. A man's. But not at all clever.

Kayo bounded in.

The shouts became yells and then screams for help.

A second later the armed seaman from around the corner bolted past me. I didn't even wait for him to get into the purser's cabin. I slipped around the corner and jabbed the button on the freight elevator before the sound of his footsteps had stopped echoing off the walls of the corridor.

This summons button wasn't keyed.

The cage didn't come soon but it came and there was no one inside.

I pushed the top button.

Every two minutes I'd open the doors and look up and down the Pisces Deck. After the umpteeth time here came Kayo. He stepped in beside me. "Any trouble?" I asked him as I sent the cage all the way down.

"No."

"Sung all right?"

"Oh, yes. She's in the room with the door locked."

"How about the purser?"

Kayo smiled. "I did like you said, Doily. I didn't hit him too hard."

"But not too soft....?"

"Not too soft. I did like you said."

The elevator opened this time in another little alcove. This one had a watertight door leading aft. It was too late to hesitate now.

Kayo spun the wheel which released the dogs. I pushed open the door.

A huge chamber, at least twenty feet in height and five times that in length was laid out below us. Kayo and I had three choices; we could descend a narrow iron stairway to the engine room. We could proceed on a catwalk. Or we could remain where we were, too shocked by what we saw even to step over the coaming. As it turned out this latter choice proved to be the best though we didn't know it at the time. We stared in speechless horror. A few yards out, the catwalk intersected another wider platform which ran athwart the ship from hull to hull. On our right was the Pacific Ocean. The wide platform breached the port hull just feet above the waterline with a gate as big as a garage door and at least as high. It opened down and outward like a drawbridge though at the moment it was only just out a few feet. But what had immobilized Kayo and me was the engine room itself. We couldn't have prepared ourselves for that.

It was a blackened hellhole. So burned was it in fact that we could only identify any of the machinery by flames from arc welding torches and portable lamps set up about a dozen work stations. Light streaming in the loading door helped too. That must have been why it was open while underway A raucous symphony of clanging steel, hissing gas and the rapid fire concussion of pneumatic tools issued from the engine room floor.

The compartment was dominated by two huge pieces of machinery which I took to be engines. These were surrounded on all sides by tanks, pipes, monitoring equipment, control stations, electrical raceways, metal walkways and ladders, winches and cables, tools and supplies. Little of this was identifiable. It looked to me like the whole engine room had been assembled from parts unearthed at ground zero, downtown Hiroshima, circa 1945. But I knew better. These engines would have been built with the same attention to quality as the rest of the ship. No, it was later, sometime around four o'clock in the mornng our second night out, that this particular blast had gone off. The fire drill that had kept the passengers huddled under the lifeboats had been no drill at all. And if the fire control crews hadn't contained this blaze when they did, the order to abandon ship could not have been minutes away.

Kayo must have been thinking the same thing that I was. We traded doubtful glances before stepping over the coaming and out onto the catwalk. We both knew a man who might have come prowling down here. He would have been looking for the same thing that we were. And he was a man whose ideas about diversions of all kinds were considerably more destructive than ours.

13. The Belowdecks

If Kayo and I had started down the ladder as soon as we opened the door we'd have made it only half way before being spotted. A cleverly concealed panel on the wall below the catwalk slid open and a big coolie stepped out. He couldn't have missed us. He'd have pulled his revolver and shouted for his mates. There would have been nowhere for us to run. I could almost see that sinister looking engine room crew swarming around us, sweating and swearing and spoiling for a fight.

But it didn't happen like that.

We didn't start down right away. Nobody caught us...not until we were leaving, that is.

By the time we'd recovered from our shock of seeing the engine room the camouflaged panel had already slid open and the coolie had already stepped out. Kayo and I crouched in the doorway over the coolie's head and watched him throw a secret switch that closed the panel again.

And then he wandered into the engine room.

I put my finger to my lips. It wasn't necessary. What with the din I could have shouted and not disturbed anybody. I pointed to my chest, made walking motions with my fingers then pointed to him and walked again. He nodded. I crept to the ladder and slunk down. Kayo joined me at the bottom seconds later. When several more coolies strolled by one of us showed the good sense to slip behind a big packing crate and drag Kayo over beside me. He's too big for hiding. He's too bold for sneakiness. To tell the truth I was starting to wonder why I'd brought him along.

Soon though the two of us were kneeling in front of the concealed panel. The thing was so cleverly designed that no one would ever realize it opened up; it looked exactly like any other watertight bulkhead between compartments or holds.

"No one's looking," said Kayo."

I activated the wall switch and the panel hummed back. We both scampered through.

Another switch inside closed the panel behind us.

We were in a small iron anteroom with a desk and filing cabinet to one side but only a single watertight door on the forward bulkhead.

I turned the wheel, pushed open the door, stepped over the coaming, and closed the door after Kayo had followed me through.

There was a light switch at my right.

I threw it.

If the Lao Shu were a naval vessel instead of a luxury liner I'd have thought we'd stumbled into the brig.

A corridor ran fifty feet to another watertight door; on each side of this corrodor, which was half the width of those on the passenger levels, were cabin doors. The deck was steel plating; the deckhead was steel plating. So were the walls and the doors of the cabins. If you could call them cabins. I stepped to the first door. It was secured from the outside with a padlock but a little Judas window at face level gave me a grim picture of the interior. It was a three by five meter room that was wall to wall people. Twenty-two of them. I counted. Nine men, seven women and the rest little kids. All of them were Chinese. I couldn't believe it. There was no furniture at all. There was no room. A few blankets were scattered about but there wasn't even enough deck space for all twenty-two to lie down at one time. I thought about dragging the purser down here and getting him to repeat his speech about how all the cabins on the Lao Shu were outside staterooms. These were outside, all right. Outside maritime law. Outside the bounds of common decency. But they looked more like prison cells than staterooms.

A stench of human odor and urine and defecation wafted out of the Judas Hole. Disinfectant, too, but not enough of it. There was little ventilation down here and the only plumbing was an open drain in the middle of the room and a single overhead pipe operated by a shutoff valve for drinking, bathing and flushing.

They were going to America. Or so they believed. But their faces were those of condemned prisoners, the faces of innocent people, falsely accused, convicted, and sentenced; faces filled with fear, confusion, and hopelessness. Worst of all though were the faces of the children. I saw hunger and thirst in them in addition to everything else.

When a little girl glanced at the door I ducked out of sight. I couldn't face her. Why, I don't know. She might think I was one of her warders and I couldn't stand that. I turned away from the window.

The next cabin held more of the same and I had to force myself to stay at the Judas hole long enough to count heads. Twenty three. And in the next, twenty-one. There were five cells on each side of the corridor. I opened the watertight door at the end of it and stepped into another compartment that was just like the first. Ten more cells. Another two hundred people. In all, there were five watertight compartments and fifty cells, though the cells themselves were not watertight. More than a thousand Chinese. On a ship with a maximum accommodation for two hundred passengers and crew.

It was a staggering discovery. I stumbled from one compartment to the next in a sullen daze.

"Shouldn't we ask around for Sha Han?" Kayo buzzed in my ear when we'd reached the last compartment.

I shook my head and whispered back.

"No. God no! As far as Han knows that damn ***Yega*** is on the ship. We know darn well he is. He started the fire in the engine room as a diversion to get in here."

My voice was breaking. That's what finding this place had done to me.

"Hell," I said, "I'll bet he did get in. If Sha Han's still alive it's only because the ***Yega*** doesn't know what he looks like. Either that or Sha Han's changed his appearance since he left school. Don't forget, Kayo, he's been running for his life for four years. Whatever the reason, the ***Yega*** must've come in here and couldn't find him."

"You could call for him, Doily. You're *saiyahn*. He wouldn't be frightened of you."

"Baloney! Sha Han knows better than to show himself until after the Lao Shu docks in Hawaii and maybe not then. Anyway, I'm not sure I want to know where he is now. We'd just be leading the***Yega*** to him.

"The ***Yega***'s not in here now."

I glared at him and shook my head. I hadn't figured it out yet…why I'd brought him along.

"How do you know he's not. Every time I turn around any more I expect to bump into him."

"Well, what should we do, Doily?"

We should have taken pictures except I hadn't brought my camera along. We should've taken notes. Except I hadn't even brought pencil and paper. Here was our story. The one I'd chased all over Hong Kong to get. Our chances of getting out of here without being seen were bad enough, coming back down again with photographic eqluipment, I didn't even want to think about. Whatever we were going to do we had to do now.

"Doily? Doyle Mulligan! Is that you?"

I whirled.

So did Kayo.

"Over here."

Our eyes swept down the row of judas holes until we found one several cells away filled by a fat little Asian face.

I moved over carefully.

"You know me?" I said squinting my eyes through the bars.

"It's me. Wu Wing. From the airport. You remember me, don't you, Doyle."

By God, it was. And I did. Wu was the old newsie who ran the magazine stand at Kai Tak, the guy I'd written the feature about and who'd sold his stand the day my airplane was blown out of the sky.

"You old fool," I practically shouted. "What are you doing here?"

"Paying the price for foolishness," he said. "Doyle, you've got to help us!"

He backed up when I put my face close to the bars to look in.

They'd obviously been told not to bring much luggage. Either that or the bulk of their luggage had been dumped in Hong Kong. The only stuff these people had with them was what they could carry under an arm or sit on. Nothing larger than an overnight bag. Small jewelry boxes. Attache cases. Satchels. I guessed they'd liquidated everything they owned: their homes, their cars, their businesses, everything. It was now in their money belts and purses and what would stop the guys who were operating this nightmare cruise from walking in and taking it away from them? I saw Mrs. Wu hunched on the floor with a gym bag between her legs. She looked worse than the others. Worse than her husband. She was too old for this kind of thing.

"They don't feed you?"

"They told us to bring enough food to last three or four days. But they brought us in here two days before sailing and our food is nearly gone." He looked down at his wife and then back at me and said in an undertone: "How much longer until…"

"We're four days out of Honolulu."

"And us? What happens to us when we get there?"

I didn't think for a moment that any of them would get there. "What did they tell you?" I asked him.

"They said they've got franchised acupuncture clinics across the United States. They said we would be moved from clinic to clinic until we found a place to settle down."

I liked him too much to lie.

"I don't believe it," I said. "There's a thousand of you on this ship alone and Zodiac ships sail three times a week. They couldn't possibly sneak that many of you off without being seen let alone hide you in Honolulu. And how do they plan to get you to the U.S. mainland?"

"They said they couldn't tell us."

That much I did believe.

Wu must have sensed what I was thinking.

"Do you know what they're going to do with us?" he asked abruptly but still in a voice to low for his wife to hear.

"I've got a pretty good idea. Don't you? This is the SS Rat, not the Good Ship Lollipop."

His face drew tighter against the bones.

"We hear rumors."

"I'll bet you do. Everything you guys own you've got in your laps. What's going to stop the bastards who run this boat from blowing your brains out, dumping your bodies into the ocean and helping themselves to your stuff. They won't even have to take you topside, they can just open up that loading door in the engine room some moonless night and toss you out."

He nodded. "That," he said, "is one rumor."

"Look, Mr. Wu—" A hand fell on my shoulder and I spun around. "What is it, Kayo?"

"Doily, we can't stay here too long. Someone may come in any time."

I almost snapped at him. This was what we got paid for, wasn't it? It was our job. At least it was mine. Why had I brought Kayo in the first place? It hadn't come to me yet.

I asked him to check out the first compartment and the engine room to make sure the way out was clear. I needed a few minutes more, I told him, but when it was time to go we would have to move fast. I suggested that while he was out there he could look around for the keys to the cells.

He lumbered off aft.

I went back to the window. "I'm looking for a guy," I told Wu. "I don't know what he looks like…all I know is his name and what he was carrying."

"I don't know any of the others," said Wu.

"He had a bag of some kind with tapes in it."

"Tapes?"

"Yeah, you know, videocassette tapes."

I saw something come over his face.

"There was someone," he said. "I don't know where he is now. Not which cell he's in."

"That's all right, Mr. Wu, I don't want to know that. And please don't try to find out. I only want to know if he's here."

"A young man? Frightened? And a thief, too, perhaps."

"He's young," I agreed, "and he's got good reason to be scared. If he's a thief though, I don't know about that." But actually, I thought, I did know. He'd stolen the tapes, hadn't he?

"Most of us," Wu went on, "perhaps a thousand of us, spent the night in a warehouse near the Tsim Sha Tsui." He started to describe it to me and I interrupted to tell him I knew about that. "This young man showed up the same day as my wife and myself," he said. "He was alone. Neither of us saw him but we heard about him the next morning, along with everyone else. You see, he'd come without food. That first evening he tried to buy rice from several of the others, but no one wanted to sell. He lay down beside an old woman for the night. When she awoke, most of her food was gone. Some of the others suspected the young man. He acted frightened. They searched his bag and found nothing but these tapes you have described."

"Then he didn't steal the food?"

"Rice, seaweed and meat were later found in the pockets of his clothing. He claimed he had bought it from a man but was not able to describe the man. Then he changed his story and said he'd paid the old woman forty dollars Hong Kong for the food. The others wanted to beat him up. They might have done so if some men from the *de ha tit* had not rushed in and taken him into another room. I heard about the story when a collection of food was taken for the old woman. Four rice rolls we gave and now my wife—also an old woman—is hungry. What's to become of us?"

Fortunately I didn't have to answer his question.

The watertight door to the compartment had banged open. Kayo rushed over beside me. He was excited.

"I found them, Doily."

He held up a ring of several dozen keys.

I stepped away from the Judas window, turned my back on Wu Wing and whispered to Kayo: "Put 'em back."

"What?"

"You heard me. Put the keys back."

"But, Doily…what you told Mr. Wu. These people don't have a chance if they stay down here. They'll be killed."

"Maybe," I agreed, "maybe not. But I've found out that Sha Han is down here somewhere. What chance will he have if we take him and the others back up—"

Kayo shook his head.

"I'm not talking about Sha Han. All of them. We can't leave them down here to starve to death or…to be drowned. We don't have to worry about the crew. Once the other passengers see them, they won't dare to do anything to them."

I could have objected to Kayo's grammar. His antecedents were hardly up the the standard of a trained reporter. His logic however, like his motives, was beyond reproach. Nevertheless, this is where I had to challenge him. I had to make him realize that saving the lives of a thousand poor slobs, many of them women and children who'd hurt no one and done nothing wrong, should take second place to protecting a selfish prick like Ping Sha Han.

"What about the ***Yega***?' I said. "Once you've freed all these guys and taken them up, he'll have no trouble finding Sha Han. Then nothing, not you, not the ship's crew, not a hundred and fifty passengers or a thousand frightened runaways, can stop him from doing to Sha Han what he did to Lee Chung and the others. Is that what you want?"

"No but—"

"Do you want to explain to five million Honkers how Sha Han couldn't keep the communists our for another four years because we set him up to be butchered?"

"No."

"We can't protect him up there. But these guys can…down here. Sha Han has to stay. Wu and his family have to stay and all of the others, too."

"Okay, Doily, whatever you say."

"Put those keys back. I'll be done in a minute."

I went back to the window to explain things to Wu Wing. We were a pair, Sha Han and I. I wasn't proud of that. But neither was I proud of my part in the deaths of Sung's aunt and uncle, so I'd made up my mind I was bringing her cousin back to Hong Kong alive.

I was telling Wu I'd do what I could to help him and the rest when the watertight door to the fourth compartment banged open. I thought it was Kayo back from returning the keys.

But it wasn't.

The big coolie thrust his head through the opening.

"Shi Shui?"

I turned away from the Judas hold and the WT door. I leaped at the light bulb and swung my fist like a hammer. The compartment was thrown into darkness.

Chinese. The coolie had spoken in Chinese. He hadn't seen my face. There was still a chance.

I tried to slip past him, to dive through the doorway and make it to the engine room, but he made a blind grab and got me. The next thing I felt was the steel deck cracking the back of my head.

Kayo later told Sung I'd gone out, but I hadn't. I saw another even larger black form move in behind the coolie. I heard a snarl. And then a cry of surprise choked off as the coolie's weight came off my chest. You can't see or hear or feel if you're out, so I wasn't out. And one other thing I did—I suddenly remembered why I'd brought Kayo along. And I thanked my lucky stars that I had.

You can't thank your lucky stars when you're out.

The dull thud of knuckles pounding against flest echoed between the steel walls. Two hundred pounds of coolie landed hard against the steel deck. A hand scooped under my trunk. Another worked under my legs. Two giant's arms lifted me up and carried me through the door like a rag doll.

I'm going back down there," said Sung. "He's my cousin and I've got a right to see him." Those are the first words I remember. The way she said it though, I knew they weren't the first words she'd spoken. It was a final appeal.

Kayo's rebuttal worked its way through my mental haze. This sounded like a rehash to me. She couldn't go below, he told her, because now the crew would be ready for intruders. If they were caught, the crew might panic. They might even start throwing people over the side right then and there, starting with Sung. Anyway (and this I sensed was his final argument too) she couldn't go down alone because, even assuming she could find the hidden dungeon and get in without being seen, she didn't know which cell Sha Han was in. She didn't even know what he looked like. Either Doily or Kayo himself would have to take her. But Doily was unconscious and Kayo wasn't going back down.

The cabin grew quiet after that and I sensed them both looking at me. I tried to open my eyes. Yup. They were looking at me.

"Doily…" Kayo started.

"Are you all right, Doyle?" asked Sung.

To her, I said I was. To Kayo, I said I wasn't unconscious. I looked back at Sung. She'd moved to the side of my bed. "But about the rest, Kayo's right," I told her. "We don't dare go down again."

"What can we do?"

"We've no choice," I said. Kayo towered over the foot of my bed now. "We've got to get to the captain."

"Nobody can get to the captain, Doily. They've blocked the door to the bridge, remember? The captain hasn't shown up for dinner since the engine room burned. He hasn't shown up anywhere. I think he knows who's on the ship."

Kayo was right again.

The captain was running scared. Like Sung's Aunt Ling and Uncle Sun. Like Huang Mu and Chang Li. But in Captain Hsiao's case there was nowhere for him to run.

I rolled to the edge of the bunk and sat up, rubbed my face with both hands and then dragged my fingers through my hair. "You're right," I said. "But this is his ship. He's the one who gives the order to kill those people down there. And he's the only one who can give the orders not to kill them. I told that old man I'd help how I could. That's about all we can do, is get to the captain. We'll bargain with him if we can, threaten him if we have to."

"What about me?" asked Sung.

"You'd better stay here. You weren't seen. They've no reason to believe you know anything that can hurt them." I looked up at Kayo. "I'd stay myself but you may want me to hold your coat while you talk with Hsiao."

He nodded.

"You do the talking, Doily. Your fighting is yin but you're yang at talking."

I stood, shook my head, walked to the door on steadier feet than I would have believed possible, and followed Kayo out and forward to the elevator.

At the passageway to the bridge we ran into the same Chinese anthropoid who'd kept us from going in before.

"Remember us?" I said. "We need to talk to the captain right away."

This ape had a yellow clock for a face with two black hands at ten minutes to two. The face told me nothing more than the time. "I'm sorry," he growled, neither looking nor sounding sorry. "The captain's busy. What do you want?"

"I told you. We need to talk to him."

"What about?"

"Stowaways," I said suddenly. "There are stowaways on the ship."

Under ordinary circumstances that should guarantee an audience with any captain.

The big ape started to say something but stopped. He didn't need to, his ten minutes-to-two clock face was saying it all. Verbal exchanges were not in his line. His answer to problems like us were more physical. But when he looked over at Kayo's clock and saw the same time of day, he knew we had that argument covered.

"I'll talk to the first officer," he said. "He may be able to get to the captain."

The ape departed with a vow to return shortly and then, after locking the door behind him, left us alone.

Two minutes later he was back.

The answer was a flat: Forget it. The captain wouldn't see us. Try the suggestion box. I wasted ten minutes arguing with him before getting it in my head I was arguing with an ape.

I turned to my left.

"Kayo, I guess my talking didn't do so good, after all. It's up to you now. I'm going inside. If this overgrown monkey tries to stop me, explain to him about yin and yang."

Before I'd taken the first step, the ape tried to stop me, but in a way I hadn't considered. His right hand flew behind his back and came out with a 45 automatic pistol. It hadn't even occurred to me that he was armed. I had to hand it to him, he was fast enough, but that was about all. Because I was moving forward he made the mistake of pointing the gun at me and I wasn't his problem. Kayo is no Albert Einstein but even a man who knows how to take orders has an edge on a trained gorilla.

Kayo knocked the guy out of his shoes. His fist caught the ape on the side of the head and sent him flying back with such force that he all but smashed the passage door off its hinges. His unconscious body slumped down to the floor where it lay in a broken heap, not even an ape any more but just a primate with holes in his socks. Beautiful.

"Now that," I said, "is what I call glib."

I picked up the 45, handed it to Kayo, told him to see that nobody followed me, then I opened the door and went in.

The passageway was long and wide with plenty of doors on both sides. I read a couple of doorplates. They were officers names. The ranks were in ascending order, which implied that the captain's cabin should be forwardmost.

I passed a medical officer's quarters, then quarters for the second officer. The first officer's quarters were just up ahead. Beyond that was the last cabin at the very end of the passageway leading into the bridge and just opposite to an exit door clearly marked.

Without warning, the captain's door swung open.

Even from down the corridor I could see the name plate which bore the words "Captain Hsiao."

I saw a black torso lean out from behind the door, the black head turned away. The hand at the end of a black arm grasped the handle of the exit door across the corridor and opened it, too.

Then the black figure stepped across the passageway and through the exit. It's hard to believe I didn't see more but I didn't. When both doors were open they blocked the whole passageway and the door openings too.

Anyway, I didn't need to see more.

My heart was already doing a drum roll. This was bad. I had no business here and no desire to be here. Anywhere but here. My pace quickened. There ws no telling how few seconds I might have. Was I several heartbeats too late? God! I thought. Nothing could be worse than that…again. Nothing except being several heartbeats too early. I broke into a run.

The cabin blew up.

A freight train roared into the corridor. It shattered the door into kindling and blasted it into my face. A ball of flames bowled me down.

It was over that quickly.

But it was over for several seconds before I knew it. My ears still roared. The fireball still stared me in the face.

The blast smothered me like a hot blanket. I couldn't get up or even move.

Smoke was everywhere. There were no flames except for some little tongues licking at the ragged opening which had once been a doorway. The dancing patterns of light from an active blaze inside the cabin shone off the opposite wall. But was I really seeing this? Two balls of fire that had once been my eyes eclipsed everything else. I rolled my head toward the lobby. The door Kayo had all but knocked off its hinges was off its hinges now. It was lying flat on the lobby floor. So were several people. Screams grew louder with every second.

But was I really hearing them? The ringing in my ears muffled every other sound. I had a vague image of people getting to their feet. Most of them began moving farther away. Kayo began moving closer.

"Doily! Doily, are you okay?"

I turned my head up. Kayo was staring down from just beyond the fireballs in my eyes. I hoped I didn't look as bad as his expression seemed to suggest. He came closer. But he couldn't get through the glare. He yelled louder.

"Are you okay, Doily?"

My throat was on fire so I thought it would be amusing to see what my voice sounded like.

"Do me a favor," I told him. "Treat for shock."

That's the way I remember it and that's what I meant to say though Kayo later told Sung he understood me to whisper, "Please, just get me out of here." I admit those two don't sound very much alike. Anyway, it's a moot point because he didn't treat me for shock and he didn't get me out of there. Not right away. When a man's in shock you don't haul him to his feet and start dragging him around. To get out of there we would have gone back to the lobby, not into the captain's cabin.

We waded through scraps of wooden door. The doorplate with the letters "…ain His…" carved in it lay on top of the mess.

A small fire burned inside but nothing like the blaze my scorched eyes had imagined. Several pieces of furniture were smoldering. The walls were badly blackened and it was a good bet the ceiling was too but so thick a layer of smoke hung down from it that Kayo had to crouch carrying me in. A massive oaken desk was piled like cordwood in the middle of the room. The battered remnants of an executive chair were crumpled against a wall. There wasn't much left of either one, the desk, the chair or the wall. That last had buckled badly. The steel plating of this outer bulkhead hadn't been holed but the blast had punched an eight-foot-wide dent in it. Both portholes had shattered.

Kayo set me down on the pile of desk, poked through a little kitchenette and then disappeared into an adjoining bedroom which he found free from damage.

"There's nobody in here," Kayo called out.

The bomb had gone off near the bulkhead. It had blown the chair against the bulkhead and the desk into the center of the room. Therefore it had gone off between the desk and the chair. I limped over and picked up a black service shoe lying near the baseboard. Either the shoe was very heavy or I was very weak or both. It was both. I felt suddenly very weak but the shoe was also heavy. They weigh more when the feet are still inside. It fell out of my hand. I stumbled into a corner to be sick.

Kayo rejoined me just as I finished. "Where is he?"

"He's here," I said.

"Where?"

The smoke was dissipating now. Charred paint and ashes failed to cover the multi-colored spatters over the walls and ceiling. The grisly dripping mess that clung to the overhead looked like the puddle of sickness I'd just laid on the floor only bigger. But it wasn't. Sickness, that is. It was a whole lot bigger. I found a fragment of bone about the size of my little finger stuck in the carpet. The carpet was sticky.

I waved a weak hand in a circle and sat down.

"He's been blown to smithereens."

Kayo looked around. "What's smithereens?"

I started to tell him it was a lot of different places at the same time but before I could say it a small party of uniformed crewmen stormed the cabin.

14. No Way to Lose

I woke up and screamed. I didn't wake up screaming—not like you do coming out of a bad dream. I woke up. I looked around. And then I started screaming.

It sounds dumb unless I explain.

Sung had urged me to go see the ship's doctor about my burns. When I refused, she pleaded with me at least to get some pain pills from the pharmacy. "You won't get any sleep if you don't," she warned me.

She was right. But I didn't dare risk it. Any member of the crew could have been involved with the *de hat tit* and most of them probably were. The doctor and the pharmacist, too. If they were, who knows what kind of pills they might have given me.

So I didn't get them.

So I didn't get any sleep.

I hurt so bad that at one point Kayo had to hold me down on the bed. Was I sorry Sung had to see that!

Captain Hsiao's death had also eliminated any doubts about whether or not the *Yega* was on the *Lao Shu.* He was. He knew that we knew he was on the *Lao Shu* just as he knew that we knew about the thousand Chinese belowdecks. If the *de hat tit* ended here in the middle of the Pacific Ocean then my investigation—and my usefulness—had come to an end too, as Macao's Superintendent of the Police Maldonado had predicted.

Kayo and Sung were in as much danger as I was. We moved their stuff into Sung's and my room. The three of us would sleep together in shifts with either Kayo or me on guard at all times. When we went out, the three of us went out together and stayed together until we got back to our cabin.

Kayo took the first watch after dinner.

I was supposed to take the second from two o'clock on.

My mind wandered all night. I kept thinking about Sung ten feet away in the other bed wearing a peach nightie that was by far my favorite of anything I'd seen her in. I kept thinking about Kayo, hunched between us in the cabin's only chair gripping my pistol like a protective big brother. He wasn't scared—Kayo never scared—but he never dozed off and he never set down the pistol. I thought about the murderous bastard who could come through that door and do whatever he wanted to us whether Kayo dozed off or not. Of course, Kayo couldn't have slept with me tossing and groaning the way I was. It seemed like the longer I lay there the more my face and hands burned. Then came that one embarrassing incident when Kayo had to hold me down on the bed. After his weight came off me and he went back to the chair I made a special effort to control my pain. I guess I did for a while but I couldn't make myself sleep. I made myself think about the ship . . . about the hundreds of desperate Chinese in the lower compartments . . . about what was going to happen to them. Somehow the night passed.

My eyes came open.

I checked the time. Damn, it was nearly five o'clock! Three hours past my turn at watch.

I started to roll out of bed.

A light came on. It must've been Sung, she was sitting in Kayo's chair with the gun in her hand. The other bed was empty. Kayo was gone. That was startling enough.

But what I saw next shocked me in a way I've never been shocked before. And that's when I screamed.

I really screamed.

Sung was beside me in an instant.

"Are you all right, Doyle?"

"I've been stabbed!"

Long, silver-colored darts were impaled in my arms and trunk. Four in my right arm. Four more in my left and six or seven in my stomach.

Sung was holding my shoulders down the way Kayo did.

"It's okay, Doyle, it's okay."

"Okay—! What d'ya mean it's okay? I've been stabbed a dozen times and the knives are still sticking in me!"

"They're acupuncture needles."

As her words sunk in I slowly stopped struggling.

I tried to relax.

"Kayo did this," I cried. "That bastard! He poked me full of holes and left us here alone. He didn't wake me up and he's not keeping watch."

"He is keeping watch, Doyle. Outside."

She asked me if I was in pain and I had to admit that I wasn't. My burns had stopped hurting. I didn't really feel the needles either. And I had slept.

"I guess, I'm okay," I told her. It didn't come easy. "What's Kayo doing outside, anyway?" I had this picture of him lurking around outside our porthole. And here we were on the bed together. Sung, in the peach nightie, was practically sitting on my lap.

After she'd told me what Kayo was doing outside I felt like a darn crybaby as well as a fool. He'd worried about the Chinese belowdecks just like I had. But he'd done something about it. After the decks cleared of strollers he'd gone out to keep a watch over the side. If one of the cargo doors came open and bodies began hitting the sea, Kayo was going to take action. What kind of action Sung didn't know.

But he couldn't take off with me waking up and howling every ten minutes so he'd jabbed me with a bunch of needles, screwed up my ch'i, and told Sung it was up to her to decide how long to let me sleep. She'd been sitting in that chair all night long.

"Don't think I don't appreciate what you did, Sung," I said, "but for Christ's sake will you please pull out these darn needles."

"I can't. I don't know how."

"Then go get Kayo."

She grabbed the hem of the peach nightie. "Go out there like this!" she said.

My voice rose an octave.

"Would you rather I go out there like this!"

As I turned out Kayo saved her the trouble of dressing or me the indignity of prowling the decks like something out of a Clive Barker film by stopping around to see how we were doing.

The needles, he said, could come out any time. I opted for immediately. He sat down beside me and pinched one with his meaty hand, rotated the shaft between a thumb and forefinger while working the head in a loop and carefully eased it out. Not even a pinpoint of blood remained. One by one he did the same with the others. When he was done, the pain was still gone. It was the damnedest thing.

"There's still an hour before daybreak," he informed me once he'd put his needles away. "I'm going back out."

"I'll go with you."

"No," he said, "it's only an hour. I'll sleep when the sun comes up."

"I've already slept," I said, reaching for my clothes, "and I can keep an eye on the port side while you watch the starboard."

Sung asked us what we would do if we saw a loading door open or heard bodies being thrown into the sea.

"I plan to raise a ruckus," I replied. "Start shouting 'Man overboard.' I'll set off a fire alarm, wake up the whole ship if I have to. They'll stop dumping fast if we make enough noise."

Kayo agreed those were good ideas. As we left I asked him what he'd planned to do and he shrugged and said that if he'd seen something like that he was going to go down there and hurt some people.

When the sun came up the three of us talked the thing over and came to the conclusion that nobody would be dumped during the day. The odds were too great one of the paying passengers might see. We also decided that they would wait until the *Lao Shu* was well into the middle of the Pacific. Even if the chance of any bodies washing to shore was only one in a thousand, when you're dumping a thousand bodies, you don't take the chance.

But we couldn't take a chance either. Even if the odds were only one in a million they would start dumping bodies near the Chinese coast, we didn't dare risk it. So Kayo and I slept that day and started pulling shifts on the rail that very next night.

Sung helped too. We couldn't have done it without her.

There were reclinable deck chairs nearby which made it easy to bundle up in blankets and pretend to be sleeping or necking whenever one of the ship's crew walked by which was not very often. Sung and I spent a lot of time together on those last few nights but it wasn't as great as it sounds. Having second-degree burns on your face and neck takes all the fun out of necking.

We ate breakfast as soon as the dining room opened.

We woke and ate dinner before going out to stand watch.

We really packed it away at lunch, away in our pockets, that is, taking enough food to last us through the following night.

It made for a different kind of a cruise.

No more suntanning by the pool. No more shooting clay pigeons or whacking golf balls off the upper deck. Shuffle board and late-night dancing was out. We didn't really care. Knowing the conditions of those people in the holds dampened our spirits for fun.

Just before dawn on the fifth day at sea, Kayo met me on my side of the ship, looking the question he'd asked twenty-four hours before, namely: how could we be sure the Chinese weren't already gone? That we were guarding an empty hold? The same thing was bothering me. We talked about going back down to check and here we disagreed. Kayo didn't want to go below again until we had some backup and I didn't want to go below again until Hell froze over.

"All we could do," I told him, "is to find out they are dead. That wouldn't help them. If we get caught again, the guys running this show might panic and start tossing people out then and there. We can't free them out here on the high seas. So let's just keep our eyes open and hope we're wrong about where the *di ha tit* ends. It may end in Hawaii, after all. I only half believed it myself but Kayo turned away, apparently satisfied for another night. But when the night passed and so had the middle of the Pacific that argument no longer even satisfied him. In another day we'd be close to the Hawaiian Ridge which extends for a thousand miles north of Honolulu. If it were unwise to have bodies washing up on the Chinese mainland, how smart could it be to let them wash up on American soil?

Twenty-four hours out of Oahu it seemed like a waste of time to be standing the night watches at all. But by then it was too late to stop.

When I woke Sung in the deck chair that last night, she pulled off her blankets—she was wearing the blue jeans and blouse—sat up and looked around. Was it already morning? No, Kayo told her. Not for two or three hours. But we had spotted the lights of Kauai off the port bow. Honolulu lay just beyond the horizon.

Kayo asked me what I planned to do when we docked and I told him plainly that I thought we had two choices: we could either go directly to the nearest police station and unload the whole story or, as an alternative, we could phone ahead first and let them know we were coming.

We were the only passengers who weren't excited about standing at the rail when the *Lao Shu* approached Oahu. Sung was down in the cabin packing; Kayo and I had had enough of rails. And yet when some Navy planes took off from the air station at Barber's Point I felt a surge of Welcome to the U.S.A. myself—I'd spent six months in Hawaii before going overseas. A few minutes later we passed the narrow inlet to Pearl Harbor and I could almost see my old stomping grounds, Hickam Air Force Base adjacent to the Honolulu International Airport. The airport runway built out into the ocean on land reclaimed by coral fill had just been completed when I'd shipped out.

As we were coming in, a brightly colored jetfoil with "Seaflite" markings came flying out of the channel laying a contrail-like wake. We followed its distinctive white path between the buoys to the harbor pinched between Sand Island on the south and downtown to the north. Modern office buildings and hotels dwarfed the Aloha Tower at the wharf's edge.

There was another cruise ship at the waterfront, some freighters docked at the mainland side, and more anchored off Sand Island which protects the tiny harbor. I saw a windjammer, too, and a tour boat just heading out . . . probably on a run to the *Arizona* memorial in Pearl Harbor bay.

The ship had been going slower and slower.

Now it stopped dead in the water.

We were still short of the docks, between Sand Island and the tower—smack in the middle of the harbor, when the anchor chains clattered down through the hawse pipes and the anchors themselves hit the water with a crash.

My blood started running.

Something was going on. There was plenty of berth for the *Lao Shu* to dock. Why would we be laying off shore?

A man near me muttered to his companion. "Now that's odd. Why would we be anchored out here?"

"This happened to me once in the Caribbean," said the woman beside him. "It turned out to be a quarantine." She laughed. "Not feeling ill, are you, Terry?"

I was feeling ill. That monkey's fist had got a grip on my intestines again. I started moving forward, shoving bewildered passengers out of my way, and ignoring their cries of protest. The next thing I knew I was running as fast as I could run. I spotted Kayo near the accommodation ladder, whirled him around, and asked him if he knew what time it was.

He checked his wristwatch.

"Just four o'clock locally."

"It's ten o'clock Hong Kong time."

I turned and sprinted for the lobby.

Kayo took off after me. He was only a step behind when I hit the stairs but by the time I'd reached the Leo Deck he was losing ground fast. He could run like a deer, but I was the one wearing Nikes. And I was the one who knew.

I'd stormed into our cabin, turned Sung around, and had her scared half to death before Kayo came racing in.

"What's going on, Doily?"

"I've been an idiot!" I said without looking away from Sung. "Honey, I want you to go up to the Pisces deck. Near the lifeboats—no, no. please don't argue with me. That's not a negative interrogative, that's a positive imperative. Don't come back here and whatever you do, don't go below."

"Why, Doyle. Why?"

"This ship is gonna blow!"

I started for the door but Kayo grabbed my arm and he knows how to grab. He demanded an explanation. And I had one. But I didn't have time to give it.

"Come with me," I ordered him. "I'll explain on the way. Sung, get up top, now!"

Kayo and I ran back to the elevator.

"I've been an absolute fool. I should have figured it out days ago."

"Figured out what?"

"Why the *Yega* killed Captain Hsiao."

The cage opened, we entered, pushed the fourth button and started to descend.

"He's closing down the *de ha tit*," said Kayo. "He's killing everybody."

"The *de ha tit* is closed," I said. "He wants to make sure it doesn't start up again, that if it does, no Chinese will dare take it. He found those people in the holds just like we did. He knew they were going to be dumped into the sea just like we knew it. Killing the captain was the only way to stop it."

"If he wanted to save them, Doily, why would he blow up the ship now?"

"He doesn't want to save them—he wants to kill them. He knows Sha Han's down there and he'd kill them all to get Han. But he's got orders to kill them here instead of out in the Pacific because Beijing wants the world to witness the shocking truth. They're to die in such a way that every Chinese in Hong Kong will know that they died and who killed them. Even though no one will ever be able to prove it."

The elevator halted. We piled out and pushed open the watertight door leading aft to the engine room and the lower holds. The din of repair work was gone now, replaced by an even greater din of both engines idling. We took the ladder in bounds. At the bottom we ran right into another coolie standing in front of the panel. He'd jumped up as we came down the stairs and started toward us, drawing a pistol out of his belt. Mine was already out. I held it in such a way that the engine room crew couldn't see what I was doing and I spoke in a quiet voice. All the same, my Cantonese was basic and to the point. He dropped his weapon. I ordered him to open the panel. We led him inside the iron box and then through the watertight door.

Once inside I checked the first few cells. They were still occupied and the occupants were still alive. But only just. I'd been right that there wasn't room for them all to lie down at one time. They were doing it. But lying on top of one another in heaps. After a seven days with only water and rice rolls they looked pretty bad. But they were still alive.

Kayo wasted no time tying the coolie's hands and feet, Using the guy's belt and shirt torn into strips to make him a nice neat package. I told him to fetch the ring of keys and meet me inside. Then I raced into the second compartment to see that Wu Wing was still hanging on.

He saw me and fought to the window. His fat face made a smile though he was too weak and too wasted to utter a sound.

"We're at Honolulu," I told him, "but we think there's a bomb somewhere down—"

Kayo's footsteps slapped the steel deck.

"Let them out—hurry!" I told him.

His face was white.

"Doily! The keys . . . they're gone!"

"What?"

"Somebody's taken them, Doily. They're not in the desk where they were before. I checked the filing cabinet, too. They're gone."

I flung my head in circles.

"What do we do, Doily?" said Kayo.

"We've no choice. We'll have to find the bomb and try to defuse it."

We left Wu Wang's cell without another word to him and side by side headed toward the next compartment, sending our eyes along all the exposed surfaces of the passageway as we moved.

"How do we know it's down here?" asked Kayo.

"It'd have to be below the water line or close to it."

"How do we know there's not more than one?"

"I guess we don't." I was just starting to realize the hopelessness of our chore when we reached the third compartment door. It was standing wide open. When we were through I tried to close it behind us but the thing wouldn't close. Somebody had hammered the dogs out of true. I doubted even Kayo could force it shut. Even if he could it would never be watertight again. I passed Kayo up and ran to the forth compartment. It was the same story there.

"This cinches it, Kayo. All these people are supposed to drown. There aren't to be any survivors. He stole the keys after sabotaging these watertight doors—"

The rest of my words were lost when the first bomb exploded.

The explosion rolled down the corridor and hit us smack in the face. It was muffled by water and steel and because of this stopped just short of deafening. The shock of the explosion was transmitted wholly intact. The steel deck shuddered at our feet; it lurched to one side as though the *Lao Shu* had been struck bows on by another vessel.

We held onto the walls until they stopped shaking, then we ran forward as fast as we could. At the last compartment seawater came at us like a flash flood down a dry wash. We waded through rushing current to the last door knowing even before we reached it what we would find. This door too had been sabotaged. Nothing would stop the lower compartments from flooding. When that happened, nothing would stop the ship from going down.

Faces rose to the Judas windows around us.

We heard shrieks and gasps of surprise as water shipped under the cell doors. One after another the cells came to life. Cries for help, hundreds of them, filled every compartment.

Kayo and I were already racing back to the engine room.

In every compartment every cell we passed was a chamber of horror. Arms reached out through the judas holes, hands clutched at our clothes as we ran by. Fists banged against the steel walls. This, and the screams were a nightmarish racket.

"Kayo!" I caught up with him, grabbed a sleeve and pulled him around. "You've got to go topsides," I shouted. "Go to the forecastle and—"

He jerked free.

"Oh, no. I'm not leaving you. Or these people." As he spoke he ducked through the next doorway. "We've got to get some pipe cutters or torches and break into the cells."

A second explosion came just as I followed him into the first compartment. Seawater was sweeping us onward now. When I grabbed his legs and we went down it washed over our backs. This second bomb had holed the starboard bow. I could tell by the way the *Lau Shu* lurched in the opposite direction.

Kayo pulled me to my feet. We were both soaked. The water level was up to our knees and rising fast.

"You can't break through these locks in time," I said, gasping for breath. "Two cells, maybe three. But there's fifty cells down here."

"I'm not leaving, Doily."

So I socked him. My wild punch caught him on the chin. He fell back, vanished under the rolling waves for a moment and then stuck up his head for a breath. He was almost as shocked as I was. Yet as he climbed to his feet and towered above me I saw the shock going and a kind of fury taking its place. I was a kid playing with matches and Kayo was a keg of dynamite with a very short fuse.

But I was mad.

"Goddammit, Tuan. You know how things stand between us—you do the fighting and I do the thinking. These people have one chance. Just one small chance. And I haven't got the time to explain it. My job is down here. Yours is to raise the anchors. Find somebody who knows how. Or do it yourself. If you don't get those anchors raised, everybody down here drowns. Have you got that?"

I've never seen him look taller. His body was rigid. His hands were stiff at his sides, almost as though he were standing at attention.

"Yes sir," he said.

"Get going!"

We waded across the compartment to the engine room door, opened it up, hefted the bound coolie out and then stepped through ourselves. Seawater was shipping over the coaming as the door closed. Closing it on those faces, on those screams was the single hardest thing I ever did. But it had to be done. When looked around, Kayo was gone and a dozen of the engine room crew were staring at me with wild expressions.

I displayed my pistol.

"Okay," I said in my best Chinese and my most official tone, "in just about two minutes we're gonna see what these babies will do. My friend wants to go waterskiing."

"What were those explosions!"

One man, who spoke with authority, a crew chief or an engineer I suppose, had stepped forward.

"We're taking water in the forward holds," I told him. "Can you turn on the bilge pumps or whatever you call them."

The guy gave the order without looking away. A crewman ran to the control panel. Others yet began forming a body edging toward the ladderway.

"Hold it, boys." I confronted the chief. "Are you in charge here?"

In answer he shouted at me, "If we are hulled badly the pumps will not save us from sinking. We must abandon ship."

I shook my head.

"We're getting underway in another minute!"

He issued some more orders and his men moved uneasily, warily back to their stations.

We heard sirens from above. A klaxon kicked in right over my head. An intercom blared instructions which were too garbled for me to catch but most of the crewman caught it all right.

Their heads swung from one to each other; they traded fearful faces and profanities.

The ship was sinking. I could feel it. I was no sailor and had no feel for the sea but I knew the ship was sinking. Maybe it was just balance. Maybe the *Lao Shu* was listing. Or getting bows heavy.

Whatever it was, I knew—we were going down.

I'd give Kayo two minutes. We couldn't wait any longer than that. I didn't know how fast he could get to the forecastle. I didn't know what he'd find when he got there. The ship's crew would be getting busy getting paying passengers into the lifeboats and would look unfavorably on the suggestion that the ship weigh anchor. It would take someone glib like Kayo to convince them.

I counted off the seconds. One hundred twenty of them.

"Okay," I cried. "Full speed ahead."

A third bomb exploded right there in the engine room. It struck like a cucussive wall of sound . . . a tidal wave of pressure that blasted us all off our feet. I came up dazed, and dizzy, my eyes swimming in their sockets, and I knew at once and exactly where the thing had exploded. On the starboard hull, halfway between deck and deckhead, a horizontal column of seawater no less than a foot in diameter shot into the compartment. It so stunned me I wasted precious seconds watching it before realizing the engine room crew had fled.

I made a mad dash for the ladderway. The door above was the only place I could hope to hold them back. I'd lost the pistol in the explosion but I had no time to turn back. Several crewmen were only yards behind me. I bounded up the steps, reached the catwalk and whirled. They weren't even slowing down. I braced my hands across the rails and lashed out with a foot. One man fell back but three more took his place. They were in a frenzy. Someone grabbed my arm and I felt myself being pulled down. I swung with the other fist, kicked with both feet, and thrashed my body like a wild man but it was no use.

The next thing I knew I was on my back sliding head first from step to step while panicked crewmen trampled over me and each other trying to reach the top.

When my back came solidly against the steel plating of the lower deck I crawled out from under the last crewman and looked up in defeat at their exodus.

Except they weren't exiting. They were still trying, but they weren't going anywhere.

In a surge and struggle of human figures up the length of the ladder only one thing remained still. A huge steady form had planted itself at the top, like a mountain where a pass should have been.

It was Kayo. Kayo had come back.

I should have climbed up to help him. I should have grabbed two or three men near the bottom and pulled them back down. But I couldn't. I sat on my butt and watched him because I knew I would never see anything like it again.

They rushed him. All at once.

The mountain became a volcano. And the volcano erupted in their faces.

One man, arms and legs flailing, came flying back down, and landed hard behind me. I saw two others rise impossibly into the air, one in each of Kayo's big hands, and be hurled backward, over the catwalk only to plunge into the knee-deep water ten feet below. The rest of the crew just went crazy. Their combined weight crushed against Kayo. They pummeled him with blows. They clutched at his legs and tried to drag him down. They might have succeeded more easily uprooting a tree. Or moving a mountain.

One by one they fell to the engine room deck until only a half dozen were left and those backed down the ladderway in terror before an advancing Kayo Tuan.

By the time Kayo reached the lower levels I had dragged the crewchief between the two engines and repeated my order. "Full speed ahead." He and his men were in no condition to argue.

I left Kayo in charge, recovered my pistol, and climbed back to the catwalk, crossed to the platform and activated the hydraulic controls for the port loading door.

When this door came open I could see smoke coming from the superstructure and pouring over the side of the ship and I knew that incendiaries had been planted topsides. For a while the purpose of this mystified me. It wasn't until I saw the fleet of fireboats hanging back that I realized the flames would keep anyone from coming close to the *Lau Shu* until it was far, far too late. It was far too late now.

The ship moved sluggishly forward.

By sticking my head out the side I was able to navigate within about twenty degrees of directly ahead. Good enough. Sand Island was right off to the south. All I had to do was guide the ship along its concrete banks shouting corrections in heading to Kayo and the engineer below. The whole harbor had been dredged; there was nothing to run into except other ships. What used to be beaches were now quayside and wharfs and the channel continued like that all the way around the island and back out into the sea.

If we turned back to the sea.

I had no intention of turning back out to sea.

Some of the fireboats had begun blowing their horns. Caught unaware by our departure they were tagging along behind now with their powerful streams of seawater falling short of our stern. A man stood on the bow of the nearest boat frantically signaling me with a pair of white flags.

When the island and the harbor doglegged to the left I leaned over the platform rail and called to Kayo, port thirty degrees. "And tell the engineer I want every damn horsepower those engines have got."

He and the crewmen were standing in two feet of water which still poured through the gash in the hull. Incoming water and those giant engines were making a hell of a noise.

By the time I got back to my position the faster, more maneuverable fireboat had pulled alongside the open freight door. The guy with the flags was using a bullhorn now but I couldn't hear a word he was saying and I couldn't care less.

We passed under a bridge. Sand Island ended abruptly and so did the harbor. The channel continued left or right. Right to more harbor which was hidden from me; left, to the sea. Dead ahead was the Reef Runway. I couldn't see coral shallows around it but they had to be there . . . just beyond the warning buoys. We were making good speed now. But it couldn't last, not as fast as we were taking on water.

We crossed over the channel. The sea color went from deep green to light green and finally to white in a matter of seconds. I could make out the coral formations beneath our keel. The bottom was coming up fast.

I threw my head inside and yelled for everyone to brace himself. But my warning came too late to do any good. They couldn't have heard me anyway. No sooner had the words left my mouth than the most awful wrenching and tearing of steel sliced through the ship. The deck shook as it had in each of the explosions. Every riveted plate in the hull shrieked with agony. It ended. And then it came again even louder, even more violently than before. I felt the bows lift a bit off the sea. Suddenly, everything stopped.

Kayo was running up the ladder. Across the catwalk and along the platform to where I stood.

I never saw such a smile.

I was smiling too.

"Good work, Tuan!" I told him.

"Yeah!" he replied. And then, putting a hurt look on his face. "Please, Doily, call me Kayo." He stuck out his big mitt.

I shook it.

I said, "Call me sir."

15. No Way to Win

Kayo and I found Sung beneath the Aloha Tower.

It was a madhouse. Harbor ferries were bringing crew and passengers to the dock as fast as they could pull them off the beached cruise liner. Medical people were treating the few that needed it, mostly Chinese who'd swallowed too much water. Fire investigators were taking statements while Customs tried to sort illegal aliens from passported passengers. Nobody had papers. Baggage wouldn't come off the ship until all the people were safe.

The three of us held a quick conference. We changed our plans about going to the nearest police station without even bothering to telephone ahead. We decide to go to the nearest United States Attorney's office...without bothering to telephone ahead. While the security people were holding back a crowd of press and public, and the Coast Guard was coordinating the rescue operation, while the harbor police were trying to round up the ship's officers and while immigration officials had their backs turned, Kayo and I used our press passes to slip into the media crowd.

We flagged a passing taxicab, told the driver: "Federal Building," and settled back for the ride. Myself, I could've felt a lot worse, We were still alive. We'd saved the IE's on the *Lao Shu.* And we were back in the United States where there are no such things as shamans or ***Yegas*** or nowhere men.

Ironically, we were to have more trouble getting to the U.S. Attorney than to anyone else we'd seen since taking on the assignment. The two security officers in the lobby of the federal building were the first hurdle. They gave us a good going over before we'd done more than walk through the door.

Routine, they told us. Even at the time it seemed to me unnecessarily thorough.

I pulled the pistol out of my belt and set it on their counter. Then I voluntarily turned out my pockets. Everything I owned made up a pile about six inches in diameter. Kayo was doing the same things beside me. "Better keep the girl's purse, too," I suggested. "I understand she carries a small bomb factory around in it."

One officer, who was examining my gun, glared at me and growled that they didn't appreciate jokes about bombs.

Fine, I muttered to myself, so drop dead!

Sung came closer. "What's this, Doyle?"

She reached over, plucked the jade ring out of my pile.

"Oh, that? It's nothing, a trinket. If you like it, Sung, you can keep it." I didn't get a chance to enjoy her reply.

The security guard was still glaring at me.

"Sir, do you have a license to carry a concealed weapon?"

"No, I couldn't get one," I said.

"Why not?"

"The gun's stolen." I was smiling as I said it but I'd forgotten that he didn't have a sense of humor.

"Let me see some identification."

I reached for the wallet. “All I have is Hong Kong ID, Hong Kong driver’s license, and my press pass.”

“Are you an American citizen?”

“Oh sure. But I’ve been out of the country for several years.”

“What about these two?”

“He’s from Hong Kong. She’s Thai.”

“Where are their passports?”

“They don’t have any. But don’t worry about it. It’s okay. I’ll vouch for them.”

“All right, all three of you step behind the counter—no, keep your hands where I can see’em.”

Yes, it was good to be back.

Eventually they sent us upstairs with an escort. He led us down a long hallway on the third floor and introduced us to the second hurdle, a glacial receptionist. I told her we wanted to see the U.S. attorney. She couldn’t believe it. “Mr. Brian Thatcher himself?” she said, drawing herself up. I told her it was extremely important, every second counted and, by golly, forty minutes later we got to meet Thatcher’s secretary, herself. After chewing the fat with her for ten minutes but trading no real meat we were taken to Thatcher’s assistant, himself. He showed us to an inner waiting room. He advised us to hang on. A plain-clothes cop and former linebacker came in and relieved the rent-a-cop to return to the lobby. I’d had my eye on a couple of the ashtrays but gave up the idea after seeing how security had been beefed up. Finally the assistant himself returned. He told us that if Kayo and Sung would be good enough to remain I’d get to have five minutes with the U.S. Attorney. Brian Thatcher. Himself.

I guess most lawyers working in the Justice Department think they’d look good in the Attorney General’s office and Brian Thatcher himself was probably no different. Though I hate to admit it, he probably would have. He certainly did look good sitting there in his own office—tall, dark hair combed back, neither too thin nor too heavy, neither too old nor too young. Wearing a conservative three-piece suit, he had it all over me in appearance.

"What's this about illegal Chinese aliens and murder, Mr. …?"

"Mulligan."

"Yes." He glanced at a slip of appointment paper, "Mulligan." Thatcher waved me to a chair across from him.

"I could tell it in five minutes," I said sitting, "but I won't, I'll just tell it. When five minutes comes you stop me if you care to." And that's what I did. An hour later I was still talking.

I told him there was a cruise ship outside the harbor, on the reefs of the international airport. He'd heard about it on a radio broadcast. I explained that there were about a hundred and fifty regular passengers aboard, about fory-five or fifty crewmen and staff, and one homicidal maniac. The announcement got no reaction. None at all. He must have figured I'd escaped from a cracker factory. "This maniac," he asked, "did he run the ship onto the reefs?" I told him, No, I did. He tried to sink it. Still no reaction.

"Why did he do that, Mr. Mulligan?'

"Because there are also about a thousand Chinese in the lower holds being smuggled into the United States." That got a reaction. "Call up the harbor master if you don't believe me. The Coast Guard should have most of them out by now."

Thatcher talked with his secretary and arranged for the call to be placed.

While we waited I explained what Kayo and I had done and why. Not until the Coast Guard had taken us off along with the other members of the engine room crew could we see the bows high on the coral reef and the two ruptures at the waterline, now just out of the water. Fortunately, the tide was going out. We'd gotten lucky there but it was our turn. I'd informed the Coast Guard captain about the aliens in the lower holds and he ordered some of his men to get cracking with bolt cutters. In the cells farthest aft, they'd found chestdeep water and adults holding children on their shoulders. It could've been worse—the engine room was flooded completely.

When the call came through, Brian Thatcher did a little talking and a lot of listening. He hung up prepared to listen some more.

"One of the Chinese on the *Lao Shu* is a guy by the name of Ping Sha Han," I said and gave him what little I knew of Han's appearance. "He'll be carrying a videocassette case; he won't let it go or set it down. Sha Han and the contents of his case are behind this whole mess."

"He's the maniac you were telling me about?"

"No. He's the target."

'You mean somebody tried to sink a ship just to get one man?"

"He would have. He practically burned Hong Kong to the ground just to keep Sha Han from getting our of town. Killing all the people on board wouldn't have bothered him any." I impressed on Thatcher how important it was that he put Sha Han in protective custody at once."

He made another phone call.

"Okay," he said when he'd hung up again. "I've gone that far on faith. Now I want the whole story, Mulligan."

I dumped it all in his lap.

I explained about the reversion of Hong Kong to China in 1997; how one man, billionaire acupuncturist Lee Chung, had assailed the sell-out and urged the people of Hong Knog to flee. I talked about Tiananmen Square. I told him kow Sha Han had sneaked out of Beijing with videotaped evidence of what had really happened that day. Four years later Lee Chung sneaked Sha Han into Hong Kong. Then I described how the massacre had already triggered an underground exodus of middle-class Chinese from Hong Kong, and how the communists, anxious to seal up the city before the money and management force had all gone, demanded the Sino-British conference to speed up their control at the ports. This was why Lee had arranged for Sha Han to escape: so he could testify at the conference. Lee had to stop the Reds from taking control. Because he was doing more than advising Chinese to get out. He was selling them tickets. He was dumping their bodies in the Pacific Ocean and taking all the cash and liquid assets they'd brought with them. And he was getting richer every day.

By the time I'd gone that far Thatcher got a call from one of his men who let him know Sha Han had been taken into custody. Thatcher told me he was being held under guard at an undisclosed location. When I asked him to disclose the location he said it was a safehouse.

"There ain't no such place," I replied.

"What do you mean?"

"What Lee Chung didn't know when he arranged for Sha Han to come to Hong Kong was that Beijing had already turned loose a killer to find him, a Chinese enforcer called the ***Yega***, bar none the most perfectly adapted killing machine that the world will ever produce. I know where he comes from," I said, "how he came to be what he is, and to some extent how he does what he does. But I've never had more than glimpse of him. I don't know of anyone who has and lived. I can almost tell you who and where he'll strike next based on my record of stumbling over his victims a matter of moments after he's diposed of them. But there's no chance anyone will ever stop him."

I gave the attorney a summary of what I'd learned from Master Wang in Kowloon, from Superintendent Maldonado in Macao, and from Ben Kao. I related everything I could recall of the ***Yega's*** capabilities. "This guy is uncanny," I told him. "I'd say he has to be seen to be believed but it doesn't come to that. You don't see him, you just believe him. He killed Lee Chung by cremating him alive. He found a ticket office on the underground railway that Sha Han had gone to and blew the conductor out the side of a DC-10 at 30,000 feet."

Thatcher had heard about that incident and recalled the photograph I'd taken. His shrewd eyes gazed at me with a wary respect. I told him about the Pings and the Pekingese, neither murder would I have supposed made the American papers but, in fact, both had. ENA had made a routine release on the four deaths aboard the jetfoil and the apparent suicides at Aberdeen and because of the eerie nature of the deaths they'd been picked up by many papers in this country. Thatcher was more than a little surprised that they were all tied together and that I had been involved in each one.

"You seem almost obsessed with this killer of yours…this nowhere man," he said. "You realize that my concern lies with illegal immigration into Hawaii and murder on the high seas. We'll put out an alert at once for the other ships in the Zodiac Line. To see that no more immigrants, illegal or not, are murdered."

I thanked him.

"As for this ***Yega***, I'll have HPD issue an island-wide bulletin for him. I can't imagine he can stay out of sight very long. They'll probably pick him up in a day or two trying to catch a flight back to Beijing."

I made a mental note right then and there to check back with Brian Thatcher in a few weeks. I was out of it now; he was in. If he'd picked up my faceless friend and in doing so became attorney general, good for him. But I would have given odds that all he'd accomplish in either direction would be to improve his imagination.

While I was thinking this over Thatcher's assistant had come in and stepped to his boss's desk. He leaned over and whispered in his boss's ear. Thatcher's face darkened.

I thought maybe his calendar was backing up. But I was wrong.

"We've had another bomb threat, Mr. Mulligan," Thatcher told me. "We're going to have to evacuate the building. No doubt it's a hoax like the others. A prank. But we have to go through the motions. With our security it's unimaginable that a bomb could be gotten into the building."

I stood up.

Every ounce of blood had drained from my body. But for some unexplainable reason my heart went on pumping. I could hear its useless pounding echo through my empty arteries. So this was the feeling. *The doctor solemnly approaches... "I'm afraid I have some bad news. You'd better sit down."* I sat down again. *The judge looks down from his bench... "The defendant will rise."* I stood up again. "*We the jury find Doyle Mulligan guilty of stupidity in the first degree.*"

"He's here," I said. "He's here now."

"Who...?"

Both men were glaring at me.

"The ***Yega***. He's followed me here."

The lawyer smiled a superior smile. "Don't worry, Mr. Mulligan," he said, "Not here. I can say that with every assurance because we had a couple of bomb threats a week or so ago and have taken precautions in the lobby downstairs. Our security is very tight. It's just some fruitcake out for a little free publicity. Scaring people appeals to his sense of humor, that's all. Your nowhere man won't stalk you here."

I barked suddenly, nervously.

It may have sounded like laughter, it wasn't.

"I don't know who made the other calls," I said, "And I don't care. I know who made this one. He doesn't need publicity and he has no sense of humor. Also he doesn't scare people—he kills them."

"But the security—"

"Forget it! If you'd surrounded the building with the Hawaiian National Guard he could have walked right through them. Your two rent-a-cops? Ha! Thatcher, you're about to get your imagination broadened."

My mind was whirling. Why had he followed me here? And why the warning call? To make us run?

Thatcher's aide was getting antsy.

"Sir, we only have a matter of minutes before this bomb is supposed to blow.: He was almost tugging at the lawyer's sleeve.

I left. People were funneling into the stairwells and lining up at the elevator. I raced up a hallway to the room where Sung and Kayo were waiting.

The sounds of restrained pandemonium died once I left the main corridor. By the time I reached the waiting room and had my hand on the doorknob, I became aware of the most frightful silence. I swung back the door.

I stepped in.

For an awful moment I just stood there.

The linebacker was balled up and packed in a corner. He had an expression of agony on his face that left little doubt as to the kind of punishment he had suffered.

Kayo was there too, stretched out on the floor in the center of the room. By contrast he was a picture of repose, lying on his back with his arms slightly away from his sides and his legs slightly apart. He looked as though he'd decided to take a short nap. But he wasn't asleep. Having spent four nights with him in a small cabin I knew he didn't sleep with his eyes wide open. He was gone. But his eyes were open.

It was different with Sung.

Sung was just gone.

I dropped to my knees beside Kayo. His stiff, lifeless body looked even bigger down than up. I heard voices behind me. Thatcher and his assistant. The two of them must have followed me in. I was too busy exploring Kayo's huge frame for wounds to bother with what they were saying.

Then one of them said clearly, "He's dead, sir."

Thatcher's assistant was still leaning over Armstrong. Thatcher was crossing over to me.

I grew frantic. I had to do something fast, find something fast before they pronounced Kayo dead, too.

But he was unbloodied. Unmarked. Outwardly unharmed. I looked at his face. Kayo's eyes, no longer trained dully at the ceiling, were staring sideways at me.

"My God, Kayo! You're alive!" I turned to Thatcher. "He's alive."

He was conscious. And yet he couldn't utter a sound; he couldn't even move his lips.

Three more plainclothes officers of Armstrong's bulk rushed into the waiting room and ordered us to evacuate at once. I stood up. One of the officers spotted Thatcher. "Just three minutes, sir. You've got to leave now."

Thatcher agreed. "All right. Mulligan, let's move."

I nodded dumbly. "Leave Armstrong for now," Thatcher snapped. "You three, bring this man, too. You'll have to carry him. He's been knocked out. Hurry."

Everyone heaved to. One of them headed for Kayo's legs and the two others took up positions at his arms. I watched them start to lift him up. I saw Kayo's eyes turned to me. He was helpless to assist them, powerless to stop them. And I saw in my mind another body in that same position while a sanguine son of a bitch standing over him, cold-bloodedly prepared a thermite explosive and laid it on his chest."

A voice was there, too "…the first person to come by and help him to his feet would have finished him off…"

"Noooo!!"

All three men froze. I rushed toward them and stopped; my words continued headlong, running together in a frantic race against reason. "You can't move him!" I cried. "Don't even touch him. I just realized why the phone call. That was the thing I couldn't figure. It was a prank after all."

"You're saying there's no bomb?"

It came from behind me. Thatcher must have stopped on his way to the door.

"I don't know. Or care. But we can't move him until an ambulance and a stretcher get here."

"Why? What are you talking about?"

"Dammit, his back is broken!"

Precious seconds passed in silence.

The lawyer's assistant had grabbed his boss by the arm. "Only two minutes, sir!" His words contained not a note but a symphony of urgency.

Thatcher tried staring me down. "You can't possibly know that. You're just guessing."

"No. I know it. You'll just have to take my word for it. The rest of you can go. I'll stay with him."

It was time for a quick decision. Five pairs of eyes turned to Thatcher to see if he was the man for making one. He was. It was the wrong decision, but he made it quickly. "Bring them both downstairs at once," he said. "If Mulligan resists, wrap him up. Come on, Denny." With that, the two men flew down the hall.

I whirled. For a moment, none of them moved. Then the necessity for haste became overwhelming and the trio bent at once to Kayo's body.

With a wild cry I was on them. My low dive hit the two at Kayo's head at waist level and all three of us went down together. We landed in a pile on the other side of his body. I whirled to face the third guy who was coming in behind me. I dodged, watched him go by and when the other two had found their feet, danced to a far corner of the room.

Any one of them could have beaten me. But their orders weren't to beat me. Their orders were to kill Kayo, though they didn't know it.

I didn't have a prayer of overpowering them.

I didn't have to. Time was on my side.

"How many seconds are left?" I taunted them.

One stood his ground. Each of the other two came at me from a side. I backed against the wall, let them come close and then sprang onto a chair, catapulted myself into the air and hit the floor rolling.

I slipped one guy's grip. Another was on me.

"I've got him. You two grab the Chinaman."

He'd bearhugged me from behind. My arms were trapped at my side. Seeing the other two reaching for Kayo got my blood running. I spun, caught the poor G-man with my knee where a knee hurts most. He doubled over and stuck out his jaw. A blind man couldn't have missed it. My haymaker had waited years to find daylight. Suddenly the sun was shining and I made hay. His head slammed back. His body went cartwheeling into a wall.

I turned with my dukes dancing.

The two officers stared at me with twin expressions of disbelief.

"Now how many seconds?" I shouted.

They charged. Again we all went down but when we came up this time they each had one of my arms. We were like that when the first explosion rocked the building.

To me it sounded as though the blast had come from just outside the door or directly down the hall but apparently it hadn't. The effect was nothing like the one in the captain's cabin on the *Lao Shu*. That had been a shattering sort of blast. This one heaved. We felt the floor shudder. Parts of the ceiling began raining down.

The roar was followed by the din of metal, glass and masonry succumbing to destruction—it was a hellish racket. But in a matter of moments it ended.

I breathed. So did the two federal officers.

We exchanged glances.

Then came the second explosion. It was louder than the first and, judging by the sound of it, even more destructive. A wave of superheated air pushed into the room which had already begun shaking so violently it was all we could do to stay on our feet.

One of the officers hot-footed it for the door. Another followed at once and then the third picked himself up and he was gone too.

Something hard struck me on the shoulder. That brought me to my senses. I leaped over to Kayo. He hadn't budged an inch during the brawl. His face was salted with ceiling plaster. Larger pieces of material were beginning to fall.

There came a third explosion. And a fourth.

I crouched over his chest with my knees to each side of him, my forearms at his shoulders. My face was close enough to his that we could have rubbed noses. But all we did was stare into each other's eyes throughout the ordeal. I'm told there were eight explosions altogether. I only remember six.

If there was one particular blow from one particular explosion that did it to me I don't recall it. I lost count of the blows. After an eternity I felt hands pulling at my body, lifting me up.

I struggled to resist.

Kayo's arms and legs were nearly buried in dry debris of every size and they were bleeding badly.

When I saw them digging him out I mumbled, "Be careful with him. His back is broken." But they already knew that. A stretcher was set on the ground beside him and he was laid on it with special care.

My mind floated away.

It should have stayed away. Instead it came back that very afternoon to visit me in the hospital. I was lying on my stomach. A nurse was adjusting some plastic bags on a rack beside my bed. Clear fluid drained from them into a tube connected to my forearm.

I asked how K'o Tuan was doing'

She didn't know. The doctor who came later didn't know either but he promised to find out and he was as good as his word. Kayo, he informed me, was still undergoing tests; his condition was listed as critical but currently stable. That made me feel a little better until I thought about the other person I'd left in that room.

Later the same evening Brian Thatcher himself paid me a visit. He asked the nurse to leave us alone as he entered, then came beside the bed where my head was facing and spent some time looking over the battlefield below my neck with an expression of genuine sympathy.

"How's the back doing?" he asked me.

"Improving. How about your imagination?"

He chuckled.

"It's improving, too." He said, but he wasn't amused.

He lay a dark bag on the tray beside my bed.

"That's Sung's purse."

"Yes. We found it in the waiting room. Identified it by its contents. What we don't understand is how she got this through security." He opened the purse and extracted an automatic pistol.

"She didn't. That's my gun, Thatcher. Just another prank by a man I didn't think could possibly possess a sense of humor. Both the purse and the pistol were left with your security staff in the lobby. You've talked to them, surely. Don't they remember that?"

"Yeah. Yeah, they remember." The lawyer cleared his throat. "See here, Mulligan, you can understand that we're on this thing now, thanks to you. It seems you brought us more than just some information. You brought us a one-man terrorist organization, too. Okay, so now we're after your assassin, this ***Yega***. We want all you've got and I know you've got more than you've told."

I said, "I want to know if you've found Sung's…if you've found her."

"Not yet. We've put out an all-island-bulletin with the State Police. She'll show up. We have the airports and the terminals watched. Where can he take her? But we can't waste any time. I've got a stenographer waiting in the hall to take your statement."

"Find Sung. Then I'll talk. Have you got anything at all?"

"I've got a federal building," Thatcher said, "that's been virtually demolished. The third floor is completely gutted. From the elevators all the way back to my office. I've got employees suffering from shock and one murdered federal officer. Ben Armstrong."

"Do they know what killed him?"

"No. The pathologists are examining him. Initially they couldn't even hazard a guess. They still don't know, but they're guessing."

It must have been the fluid going into my arm. Did they refrigerate the damn stuff? How else could I explain the chill I was feeling? Of course, I had Armstrong on my conscience now in addition to all the others. And there was Kayo. I couldn't ever…no, not Kayo. But worst of all was Sung. I didn't know how much I loved her until she was gone. She had reached in and clutched my soul. When she left she'd taken it with her. And I was cold.

So perhaps it wasn't the clear fluid in my arm. I was too Emotionally destroyed to think clearly but some things were coming together.

"Well, I can guess," I told him. "In a way that was part of the prank. You see, he was poisoned…when somebody touched him. Armstrong had nothing apparently wrong with him, and yet he was dead. Kayo had a potentially fatal injury to his spine but he was alive. Don't you get it? I don't know if the ***Yega*** knew about the previous bomb threats, but I don't doubt he made this last one. And he planted the bombs. The idea was to scare us into moving Kayo to safety, and in the process of moving him, causing the final damage that would kill him. Then the real laugh would come when the bombs would literally wipe out much of the entire floor of the building but spare those of us in the waiting room. Kayo was to have died by our hands and not until later were we to have known that only by leaving him exactly where he was could he have survived."

"Why kidnap the girl?"

"To stop me from talking. He has distinctive style. He knew I'd recognize it and know he has Sung. He thinks I won't do any talking until we get her back. And you know something? He's right!"

Thatcher hung around for nearly another half an hour trying to get me to change my mind. Finally he picked up the purse and gun and readied to leave. But he paussed at the door, turned, and cocked his head to ask me:

"Then why didn't this guy just kill you?"

He didn't wait for an answer. He'd have had to wait a long time.

I didn't see him again until the next morning.

This time I was the guy standing at the bedside and Kayo was wearing the smock. He didn't look very good but then having one's spine broken in two places is a hard one to bounce back from. He was supine and strapped down so he couldn't have moved even if he'd been able to and my understanding is that he wouldn't have been able. He could shift his eyes around and work his lips a little but everything else was out of the question.

Our meeting probably did more good for me than for him. At least until Thatcher made his appearance. I thanked the lawyer for the two armed guards he'd assigned to Kayo's door but secretly I didn't think they were worth the taxpayers' money. Only one man wished Kayo harm and those two guards wouldn't stop him. Nothing would every stop him.

Thatcher accepted my remarks stone-faced.

Then he reached out. A small object was pinched between his thumb and forefinger. Slowly my hand extended until it was just under his and only then did the jade ring drop into my palm.

A chill flushed through me.

"Where...where did you find her?"

"We didn't exactly find her." He went to the one chair in the room and dropped down. "We believe she may have been seen in Hong Kong."

"You mean she's alive? She's alive in Hong Kong?"

"We don't really know?"

I was sorry there was no other chair.

"That ring and a message to you came in this morning on the red-eye flight from Hong Kong. Your office has received word—in what, I understand, was a most mysterious fashion—that the girl will be exchanged...." Thatcher shifted in his chair. "For Ping Sha Han and the videotapes. You're instructed to arrange it. If you can't get Sha Han to the exchange site on time you're to be there yourself. With the videotapes. One of you with the tapes. Otherwise, the girl dies."

The most frigid of waves surged over me. I couldn't move. I couldn't speak. What do they call it when things get so cold that no heat exists. When movement, even atomic activity ceases? Absolute zero? I shivered. I'd thought I had it bad before but until that moment I didn't even know what cold was.

16. No Way to Live

Victoria Peak loomed gray and ghostly over Hong Kong. Hovering there, shrouded in a cape of morning mist that was giving everything above the skyline a static drenching, the Peak looked like a Chinese Asgard or even a Mount Oylmpus, one that had been abandoned by the gods and taken over by ghouls.

The residents of the Peak were used to dawn drizzles like this one. It didn't dampen their spirits the way it did mine. I felt like the gods had abandoned me, too. The headlights of Kayo's little Subaru barely kept the gloom at bay by boring a narrow tunnel of visibility up the winding Magazine Gap Road.

* * *

I now had the answer to Thatcher's question. About why the ***Yega*** hadn't killed me. He wanted more than my silence. He wanted the tapes. And he wanted Sha Han although I wasn't convinved at this point that he didn't want me even more. I'd ruined his big plans with the Lao Shu. I'd saved the Chinese in the holds. On top of that I knew more about him and what he'd done in the last few days than any man alive. Oh, he wanted me dead, all right. But he realized that as long as he had Sung, I'd stop at nothing to see that either Sha Han or I showed up at the exchange with the tapes.

He was right about that.

I went to the safehouse to talk to Sha Han. After all the searching, Sung's cousin turned out to be a big disappointment. He was some taller than Sung but not much; heavier than her but not much. A skinny guy with a gaunt face and big eyes set deep in their sockets; he was not much in the way of a savior for Hong Kong. If anyone had asked what I thought of him I'd have said just that: not much. The most impressive thing about him was the black leather carrying bag under his arm. He never let go of it. He never set it down.

"Are those the tapes?" I asked.

His head dipped. His eyes never left mine.

"Has anyone seen them? Besides you."

His head moved back and forth. Once each direction.

I said: "We need to make some copies. In case anything happens to these originals."

"No. The value of these tapes is that they're the only ones in existence. No copies."

"The value of these tapes," I said slowly and clearly, "is that they can prove to the world what Beijing did."

"I don't care about the world," he replied.

"You don't?"

"No. I only care about me."

I found myself shaking my head in disbelief. But however much as I objected to his attitude it did answer another question: how the Yega could feel certain we wouldn't show up with duplicates. That was the answer. Sha Han wouldn't allow anyone to copy the tapes. And before I could come up with an argument he had his rebuttal.

"These tapes are mine," he told me with feeling, "they're all I've got left."

He was almost right. He was playing a high-stakes game with bad cards and bad luck and only one chip left to ante, the tapes.

"Not quite, buster. What about Sung?"

"Sung? She's here?"

"No. She was. She came here to help you. But she got burned in your place."

His eyes grew huge.

He didn't do it like Sung did it though. In fact, if I hadn't known they were cousins I wouldn't have believed they had any genes in common. I'll admit I was prejudiced. I liked the way Sung had stuck by her people in Bangkok even though she had the money to get out. I didn't like the way Han had stayed communist as long as it meant a free college degree and then run straight to the capital of Chinese capitalism to cash in.

"What are you talking about?" he hissed.

"You know what I'm talking about. What you told your mother about that made her run away. What you must have let slip to Huang Mu and Chang Li that made them try to get away too. But they didn't get away. None of them. Not Huang or Chang or even Lee Chung. Or your mother either. Don't kid me, you know what I'm talking about. You wear the ***Yega*** on your face like a death mask.

Hearing about his mother didn't faze him.

Hearing about the ***Yega*** did.

Sha Han made a noise in his throat.

"The…! He's….he's here."

"He was here. He grabbed Sung and went back to Hong Kong. The British government wants you back there to tell the conference what you know. The ***Yega*** has ordered me to take you back so he can trade you and these tapes for Sung."

"It's suicide. I'm not going back. Not to testify. Not for anything."

"He'll kill Sung if we don't go back."

"You're just thinking about her. What about me? He'll kill her anyway. Nothing can save her."

"She's your cousin," I said.

"I'm not going back."

But he was going back. He was an illegal immigrant. All the Chinese in the holds of the Lao Shu were going back. As citizens of Hong Kong they could hardly claim a refugee status. Sha Han's case was different. He could. He'd fled from China because of the Tiananmen Square incident and a death sentence waited for him if he went back. However once Thatcher got on the horn to Washington and Washinton had conferred with London it was decided that Han should also be deported to Hong Kong where he was a material witness in the murders of nine people. The Hong Kong government would have to decide what to do with him.

We'd flown back to Hong Kong together in the company of four armed sky marshals. They'd commandeered the first class section of a United flight, bumped the other passengers into coach, surrounded Han and me and kept their guns handy throughout the flight.

A battalion of Gurkhas met us at Kai Tak and escorted us to a blockhouse inside a garrison near Government House.

* * *

I wrapped the Subaru's four tiny cylinders all the way up until, screaming, it topped the last rise of the Magazine Gap. Then I followed Peak Road and wound into the open book formation which separated the mountain's two summits. I was heading for the Victoria Peak Garden. It was there on the westernmost summit and the higher of the two that Sung and I had walked hand in hand while I told her my big plans for finding her cousin. From the garden we'd watched the hundred fires light up the city and ruin my plans. Today there was the mist. The residents of the

Peak, the godly and ungodly alike, had fled. And I'd come back to give my big plan one last chance.

"Don't be an idiot," Stringer had implored me. "What can you hope to accomplish besides getting yourself killed? Let the police handle it."

"And what will happen to Sung when Sha Han doesn't show?"

"The same thing that will happen to her if he does show. Doyle, be reasonable; your girlfriend is probably dead now. If she's not, nothing you or Sha Han do can save her. I'm sorry to say that. It sounds harsh. But it's true."

"You said Ben saw her. She talked to him."

Stringer waved it away.

"It was crazy! He swears the girl came to the office. During hours for Christ's sake! His door was closed but he looked up and there she was standing in front of his desk. Told him to have Sha Han return here from Honolulu without giving the authorities there any more information and to await further word about a time and place for an exchange. The tapes in exchange for her. Then she disappeared. No smoke, no cape, not even a magic hat. She just vanished. According to Ben. We would have thought he'd been napping but you know Ben, he never naps. Anyway, after the girl left he found that jade ring on his desk. We sent it and the message to Honolulu on the first flight."

"Where's Ben now?"

"Gone. He didn't tell us where he was going or when he'd be back. He had several days leave coming and he took it. I couldn't stop him. He was scared, Doyle. He said you'd understand. And then he practically ran out of here. Can you believe that?"

"Yeah."

"But I mean his running out?"

"I'm glad he made it out, that's all. The Yega could just as easily have written the message in Ben's blood."

"Goddammit, Doyle, you're starting to sound like Ben."

I shook my head. "No, no. I know more about this guy now than Ben does. However scared you might think Ben Kao is, multiply it by ten and you've got Doyle Mulligan. But I'm not quitting until I've got Sung back."

Stringer threw up his hands. "Ben was hallucinating. We don't even know the girl's on the island and we certainly don't have any reason to believe she's alive. The only way they could've made it back to Hong Kong so fast is to fly. How in the world could your have gotten an unwilling or unconscious girl through the Honolulu Airport, onto an airplane and then off again without anyone knowing. Hell, they didn't even purchase a ticket. We've checked. And no one answering their description went through customs at Kai Tak. Nobody's capable of that."

"He is."

"If that's true then my advice is even more imperative. Go to the police!"

* * *

The tortuous Peak Road dipped and climbed through the open book formation past equally twisting lanes heading up or down the hill. The road neither gains nor loses much altitude from one end to the other but that utterly fails to describe the roller coaster route it takes to get there. When my headlights found the upper tram station hiding in the mist I knew the garden lay just beyond. The station was empty. As empty as the streets. I hadn't passed a single vehicle since topping the peak or seen a living soul.

* * *

As soon as I could get to a phone after leaving Stringer I'd called Superintendent of Police Maldonado in Macao.

"Mulligan?" he said. "How did you know I was trying to reach you?" His quack of a voice was even harder to believe over the telephone.

"I didn't," I said. "I need to talk to you."

"Don't bother going into it. I already know. I took a message for you two hours ago and was told to get in touch with you—"

"Who gave you the message?"

"Just listen. The girl, Sung what's-her-name, will be at the Victoria Peak Garden at first light tomorrow inside the pagoda midway along the Governor's Walk. Sha Han or you are to go there, alone, with the videotapes. If nobody shows up, the girl dies. If anyone other than you or Sha Han shows, the girl dies. That's the message."

"But who? How did—"

"You know who it was. The gentleman whose extra-ordinary talents we discussed."

"You mean he phoned...?"

"No, he came to the police station. Walked right into my office disguised as a policeman. I managed to set off an alarm when he left and as a result, four of my best men are dead."

My hopes evaporated. I'd thought that Maldonado might be able to help me. I'd thought he would want to. And I'd believed, because he wasn't from Hong Kong, that he was one cop who could help me without the ***Yega*** finding out about it. I was wrong. The ***Yega*** knew about my talk with Maldonado and he'd taken this way to tell me that he knew. He knew I'd go to Maldonado for help and this was his way of seeing that I wouldn't get it. There didn't seem to be any point in going on but for Sung's sake I had to try. "Donado," I said with urgency, "I need your help."

"I'm sorry, Mulligan."

"You're a policeman, aren't you?"

"For another four months. Then I retire and go back to Lisbon. Look, Mulligan. I've got nothing against you. I'd like to help."

"You said you were tired of looking over your shoulder, didn't you?"

"It's better than being dead."

* * *

A funereal gloom had settled over the garden. It was a gray damp gloom like the mist but more so. My headlights could cut through the mist. The gloom was impenetrable. The windshield wipers would burp if I left them on for more than a few seconds at a time. No amount of wiping could clear the gloom. It was as much a part of the peak as the air itslf.

I shut down the engine in the garden parking lot.

The gloom was a musty thing, too.

The staleness of it struck me as I climbed from the car and started along the gravel walk. I'd gone only a few feet before looking back. The Subaru was gone, vanished behind a gray curtain. But I knew it was still there. I was the one who'd disappeared.

The gloom—gray, damp and stinking of must—had swallowed me up.

* * *

After three years in Hong Kong I thought I new someone I could go to for almost any problem. But after talking with Maldonado I considered my short list of friends and acquaintances. I couldn't come up with one guy I disliked enough to ask or who liked me well enough to agree. This failure took me back to Reclamation Street and the martial arts studio of Master Wang Chen.

Later afternoon should have been the peak period for classes and yet a sign saying: “Closed until further notice” hung over the front door.

I went inside. The lobby was empty. So was the inner office as were two small classrooms I came to down the hall. I stopped to look through the viewing glass where Dennis had been putting his two dozen black belt hopefuls through their paces. Unoccupied but not empty.

In fact, it was an unholy clutter.

The heavy leather bag had been hung in the middle of the room as it had been on my last visit. The top half was still there. The bottom half lay on the floor under a pile of sawdust. Sawdust had been scattered over the classroom. Torn pieces of leather had been thrown to every side in what must have been a maelstrom of madness. The heavy leather bag had been literally hacked to shreds. There was something about it, an undefinable savagery that was so staggering, I didn’t hear footsteps coming from the hall. I even failed to hear the words spoken directly in my ear.

“I said, ‘Some mess, huh?’”

I turned. It was Dennis.

“It was like that,” he said, “when Master Wang came in early this morning.”

“What does it mean?”

“I don’t know. He knows. The master had a dream last night. About that legend of yours that the two of you gave life to, remember? You were in the dream too. He told me that he knew you would be coming here today and that you were not to see him. At any cost. I’m sorry, pal. Nothing personal, you know, but I’ll do what the master tells me to. If you don’t leave on your own then…”

There was no hope at all. But I had to try. “Look, Dennis. My girl’s been kidnapped. It’s the same guy that’s been in the papers. I can’t deal with him by myself. Maybe you can’t either, or even Wang. But if the two of you and a bunch of your better fighters, black belts or whatever, went after him together we might be able to do it. It's the only way. I can't go to the police. If he finds out, he'll kill her for sure."

"Don't be a sap," he said. "he'll find out if we try to help. Hell, he knew this morning that you were coming here. Anyhow, there's no point in arguing. The master won't even talk about it and I'll guarantee you no one else here will either. Including me."

And true to his word, Dennis wouldn't say another word. I left, moments later, with the feeling that I had exhausted my chances for getting Sung back alive.

* * *

I couldn't see the path beneath my feet, the garden was as dark as that; the fog, that thick. Though dawn was only minutes away I felt it was darker and wetter than ever. The gloom was slowly dissipating. But fear was taking its place.

The closer I got to the pagoda the more scared I got.

Where gloom is gray, fear is black. Fear is wetter than gloom, too, and even more rancid.

Fear turned the meandering path into the deepest and darkest of caves.

Fear ran down my face like sweat.

The stench of fear clung to my body; no matter how fast I moved I couldn't outrun it.

The Governor's Walk winds all through the garden. I'd been on the walk several times, usually in the company of an interesting gender, but I'd never seen the governor around. Just about then I'd have given anything to have had someone with me: a girl, a man, even a Manuel, for it's harder to be brave when you've only your own ego for an audience and it knows better.

It knows that dark soggy odor around you is fear.

* * *

I'd gone to the cops.

At least I'd gone to Inspector Hawthorne.

"Ping's not going to go to that rendez-vous," he said. "He absolutely refuses. Can't say I blame him too much. But even if he were willing to go, the Governor wouldn't allow it. His testimony's too valuable. And tomorrow is the last day of the conference. Neither side can stall any longer.

"Someone has to go…"

"Someone to take his place, you mean? There's several million Chinese in this town to choose from including a few thousand Chinese policemen. Do you think you can talk some poor sucker into it. Going up there with some dummy tapes, pray the ***Yega*** doesn't know what this Ping fellow looks like and try to distract him long enough for your girlfriend to get away." He snorted. "You'd have to find some chap who's not married. Someone with no relatives and no obligations and no reason for living. You know as well as I do that he'd be meat as soon as he walked in the door of that pagoda."

I grabbed his jacket.

"I'm going, dammit!"

He drew back in surprise

"I don't want someone to take Sha Han's place or mine. That's not what I need from the police. He'd be meat like you said, and he'll have Sung for dessert. I want somebody to go with me. A sharpshooter, a sniper, whatever you call him. To hide himself up there in the garden and pick off the ***Yega*** before he can kill me and Sung."

* * *

I passed trees and shrubbery, benches and sculptures, fountains and flowers, all of them skulking in the darkness mere yards to the side of the Governor's Walk. About half way up the hill I spotted the pagoda. It didn't look very inviting but then, in all fairness I was here not by invitation but by extortion. It was just a small four wall structure about twenty feet square with a three layer roof, upturned corners in the traditional Oriental design that was topped by a point. The exterior was blood red and garishly ornate.

My right hand moved to my belt. The automatic pistol was there. I knew it was there—the barrel was digging into my stomach—but my right hand had to be sure.

My left hand gripped the handle of the videocassette case. It contained my collection of old movies. Alan Ladd. Humphrey Bogart. John Garfield. I'd spent seven years and God knows how many paychecks filling it out. It hurt to throw them away.

Those last thirty yards were up good slope and my pace got slower and slower. Twice, I almost slipped and fell on the slick stones. My back let me hear about it. That hurt even more.

But I figured, what the hell?

In another two minutes, it wouldn't hurt any more.

* * *

"The Chief of Police had refused your request for a sharpshooter," said Hawthorne later that same afternoon.

I swallowed hard.

"More accurately," Hawthorne went on, "the chief asked for volunteers and didn't get any. Not one. And he refused to order any of his men to do it."

"I don't blame him," I said.

I really didn't.

"He believes, like I do, that any single sharpshooter or even a team of sharpshooters, would get torn to pieces. Don't forget, man, they're all Chinese. The police chief, too. He's Chinese. He can't stand by and do nothing. But he won't send a small force out to be slaughtered. He says it's either nobody at all or a full-scale operation."

"What kind of operaton?"

"One involving every police officer on the force except those on vital assignments elsewhere in the city. He suggests we barricade off the whole summit and let nobody in or out without going through our checkpoints.

"How would you do it?"

"We'll make a human wall that completely surrounds the Peak Gardens. Only you, the Chinese girl, and our man will be inside."

"Our man?"

"This ***Yega*** chap."

My main objection I put in the form of a question. If nobody was going to get into the gardens, then how did they plan to get either Sung or "their man"? Hawthorne admitted that the efforts to clear the summit would be largely for show. "We'll do our best" he assured me. "but this fellow's record would lead us to believe he'll get through somehow. You'll go in. Get him to show himself. Then you give us a signal and we'll all move in. He can't get through that."

I was not impressed but Hawthorne convinced me the Hong Kong police were not going to be budged from their position: it would be all their force…or none. There would be no heroes.

I asked Hawthorne if he thought it would work.

"Yes," he answered a little reluctantly. "I think it just might. Don't you?"

"No," I replied. "Neither do I."

He said he'd get Sha Han's tape case for me as a stall and even have it filled with dummy tapes. It might give me the few extra seconds I'd need. But I'd told him no, I had my own tapes to put in it and I'd rather go in with them.

Hawthorne hadn't objected.

Even in Hong Kong a condemned man gets his last request granted.

Well before daybreak a cordon of police made a sweep across the Peak. They walked side by side in a single mile-long rank with only a few feet between them. Harlech, Old Peak and

Findlay Roads were barricaded. Only I was allowed to pass via the Magazine Gap.

They had found nothing. But then, they hadn't expected to find anything. They were out there now, waiting, beneath the summit but surrounding the garden like a garrote waiting my signal to begin tightening the loop.

* * *

I couldn't have walked through that door alone. The four of us walked in together: Alan Ladd, Humphrey Bogart, John Garfield and me. Once inside we froze.

It was a bare expanse of concrete floor and plastered walls as gray as the weather.

That didn't even register. Sung was lying on her side in a corner, tied hands and feet and either unconscious or asleep or… With her long dark hair falling over her face, I couldn't tell which.

I rushed to her. But I never made it. Halfway across the room I heard footsteps and I turned around.

A stranger had stepped in behind me.

Turning to face him was the second dumbest mistake in my life. I looked the stranger square in the eyes. That was the dumbest.

He was about my size, maybe a little shorter, wearing dark loose clothing. His face was an Oriental face with big black balls of glass for eyes, eyes aflame and yet without a trace of light.

I should have looked away.

I should have run away, but I was literally petrified. I was too afraid to run and too captivated to look in any other direction.

Here was the shadow I'd glimpsed in Kowloon City, the whisp of smoke in the Aberdeen junk, the formless figure slipping out of the captain's cabin on the Lao Shu. Now, for the first time, I was seeing him clearly. But was it the first time? Hadn't I seen this face before? On the roof of the Macao hydrofoil? The image had been buried in my mind until that moment. Now I remembered.

Slowly the stranger began moving toward me.

That's when it hit me. The ***Yega*** was attacking! My hand fell to my belt and I drew out my pistol. But before I could even pull back the hammer he looked into my brain and smiled because he knew I'd never pull the trigger.

And he was right.

Because it wasn't a he. It was a she.

And it wasn't a stranger.

It was Sung.

17. No Way to Die

It didn't happen like that all at once.

One by one my senses ran out on me. At first I only felt a bit dizzy. Before I knew it I'd become completely disoriented. My balance, mental and physical, tettered on the brim of a bottomless pit.

"Doyle, it's me. It's Sung."

I could hardly hear her. The words sounded faint and distant and yet they seemed to come from inside my head. I tried to turn around because I knew that Sung was supposed to be somewhere behind me.

"No, here. I'm over here, Doyle."

I turned clumsily back.

It didn't sound like Sung's voice. And yet I couldn't be sure. There was a bonfire in my brain. I was numb from the neck down but my brain was burning up.

"Look at me, Doyle."

To my everlasting sorrow, I looked. "It can't be," I said.

My own voice sounded strange, too.

"It is me, Doyle."

It didn't look like Sung either. But I'd no sense left I could trust. Certainly not my vision. My eyes cooked in their sockets like a pair of poached eggs. Hot tears seared twin scars down my cheeks and sweat boiled from my face like steam.

"Just look into my eyes, Doyle."

I looked into her eyes.

"It can't be," I said again.

But it could be. I looked again because I knew that it could be. I'd known all along that it could be Sung, I just hadn't wanted to face it.

"Look into my eyes, Doyle."

Like a fool I stared into her eyes, those two black balls of glass.

"Have you brought the tapes?"

"Yes, I…" I stopped. What was the point of lying? "Is it really you, Sung?"

"Yes, it is me."

She took two steps forward. I raised the automatic to waist level and she stopped.

"You can't kill me, Doyle. You don't want to. You're only frightened because you're so tired."

It was true. I couldn't. I knew it was the only thing that would save me. But I couldn't.

Sung took a step. I backed up. She smiled. She moved in and again I moved back. This couldn't go on forever. The pagoda wasn't big enough for that.

She smiled again. They were the same full lips that I knew. The eyes I looked into were the same bright eyes as before. Her skin was the same butterscotch; her hair, the same violent black. She was every bit as gorgeous as ever. And as innocent.

"You're just very tired," she said as she turned at right angles to me and began circling. "I wouldn't hurt you, would I?" As she circled past my shoulder, I turned. She kept talking as she walked around me. I kept turning to watch her. "I only wanted to find Sha Han. To get back the tapes that he stole. He shouldn't have done that, you know. We trusted him. And he betrayed us. But it's over now. You can give me the tapes. Then you can rest."

She was right about being tired. The tape case seemed to weigh fifty pounds. Even the pistol hung at my side now.

On the third lap I stopped pivoting. I followed her by turning my head. When she moved directly behind me I swung my head to the other side and picked her up coming around. She was closer now. On each lap she'd closed up the distance between us.

"You don't have to worry about Sha Han. He's one of us. Didn't he come to us with the names of the student leaders? Didn't he help us to find them? Didn't he film that last day at Tiananmen Square for us."

And then I grew too tired even to move even my head. When she went past my shoulder I watched her from the corner of my eye, so close I could have reached out and touched her.

And she could reach out and touch me.

Hysteria screamed at the shreds of my consciousness.

I had to do something. But I couldn't move. I had to know something. There was a question I had to ask her. A certain question.

I said. "Then you're not going to kill me?"

She was directly behind me when I heard:

"No."

Wrong answer!

Certainty, sudden horrifying certainty, jarred me free from the spell. I threw myself forward...not a moment to soon. A blow like the butt of a charging bull skidded over my spine and across my left shoulder; it was all but spent bfore it hit me. And it was staggering. It knocked the gun out of my hand. And the case. It drove me against the wall below one of the windows. I caught the sill with both hands and launched myself into the air. The window pane shattered. I landed hard on my side in a shower of glass, rolled to my feet and raced into a small stand of trees with a speed born to the mother and father of all panic.

Fresh air, warm fresh air flooded my lungs as I ran. It thawed my frozen limbs. A glorious drizzle doused the fire in my brain.

Only then did I think of Sung.

If he wasn't Sung, then she must have been. The girl in the corner. But I never slowed down or looked back.

I hurdled a park bench, skirted a rock wall and dove into thick shrubbery to the side of the Goveror's Walk. The branches caught at my legs, tore at my clothing. But I didn't slow down.

I was terrified that he was chasing me. Sung was still back in the pagoda. I prayed that he was chasing me.

I dodged behind an acacia and fell to hands and knees. My lungs heaved. A mixture of sweat and drizzle ran off my face in buckets. Nobody was following me that I could see. I swallowed an hysterical giggle. The ***Yega*** had trailed me around for two weeks without my seeing him, using me to find the names he scratched off his list. And now, when I knew that mine was the last name to be scratched, I expected to see him?

What a laugh!

I clawed my hair out of my face and then drove the heels of both palms into my eyes. This hysteria was getting me nowhere.

I looked around. I was within a few yards of the overlook where Sung and I had watched the burning of Hong Kong. I could go east or west along the treeless bluff and let him spot me. Or I could take the cliff.

The sound of a twig snapping off the right made up my mind.

I bounded from cover land and raced to the edge. Down there were several hundred police as well as several million Honkers and I wanted all the help I could get. I got a quick view of the gray cityscape beneath the clouds before throwing myself over the side.

Boulders and wet grass flew under my feet.

The mountainside got so steep so fast it was like the bottom had dropped out of the world. When it turned into a vertical wall of rock I dug in my heels and sidestepped like a maniac along the top of the wall. I slipped and fell onto an overhanging stratum of rock that ran around the ridge of the mountain. I scampered along it, hoping against the odds it would lead me farther down.

Around the ridge the trail ended, and so did my hopes. Climbing down was impossible. It was a vertical drop of at least fifty feet. I looked up the side of the hill but that wasn't climbable either. It was nothing but mud. The same for below. Clay soil turned to the consistency of lubricating oil by constant drizzle. I would have to turn back.

I'd just rounded the ridge when I saw him. He was on the trail walking toward me. His form was still obscure. Still hazy. But it wasn't the fire in my brain this time. It was the rain. I froze.

I'd been wrong about everything. He was taller than me, not shorter. A little heavier, too. His clothes were black and loose fitting like the samfoo pants and tops worn by the Hakkas. A black shock of ragged hair hung over his forehead. He had lean muscular features and a slash of a mouth. All that was incidental. What was in the Yega was in his eyes.

I remembered saying much the same thing about the Pekingese. About old man Ping, too. But there all similarity ended.

These eyes were like no eyes that I'd ever seen.

They were devoid of light. Of life. They were utterly black. Eerier still, they were completely black. No white showed in them at all. His was a dual aberration, oversized irises that filled the whole of his eyes and irises as black as puddles of India ink.

If I'd any notions about talking to him, trying to reason with him, I abandoned them. No words would ever affect him. The pure malevolence I was seeing, the evil, it was not just in his eyes. I was looking directly into his black soul.

I stepped back. But my foot searched behind me in vain until, at the point of overbalancing I turned to see myself standing at the very lip of the overhang. I'd backed up six paces without even knowing.

The black eyes came closer.

I opened my mouth and filled my lungs. My only hope now was to call out for help.

The cry lodged in my chest when I saw his right hand reach out. I thought at first he was going to push me over the side. He wasn't. But once I realized what his movement meant I was too frightened to utter a sound.

The ***Yega*** closed on me. His hand came within inches of my chest. I found myself flowing into his eyes. Sinking into them, deeper and deeper. I would drown there unless I could climb out or…

His palm pressed against my sternum.

I screamed a wild scream.

Not a soul could have heard me. My chest seemed to eplode. My heart and lungs swelled in a kind of eruption and then simply exploded. My scream had been real. But so was the blast. And it smothered all other sounds.

I don't know what he did or how he did it. I do know that if his hand had touched my chest for another moment I would have died there instead of—

Anyway, it didn't. I went over the cliff.

I have no memory of the fall. Even of my crippling landing in the muddy scree at the bottom I remember nothing.

I was looking up. Rain washed the mud from my face. The sky was half my view, the cliff face high overhead was the other. Several moments passed before I was aware that I was looking up and seeing that cliff. And then I was aware of more. My right leg was twisted underneath me. My back was a mass of tortured muscles and bones from my neck to my hips. My stitched wounds had opened up, too.

Painfully I brought my leg out from under. As I did several kindling-sized pieces of wood fell off my stomach and head. I looked around. They were everywhere. Scraps of the pagoda. Something inside of me died. He had blown it up. He had killed Sung!

My smothered scream on the cliff face was nothing compred to the one I screamed then. I fell back in the mud and vented my soul.

It would have been better if he'd killed me, too.

I lay there waiting for him, long after I knew that he wasn't coming. He couldn't climb down any more than I could climb up.

I was in anguish putting my weight on my twisted leg; I stood willingly. Each step along the uneven ground sent lances of pain up my spine. I struck out eagerly. My incompetence had meant months of pain and rehabilitation for Kayo if he lived at all. My impotence had brought death to Sung. I hadn't even managed to sound the alarm that would bring the cops. Of course the explosion itself would have alerted them but I could hardly take credit for that…it had also killed Sung.

I reached the road which circles the peak on the north. I followed this road east toward the garden entrance and ran right into the cordon of police. They were moving almost arm in arm diagonally across the road toward the bluff.

They didn't like the looks of me. They allowed me to pass only after seeing my wounds, telling me I needed medical attention. I didn't care about that.

A couple of them escorted me to the entrance of the garden. Cops were coming from and heading into the upper tram station. It had been turned into a headquarters for the operation. We went directly inside.

A captain in command and his senior officers provided me with an audience of mixed reactions for my report. Some were nervous. A few were openly hostile if only because of this trouble they viewed as one of my making. But I didn't care about that either.

After a little while I located a chair in the vacated station manager's office. I buried my head in my hands.

Reports were constantly coming in for the captain by runner and walkie-talkie. The one about me I missed, only because I didn't care enough to listen.

The captain came into the office flanked by four of his men. There were five handguns pointed at my heart.

"Stand up," ordered the captain.

I stood up.

"What's wrong?" I asked.

He told me to turn around.

The shirt, already in tatters, was ripped from my back. The five men stood away and regarded the canvas of colors with distaste.

"Okay," said the captain at last.

I asked him again what was wrong.

"We just got a message from the southern cordon. Doyle Mulligan crossed through," he said, "two minutes ago."

"I passed through your line on the north side and it was more like twenty minutes."

But they already knew that.

"You back is in bad shape, Mr. Mulligan," the captain told me. "We'd better get you to a doctor. "When I reminded him that my car, Kayo's Subaru, was still up in the garden parking lot he let me know that the parking lot was inside the cordon and that I was in no condition to drive anyway. He offered to send me down on the tram with one of his men.

I turned and limped through a set of doors to the station's platform. It was empty. The tramway wouldn't start running until 7 a.m. The trolley-like car perched at the room's edge with its nose pointed down the hill.

A young policeman entered and gestured to the car door. I went in. As I stepped to the front I heard the door being closed behind us. Motors began to whine. The car lurched ahead and dipped out of the station. As soon as we cleared the overhang, mistlike drops covered the windscreen and made the glass barely translucent.

The skyscrapers, trees and even the rails disappeared behind the diffusion of drops. And I was alone.

So the ***Yega*** had given several hundred cops the slip. Well, it didn't surprise me.

Tiny drops collected and ran down the glass. In their trails the glass became almost transparent again. The tram passed directly over the Old Peak Road which weaved its way down the mountain. As I watched, a little brown sedan shot out from the cover of trees. It was doing a criminal speed considering the incline, the sharp corners and the weather conditions. It took the first switchback on two wheels, barely regaining the slick road before vanishing beneath the next trestle down. It was a maniac at the wheel of that car. And it was Kayo's car.

A sudden pang caught my chest.

And then it passed. I smiled the kind of morbid smile an undertaker applies to a corpse at an open casket affair.

The ***Yega*** wasn't escaping. He was coming after me.

I couldn't stop or speed up or get off. I don't know that I would have if I could. I watched the brown smudge of car disappear in the gloom of mist on a wide loop that would bring it back on Tregunter Path. It was going to be a close race. The driver was going a lot faster than the tram but the road wound all over the mountain while the tram descended straight down.

My role seemed to be limited to that of spectator.

But for whom should I root?

I brought out a coin and flipped it into the air.

Heads for him; tails for me.

It was tails.

That didn't make any sense. Why root for a loser? I fllpped agin. Tails. "Stupid Hong Kong money," I muttered. I knew there was only one way to go out a winner and that was to bet on anybody but me. Because when you came right down to it, it didn't matter what I wanted or which side I rooted for. This ***Yega*** wasn't the Old Boy himself but he was grim and he reaped and when he crooked his boney finger in your direction you died.

I had avoided it once by my wits and once again by luck but Death could only be avoided so long. When I met him the next time—

The car appeared again for a moment and was as quickly gone, flying behind a ridge of the mountain. I remained at the glass as the tram entered the Tregunter access, watching the up-bound tram climbing to meet us.

I heard footsteps behind me and saw a reflection of movement in the glass.

"You better get out of here," I said over my shoulder, "as soon as we reach the base station." The reflected image of the policeman grew larger.

"What about you?" he asked. I should have recognized the voice. But I didn't. The only other time I'd heard it he'd sounded like Sung in my mind. He didn't sound like Sung now.

The interlocking rails separated as the two trams met, passed one another and went their own ways. We'd passed the halfway point. Another five minutes of life for Doyle Mulligan, I thought. Who cares?

"I guess I'll stick around," I said.

I watched a mirror image of the cop move in behind me. His face was an indistinct smear of unfocused malevolence with two black glass balls for eyes that made me stop and swallow hard.

And then I rolled back my head and I laughed. If the laugh sounded a bit hollow I'm sorry but I'd only gone to the wall twice before and they were both in the last thirty minutes.

He had stopped midway down the car.

I turned.

I couldn't look at his eyes—I couldn't let myself look at them. "You're in big trouble now," I said. "It's just you and me and you can't get away."

"Where is Sha Han?"

I looked at my watch. But that was just for effect—I didn't need to know the time to know where Sha Han was now. "He's under police guard in Government House," I said. "In a cell next to the conference room surrounded by a few dozen policemen. He's going to testify…" I checked my watch again. For effect. "In about two hours."

His snarl came from beyond the banging of the tram on its rails.

"You can kill me," I said. "But you can't win. Those tapes you've got are just a bunch of old Hollywood movies. After Honolulu, your god image is finished. And after today, the Chinese will know you're no more infallible than anyone else."

He moved toward me.

"You can kill me," I said again, "Like you killed Kayo and Sung." I raced to finish my little speech before he closed the distance between us. "But you can't win," I said, "because I've already beaten you."

I never saw him hit me. A judo practitioner believes that by watching an opponent's sternum he can see the first nuance of movement that precedes a strike. Some styles of combat teach concentrating on an opponent's eyes will often signal an attack before it is launched. It's all rubbish. I was looking for what I knew darn well as coming and I didn't see it before, during or after. One second I was in front of him and the next I was piled up on the floor near the front of the tram. My head was ringing and the side of my head felt like someone had given me a prefrontal lobotomy without benefit of anesthetic. I covered it with a hand and then brought my palm, smeared with blood in front of my eyes.

Apparently we'd gotten started.

"Is that the best you can do?" I said. My brain was doing loops inside my skull. "The doctors said you only hit Kayo once. How may blows do you think it'll take to kill me?"

He was standing over me as I worked to hands and knees and then fought dizzily to my feet. His chest swung wildly before my eyes but I doubt he was actually moving.

"No. Not for you," he said savagely. "Rather than seeing how quickly you can be killed, I believe I will see how long the process can be prolonged."

"You'd better hurry."

"Fool! You think Inspector Hawthorne will save you? He's as big a fool as you are! He may beat us to the bottom but he'll die for his trouble."

Suddenly the Yega was on me. His fingertips jabbed me in the solar plexus. My lungs seized. I couldn't breathe. I couldn't even stand up straight. I just wrapped my stomach with my arms and fell to a knee. I've been hit there before but never so perfectly. Never so casually. He wrenched my left arm outward, twisted it behind my back and held it there with a one-handed but iron grip on my wrist. When he lifted it high, I dropped to one knee.

I was absolutely powerless to resist.

While I don't say I'd changed my mind about throwing it in, I was still mindless with fear. He could break my neck—it was open to him. He could strike me in the chest or stomach or face, all within easy reach of his knees and feet. He undoubtedly had an assortment of techniques, any one of which could kill me instantly, that could be used from that one position.

Waiting for him to strike, my body began to shake like a baby's. At last he uttered a single word:

"Thumb."

I saw his other hand raised high above his head and I saw his knife chop start down. Somehow I was thrown to one side. A sea of pain had swallowed my hand and washed up my arm and shoulder. He had broken my thumb. I contracted my body into a fetal position letting my legs bring the numbed left hand in front of my face. I wanted to see how bad my thumb was but my eyes were so clouded I couldn't even find the damn thing. Then I knew. He hadn't broken it—he'd whacked it off! Blood spurted sickeningly from the open wound.

The Yega was back, standing over me again. The fingers of his hands, hanging loosely at his sides, flicked upward in a gesture of impatience.

Come on, you asshole, I growled to myself. You wanted him to kill you and this is it. I got my legs under me and staggered to my feet with my left hand tucked into my chest.

He struck me twice more. Neither blow was intended to kill me. I know that because neither one did and his blows always did as they were intended. On the third attack, I shrank back and instinctively raised my hands to protect my head. He'd been waiting for that. By then I was too groggy to be aware of technique but I vaguely recall his grabbing my left arm at the wrist and tossing me rather rag-dollishly over his side. I landed back on the floor in a heap but my wrist was still securely in his grasp. And again he paused until I forced myself to look around.

Then I heard him say clearly:

"Hand."

A bolt of terror electrified me. It was short-lived.

The sudden searing pain wiped out all other feelings. I lost myself in screams. What happened right after that I don't know. And I don't know how long my senselessness lasted. It couldn't have been long for we were still moving. The tram wall banged against my head as it rattled down the mountain. I wanted to vomit. My stomach heaved but there was nothing in me. An unimaginable pain had swallowed my arm. I became aware that my left shoulder was hanging low. I didn't dare look. I didn't have to. I could hear the scrape of bone on metal. I didn't need to look at my arm to know there was no hand on the end of it. And so I forced myself to look down. The wrist seemed to disappear into the floor plate. A red pool had gathered around it.

I was swaying between unconsciousness and death. I was in more pain than I would have thought it possible for me to endure. Shock would take me soon. Or just a loss of blood. But my mind was beginning to set the suffering aside.

I was starting to get mad.

It was a long time coming. I'd been angry with myself for the stupidity which had led to Sung's death. That was an error which could never be forgiven and one that could only be repaid with my own life. And I was willing to let Death come. That's how I thought of the ***Yega***: as a force of nature like a cyclone, an earthquake or a volcano. When someone is struck by lightning you don't blame the thunderstorm. So I'd blamed myself. Let it take me.

But this was not natural. This was no way to die.

Fear and then terror had replaced my feelings of guilt. But now that was going too.

The Yega hauled me to my feet, impatient at my slow return to sensibility. My left arm was wrenched outward. I watched in a kind of stupor as his hand held my stump of a wrist, pulled the forearm straight and twisted the elbow until my arm was locked.

He raised his other hand high.

His voice came agan.

"Arm."

I threw my weight against him and shouted: "Enough!" at the top of my lungs.

Anyway, I tried to. All I heard was a shout; I suppose that's all he heard too.

He'd expected nothing. Even so my lunge wouldn't have upset him if the tram hadn't shifted on a rail just enough to make him lose his balance. I went down. He didn't. As I looked up he was turning to face me again.

I climbed the dizzying heights to my feet.

My lungs were gulping in air by the peck. I should've been hyperventilated, but I wasn't. Sweat came pouring off my face and neck. I should've been in shock; but I wasn't. My heart pounded against my chest like a sledge hammer with pneumatic velocity. And all the while the blood poured from my stump of an arm. I should've been dead. But I wasn't.

I raised my eyes to the face of the ***Yega***.

This was the guy I should be mad at. Doyle Mulligan had been stupid, okay, and his impotence had gotten Sung killed, yeah. But this was the guy that had killed her.

I could die, that part was all right. But my brain, driven to the edge by anger and fear and desperation, had decided that this ***Yega*** was going with me. He deserved it as much as I did. I knew I couldn't outsmart him again. I couldn't depend on any more luck. I was out of luck.

Nevertheless, he was going.

If I had to beat him to death he was going.

Maybe he sensed my irrational intentions as he stalked over to finish me off and maybe he was amused.

I didn't care. And I didn't wait. I went to meet him.

He was too fast for me to avoid. I wouldn't be able to dodge his attacks so I'd have to attack him.

That's what I did. It must have seemed like a joke to him. I swung like a madman, wildly, ineptly with the right and then the left, mindless to the hopelessness of the technique. He had blocked ten thousand blows. Even ten thousand times ten thousand blows that were better skilled than mine. As Master Wang had swatted my fist aside, the ***Yega*** could swat Wang's. He didn't even look at my punches. He didn't need to.

His hand flashed up and waved my right first away like a bothersome mosquito. The same hand whipped in front of his face to execute a textbook deflection of my left. He had done it that way on his thousands of battles and on every occasion it had worked to utter perfection.

But this time it missed completely.

His block caught the point in space where my left fist would have been as it raced toward his face, and with his unmatched speed, whisked just in front of my bloodied wrist.

…my hand wasn't there.

In his favor, I suppose that no one whose hand he had just dismembered had ever tried to punch him with the stump that remained.

I was looking at his face when he saw it.

In the instant before my wrist, with a wicked section of bone protruding, caught him precisely in his right eye, it opened in abrupt astonishment and I had a flash of white circumference around the oversized iris. And then the eye vanished. I'll bet it hurt me every bit as much as it hurt him. More. I fell back in anguish, gripping my wrist with my right hand and fighting to stay on my feet. Nightfall closed in. When I saw the ***Yega*** also holding his wound, the night temporarily retreated. He was bent over. His head was in both hands with his fingers covering his eye.

His cry of pain filled the tram.

It was my only chance. Nothing like it would ever come again. I balled my right fist and threw the haymaker. Every ounce of my weight was behind it. I landed on my back in the darkness but somehow fought back the night once more and started to my feet. The Yega had only been knocked back against a window. Though he wasn't down, he was staggered. I guess I'd busted his nose. Blood sprayed from both nostrils.

It wasn't victory. But whatever it was, I felt like dying after that would be something I could live with.

I laughed as the thought struck me.

I laughed aloud because I wanted him to hear it.

He was squaring off at me again in only a moment. He made and unmade his fists so tight the veins popped on his forearms. But I was staring at his face. I was seeing it clearly for the first time and I didn't want to look away. For the first time I didn't have to. His right eyeball was gone. Clear flud drained from the open socket and blood was spattered over his nose and mouth. Some of it may have been mine. Most of it must have been his. I knew he'd never see out of that eye again. And no one, I suspected would ever again be mesmerized by looking upon it.

We were approaching the station. The tram was slowing more and more all the time. But we'd never make it. Not both of us. I saw him fill his lungs. Eyes or no eyes this assassin had never lost a fight. I was the kid who'd never won. He was the most dangerous man alive. And I was only the maddest.

The *Yega* began a long cry of attack. I'd never heard anything like it. But when he charged me, I knew what it reminded me of. He was like a wounded tiger, roaring and springing at his even more weakened prey.

I guess I screamed too. I must have matched him for volume because the noise in that tram was twice as loud as any single madman could have made. And I attacked. I leapt at him with a fury I would not have believed possible.

It ended right there. In that space between us.

He made a gesture of blocking but it never came close. I doubt he even saw my right hand reaching out for his neck. I never saw his strike either. The last thing I sensed was a blow to my stomach just under the rib cage. But the blow didn't stop. It kept coming. It invaded my body and tore through my insides.

My left stump hammered his face.

My right hand clawed at his throat.

There was another explosion. I heard it. I felt it in my chest. The Yega had grabbed my guts in his fist.

I dug my fingers into his windpipe and ripped with all my strength.

And then I let the night come.

18. Day after Night

BEIJING PACKS UP, LEAVES HONG KONG
By Manuel Fuentes
ENA Reporter

HONG KONG (ENA)—Beijing learned its first lesson in capitalism today when the British sent them packing at the close of the Hong Kong conference. "They made a deal…and they'll have to live up to it," the Colonial Governor told a jubilant assembly of Chinese outside Government House. "The deal," he said, "was 1997."

Governor C.Y. Montague praised the British negotiating team for remaining steadfast.

"And we'll be just as firm in seeing Beijing adheres to its obligations under the terms of the Bacis Law," Governor Montague added, referring to the turnover settlement which requires the communists to respect Hong Hong's free market system until 2047."

The failed attempt by the People's Republic for early control of the ports of entry was met with widespread joy in this jewel of British crown colonies. An unofficial holiday was immediately declared throughout Hong Kong but many Chinese, former refugees, had already begun their celebrations.

No one expected this outcome. As little as twenty-four hours before even the risk-loving, gambling-crazy Chinese of Hong Kong would have considered the odds of keeping the communists out even a few more weeks as too remote to consider.

Beijing had charged that many thousands of middle class Chinese were being allowed to leave the colony illegally. Capital flight and loss of a managerial base second to none were Beijing's stated concerns. They had promised to provide proof of the Chinese exodus and Monday the proof had come, unexpectedly, from the burning and near-sinking of a Hong Hong-to-Hawaii cruise ship in Honolulu Harbor. More than a thousand illegal immigrants were rescued from the ship's lower holds. Authorities here and in the United States are investigating the possibility that hundreds of thousands of others were spirited out of Hong Kong in similar fashion over the past several months only to be killed and dumped into the Pacific Ocean. The ship, *Lao Shu*, of the Zodiac Cruise Line, had been previously inspected and cleared by the Royal Hong Kong Police before sailing.

These revelations had bolstered Beijing's position at the conference. British negotiators were at the point of allowing a Red Chinese presence in Hong Kong government.

However, the final day of negotiations was highlighted by the testimony of the last surviving student leader of the prodemocaracy movement in China two years before, a movement which had culminated in the massacre of hundreds of students at Tienanmen Square. Former Beijing University student Ping Sha Han provided videotaped evidence of communist brutality on May 4, 1989, which shocked even the normally unflappable Britsh team. After this, Beijing could not regain its initiative.

Equally damning was evidence submitted by Inspector Llewellyn Hawthorne of Scotland Yard, London, that Beijing had taken steps to close down the underground railway even while the conference was in progress. Hawthorne testified that a Red Chinese enforcer known only as the ***Yega*** had murdered a dozen members of the underground and burned nearly a hundred Hong Kong acupuncture clinics in an almost successful attempt to prevent Ping and other Chinese from leaving.

The ***Yega***, Hawthorne told the conference, had tracked Ping out of China in order to kill him and keep the tapes he had stolen from reaching the West. When Ping boarded the under-ground, the ***Yega*** followed him. Burnings, bombings, and brutal murders carved a trail from Hong Kong to Honolulu. The sinking of the *Lao Shu* in Honolulu Harbor was the work of the ***Yega***, according to Hawthorne. The eleven hundred Hong Kong Chinese in its hold were to have drowned as a warning to would-be emigrants.

Billionaire businessman an author Lee Chung, who owned the Zodiac Cruise Line as well as the string of razed Celestial Acupuncture Clinics, was burned to death in his Victoria Peak mansion by the ***Yega***, according to police.

One of his acupuncture clinic operators and a ticket seller in the underground railway—which is know here as the *de ha tit*—was blown out the side of the DC-10 over the South China Sea last week. Officials are still looking into the cause of that near-disaster.

ENA reporter Doyle Mulligan followed the *de ha tit* from the mansion home of Lee Chung to Kowloon City, Aberdeen, the waterfront warehouses, to the Portuguese colony of Macao, and finally to Honolulu. Mulligan was himself the last vicitim of the ***Yega***. Another ENA reporter working with Mulligan, K'o Tuan, was murdered in Hawaii and Sung Kwon, Ping Sha Han's cousin, was killed here in Hong Kong.

In a most unorthodox move Government House placed the body of the ***Yega*** on public sidplay. Thousands lined up to assure themselves that the reign of terror had ended.

Meanwhile, Zodiac Cruise Lines has been forced to cease operations indefinitely pending an investigation by American and British authorities. Officers and crewmen of the twelve member Zodiac shipline are being sought for questioning by the

(Continued on page A12)

"That's the third time you've read it through," growled Stringer. "Don't you have something to say? Aren't you going to make some kind of a crack?"

"One gains no knowledge while speaking. Confucious pointed that out in the I-Ching. A wise man listens. A fool speaks."

Stringer shook his head. "Don't hand me that crap. You're too egoistic for Confucious. I'll bet you've never read a page of the I-Ching."

"And Manuel never wrote a word of this story!" I threw the newspaper across the length of my hospital bed. "Dammit, Alex, I can understand your writing me off as dead so Beijing wouldn't have a target for their revenge. That makes sense. But why in hell did you have to give Manuel a byline on my story for Christ's sake?"

"Dead men can't write stories."

"But why Manuel?"

Of course at that point I'd already lost it.

Stringer shook his head: "Don't be a hog. There's enough credit to go around. Manuel did a lot of legwork out at the airport and some of the other guys spent the week in the New Territories checking out Lee's containerized firm. It was just your good luck that you landed into the right one."

Good luck. That's not how I'd seen it. I felt lucky to be alive. When Hathorne had burst into the tram after firing through the glass, he'd found the ***Yega*** and me locked together on the floor. The ***Yega***'s hand was embedded in my stomach up to the thumb and within an inch, I am told, of my heart. The doctors had not yet determined whether he'd died by having the back of his head blown open or because I'd dislodged his windpipe. Both had occurred within an instant of each other. By one or by both the guy had died.

With characteristic British cool, the inspector had gathered up Doyle Mulligan, a thumb and a hand he'd found lying around, wrapped up the three of me and sped us to the hospital at a velocity matched only by his insane descent off the Peak

I owed Hawthorne everything. More than just my life.

Sung's life, too.

He'd seen me race out of the pagoda. He'd seen the ***Yega*** streak out a few seconds later. Hawthorne had looked inside and found Sung beside an explosive device about to blow. By the time he'd dragged her out it was too late to help me. He'd reached the upper tram station just as I was heading to the bottom and learned that the ***Yega*** had slipped through the cordon. The unconscious body of the policeman whose clothes and face the ***Yega*** had borrowed lay in the next room.

That was two days ago.

"Speaking of luck," said Alex Stringer, "guess what? This damn story had generated some much needed publicity for the office and I'm being reassigned early. Know where? Tokyo! They even had the nerve to call it a promotion. Can you believe they'd do that?"

"You'll be right at home, Alex. I understand you also don't speak a word of Japanese."

"Your name came up as my replacement, but naturally I had to kill it."

Naturally, I thought; if I couldn't write a news story how could I oversee the Hong Kong office. The Chinese have long memories.

"And that means Manuel will probably get the job," he continued, "at least on an interim basis. But I want you to know, Doyle, that when Kayo flies back next month I'm going to give him your desk. He's earned the promotion."

"My desk?"

Stringer was going on.

"His first big story is going to be the new spirit in Hong Kong. The evil spirit is dead. And an optimistic one has taken its place. The borders are open now for Chinese to leave if they want to. There are even rumblings in the Britih parliament that Great Britain will lift its Chinese immigration quotas to allow more Honkers to emigrate. My instincts tell me, however that the exodus has ended."

I thought I knew what he was getting at but I asked him to explain because I saw a speech coming again and this time I didn't want to stop him. He'd been right about our job as members of the press. It was his turn to gloat.

"The ***Yega*** symbolized something," said Stringer. "Something that couldn't be beaten. But we beat it. In the same way a few thousand students with little or no idea of what freedom is all about nearly brought Red China to its knees. Now, in a few years China is going to absorb five million of the most industrious, the most enterprising and resouorceful people on the planet. And those five million people know exactly what freedom is. I think it's very possible China is biting off more than it can chew. And I almost regret that you and I won't be here to see it. In fact—"

"Hold it, Alex."

"What's wrong?"

"Let me get this straight. I lost the byline. I don't get the promotion, I get my desk taken away from me and now you're making noises like I don't even get to hang around town."

"You don't."

"Where do I go?"

"I thought I told you, Australia. The office in Sydney can use a wise ass like you."

He went on to make it sound like a big deal but I was hardly listening. I didn't care about Australia. I'd lost the byline, the promotion, the job, and the town but I did get something, something Alan Ladd, Humphrey Bogart and John Garfield might have appreciated. I got the girl. I hoped.

The door opened and in she came.

Stringer made some closing comments but I didn't hear them. When I looked over at him he was gone.

Sung had needed the two days recuperation as much as I had. She was wearing a ponytail and some ridiculous hospital gown that was at least four sizes too large for her. On her it looked as fashionable as a two-man arctic tent. Hospital green ballooned to the floor.

It was my favorite of anything I'd seen her in.

"You look great!" I told her.

"That's very kind of you," she said shyly.

"I'm a kind kind of guy," I replied.

She came to my bedside.

After a moment she asked me about the hand.

"The doctor gives it a fifty-fifty chance," I told her. "He said it would have been better odds if I hadn't used it as a hammer. But I don't know, I like fifty-fifty. That way I can flip a coin."

"You were very brave, Doyle."

"Can I help it," I asked her, "if bravery runs in my family?"

"The inspector said he was sorry he couldn't delay his return to London. He thinks that you are a very good man and so do I."

"Hawthorne has his faults, I guess, but he knows a good man when he sees one."

"He said to tell you that if you were ever in England to look him up."

I said, "He didn't say that."

"It was something like that," she lied.

"But not exactly like that?"

"No, actually it was more like; Tell Doyle that if he ever comes to England . . . tell him to go to Ireland instead."

We laughed.

"Sung?"

"Yes, Doyle?"

I handed her the little jade engagement ring. It had been in my pocket for days. It had not left my bedside in the last two. "I never really got a chance to give this to you properly. I kept waiting for the right time."

"You were very patient with me."

"That's me. Patience personified." I held it out to her. "Well, I have the time now, but I'm not sure I've got the right. You wouldn't want to get serious with a one-handed touch typist, would you?"

Her enormous eyes opened even wider.

"It would depend," she said, "on whether or not he was kind and good and brave and patient."

"And humble," I reminded her. "Don't forget humble."

"Yes," she agreed reluctantly, "And humble." All of a sudden she smiled. "Well, maybe humble is not so important."

"Then the answer is no?"

"Yes," she said. "The answer is no."

I didn't even try to restrain the grin.

Sung and I understood each other at last.

An excerpt from:

F2
(Effay Dos)
By Steve Forbes

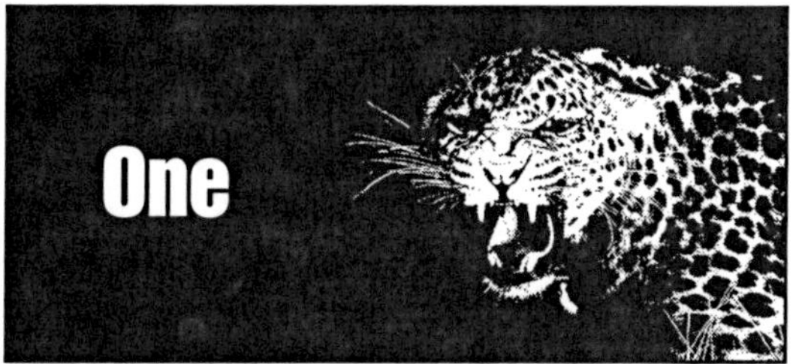

Michael Martin's aviophobia came in three stages:

What, during take off, had him bolted to his seat like a condemned man, gulping air by the peck, his heartbeat and blood pressure climbing to uncharted heights at speeds that seemed somehow tied in with the aircraft's rate of ascent, characterized itself quite differently in level flight. The rigor withdrew and he collapsed. His heartbeat fibrillated. He showed difficulty breathing or swallowing. Any reasonably competent physician might have incorrectly diagnosed stroke and surmised, correctly, that only an inordinately tightened seat belt—which was never loosened—restrained incontinent movement. By the time the landing gear was lowered and a descent begun this condition had come full circle. Martin's face blanched. His lips turned blue and sweat ran freely from his brow. In one sense he hadn't lost his grip. He clutched four air sick bags—donated by nervous neighbors—with such a tenacity they threatened to rupture, scattering their contents into the aisles. Cautious approaches by stewardesses only served to tighten his stranglehold on the bags. The stewardesses retreated. A member of the flight crew, trained in hostage negotiation, had stepped into the tourist compartment, taken one look at Martin's face and wheeled without a word into the cockpit. There, his recommendations to the crew and by radio to the tower officials were brief and to the point. Land. With all possible speed. Call it aviophobia or just a fear of flying, everyone agreed Michael Martin had a bad case.

The Aerocondor flight from Miami had taken six hours. That included two stops on the island of Hispaniola which only added to the misery. In Port-au-Prince, Martin nearly balked at the mandatory deplaning, a curious malpractice held over from Papa Doc's little black bag of tricks. While black-faced government officials herded them on, the passengers had filed unmolested through the customs facility and exited by way of the state-owned souvenir shop before charging the ramp to reboard. Despite the store's being eradicated of all traces of the Emperor for Life—or perhaps because of this—the cash register had rung no sales.

It had been the opposite in Santo Domingo. Here troops clad in desert khaki and wielding antiquated weaponry took up positions on each side of the aircraft in order to discourage any passengers from trying to slip off the plane. Stowaways were the real concern. Haitian stowaways. Neither political oppression nor the practice of escaping it by hiding in aircraft wheel wells had originated in Haiti, a mere twenty minutes away by air, but both had been perfected there and only a Haitian could consider coming to the Dominican Republic as political progress.

Now the Colombian airliner dipped its nose a third time as the horizon changed from blue to gray and finally green at the southernmost limits of the Caribbean Sea. A continent swept under their wings. To the west, an ocean of vegetation extended from the tide line to infinity. To the east, the green gathered wings and soared into the high Sierra Nevadas de Santa Marta. An ugly smudge of brown dirtied the coastline between the two. This was the aircraft's destination.

The no-smoking signs were lit.

Tray tables were raised. The seat backs came forward.

Michael Martin shivered, mopped his brow, tightened his grip on the air sick bags and inhaled a mighty breath. All of the vents on the overhead panel had been commandeered and redirected onto him but their combined volumes seemed hardly up to the task.

"My macho Mikey Martin," laughed Gayle Saunders.

It had been a brave attempt at humor for here was a lady with a job to do. More than a mere errand—a mission of mercy.

She was at the window separated from him by the center seat and several generations of selective breeding. Gayle's delicate hands lay like tastefully folded gloves on the chair arms. Stockingless white legs were crossed in such a way as to emphasize their perfection of contour and color. And her flawless face, applied eight hours before, showed no signs of tropical wear. It was not a gay face; that much was clear by the severe sweep of her blonde hair under the jaguar bandana, the determined—but optimistic—"peek-a-boo blue" shading to her eyes and brows, and the no-nonsense cherry chap-free gloss on her wide lips. Cosmetics aside, Miss Saunders cut a very fashionable figure. A tailored Andes Trek shirt had been let out in the bosom and tucked into tight outback shorts the waist of which was cinched to twenty-two inches by a jute twice-buckled belt. She wore knee-length safari socks and chic traveling boots, all color-coordinated in pith with pewter piping.

The perfect outfit for rescuing a lover from the bush.

Or, more accurately, traveling by air to South America in order to rescue a lover from the bush. Men who passed her in the aisle or had stood beside her in the terminal could sense urgency in her manner. "A lady with a mission," they might think to themselves and then, after a wistful pause, "Good luck, lass."

When they turned—as inevitably they did—to regard Martin with something less than generosity, one could see him being written off as another example of the peculiar taste in males by the female of the species. Or worse, as a stooge along for the ride.

Martin faced her with a wan expression.

"I warned you. We should never have flown."

"You refused even to discuss sailing."

With a grimace he turned quickly around, fighting to control the abdominal urges evoked by the mere suggestion of an ocean passage. "It's no secret I'm not a good traveler."

A foul cap of smog lay over the soiled cityscape like work clothes thrown into a corner. Dirty low rises were the first structures to come into view. Brown houses and brown streets resolved from the ground and finally brown vehicles and evidence of three quarters of a million brown residents. South of the city a dusty tarmac reached out and pulled the jet down. Even the airport terminal was a drab off-white structure that could have doubled as an armory. The sides wanted so badly a cleaning that the airport letters were only just discernable. In the absence of a jetway, a platform was rolled to the side of the plane and the American couple was among the first to disembark.

Martin had thrown off his distress.

It might have taken hours for his condition to improve but it didn't. Michael Martin never convalesced. The only thing more startling to witness than his swift descent to death's door was his capacity to rebound.

Following at her heels he stepped gratefully from the crowded confines of the 707, paused for a moment at the head of the platform steeling himself for a hike the length of the tar macadam, and then started down. To Martin, the ideal environment was his apartment, big—but not too big—open—but with windows barred—and with just the right population: himself and a pair of goldfish (the three of whom shared may characteristics not least among them an abject fear of cats; in the latter it was a matter of instinct; in the former, classic ailurophobia). Three weeks earlier their household number had doubled when Gayle Saunders had moved in with Kit and Kaboodle, her two royal Siamese.

The terminal was open air. Chipped masonry, cracking concrete throughout. The dozen ticket counters were small and for the most part, unmanned. What few passengers were in sight lounged on the wooden benches with practiced patience. Soldiers in uniform strolled about, slumped against the faded and peeling pastel walls, or merely basked in military might, their presence lending the facility all the charm of an induction center. Arriving passengers, having acquired their luggage, queued up before a single official in an elevated kiosk whose customs fatigues were indistinguishable from those of other military personnel.

Beyond were rows of tables for luggage inspection. A documents check would be largely perfunctory; the baggage inspection, routine. Other than determining that contraband arms were not being imported to insurgent groups, the government had little concern. Colombia is a contraband exporting nation. Martin knew that this inspection would bear little similarity to the one they would undergo leaving for home. He could almost visualize the customs facilities for outbound passengers. The probing questions. The strip searches. "How much Colombian money are you carrying, mister? You cannot take this out of the country; you must convert it before departing. I'm sorry, there is no time, if you want to catch the next flight you must leave it with someone here…?" "Is this your luggage? I know it was already examined; favor me to open it again." "You are Mrs. Brewster? Would you mind stepping into the next room? No, your husband must wait here."

Martin's mind play ended suddenly.

"Welcome to Barranquilla." The official spoke English by rote. "Is this veesit business or playsure?"

"Are you kidding?" Martin asked.

"Gayle Saunders moved in at once: "Pleasure," she said. "We're strictly tourists."

"Speak for yourself," he muttered. "I was born here."

Made in the USA